There was an instant of utter stillness when the boundary reached me. Then a roar out of hell. The winds inside were ferocious. I thought of nothing but getting down and hanging on. Around me gear was flying about, changing shape as it flew. Then I spied Goblin. And nearly threw up.

Goblin indeed. His head had swelled ten times normal size. The rest of him looked inside out. Around him swarmed a horde of the parasites that live on a windwhale's back, some as big as pigeons.

Tracker and Toadkiller Dog were worse. The mutt had become something half as big as an elephant, fanged, possessed of the most evil eyes I've ever seen. He looked at me with a starved lust that chilled my soul. And Tracker had become something demonic, vaguely apelike yet certainly much more. Both looked like creatures from an artist's or sorcerer's nightmares.

THE WHITE ROSE

GLEN COOK

THE THIRD CHRONICLE OF
THE BLACK COMPANY

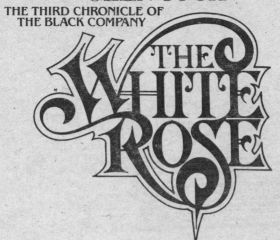

THE
WHITE
ROSE

TOR®
fantasy

A TOM DOHERTY ASSOCIATES BOOK
NEW YORK

This is a work of fiction. All the characters and events portrayed in this book are either products of the author's imagination or are used fictitiously.

THE WHITE ROSE

A Tor Book
Published by Tom Doherty Associates, LLC
175 Fifth Avenue
New York, NY 10010

www.tor.com

Tor® is a registered trademark of Tom Doherty Associates, LLC.

ISBN: 0-812-50844-0

First edition: April 1985

Printed in the United States of America

0   9   8   7   6

DEDICATION

For Nancy Edwards, just because.

Chapter One: THE PLAIN OF FEAR

The still desert air had a lenselike quality. The riders seemed frozen in time, moving without drawing closer. We took turns counting. I could not get the same number twice running.

A breath of a breeze whined in the coral, stirred the leaves of Old Father Tree. They tinkled off one another with the song of wind chimes. To the north, the glimmer of change lightning limned the horizon like the far clash of warring gods.

A foot crunched sand. I turned. Silent gawked at a talking menhir. It had appeared in the past few seconds, startling him. Sneaky rocks. Like to play games.

"There are strangers on the Plain," it said.

I jumped. It chuckled. Menhirs have the most malevolent laughs this side of fairy stories. Snarling, I ducked into its shadow. "Hot out here already." And: "That's One-Eye and Goblin, back from Tanner."

It was right and I was wrong. I was too narrowly focused. The patrol had been away a month longer than planned. We were worried. Lately the Lady's troops have been more active along the bounds of the Plain of Fear.

Another chuckle from the block of stone.

It towered over me, thirteen feet tall. A middle-sized one. Those over fifteen feet seldom move.

The riders were closer, yet seemed no nearer. Blame nerves. Times are desperate for the Black Company. We cannot afford casualties. Any man lost would be a friend of many years. I counted again. Seemed right this time. But there was a riderless mount. . . . I shivered despite the heat.

They were on the downtrail leading to a creek three hundred yards from where we watched, concealed within a great reef. The walking trees beside the ford stirred, though the breeze had failed.

The riders urged their mounts to hurry. The animals were tired. They were reluctant, though they knew they were almost home. Into the creek. Water splashing. I grinned, pounded Silent's back. They were all there. Every man, and another.

Silent shed his customary cool, returned a smile. Elmo slipped out of the coral and went to meet our brethren. Otto, Silent, and I hurried after him.

Behind us, the morning sun was a great seething ball of blood.

Men piled off horses, grinning. But they looked bad. Goblin and One-Eye worst of all. But they had come back to territory where their wizards' powers were useless. This near Darling they are no greater than the rest of us.

I glanced back. Darling had come to the head of the tunnel, stood like a phantom in its shadow, all in white.

Men hugged men; then old habit took charge. Everybody pretended it was just another day. "Rough out there?" I asked One-Eye. I considered the man accompanying them. He was not familiar.

"Yes." The dried-up little black man was more diminished than first I had thought.

"You all right?"

"Took an arrow." He rubbed his side. "Flesh wound."

From behind One-Eye, Goblin squeaked, "They almost got us. Been chasing us a month. We couldn't shake them."

"Let's get you down in the Hole," I told One-Eye.

"Not infected. I cleared it."

"I still want a look." He has been my assistant since I enlisted as Company physician. His judgment is sound. Yet health is my responsibility, ultimately.

"They were waiting for us, Croaker." Darling was gone from the mouth of the tunnel, back to the stomach of our subterranean fastness. The sun remained bloody in the east, legacy of the change storm's passing. Something big drifted across its face. Windwhale?

"Ambush?" I glanced back at the patrol.

"Not us specifically. For trouble. They were on the ball."
The patrol had had a double mission: to contact our sympathizers in Tanner to find out if the Lady's people were coming
alive after a long hiatus, and to raid the garrison there in order
to prove we could hurt an empire that bestrides half a world.

As we passed it the menhir said, "There are strangers on
the Plain, Croaker."

Why do these things happen to me? The big stones talk to
me more than to anyone else.

Twice a charm? I paid attention. For a menhir to repeat
itself meant it considered its message critical. "The men
hunting you?" I asked One-Eye.

He shrugged. "They wouldn't give up."

"What's happening out there?" Hiding on the Plain, I
might as well be buried alive.

One-Eye's face remained unreadable. "Corder will tell it."

"Corder? That the guy you brought in?" I knew the name
though not the man. One of our best informants.

"Yeah."

"No good news, eh?"

"No."

We slipped into the tunnel which leads down to our warren,
our stinking, moldering, damp, tight little rabbit-hole fortress.
It is disgusting, but it is the heart and soul of the New White
Rose Rebellion. The New Hope, as it is whispered among the
captive nations. The Joke Hope to those of us who live here.
It is as bad as any rat-infested dungeon—though a man *can*
leave. If he does not mind a venture into a world where all
the might of an empire is turned upon him.

Chapter Two: THE PLAIN OF FEAR

Corder was our eyes and ears in Tanner. He had contacts everywhere. His work against the Lady goes back decades. He is one of the few who escaped her wrath at Charm, where she obliterated the Rebel of old. In great part, the Company was responsible. In those days we were her strong right arm. We piloted her enemies into the trap.

A quarter million men died at Charm. Never was there a battle so vast or grim, nor of outcome so definitive. Even the Dominator's bloody failure in the Old Forest consumed but half as many lives.

Fate compelled us to switch sides—once there was no one left to help us in our fight.

One-Eye's wound was as clean as he claimed. I cut him loose, ambled off to my quarters. Word was, Darling wanted the patrol rested before she accepted its report. I shivered with premonition, afraid to hear their tidings.

An old, tired man. That is what I am. What became of the old fire, drive, ambition? There were dreams once upon a time, dreams now all but forgotten. On sad days I dust them off and fondle them nostalgically, with a patronizing wonder at the naivete of the youth who dreamed them.

Old infests my quarters. My great project. Eighty pounds of ancient documents, captured from the general Whisper when we served the Lady and she the Rebel. They are supposed to contain the key to breaking the Lady and the Taken. I have had them six years. And in six years I have found nothing. So much failure. Depressing. Nowadays, more often than not I merely shuffle them, then turn to these Annals.

Since our escape from Juniper they have been little more than a personal journal. The remnant of the Company generates little excitement. What outside news we get is so slim and unreliable I seldom bother recording it. Moreover, since her victory over her husband in Juniper, the Lady seems to be in stasis even more than we, running on inertia.

Appearances deceive, of course. And the Lady's essence is illusion.

"Croaker."

I looked up from a page of Old TelleKurre already studied a hundred times. Goblin stood in the doorway. He looked like an old toad. "Yeah?"

"Something happening up top. Grab a sword."

I grabbed my bow and a leather cuirass. I am too ancient for hand-to-hand. I'd rather stand off and plink if I have to fight at all. I considered the bow as I followed Goblin. It had been given me by the Lady herself, during the battle at Charm. Oh, the memories. With it I helped slay Soulcatcher, the Taken who brought the Company into the Lady's service. Those days now seemed almost prehistoric.

We galloped into sunlight. Others came out with us, dispersed amidst cactus and coral. The rider coming down the trail—the only path in here—would not see us.

He rode alone, on a moth-eaten mule. He was not armed. "All this for an old man on a mule?" I asked. Men scooted through coral and between cacti, making one hell of a racket. The old-timer had to know we were there. "We'd better work on getting out here more quietly."

"Yeah."

Startled, I whirled. Elmo was behind me, one hand shading his eyes. He looked as old and tired as I felt. Each day something reminds me that none of us are young anymore. Hell, none of us were young when we came north, over the Sea of Torments. "We need new blood, Elmo."

He sneered.

Yes. We will be a lot older before this is done. If we last. For we are buying time. Decades, hopefully.

The rider crossed the creek, stopped. He raised his hands.

Men materialized, weapons held negligently. One old man alone, at the heart of Darling's null, presented no danger.

Elmo, Goblin, and I strolled down. As we went I asked Goblin, "You and One-Eye have fun while you were gone?" They have been feuding for ages. But here, where Darling's presence forbids it, they cannot play sorcerous tricks.

Goblin grinned. When he grins, his mouth spreads from ear to ear. "I loosened him up."

We reached the rider. "Tell me later."

Goblin giggled, a squeaking noise like water bubbling in a teakettle. "Yeah."

"Who are you?" Elmo asked the mule rider.

"Tokens."

That was not a name. It was a password for a courier from the far west. We had not heard it for a long time. Western messengers had to reach the Plain through the Lady's most tamed provinces.

"Yeah?" Elmo said. "How about that? Want to step down?"

The old man eased off his mount, presented his bonafides. Elmo found them acceptable. Then he announced, "I've got twenty pounds of stuff here." He tapped a case behind his saddle. "Every damn town added to the load."

"Make the whole trip yourself?" I asked.

"Every foot from Oar."

"Oar? That's . . ."

More than a thousand miles. I hadn't known we had anyone up there. But there is a lot I do not know about the organization Darling has assembled. I spend my time trying to get those damned papers to tell me something that may not be there.

The old man looked at me as though subjecting my soul to an accounting. "You the physician? Croaker?"

"Yeah. So?"

"Got something for you. Personal." He opened his courier case. For a moment everyone was alert. You never know. But he brought out an oilskin packet wrapped to protect something against the end of the world. "Rains all the time up there," he explained. He gave me the packet.

I weighed it. Not that heavy, oilskin aside. "Who's it from?"

The old man shrugged.

"Where'd you get it?"

"From my cell captain."

Of course. Darling has built with care, structuring her organization so that it is almost impossible for the Lady to break more than a fraction. The child is a genius.

Elmo accepted the rest, told Otto, "Take him down and find him a bunk. Get some rest, old-timer. The White Rose will question you later."

An interesting afternoon upcoming, maybe, what with this guy and Corder both to report. I hefted the mystery packet, told Elmo, "I'll go give this a look." Who could have sent it? I knew no one outside the Plain. Well . . . But the Lady would not inject a letter into the underground. Would she?

Twinge of fear. It had been a while, but she *had* promised to keep in touch.

The talking menhir that had forewarned us about the messenger remained rooted beside the path. As I passed, it said, "There are strangers on the Plain, Croaker."

I halted. "What? More of them?"

It reverted to character, would say no more.

Never will I comprehend those old stones. Hell, I still don't understand why they are on our side. They hate all outsiders separately but equally. They and every one of the weird sentiences out here.

I slipped into my quarters, unstrung my bow, left it leaning against the earth wall. I settled at my worktable and opened the packet.

I did not recognize the hand. I found the ending was not signed. I began to read.

Chapter Three: STORY FROM YESTERYEAR

Croaker:

The woman was bitching again. Bomanz massaged his temples. The throbbing did not slacken. He covered his eyes. "Saita, sayta, suta," he murmured, his sibilants angry and ophidian.

He bit his tongue. One did not make a sending upon one's wife. One endured with humbled dignity the consequences of youthful folly. Ah, but what temptation! What provocation!

Enough, fool! Study the damned chart.

Neither Jasmine nor the headache relented.

"Bloody hell!" He slapped the weights off the corners of the chart, rolled the thin silk around a wisp of glass rod. He slipped the rod inside the shaft of a fake antique spear. That shaft was shiny with handling. "Besand would spot it in a minute," he grumbled.

He ground his teeth as his ulcer took a bite of gut. The closer the end drew, the greater was the danger. His nerves were shot. He was afraid he might crack at the last barrier, that cowardice would devour him and he would have lived in vain.

Thirty-seven years was a long time to live in the shadow of the headsman's axe.

"Jasmine," he muttered. "And call a sow Beauty." He flung the door-hanging aside, shouted downstairs, "What is it now?"

It was what it always was. Nagging unconnected with the root of her dissatisfaction. An interruption of his studies as a payback for what she fancied was his having misspent their lives.

He could have become a man of consequence in Oar. He could have given her a great house overstuffed with fawning servants. He could have draped her in cloth-of-gold. He could have fed her tumble-down fat with meat at every meal. Instead, he had chosen a scholar's life, disguising his name and profession, dragging her to this bleak, haunted break in the Old Forest. He had given her nothing but squalor, icy winters, and indignities perpetrated by the Eternal Guard.

Bomanz stamped down the narrow, squeaky, treacherous stairway. He cursed the woman, spat on the floor, thrust silver into her desiccated paw, drove her away with a plea that supper, for once, be a decent meal. Indignity? he thought. I'll tell you about indignity, you old crow. I'll tell you what it's like to live with a perpetual whiner, a hideous old bag of vapid, juvenile dreams. . . .

"Stop it, Bomanz," he muttered. "She's the mother of your son. Give her her due. She hasn't betrayed you." If nothing else, they still shared the hope represented by the map on silk. It was hard for her, waiting, unaware of his progress, knowing only that nearly four decades had yielded no tangible result.

The bell on the shop door tinkled. Bomanz clutched at his shopkeeper persona. He scuttled forward, a fat, bald little man with blue-veined hands folded before his chest. "Tokar." He bowed slightly. "I didn't expect you so soon."

Tokar was a trader from Oar, a friend of Bomanz's son Stancil. He had a bluff, honest, irreverent manner Bomanz deluded himself into seeing as the ghost of his own at a younger age.

"Didn't plan to be back so soon, Bo. But antiques are the rage. It surpasses comprehension."

"You want another lot? Already? You'll clean me out." Unsaid, the silent complaint: Bomanz, this means replenishment work. Time lost from research.

"The Domination is hot this year. Stop pottering around, Bo. Make hay, and all that. Next year the market could be as dead as the Taken."

"They're not . . . Maybe I'm getting too old, Tokar. I

don't enjoy the rows with Besand anymore. Hell. Ten years ago I went looking for him. A good squabble killed boredom. The digging grinds me down, too. I'm used up. I just want to sit on the stoop and watch life go by." While he chattered, Bomanz set out his best antique swords, pieces of armor, soldiers' amulets, and an almost perfectly preserved shield. A box of arrowheads with roses engraved. A pair of broad-bladed thrusting spears, ancient heads mounted on replica shafts.

"I can send you some men. Show them where to dig. I'll pay you commission. You won't have to do anything. That's a damned fine axe, Bo. TelleKurre? I could sell a bargeload of TelleKurre weaponry."

"UchiTelle, actually." A twinge from his ulcer. "No. No helpers." That was all he needed. A bunch of young hotshots hanging over his shoulder while he made his field calculations.

"Just a suggestion."

"Sorry. Don't mind me. Jasmine was on me this morning."

Softly, Tokar asked, "Found anything connected with the Taken?"

With the ease of decades, Bomanz dissembled, feigning horror. "The Taken? Am I a fool? I wouldn't touch it if I *could* get it past the Monitor."

Tokar smiled conspiratorily. "Sure. We don't want to offend the Eternal Guard. Nevertheless . . . There's one man in Oar who would pay well for something that could be ascribed to one of the Taken. He'd sell his soul for something that belonged to the Lady. He's in love with her."

"She was known for that." Bomanz avoided the younger man's gaze. How much had Stance revealed? Was this one of Besand's fishing expeditions? The older Bomanz became, the less he enjoyed the game. His nerves could not take this double life. He was tempted to confess just for the relief.

No, damnit! He had too much invested. Thirty-seven years. Digging and scratching every minute. Sneaking and pretending. The most abject poverty. No. He would not give up. Not now. Not when he was this close.

"In my way, I love her, too," he admitted. "But I haven't abandoned good sense. I'd scream for Besand if I found anything. So loud you'd hear me in Oar."

"All right. Whatever you say." Tokar grinned. "Enough suspense." He produced a leather wallet. "Letters from Stancil."

Bomanz seized the wallet. "Haven't heard from him since last time you were here."

"Can I start loading, Bo?"

"Sure. Go ahead." Absently, Bomanz took his current inventory list from a pigeonhole. "Mark off whatever you take."

Tokar laughed gently. "All of it this time, Bo. Just quote me a price."

"Everything? Half is junk."

"I told you, the Domination is hot."

"You saw Stance? How is he?" He was halfway through the first letter. His son had nothing substantial to relate. His missives were filled with daily trivia. Duty letters. Letters from a son to his parents, unable to span the timeless chasm.

"Sickeningly healthy. Bored with the university. Read on. There's a surprise."

"Tokar was here," Bomanz said. He grinned, danced from foot to foot.

"That thief?" Jasmine scowled. "Did you remember to get paid?" Her fat, sagging face was set in perpetual disapproval. Generally her mouth was open in the same vein.

"He brought letters from Stance. Here." He offered the packet. He could not contain himself. "Stance is coming home."

"Home? He can't. He has his position at the university."

"He's taking a sabbatical. He's coming for the summer."

"Why?"

"To see us. To help with the shop. To get away so he can finish a thesis."

Jasmine grumbled. She did not read the letters. She had not forgiven her son for sharing his father's interest in the Domination. "What he's doing is coming here to help you poke around where you're not supposed to poke, isn't he?"

Bomanz darted furtive glances at the shop's windows. His was an existence of justifiable paranoia. "It's the Year of the

Comet. The ghosts of the Taken will rise to mourn the passing of the Domination.''

This summer would mark the tenth return of the comet which had appeared at the hour of the Dominator's fall. The Ten Who Were Taken would manifest strongly.

Bomanz had witnessed one passage the summer he had come to the Old Forest, long before Stancil's birth. The Barrowland had been impressive with ghosts walking.

Excitement tightened his belly. Jasmine would not appreciate it, but this was the summer. End of the long quest. He lacked only one key. Find it and he could make contact, could begin drawing out instead of putting in.

Jasmine sneered. ''Why did I get into this? My mother warned me.''

''It's Stancil we're talking about, woman. Our only.''

''Ah, Bo, don't call me a cruel old lady. Of course I'll welcome him. Don't I cherish him, too?''

''Wouldn't hurt to show it.'' Bomanz examined the remnants of his inventory. ''Nothing left but the worst junk. These old bones ache just thinking of the digging I'll have to do.''

His bones ached, but his spirit was eager. Restocking was a plausible excuse for wandering the edges of the Barrowland.

''No time like now to start.''

''You trying to get me out of the house?''

''That wouldn't hurt my feelings.''

Sighing, Bomanz surveyed his shop. A few pieces of time-rotted gear, broken weapons, a skull that could not be attributed because it lacked the triangular inset characteristic of Domination officers. Collectors were not interested in the bones of kerns or in those of followers of the White Rose.

Curious, he thought. Why are we so intrigued by evil? The White Rose was more heroic than the Dominator or Taken. She has been forgotten by everybody but the Monitor's men. Any peasant can name half the Taken. The Barrowland, where evil lies restless, is guarded, and the grave of the White Rose is lost.

''Neither here nor there,'' Bomanz grumbled. ''Time to hit the field. Here. Here. Spade. Divining wand. Bags. . . . Maybe Tokar was right. Maybe I should get a helper. Brushes.

Help carry that stuff around. Transit. Maps. Can't forget those. What else? Claim ribbons. Of course. That wretched Men·fu.''

He stuffed things into a pack and hung equipment all about himself. He gathered spade and rake and transit. ''Jasmine. Jasmine! Open the damned door.''

She peeped through the curtains masking their living quarters. ''Should've opened it first, dimwit.'' She stalked across the shop. ''One of these days, Bo, you're going to get organized. Probably the day after my funeral.''

He stumbled down the street grumbling, ''I'll get organized the day you die. Damned well better believe. I want you in the ground before you change your mind.''

Chapter Four: THE NEAR PAST: CORBIE

The Barrowland lies far north of Charm, in the Old Forest so storied in the legends of the White Rose. Corbie came to the town there the summer after the Dominator failed to escape his grave through Juniper. He found the Lady's minions in high morale. The grand evil in the Great Barrow was no longer to be feared. The dregs of the Rebel had been routed. The empire had no more enemies of consequence. The Great Comet, harbinger of all catastrophes, would not return for decades.

One lone focus of resistance remained, a child claimed to be the reincarnation of the White Rose. But she was a fugitive, running with the remnants of the traitorous Black Company. Nothing to fear there. The Lady's overwhelming resources would swamp them.

Corbie came limping up the road from Oar, alone, a pack

on his back, a staff gripped tightly. He claimed to be a disabled veteran of the Limper's Forsberg campaigns. He wanted work. There was work aplenty for a man not too proud. The Eternal Guard were well-paid. Many hired drudgework taken off their duties.

At that time a regiment garrisoned the Barrowland. Countless civilians orbited its compound. Corbie vanished among those. When companies and battalions transferred out, he was an established part of the landscape.

He washed dishes, curried horses, cleaned stables, carried messages, mopped floors, peeled vegetables, assumed any burden for which he might earn a few coppers. He was a quiet, tall, dusky, brooding sort who made no special friends, but made no enemies either. Seldom did he socialize.

After a few months he asked for and received permission to occupy a ramshackle house long shunned because once it belonged to a sorcerer from Oar. As time and resources permitted, he restored the place. And like the sorcerer before him, he pursued the mission that had brought him north.

Ten, twelve, fourteen hours a day Corbie worked around town, then went home and worked some more. People wondered when he rested.

If there was anything that detracted from Corbie, it was that he refused to assume his role completely. Most scutboys had to endure a lot of personal abuse. Corbie would not accept it. Victimize him and his eyes went cold as winter steel. Only one man ever pressed Corbie once he got that look. Corbie beat him with ruthless, relentless efficiency.

No one suspected him of leading a double life. Outside his home he was Corbie the swamper, nothing more. He lived the role to his heart. When he was home, in the more public hours, he was Corbie the renovator, creating a new home from an old. Only in the wee hours, while all but the night patrol slept, did he become Corbie the man with a mission.

Corbie the renovator found a treasure in a wall of the wizard's kitchen. He took it upstairs, where Corbie the driven came up from the deeps.

The scrap of paper bore a dozen words scribbled in a shaky hand. A cipher key.

That lean, dusky, long-unsmiling face shed its ice. Dark

eyes sparkled, Fingers turned up a lamp. Corbie sat, and for an hour stared at nothing. Then, still smiling, he went downstairs and out into the night. He raised a hand in gentle greeting whenever he encountered the night patrol.

He was known now. No one challenged his right to limp about and watch the constellations wheel.

He went home when his nerves settled. There would be no sleep for him. He scattered papers, began to study, to decipher, to translate, to write a story-letter that would not reach its destination for years.

Chapter Five: THE PLAIN OF FEAR

One-Eye stopped by to tell me Darling was about to interview Corder and the messenger. "She's looking peaked, Croaker. You been watching her?"

"I watch. I advise. She ignores. What can I do?"

"We got twenty-some years till the comet shows. No point her working herself to death, is there?"

"Tell *her* that. She just tells me this mess will be settled long before the comet comes around again. That it's a race against time."

She believes that. But the rest of us cannot catch her fire. Isolated in the Plain of Fear, cut off from the world, the struggle with the Lady sometimes slips in importance. The Plain itself too often preoccupies us.

I caught myself outdistancing One-Eye. This premature burial has not been good for him. Without his skills he has weakened physically. He is beginning to show his age. I let him catch up.

"You and Goblin enjoy your adventure?"

He could not choose between a smirk or scowl.

"Got you again, eh?" Their battle has been on since the dawn. One-Eye starts each skirmish. Goblin usually finishes.

He grumbled something.

"What?"

"Yo!" someone shouted. "Everybody up top! Alert! Alert!"

One-Eye spat. "Twice in one day? What the hell?"

I knew what he meant. We have not had twenty alerts our whole two years out here. Now two in one day? Improbable.

I dashed back for my bow.

This time we went out with less clatter. Elmo had made his displeasure painfully apparent in a few private conversations.

Sunlight again. Like a blow. The entrance to the Hole faces westward. The sun was in our eyes when we emerged.

"You damned fool!" Elmo was yelling. "What the hell you doing?" A young soldier stood in the open, pointing. I let my gaze follow.

"Oh, damn," I whispered. "Oh, double bloody damn."

One-Eye saw it too. "Taken."

The airborne dot drifted higher, circling our hideout, spiraling inward. It wobbled suddenly.

"Yeah. Taken. Whisper or Journey?"

"Good to see old friends," Goblin said as he joined us.

We had not seen the Taken since reaching the Plain. Before that they had been in our hair constantly, having pursued us all the four years it had taken us to get here from Juniper.

They are the Lady's satraps, her understudies in terror. Once there were ten. In the time of the Domination, the Lady and her husband enslaved the greatest of their contemporaries, making them their instruments: the Ten Who Were Taken. The Taken went into the ground with their masters when the White Rose defeated the Dominator four centuries ago. And they arose with the Lady, two turns of the comet back. And in fighting among themselves—for some remained loyal to the Dominator—most perished.

But the Lady obtained new slaves. Feather. Whisper. Journey. Feather and the last of the old ones, the Limper, went down at Juniper, when we overcame the Dominator's bid for his own resurrection. Two are left. Whisper. Journey.

The flying carpet wobbled because it had reached the boun-

dary where Darling's null was enough to overpower its buoyancy.
The Taken turned away, falling outward, got far enough to
recover complete control. "Pity it didn't come straight in," I
said. "And come down like a rock."

"They're not stupid," Goblin said. "They're just scouting
us now." He shook his head, shuddered. He knew something
I did not. Probably something learned during his venture
outside the Plain.

"Campaign heating up?" I asked.

"Yep. What're you doing, bat-breath?" he snapped at
One-Eye. "Pay attention."

The little black man was ignoring the Taken. He stared at
the wild wind-carved bluffs south of us.

"Our job is to stay alive," One-Eye said, so smug you
knew he had something to get Goblin's goat. "That means
don't get distracted by the first flashy show you see."

"What the hell does that mean?"

"Means while the rest of you are eyeballing that clown up
there another one sneaked up behind the bluffs and put somebody down."

Goblin and I glared at the red cliffs. We saw nothing.

"Too late," One-Eye said. "It's gone. But I reckon somebody should go collect the spy."

I believed One-Eye. "Elmo! Get over here." I explained.

"Beginning to move," he murmured. "Just when I was
hoping they'd forgotten us."

"Oh, they haven't," Goblin said. "They most certainly
haven't." Again I felt he had something on his mind.

Elmo scanned the ground between us and the bluffs. He
knew it well. We all do. One day our lives may depend on
our knowing it better than someone hunting us. "Okay," he
told himself. "I see it. I'll take four men. After I see the
Lieutenant."

The Lieutenant does not come up for alerts. He and two
other men camp in the doorway to Darling's quarters. If ever
the enemy reaches Darling, it will be over their bodies.

The flying carpet went away westward. I wondered why it
had gone unchallenged by the creatures of the Plain. I went to
the menhir that had spoken to me earlier. I asked. Instead of
answering, it said, "It begins, Croaker. Mark this day."

"Yeah. Right." And I do call that day the beginning, though parts of it started years before. That was the day of the first letter, the day of the Taken, and the day of Tracker and Toadkiller Dog.

The menhir had a final remark. "There are strangers on the Plain." It would not defend the various flyers for not resisting the Taken.

Elmo returned. I said, "The menhir says we might have more visitors."

Elmo raised an eyebrow. "You and Silent have the next two watches?"

"Yep."

"Be careful. Goblin. One-Eye. Come here." They put their heads together. Then Elmo picked four youngsters and went hunting.

Chapter Six: THE PLAIN OF FEAR

I went up top for my watch. There was no sign of Elmo and his men. The sun was low. The menhir was gone. There was no sound but the voice of the wind.

Silent sat in shadow inside a reef of thousand-coral, dappled by sunlight come through twisted branches. Coral makes good cover. Few of the Plain's denizens dare its poisons. The watch is always in more danger from native exotica than from our enemies.

I twisted and ducked between deadly spines, joined Silent. He is a long, lean, aging man. His dark eyes seemed focused on dreams that had died. I deposited my weapons. "Anything?"

He shook his head, a single miniscule negative. I arranged the pads I had brought. The coral twisted around us, branches and fans climbing twenty feet high. We could see little but the creek crossing and a few dead menhirs, and the walking trees on the far slope. One tree stood beside the brook, taproot in the water. As though sensing my attention, it began a slow retreat.

The visible Plain is barren. The usual desert life—lichens and scrub brush, snakes and lizards, scorpions and spiders, wild dogs and ground squirrels—is present but scarce. You encounter it mainly when that is inconvenient. Which sums up Plain life generally. You encounter the real strangeness only when that is most inopportune. The Lieutenant claims a man trying to commit suicide here could spend years without becoming uncomfortable.

The predominant colors are reds and browns, rust, ochre, blood- and wine-shaded sandstones like the bluffs, with here and there the random stratum of orange. The corals lay down scattered white and pink reefs. True verdance is absent. Both walking trees and scrub plants have leaves a dusty grey-green, in which green exists mainly by acclamation. The menhirs, living and dead, are a stark grey-brown unlike any stone native to the Plain.

A bloated shadow drifted across the wild scree skirting the cliffs. It covered many acres, was too dark to be the shadow of a cloud. "Windwhale?"

Silent nodded.

It cruised the upper air between us and the sun, but I could not spot it. I had not seen one in years. Last time Elmo and I were crossing the Plain with Whisper, on the Lady's behalf. . . . That long ago? Time does flee, and with little fun in it. "Strange waters under the bridge, my friend. Strange waters under."

He nodded, but he did not speak. He is Silent.

He has not spoken in all the years I have known him. Nor in the years he has been with the Company. Yet both One-Eye and my predecessor as Annalist say he is quite capable of speech. From hints accumulated over the years, it has become my firm conviction that in his youth, before he signed on, he swore a great oath never to speak. It being the iron law of the Company not to pry into a man's life before he enlisted, I have been unable to learn anything about the circumstances.

I have seen him come close to speaking, when he was angry enough, or amused enough, but always he caught himself at the last instant. For a long time men made a game of baiting him, trying to get him to break his vow, but most abandoned the effort quickly. Silent had a hundred little ways of discouraging a man, like filling his bedroll with ticks.

Shadows lengthened. Stains of darkness spread. At last Silent rose, stepped over me, returned to the Hole, a darkly clad shadow moving through darkness. A strange man, Silent. Not only does he not talk; he does not gossip. How can you get a handle on a guy like that?

Yet he is one of my oldest and closest friends. Go explain that.

"Well, Croaker." The voice was as hollow as a ghost's. I started. Malicious laughter rattled through the coral reef. A menhir had slipped up on me. I turned slightly. It stood square on the path Silent had taken, twelve feet tall and ugly. A runt of its kind.

"Hello, rock."

Having amused itself at my expense, it now ignored me. Stayed as silent as a stone. Ha-ha.

The menhirs are our principal allies upon the Plain. They interlocute for the other sentient species. They let us know what is happening only when it suits them, however.

"What's happening with Elmo?" I asked.

Nothing.

Are they magic? I guess not. Otherwise they would not survive inside the nullity Darling radiates. But what are they? Mysteries. Like most of the bizarre creatures out here.

"There are strangers on the Plain."

"I know. I know."

Night creatures came out. Dots of luminescence fluttered and swooped above. The windwhale whose shadow I saw came far enough eastward to show me its glimmering underbelly. It would descend soon, trailing tendrils to trap whatever came its way. A breeze rose.

Sagey scents trickled across my nostrils. Air chuckled and whispered and murmured and whistled in the coral. From farther away came the wind-chimes tinkle of Old Father Tree.

He is unique. First or last of his kind, I do not know. There he stands, twenty feet tall and ten thick, brooding beside the creek, radiating something akin to dread, his roots planted on the geographical center of the Plain. Silent, Goblin, and One-Eye have all tried to unravel his significance. They have gotten nowhere. The scarce wild human tribesmen of the Plain worship him. They say he has been here since the dawn. He does have that timeless feel.

The moon rose. While it lay torpid and pregnant on the horizon I thought I saw something cross it. Taken? Or one of the Plain creatures?

A racket rose round the mouth of the Hole. I groaned. I did not need this. Goblin and One-Eye. For half a minute, uncharitably, I wished they had not come back. "Knock it off. I don't want to hear that crap."

Goblin scooted up outside the coral, grinned, dared me to do something. He looked rested, recuperated. One-Eye asked, "Feeling cranky, Croaker?"

"Damned straight. What're you doing out here?"

"Needed some fresh air." He cocked his head, stared at the line of cliffs. So. Worried about Elmo.

"He'll be all right," I said.

"I know." One-Eye added, "I lied. Darling sent us. She felt something stir at the west edge of the null."

"Ah?"

"I don't know what it was, Croaker." Suddenly he was defensive. Pained. He would have known but for Darling. He stands where I would were I stripped of my medical gear. Helpless to do what he has trained at all his life.

"What're you going to do?"

"Build a fire."

"What?"

That fire roared. One-Eye got so ambitious he dragged in enough deadwood to serve half a legion. The flames beat back the darkness till I could see fifty yards beyond the creek. The last walking trees had departed. Probably smelled One-Eye coming.

He and Goblin dragged in a fallen tree of the ordinary sort. We leave the walkers alone, except to right clumsies that trip on their own roots. Not that that happens often. They do not travel much.

They were bickering about who was dogging his share of work. They dropped the tree. "Fade," Goblin said, and in a moment there was no sign of them. Baffled, I surveyed the darkness. I saw nothing, heard nothing.

I found myself having trouble remaining awake. I broke up the dead tree for something to do. Then I felt the oddness.

I stopped in midbreak. How long had the menhirs been gathering? I counted fourteen on the verges of the light. They cast long, deep shadows. "What's up?" I asked, my nerves a bit frayed.

"There are strangers on the Plain."

Hell of a tune they played. I settled near the fire, back to it, tossed wood over my shoulder, building the flames. The light spread. I counted another ten menhirs. After a time I said, "That's not exactly news."

"One comes."

That *was* new. And spoken with passion, something I had not witnessed before. Once, twice, I thought I caught a flicker of motion, but I could not be sure. Firelight is tricky. I piled on more wood.

Movement for sure. Beyond the creek. Manshape coming toward me, slowly. Wearily. I settled in pretended boredom. He came nearer. Across his right shoulder he carried a saddle and blanket held with his left hand. In his right he carried a long wooden case, its polish gleaming in the firelight. It was seven feet long and four inches by eight. Curious.

I noticed the dog as they crossed the creek. A mongrel, ragged, mangy, mostly a dirty white but with a black circle around one eye and a few daubs of black on its flanks. It limped, carrying one forepaw off the ground. The fire caught its eyes. They burned bright red.

The man was over six feet, maybe thirty. He moved lithely even in his weariness. He had muscles on muscles. His tattered shirt revealed arms and chest crisscrossed with scars. His face was empty of emotion. He met my gaze as he approached the fire, neither smiling nor betraying unfriendly intent.

Chill touched me, lightly. He looked tough, but not tough enough to negotiate the Plain of Fear alone.

First order of business would be to stall. Otto was due out

to relieve me soon. The fire would alert him. He would see the stranger, then duck down and rouse the Hole.

"Hello," I said.

He halted, exchanged glances with his mongrel. The dog came forward slowly, sniffing the air, searching the surrounding night. It stopped a few feet away, shook as though wet, settled on its belly.

The stranger came forward just that far. "Take a load off," I invited.

He swung his saddle down, lowered his case, sat. He was stiff. He had trouble crossing his legs.

"Lose your horse?"

He nodded. "Broke a leg. West of here, five, six miles. I lost the trail."

There *are* trails through the Plain. Some of them the Plain honors as safe. Sometimes. According to a formula known only to its denizens. Only someone desperate or stupid hazards them alone, though. This fellow did not look like an idiot.

The dog made a whuffling sound. The man scratched its ears.

"Where you headed?"

"Place called the Fastness."

That is the legend-name, the propaganda name, for the Hole. A calculated bit of glamor for the troops in faraway places.

"Name?"

"Tracker. This is Toadkiller Dog."

"Pleased to meet you, Tracker. Toadkiller."

The dog grumbled. Tracker said, "You have to use his whole name. Toadkiller Dog."

I kept a straight face only because he was such a big, grim, tough-looking man. "What's this Fastness?" I asked. "I never heard of it."

He lifted hard, dark eyes from the mutt, smiled. "I've heard it lies near Tokens."

Twice in one day? Was it the day of twos? No. Not bloody likely. I did not like the look of the man, either. Reminded me too much of our one-time brother Raven. Ice and iron. I donned my baffled face. It is a good one. "Tokens? That's a new one on me. Must be somewhere way the hell out east. What are you headed there for, anyway?''

He smiled again. His dog opened one eye, gave me a baleful look. They did not believe me.

"Carrying messages.''

"I see.''

"Mainly a packet. Addressed to somebody named Croaker.''

I sucked spittle between teeth, slowly scanned the surrounding darkness. The circle of light had shrunk, but the number of menhirs remained undiminished. I wondered about One-Eye and Goblin. "Now there's a name I've heard,'' I said. "Some kind of sawbones.'' Again the dog gave me that look. This time, I decided, it was sarcastic.

One-Eye stepped out of the darkness behind Tracker, sword ready to do the dirty deed. Damn, but he came quiet. Witchery or no.

I gave him away with a flicker of surprise. Tracker and his dog looked back. Both were startled to see someone there. The dog rose. Its hackles lifted. Then it sank to the ground again, having twisted till it could keep us both in sight.

But then Goblin appeared, just as quietly. I smiled. Tracker glanced over. His eyes narrowed. He looked thoughtful, like a man discovering he was in a card game with rogues sharper than he had expected. Goblin chuckled. "He wants in, Croaker. I say we take him down.''

Tracker's hand twitched toward the case he had carried. His animal growled. Tracker closed his eyes. When they opened, he was in control. His smile returned. "Croaker, eh? Then I've found the Fastness.''

"You've found it, friend.''

Slowly, so as not to alarm anyone, Tracker took an oilskin packet from his saddlebag. It was the twin of that I had received only half a day before. He offered it to me. I tucked it inside my shirt. "Where'd you get it?''

"Oar.'' He told the same story as the other messenger.

I nodded. "You've come that far, then?''

"Yes.''

"We *should* take him in, then,'' I told One-Eye. He caught my meaning. We would let this messenger come face to face with the other. See if sparks flew. One-Eye grinned.

I glanced at Goblin. He approved.

None of us felt quite right about Tracker. I am not sure why.

"Let's go," I said. I hoisted myself off the ground with my bow.

Tracker eyed the stave. He started to say something, shut up. As though he recognized it. I smiled as I turned away. Maybe he thought he had fallen foul of the Lady. "Follow me."

He did. And Goblin and One-Eye followed him, neither helping with his gear. His dog limped beside him, nose to the ground. Before we went inside, I glanced southward, concerned. When would Elmo come home?

We put Tracker and mutt into a guarded cell. They did not protest. I went to my quarters after wakening Otto, who was overdue. I tried to sleep, but that damned packet lay on the table screaming.

I was not sure I wanted to read its contents.

It won the battle.

Chapter Seven: THE SECOND LETTER

Croaker:

Bomanz peered through his transit, sighting on the prow of the Great Barrow. He stepped back, noted the angle, opened one of his crude field maps. This was where he had unearthed the TelleKurre axe. "Wish Occules' descriptions weren't so vague. This must have been the flank of their formation. The axis of their line should have paralleled the others, so. Shifter and the knights would have bunched up over there. I'll be damned."

The ground there humped slightly. Good. Less ground water to damage buried artifacts. But the overgrowth was dense. Scrub oak. Wild roses. Poison ivy. Especially poison ivy. Bomanz hated that pestilential weed. He started scratching just thinking about it.

"Bomanz."

"What?" He whirled, raising his rake.

"Whoa! Take it easy, Bo."

"What's the matter with you? Sneaking up like that. Ain't funny, Besand. Want me to rake that idiot grin off your face?"

"Ooh! Nasty today, aren't we?" Besand was a lean old man approximately Bomanz's age. His shoulders slumped, following his head, which thrust forward as though he was sniffing a trail. Great blue veins humped the backs of his hands. Liver spots dotted his skin.

"What the hell do you expect? Come jumping out of the bushes at a man."

"Bushes? What bushes? Your conscience bothering you, Bo?"

"Besand, you've been trying to trap me since the moon was green. Why don't you give up? First Jasmine gives me a hard way to go, then Tokar buys me out so I have to go digging fresh stock, and now I have to dance with you? Go away. I'm not in the mood."

Besand grinned a big, lopsided grin, revealing pickets of rotten teeth. "I haven't caught you, Bo, but that don't mean you're innocent. It just means I never caught you."

"If I'm not innocent, you must be damned stupid not to catch me in forty years. Damn, man, why the hell can't you make life easy for both of us?"

Besand laughed. "Real soon now I'll be out of your hair for good. They're putting me out to pasture."

Bomanz leaned on his rake, considered the Guardsman. Besand exuded a sour odor of pain. "Really? I'm sorry."

"Bet you are. My replacement might be smart enough to catch you."

"Give it a rest. You want to know what I'm doing? Figuring where the TelleKurre knights went down. Tokar wants spectacular stuff. That's the best I can do. Short of going over there and giving you an excuse to hang me. Hand me that dowser.''

Besand passed the divining rod. ''Mound robbing, eh? Tokar suggest that?''

Icy needles burrowed into Bomanz's spine. This was more than a casual question. ''We have to do this constantly? Haven't we known each other long enough to do without the cat-and-mouse?''

''I enjoy it, Bo.'' Besand trailed him to the overgrown hummock. ''Going to have to clear this out. Just can't keep up anymore. Not enough men, not enough money.''

''Could you get it right away? That's where I want to dig, I think. Poison ivy.''

''Oh, 'ware poison ivy, Bo.'' Besand snickered. Each summer Bomanz cursed his way through numerous botanical afflictions. ''About Tokar . . .''

''I don't deal with people who want to break the law. That's been my rule forever. Nobody bothers me anymore.''

''Oblique but acceptable.''

Bomanz's wand twitched. ''I'll be dipped in sheep shit. Right in the middle.''

''Sure?''

''Look at it jump. Must've buried them in one big hole.''

''About Tokar . . .''

''What about him, dammit? You want to hang him, go ahead. Just give me time to hook up with somebody else who can handle my business as good.''

''I don't want to hang anybody, Bo. I just want to warn you. There's a rumor out of Oar that says he's a Resurrectionist.''

Bomanz dropped his rod. He gobbled air. ''Really? A Resurrectionist?''

The Monitor scrutinized him intently. ''Just a rumor. I hear all kinds. Thought you might want to know. We're as close as two men get around here.''

Bomanz accepted the olive branch. ''Yeah. Honestly, he's never dropped a hint. Whew! That's a load to drop on a man.'' A load which deserved some heavy thinking. ''Don't tell anybody what I found. That thief Men fu . . .''

Besand laughed yet again. His mirth had a sephulchral quality.

"You enjoy your work, don't you? I mean, harassing people who don't dare fight back."

"Careful, Bo. I could drag you in for questioning." Besand spun, stalked away.

Bomanz sneered at his back. Of course Besand enjoyed his job. It let him play dictator. He could do anything to anyone without having to answer for it.

Once the Dominator and his minions fell and were buried in their mounds behind barriers wrought of the finest magicks of their day, the White Rose decreed that an eternal guard be posted. A guard beholden to none, charged with preventing the resurrection of the undead evil beneath the mounds. The White Rose understood human nature. Always there would be those who would see profit in using or following the Dominator. Always there would be worshippers of evil who wished their champion freed.

The Resurrectionists appeared almost before the grass sprouted on the barrows.

Tokar a Resurrectionist? Bomanz thought. Don't I have enough trouble? Besand will pitch his tent in my pocket now.

Bomanz had no interest in reviving the old evils. He merely wanted to make contact with one of them so as to illuminate several ancient mysteries.

Besand was out of sight. He should stomp all the way back to his quarters. There would be time for a few forbidden observations. Bomanz realigned his transit.

The Barrowland did not have the look of great evil, only of neglect. Four hundred years of vegetation and weather had restructured that once marvelous work. The barrows and mystical landscaping were all but lost amidst the brush covering them. The Eternal Guard no longer had the wherewithal to perform adequate upkeep. Monitor Besand was fighting a desperate rearguard action against time itself.

Nothing grew well on the Barrowland. The vegetation was

twisted and stunted. Still, the shapes of the mounds, and the menhirs and fetishes which bound the Taken, were often concealed.

Bomanz had spent a lifetime sorting out which mound was which, who lay where, and where each menhir and fetish stood. His master chart, his silken treasure, was nearly complete. He could, almost, thread the maze. He was so close he was tempted to try before he was truly ready. But he was no fool. He meant to try nursing sweet milk from the blackest of cows. He dared make no mistake. He had Besand on the one hand, the poisonous old wickedness on the other.

But if he succeeded. . . . Ah, if he succeeded. If he made contact and nursed away the secrets. . . . Man's knowledge would be extended dramatically. He would become the mightiest of living mages. His fame would course with the wind. Jasmine would have everything she quarreled about sacrificing. *If* he made contact.

He would, by damn! Neither fear nor the infirmity of age would stay him now. A few months and he would have the last key.

Bomanz had lived his lies so long he often lied to himself. Even in his honest moments he never confessed his most powerful motive, his intellectual affair with the Lady. It was she who had intrigued him from the beginning, she whom he was trying to contact, she who made the literature endlessly fascinating. Of all the lords of the Domination she was the most shadowed, the most surrounded by myth, the least encumbered by historical fact. Some scholars called her the greatest beauty ever to have lived, claiming that simply to have seen her was to have fallen into her thrall. Some called her the true motive force of the Domination. A few admitted that their documentaries were really little more than romantic fantasies. Others admitted nothing while demonstrably embellishing. Bomanz had become perpetually bemused while still a student.

Back in his attic, he spread his silken chart. His day had not been a complete waste. He had located a previously unknown menhir and had identified the spells it anchored. And he had found the TelleKurre site. That would buy the mutton and beans.

He glared at the chart, as if pure will might conjure the information he needed.

There were two diagrams. The upper was a five-pointed star within a slightly larger circle. Such had been the shape of the Barrowland when newly constructed. The star had stood a fathom above the surrounding terrain, retained by limestone walls. The circle represented the outer bank of a moat, the earth from which had been used to build the barrows, the star, and a pentagon within the star. Today the moat was little more than boggy ground. Besand's predecessors had been unable to keep up with Nature.

Within the star, drawn off the points where the arms met, was a pentagon another fathom high. It, too, had been retained, but the walls had fallen and become overgrown. Central to the pentagon, on a north-south axis, lay the Great Barrow where the Dominator slept.

At the points of his chart star, clockwise from the top, Bomanz had penned the odd numbers from one to nine. Accompanying each was a name: Soulcatcher, Shapeshifter, Nightcrawler, Stormbringer, Bonegnasher. The occupants of the five outer barrows had been identified. The five inner points were numbered evenly, beginning at the right foot of the arm of the star pointing northward. At four was the Howler, at eight the Limper. The graves of three of the Ten Who Were Taken remained unidentified.

"Who's in that damned six spot?" Bomanz muttered. He slammed a fist against the table. "Dammit!" Four years and he was no closer to that name. The mask concealing that identity was the one remaining substantial barrier. Everything else was plain technical application, a matter of negating wardspells, then of contacting the great one in the central mound.

The wizards of the White Rose had left volumes bragging about their performances of their art, but not one word of where their victims lay. Such was human nature. Besand bragged about the fish he caught, the bait he used, and seldom produced the veritable piscine trophy.

Below his star chart Bomanz had drawn a second portraying the central mound. It was a rectangle on a north-south axis surrounded by and filled with ranks of symbols. Outside each corner was a representation of a menhir which, on the Barrowland, was a twelve-foot pillar topped by a two-faced owl's head. One face glared inward, the other out. The menhirs formed the corner posts anchoring the first line of spells warding the Great Barrow.

Along the sides were the line posts, little circles representing wooden fetish poles. Most had rotted and fallen, their spells drooping with them. The Eternal Guard had no staff wizard capable of restoring or replacing them.

Within the mound proper there were symbols ranked in three rectangles of declining size. The outermost resembled pawns, the next knights, and the inner, elephants. The crypt of the Dominator was surrounded by men who had given their lives to bring him down. Ghosts were the middle line between old evil and a world capable of recalling it. Bomanz anticipated no difficulty getting past them. The ghosts were there, in his opinion, to discourage common grave robbers.

Within the three rectangles Bomanz had drawn a dragon with its tail in its mouth. Legend said a great dragon lay curled round the crypt, more alive than the Lady or Dominator, catnapping the centuries away while awaiting an attempt to recall the trapped evil.

Bomanz had no way of coping with the dragon, but he had no need, either. He meant to communicate with the crypt, not to open it.

Damn! If he could only lay hands on an old Guardsman's amulet. . . . The early Guards had worn amulets which had allowed them to go into the Barrowland to keep it up. The amulets still existed, though they were no longer used. Besand wore one. The others he kept squirreled away.

Besand. That madman. That sadist.

Bomanz considered the Monitor his closest acquaintance— but a friend, never. No, never a friend. Sad commentary on his life, that the man nearest him would be one who would jump at a chance to torture or hang him.

What was that about retirement? Someone outside this forsaken forest had recalled the Barrowland?

"Bomanz! Are you going to eat?"

Bomanz muttered imprecations and rolled his chart.

* * *

The Dream came that night. Something sirenic called him. He was young again, single, strolling the lane that passed his house. A woman waved. Who was she? He didn't know. He didn't care. He loved her. Laughing, he ran toward her. . . . Floating steps. Effort took him no nearer. Her face saddened. She faded. . . . "Don't go!" he called. "Please!" But she disappeared, and took with her his sun.

A vast starless night devoured his dream. He floated in a clearing within a forest unseen. Slowly, slowly, a diffuse silver something limned the trees. A big star with a long silver mane. He watched it grow till its tail spanned the sky.

Twinge of uncertainty. Shadow of fear. "It's coming right at me!" He cringed, threw his arm across his face. The silver ball filled the sky. It had a face. The woman's face. . . .

"Bo! Stop it!" Jasmine punched him again.

He sat up. "Uhn? What?"

"You were yelling. That nightmare again?"

He listened to his heart hammer, sighed. Could it take much more? He was an old man. "The same one." It recurred at unpredictable intervals. "It was stronger this time."

"Maybe you ought to see a dream doctor."

"Out here?" He snorted disgustedly. "I don't need a dream doctor anyway."

"No. Probably just your conscience. Nagging you for luring Stancil back from Oar."

"I didn't lure . . . Go to sleep." To his amazement, she rolled over, for once unwilling to pursue their squabble.

He stared into the darkness. It had been so much clearer. Almost too crisp and obvious. Was there a meaning hidden behind the dream's warning against tampering?

Slowly, slowly, the mood of the beginning of the dream returned. That sense of being summoned, of being but one intuitive step from heart's desire. It felt good. His tension drained away. He fell asleep smiling.

Besand and Bomanz stood watching Guardsmen clear the brush from Bomanz's site. Bomanz suddenly spat, "Don't burn it, you idiot! Stop him, Besand."

Besand shook his head. A Guard with a torch backed away from the brush pile. "Son, you don't burn poison ivy. The smoke spreads the poison."

Bomanz was scratching. And wondering why his companion was being so reasonable. Besand smirked. "Get itchy just thinking about it, don't you?"

"Yes."

"There's your other itch." He pointed. Bomanz saw his competitor Men fu observing from a safe distance. He growled, "I never hated anybody, but he tempts me. He has no ethics, no scruples, and no conscience. He's a thief and a liar."

"I know him, Bo. And lucky for you I do."

"Let me ask you something, Besand. *Monitor* Besand. How come you don't aggravate him the way you do me? What do you mean, lucky?"

"He accused you of Resurrectionist tendencies. I don't shadow him because his many virtues include cowardice. He doesn't have the hair to recover proscribed artifacts."

"And I do? That little wart libeled me? With capital crimes? If I weren't an old man. . . ."

"He'll get his, Bo. And you do have the guts. I've just never caught you with the inclination."

Bomanz rolled his eyes. "Here we go. The veiled accusations. . . ."

"Not so veiled, my friend. There's a moral laxness in you, an unwillingness to accept the existence of evil, that stinks like an old corpse. Give it its head and I'll catch you, Bo. The wicked are cunning, but they always betray themselves."

For an instant Bomanz thought his world was falling apart. Then he realized Besand was fishing. A dedicated fisherman, the Monitor. Shaken, he countered, "I'm sick of your sadism. If you really suspected anything, you'd be on me like a snake on shit. Legalities never meant anything to you Guards. You're probably lying about Men fu. You'd haul your own mother in on the word of a sorrier villain than him. You're sick, Besand. You know that? Diseased. Right here." He tapped his temple. "You can't relate without cruelty."

"You're pushing your luck again, Bo."

Bomanz backed down. Fright and temper had been talking. In his own odd way Besand had shown him special tolerance.

It was as though he were necessary to the Monitor's emotional health. Besand needed one person, outside the Guard, whom he did not victimize. Someone whose immunity repaid him in a sort of validation. . . . I'm symbolic of the people he defends? Bomanz snorted. That was rich.

That business about being retired. Did he say more than I heard? Is he calling off all bets because he's leaving? Maybe he does have a sense for scofflaws. Maybe he wants to go out with a flash.

What about the new man? Another monster, unblinkered by the gossamer I've spun across Besand's eyes? Maybe someone who will come in like the bull into the corrida? And Tokar, the possible Resurrectionist. . . . How does he fit?

"What's the matter?" Besand asked. Concern colored his words.

"Ulcer's bothering me." Bomanz massaged his temples, hoping the headache would not come too.

"Plant your markers. Men fu might jump you right here."

"Yeah." Bomanz took a half dozen stakes from his pack. Each trailed a strip of yellow cloth. He planted them. Custom dictated that the ground so circumscribed was his to exploit.

Men fu could make night raids, or whatever, and Bomanz would have no legal recourse. Claims had no standing in law, only in private treaty. The antique miners exercised their own sanctions.

Men fu was under every sanction but violence. Nothing altered his thieving ways.

"Wish Stancil was here," Bomanz said. "He could watch at night."

"I'll growl at him. That's always good for a few days. I heard Stance was coming home."

"Yeah. For the summer. We're excited. We haven't seen him in four years."

"Friend of Tokar, isn't he?"

Bomanz whirled. "Damn you! You never let up, do you?" He spoke softly, in genuine rage, without the shouts and curses and dramatic gestures of his habitual semi-rage.

"All right, Bo. I'll drop it."

"You'd better. You'd damned well better. I won't have you crawling all over him all summer. Won't have it, you hear?"

"I said I'd drop it."

Chapter Eight: THE BARROWLAND

Corbie came and went at will around the Guard compound. The walls inside the headquarters building boasted several dozen old paintings of the Barrowland. He studied those often while he cleaned, shivering. His reaction was not unique. The Dominator's attempt to escape through Juniper had rocked the Lady's empire. Stories of his cruelties had fed upon themselves and grown fat in the centuries since the White Rose laid him down.

The Barrowland remained quiet. Those who watched saw nothing untoward. Morale rose. The old evil had shot its bolt.

But it waited.

It would wait throughout eternity if need be. It could not die. Its apparent last hope was no hope. The Lady was immortal, too. She would allow nothing to open her husband's grave.

The paintings recorded progressive decay. The latest dated from shortly after the Lady's resurrection. Even then the Barrowland had been much more whole.

Sometimes Corbie went to the edge of town, stared at the Great Barrow, shook his head.

Once there had been amulets which permitted Guards safely within the spells making the Barrowland lethal, to allow for upkeep. But those had disappeared. The Guard could but watch and wait now.

Time ambled. Slow and grey and limping, Corbie became a town fixture. He spoke seldom, but occasionally enlivened the lie sessions at Blue Willy with a wooly anecdote from the Forsberg campaigns. The fire blazed in his eyes then. No one doubted he had been there, even if he saw those days a little walleyed.

He made no true friends. Rumor said he did share the occasional private chess game with the Monitor, Colonel Sweet, for whom he had done some special small services. And of course, there was the recruit Case, who devoured his tales and accompanied him on his hobbling walks. Rumor said Corbie could read. Case hoped to learn.

No one ever visited the second floor of Corbie's home. There, in the heart of the night, he slowly unravelled the treacherous mare's nest of a tale that time and dishonesty had distorted out of any parallel with truth.

Only parts were encrypted. Most was hastily scribbled in TelleKurre, the principal language of the Domination era. But scattered passages were in UchiTelle, a TelleKurre regional vulgate. Times were, when battling those passages, Corbie smiled grimly. He might be the only man alive able to puzzle through those sometimes fragmentary sentences. "Benefit of a classical education," he would murmur with a certain sarcasm. Then he would become reflective, introspective. He would take one of his late night walks to shake revenant memory. One's own yesterday is a ghost that will not be laid. Death is the only exorcism.

He saw himself as a craftsman, did Corbie. A smith. An armorer cautiously forging a lethal sword. Like his predecessor in that house, he had dedicated his life to the search for a fragment of knowledge.

The winter was astonishing. The first snows came early, after an early and unusually damp autumn. It snowed often and heavily. Spring came late.

In the forests north of the Barrowland, where only scattered clans dwelt, life was harsh. Tribesmen appeared bearing furs to trade for food. Factors for the furriers of Oar were ecstatic.

Old folks called the winter a harbinger of worse to come. But old folks always see today's weather as more harsh than that of yore. Or milder. Never, never the same.

Spring sprung. A swift thaw set the creeks and rivers raging. The Great Tragic, which looped within three miles of the Barrowland, spread miles beyond its banks. It abducted ten's and hundreds of thousands of trees. The flood was so spectacular that scores from town wandered out to watch it from a hilltop.

For most, the novelty faded. But Corbie limped out any day Case could accompany him. Case was yet possessed of dreams. Corbie indulged him.

"Why so interested in the river, Corbie?"

"I don't know. Maybe because of its grand statement."

"What?"

Corbie swung an encompassing hand. "The vastness. The ongoing rage. See how significant we are?" Brown water gnawed at the hill, furious, fumbling forests of driftwood. Less turbulent arms hugged the hill, probed the woods behind.

Case nodded. "Like the feeling I get when I look at the stars."

"Yes. Yes. But this is more personal. Closer to home. Not so?"

"I guess." Case sounded baffled. Corbie smiled. Legacy of a farm youth.

"Let's go back. It's peaked. But I don't trust it with those clouds rolling in."

Rain did threaten. Were the river to rise much more, the hill would become an island.

Case helped Corbie cross the boggy parts and up to the crest of the low rise which kept the flood from reaching cleared land. Much of that was a lake now, shallow enough to be waded if some fool dared. Under grey skies the Great Barrow stood out poorly, reflecting off the water as a dark lump. Corbie shuddered. "Case. He's still there."

The youth leaned on his spear, interested only because Corbie was interested. He wanted to get out of the drizzle.

"The Dominator, lad. Whatever else did not escape. Waiting. Filling with ever more hatred for the living."

Case looked at Corbie. The older man was taut with tension. He seemed frightened.

"If he gets loose, pity the world."

"But didn't the Lady finish him in Juniper?"

"She stopped him. She didn't destroy him. That may not be possible. . . . Well, it must be. He has to be vulnerable somehow. But if the White Rose couldn't harm him. . . ."

"The Rose wasn't so strong, Corbie. She couldn't even hurt the Taken. Or even *their* minions. All she could do was bind and bury them. It took the Lady and the Rebel. . . ."

"The Rebel? I doubt that. *She* did it." Corbie lunged forward, forcing his leg. He marched along the edge of the lake. His gaze remained fixed on the Great Barrow.

Case feared Corbie was obsessed with the Barrowland. As a Guard, he had to be concerned. Though the Lady had exterminated the Resurrectionists in his grandfather's time, still that mound exerted its dark attraction. Monitor Sweet remained frightened someone would revive that idiocy. He wanted to caution Corbie, could think of no polite way to phrase himself.

Wind stirred the lake. Ripples ran from the Barrow toward them. Both shivered. "Wish this weather would break," Corbie muttered. "Time for tea?"

"Yes."

The weather continued chill and wet. Summer came late. Autumn arrived early. When the Great Tragic did at last recede, it left a mud plain strewn with the wrecks of grand trees. Its channel had shifted a half mile westward.

The woodland tribes continued selling furs.

Serendipity. Corbie was near done renovating. He was restoring a closet. In removing a wooden clothes rod he fumbled. The rod separated into parts when it hit the floor.

He knelt. He stared. His heart hammered. A slim spindle of white silk lay exposed. . . . Gently, gently, he put the rod back together, carried it upstairs.

Carefully, carefully, he removed the silk, unrolled it. His stomach knotted.

It was Bomanz's chart of the Barrowland, complete with notes about which Taken lay where, where fetishes were located and why, the puissance of protective spells, and a scatter of known resting places of minions of the Taken who had gone into the ground with their captains. A cluttered chart indeed. Mostly annotated in TelleKurre.

Also noted were burial sites outside the Barrowland proper. Most of the ordinary fallen had gone into mass graves.

The battle fired Corbie's imagination. For a moment he saw the Dominator's forces standing firm, dying to the last man. He saw wave after wave of the White Rose horde give themselves up to contain the shadow within the trap. Overhead, the Great Comet seared the sky, a vast flaming scimitar.

He could only imagine, though. There were no reliable histories.

He commiserated with Bomanz. Poor foolish little man, dreaming, seeking the truth. He had not earned his dark legend.

Corbie remained fixed over the chart all night, letting it seep into bone and soul. It did little to help him translate, but it did illuminate the Barrowland some. And even more, it illuminated a wizard so dedicated he had spent his entire adult life studying the Barrowland.

Dawn's light stirred Corbie. For a moment he doubted himself. Could he become prey to the same fatal passion?

Chapter Nine: THE PLAIN OF FEAR

The Lieutenant himself stirred me out. "Elmo's back, Croaker. Eat some breakfast, then report to the conference room." He was a sour man getting sourer every day. Sometimes I regret having voted for him after the Captain died in Juniper. But the Captain wished it. It was his dying request.

"Be there soonest," I said, piling out without my customary growl. I grabbed clothing, stirred papers, silently mocked myself. How often did I doubt voting for the Captain himself? Yet when he wanted to resign, we did not let him.

My quarters look nothing like a physician's den. The walls are floor to ceiling with old books. I have read most, after having studied the languages in which they are written. Some are as old as the Company itself, recounting ancient histories. Some are noble genealogies, stolen from widely dispersed old temples and civil offices. The rarest, and most interesting, chronicle the rise and growth of the Domination.

The rarest of all are those in TelleKurre. The followers of the White Rose were not gentle victors. They burned books and cities, transported women and children, profaned ancient works of art and famous shrines. The customary afterglow of a great conflagration.

So there is little left to key one into the languages and thinking and history of the losers. Some of the most plainly written documents I possess remain totally inaccessible.

How I wish Raven were with us still, instead of dwelling among the dead men. He had a passing familiarity with written TelleKurre. Few outside the Lady's intimate circle do.

Goblin stuck his head in. "You coming or not?"

I cried on his shoulder. It was the old lament. No progress. He laughed. "Go blow in your girlfriend's ear. She might help."

"When will you guys let up?" It had been fifteen years since I wrote my last simpleminded romance about the Lady. That was before the long retreat which led the Rebel to his doom before the Tower at Charm. They do not let you forget.

"Never, Croaker. Never. Who else has spent the night with her? Who else goes carpet-flying with her?"

I would rather forget. Those were times of terror, not romance.

She became aware of my annalistic endeavors and asked me to show her side. More or less. She did not censor or dictate, but did insist I remain factual and impartial. I recall thinking she expected defeat, wanted an unbiased history set down somewhere.

Goblin glanced at the mound of documents. "You can't get any handle on it?"

"I don't think there is a handle. Everything I do translate turns out a big nothing. Somebody's expense record. An appointment calendar. A promotions list. A letter from some officer to a friend at court. Everything way older than what I'm looking for."

Goblin raised an eyebrow.

"I'll keep on trying." There was *something* there. We took them from Whisper, when she was a Rebel. They meant a lot to her. And our mentor then, Soulcatcher, thought them of empire-toppling significance.

Thoughtfully, Goblin remarked, "Sometimes the whole is greater than the sum of its parts. Maybe you should look for what ties it all together."

The thought had occurred to me. A name here, there, elsewhere, revealing the wake of someone through his or her earlier days. Maybe I would find it. The comet would not return for a long time.

But I had my doubts.

Darling is a young thing yet, just into her middle twenties. But the bloom of youth has abandoned her. Hard years have piled on hard years. There is little feminine about her. She had no chance to develop in that direction. Even after two years on the Plain none of us think of her as Woman.

She is tall, maybe two inches under six feet. Her eyes are a washed-out blue that often seems vacant, but they become swords of ice when she is thwarted. Her hair is blonde, as from much exposure to the sun. Without continuous attention it hangs in straggles and strings. Not vain, she keeps it shorter than is stylish. In dress, too, she leans toward the utilitarian. Some first-time visitors are offended because she dresses so masculine. But she leaves them with no doubts that she can handle business.

Her role came to her unwanted, but she has made peace with it, has assumed it with stubborn determination. She shows a wisdom remarkable for her age, and for one handicapped as she is. Raven taught her well during those few years he was her guardian.

She was pacing when I arrived. The conference room is earth-sided, smokey, crowded even when empty. It smells of long occupation by too many unclean men. The old messenger from Oar was there. So were Tracker and Corder and several other outsiders. Most of the Company were present. I finger-signed a greeting. Darling gave me a sisterly hug, asked if I had any progress to report.

I spoke for the group and signed for her. "I am sure we don't have all the documents we found in the Forest of Cloud. Not just because I can't identify what I'm looking for, either. Everything I do have is too old."

Darling's features are regular. Nothing stands out. Yet you sense character, will, that this woman cannot be broken. She has been to Hell already. It did not touch her as a child. She will not be touched now.

She was not pleased. She signed, "We will not have the time we thought."

My attention was half elsewhere. I had hoped for sparks between Tracker and the other westerner. On a gut level I had responded negatively to Tracker. I found myself with an irrational hope for evidence to sustain that reaction.

Nothing.

Not surprising. The cell structure of the movement keeps our sympathizers insulated from one another.

Darling wanted to hear from Goblin and One-Eye next.

Goblin used his squeakiest voice. "Everything we heard is true. They are reinforcing their garrisons. But Corder can tell you better. For us, the mission was a bust. They were ready. They chased us all over the Plain. We were lucky to get away. We didn't get no help, either."

The menhirs and their weird pals are on our side, supposedly. Sometimes I wonder. They are unpredictable. They help or don't according to a formula only they understand.

Darling was little interested in details of the failed raid. She moved on to Corder. He said, "Armies are gathering on both sides of the Plain. Under command of the Taken."

"Taken?" I asked. I knew of only the two. He sounded like he meant many.

A chill then. There is a longtime rumor that the Lady has been quiet so long because she is raising a new crop of Taken. I had not believed it. The age is sorrowfully short of characters of the magnificently villainous vitality of those the Dominator took in olden times: Soulcatcher, the Hanged Man, Nightcrawler, Shapeshifter, the Limper, and such. Those were nastymen of the grand scope, nearly as wild and hairy in their wickedness as the Lady and Dominator themselves. This is the era of the weak sister, excepting only Darling and Whisper.

Corder responded shyly. "The rumors are true, Lord."

Lord. Me. Because I stand near the heart of the dream. I hate it, yet eat it up. "Yes?"

"They may not be Stormbringers or Howlers, these new Taken." He smiled feebly. "Sir Tucker observed that the old Taken were wild devils as unpredictable as the lightning, and the new ones are the predictable tame thunder of bureaucracy. If you follow my meaning."

"I do. Go on."

"It is believed that there are six new ones, Lord. Sir Tucker believes they are about to be unleashed. Thus the great buildup around the Plain. Sir Tucker believes the Lady has made a competition of our destruction."

Tucker. Our most dedicated agent. One of the few survivors of the long siege of Rust. His hatred knows no bounds.

Corder had a strange look. A green-around-the-edges look. A look that said there was more, and all bad. "Well?" I said. "Spit it out."

"The names of the Taken have been enscribed on stellae raised in their respective demenses. At Rust the army commander is named Benefice. His stella appeared after a carpet arrived by night. He has not actually been seen."

That bore investigation. Only the Taken can manage a carpet. But no carpet can reach Rust without crossing the Plain of Fear. The menhirs have reported no such passage. "Benefice? Interesting name. The others?"

"In Thud the stella bears the name Blister."

Chuckles. I said, "I liked it better when the names were descriptive. Like the Limper, Moonbiter, the Faceless Man."

"At Frost we have one called the Creeper."

"That's better." Darling gave me a cautionary look.

"At Rue there is one called Learned. And at Hull, one called Scorn."

"Scorn. I like that, too."

"The western bounds of the Plain are held by Whisper and Journey, both operating from a village called Spit."

Being a natural mathematical phenom, I summed and said, "That's five new ones and two old. Where is the other new one?"

"I don't know. The only other is the commander over all. His stella stands in the military compound outside Rust."

The way he said that abraded my nerves. He was pale. He started shaking. A premonition gripped me. I knew I would not like what he said next. But, "Well?"

"That stella bears the sigil of the Limper."

Right. So right. I did not like it at all.

The feeling was universal.

"Oh!" Goblin shrieked.

One-Eye said, "Holy shit," in a soft awed tone that was all the more meaningful for its reserve.

I sat down. Right there. Right in the middle of the floor. I folded my head in my hands. I wanted to cry. "Impossible," I said. "I killed him. With my own hands." And saying it, I did not believe it anymore, though I had had faith in that fact for years. "But how?"

"Can't keep a good man down," Elmo chided. That he was shaken was evidenced by the smart remark. Elmo says nothing gratuitously.

The feud between the Limper and the Company dates to our arrival north of the Sea of Torments, for it was then that we enlisted Raven, a mysterious native of Opal, a man of former high estate who had been done out of his titles and livings by minions of the Limper. Raven was as tough as they come, and utterly fearless. The robbery sanctioned by Taken or not, he struck back. He slew the villains, among them the Limper's most competent people. Then our path kept crossing the Limper's. Each time something worsened the weather between us. . . .

In the confusion after Juniper, Limper thought to settle with us. I engineered an ambush. He charged in. "I would have bet anything I killed him." I tell you, at that moment I was as rattled as ever I have been. I was on the precipice of panic.

One-Eye noticed. "Don't get hysterical, Croaker. We survived him before."

"He's one of the old ones, idiot! One of the real Taken. From times when they had real wizards. And he's never really been allowed to go full speed at us before. And with all that help." Eight Taken and five armies to assault the Plain of Fear. Seldom were there more than seventy of us here in the Hole.

My head filled with terrible visions. Those Taken might be second-rate, but they were so many. Their fury would fire the Plain. Whisper and the Limper have campaigned here before. They are not ignorant of the Plain's perils. In fact, Whisper battled here both as a Rebel and as Taken. She won most of the most famous battles of the eastern war.

Reason reasserted itself but did little to brighten tomorrow. Once I thought, I reached the inescapeable conclusion that Whisper knows the Plain too well. Might even have allies out here.

Darling touched my shoulder. That was more calming than

any words from friends. Her confidence is contagious. She signed, "Now we know," and smiled.

Still, time has become a hanging hammer about to fall. The long wait for the comet has been rendered irrelevant. We have to survive right now. Trying for a bright side, I said, "The Limper's true name is somewhere in my document collection."

But that recalled my problem. "Darling, the specific document I want is not there."

She raised an eyebrow. Unable to speak, she has developed one of the most expressive faces I've ever seen.

"We have to have a sit-down. When you have time. To go over exactly what happened to those papers while Raven had them. Some are missing. They were there when I turned them over to Soulcatcher. They were there when I got them back from her. I am sure they were there when Raven took them. What happened to them later?"

"Tonight," she signed. "I will make time." She seemed distracted suddenly. Because I mentioned Raven? He meant a lot to her, but you'd think the edge would be off by now. Unless there was more to the story than I knew. And that was plenty possible. I really have no idea what their relationship became in the years after Raven left the Company. His death certainly bothers her still. Because it was so pointless. I mean, after surviving everything the shadow threw his way, he drowned in a public bath.

The Lieutenant says there are nights she cries herself to sleep. He does not know why, but he suspects Raven is at the root.

I have asked her about those years when they were on their own, but she will not tell the tale. The emotional impression I get is one of sorrow and grave disappointment.

She pushed her troubles away now, turned to Tracker and his mutt. Behind them, the men Elmo caught on the bluff squirmed. Their turn was coming. They knew the reputation of the Black Company.

But we did not get to them. Nor even to Tracker and Toadkiller Dog. For the watch above shrieked another alert.

This was getting tiresome.

*   *   *

The rider crossed the stream as I entered the coral. Water splashed. His mount staggered. It was covered with foam. Never again would it run well. It hurt me to see an animal so broken. But its rider had cause.

Two Taken darted about just beyond the bound of the null. One flung a violet bolt. It perished long before it reached us. One-Eye cackled and raised a middle finger. "Always wanted to do that."

"Oh, wonder of wonders," Goblin squeaked, looking the other way. A number of mantas, big blue-blacks, soared off the rosy bluffs, caught updrafts. Must have been a dozen, though they were hard to count, maneuvering as they did to avoid stealing one another's wind. These were giants of their kind. Their wings spanned almost a hundred feet. When they were high enough, they dove at the Taken in pairs.

The rider halted, fell. He had an arrow in his back. He remained conscious just long enough to gasp, "Tokens!"

The first manta pair, seeming to move with slow stately grace, though actually they streaked ten times faster than a man can run, ripped past the nearer Taken just inside Darling's null. Each loosed a brilliant lightning bolt. Lightning could speed where Taken witchery would not survive.

One bolt hit. Taken and carpet reeled, glowed briefly. Smoke appeared. The carpet twisted and spun earthward. We sent up a ragged cheer.

The Taken regained control, rose clumsily, drifted away.

I knelt by the messenger. He was little more than a boy. He was alive. He had a chance if I got to work. "A little help here, One-Eye."

Manta pairs ripped along the boundary of the null, blasting away at the second Taken. This one evaded effortlessly, did nothing to fight back. "That's Whisper," Elmo said.

"Yeah," I said. She knows her way around.

One-Eye grumbled, "You going to help this kid or not, Croaker?"

"All right. All right." I hated to miss the show. It was the first I had seen so many mantas, the first I had seen them support us. I wanted to see more.

"Well," said Elmo, while calming the boy's horse and

going through his saddlebags, "another missive for our esteemed annalist." He proffered another oilskin packet. Baffled, I tucked it under my arm, then helped One-Eye carry the messenger down into the Hole.

Chapter Ten:
BOMANZ'S STORY

Croaker:

Jasmine's squeal rattled the windows and doors. "Bomanz! You come down here! Come down right now, you hear me?"

Bomanz sighed. A man couldn't get five minutes alone. What the hell did he get married for? Why did any man? You spent the rest of your life doing hard time, doing what other people wanted, not what you wanted.

"Bomanz!"

"I'm coming, dammit! Damned woman can't blow her nose without me there to hold her hand," he added sotto voce. He did a lot of talking under his breath. He had feelings to vent, and peace to maintain. He compromised. Always, he compromised.

He stamped downstairs, each footfall a declaration of irritation. He mocked himself as he went: You know you're getting old when everything aggravates you.

"What do you want? Where are you?"

"In the shop." There was an odd note in her voice. Suppressed excitement, he decided. He entered the shop warily.

"Surprise!"

His world came alive. Grouchiness deserted him. "Stance!" He flung himself at his son. Powerful arms crushed him. "Here already? We didn't expect you till next week."

"I got away early. You're getting pudgy, Pop." Stancil opened his arms to include Jasmine in a three-way hug.

"That's your mother's cooking. Times are good. We're eating regular. Tokar's been . . ." He glimpsed a faded, ugly shadow. "So how are you? Back up. Let me look at you. You were still a boy when you left."

And Jasmine: "Doesn't he look great? So tall and healthy. And such nice clothes." Mock concern. "You haven't been up to any funny business, have you?"

"Mother! What could a junior instructor get up to?" He met his father's eye, smiled a smile that said "Same old Mom."

Stancil was four inches taller than his father, in his middle twenties, and looked athletic despite his profession. More like an adventurer than a would-be don, Bomanz thought. Of course, times changed. It had been eons since his own university days. Maybe standards had changed.

He recalled the laughter and pranks and all-night, dreadfully serious debates on the meaning of it all, and was bitten by an imp of nostalgia. What had become of that mentally quick, foxy young Bomanz? Some silent, unseen Guardsman of the mind had interred him in a barrow in the back of his brain, and there he lay dreaming, while a bald, jowly, potbellied gnome gradually usurped him. . . . They steal our yesterdays and leave us no youth but that of our children. . . .

"Well, come on. Tell us about your studies." Get out of that self-pitying mindset, Bomanz, you old fool. "Four years and nothing but letters about doing laundry and debates at the Stranded Dolphin. Stranded he would be in Oar. Before I die I want to see the sea. I never have." Old fool. Dream out loud and that's the best you can do? Would they really laugh if you told them the youth is still alive in there somewhere?

"His mind wanders," Jasmine explained.

"Who are you calling senile?" Bomanz snapped.

"Pop. Mom. Give me a break. I just got here."

Bomanz gobbled air. "He's right. Peace. Truce. Armistice. You referee, Stance. Two old warhorses like us are set in their ways."

Jasmine said, "Stance promised me a surprise before you came down."

"Well?" Bomanz asked.

"I'm engaged. To be married."

How can this be? This is my son. My baby. I was changing his diapers last week. . . . Time, thou unspeakable assassin, I feel thy cold breath. I hear thine iron-shod hooves. . . .

"Hmph. Young fool. Sorry. Tell us about her, since you won't tell us about anything else."

"I would if I could get a word in."

"Bomanz, be quiet. Tell us about her, Stance."

"You probably know something already. She's Tokar's sister, Glory."

Bomanz's stomach plunged to the level of his heels. Tokar's sister. Tokar, who might be a Resurrectionist.

"What's the matter now, Pop?"

"Tokar's sister, eh? What do you know about that family?"

"What's wrong with them?"

"I didn't say anything was. I asked you what you know about them."

"Enough to know I want to marry Glory. Enough to know Tokar is my best friend."

"Enough to know if they're Resurrectionists?"

Silence slammed into the shop. Bomanz stared at his son. Stancil stared back. Twice he started to respond, changed his mind. Tension rasped the air. "Pop . . ."

"That's what Besand thinks. The Guard is watching Tokar. And me, now. It's the time of the comet, Stance. The tenth passage. Besand smells some big Resurrectionist plot. He's making life hard. This thing about Tokar will make it worse."

Stancil sucked spittle between his teeth. He sighed. "Maybe it was a mistake, coming home. I won't get anything done wasting time ducking Besand and fighting with you."

"No, Stance," Jasmine said. "Your father won't start anything. Bo, you weren't starting a fight. You're not going to start one."

"Uhm." My son engaged to a Resurrectionist? He turned away, took a deep breath, quietly berated himself. Jumping to conclusions. On word no better than Besand's. "Son, I'm sorry. He's been riding me." He glanced at Jasmine. Besand wasn't his only persecutor.

"Thanks, Pop. How's the research coming?"

Jasmine grumbled and muttered. Bomanz said, "This conversation is crazy. We're all asking questions and nobody is answering."

"Give me some money, Bo," Jasmine said.

"What for?"

"You two won't say hello before you start your plotting. I might as well go marketing."

Bomanz waited. She eschewed her arsenal of pointed remarks about Woman's lot. He shrugged, dribbled coins into her palm. "Let's go upstairs, Stance."

"She's mellowed," Stancil said as they entered the attic room.

"I hadn't noticed."

"So have you. But the house hasn't changed."

Bomanz lighted the lamp. "Cluttered as ever," he admitted. He grabbed his hiding spear. "Got to make a new one of these. It's getting worn." He spread his chart on the little table.

"Not much improvement, Pop."

"Get rid of Besand." He tapped the sixth barrow. "Right there. The only thing standing in my way."

"That route the only option, Pop? Could you get the top two? Or even one. That would leave you a fifty-fifty chance of guessing the other two."

"I don't guess. This isn't a card game. You can't deal a new hand if you play your first one wrong."

Stancil took the one chair, stared at the chart. He drummed the tabletop with his fingers. Bomanz fidgeted.

A week passed. The family settled into new rhythms, including living with the Monitor's intensified surveillance.

Bomanz was cleaning a weapon from the TelleKurre site. A trove, that was. A veritable trove. A mass burial, with weapons and armor almost perfectly preserved. Stancil entered the shop. Bomanz looked up. "Rough night?"

"Not bad. He's ready to give up. Only came round once."

"Men fu or Besand?"

"Men fu. Besand was there a half dozen times."

They were working shifts. Men fu was the public excuse.

In reality, Bomanz hoped to wear Besand down before the comet's return. It was not working.

"Your mother has breakfast ready." Bomanz began assembling his pack.

"Wait up, Pop. I'll go too."

"You need to rest."

"That's all right. I feel like digging."

"Okay." Something was bothering the boy. Maybe he was ready to talk.

They'd never done much of that. Their pre-university relationship had been one of confrontation, with Stance always on the defensive. . . . He had grown, these four years, but the boy was still there inside. He was not yet ready to face his father man-to-man. And Bomanz had not grown enough to forget that Stancil was his little boy. Those growths sometimes never come. One day the son is looking back at his own son, wondering what happened.

Bomanz resumed rubbing flakes off a mace. He sneered at himself. Thinking about relationships. This isn't like you, you old coot.

"Hey, Pop," Stance called from the kitchen. "Almost forgot. I spotted the comet last night."

A claw reached in and grabbed a handful of Bomanz's guts. The comet! Couldn't be. Not already. He was not ready for it.

"Nervy little bastard," Bomanz spat. He and Stancil knelt in the brush, watching Men fu toss artifacts from their diggings. "I ought to break his leg."

"Wait here a minute. I'll circle around and cut him off when he runs."

Bomanz snorted. "Not worth the trouble."

"It's worth it to me, Pop. Just to keep the balance."

"All right." Bomanz watched Men fu pop up to look around, ugly little head jerking like that of a nervous pigeon. He dropped back into the excavation. Bomanz stalked forward.

He drew close enough to hear the thief talking to himself. "Oh. Lovely. Lovely. A stone fortune. Stone fortune. That fat little ape don't deserve it. All the time sucking up to Besand. That creep."

"Fat little ape? You asked for it." Bomanz shed his pack and tools, got a firm grip on his spade.

Men fu came up out of the pit, his arms filled. His eyes grew huge. His mouth worked soundlessly.

Bomanz wound up.

"Now Bo, don't be . . ."

Bomanz swung. Men fu danced, took the blow on his hip, squawked, dropped his burden, flailed the air, and toppled into the pit. He scrambled out the far side, squealing like a wounded hog. Bomanz wobbled after him, landed a mighty stroke across his behind. Men fu ran. Bomanz charged after him, spade high, yelling, "Stand still, you thieving son-of-a-bitch! Take it like a man."

He took a last mighty swing. It missed. It flung him around. He fell, bounced back up, continued the chase sans avenging spade.

Stancil threw himself into Men fu's way. The thief put his head down and bulled through. Bomanz ploughed into Stancil. Father and son rolled in a tangle of limbs.

Bomanz gasped, "What the hell? He's gone now." He sprawled on his back, panted. Stancil started laughing. "What's so damned funny?"

"The look on his face."

Bomanz sniggered. "You weren't much help." They guffawed. Finally, Bomanz gasped, "I'd better find my spade."

Stancil helped his father stand. "Pop, I wish you could have seen yourself."

"Glad I didn't. Lucky I didn't have a stroke." He lapsed into a fit of giggles.

"You all right, Pop?"

"Sure. Just can't laugh and catch my breath at the same time. Oh. Oh, my. I won't be able to move again if I sit down."

"Let's go dig. That'll keep you loose. You dropped the spade around here, didn't you?"

"There it is."

The giggles haunted Bomanz all morning. He would recall Men fu's flailing retreat and his self-control would go.

"Pop?" Stancil was working the far side of the pit. "Look here. This may be why he didn't notice you coming."

Bomanz limped over, watched Stancil brush loose soil off a perfectly preserved breastplate. It was as black and shiny as rubbed ebony. An ornate ornament in silver bossed its center. "Uhm." Bomanz popped out of the pit. "Nobody around. That half-man, half-beast design. That's Shapeshifter."

"He led the TelleKurre."

"He wouldn't be buried here, though."

"It's his armor, Pop."

"I can see that, dammit." He popped up like a curious groundhog. No one in sight. "Sit up here and keep watch. I'll dig it out."

"You sit, Pop."

"You were up all night."

"I'm a lot younger than you are."

"I'm feeling just fine, thank you."

"What color is the sky, Pop?"

"Blue. What kind of question . . ."

"Hallelujah. We agree on something. You're the most contrary old goat . . ."

"Stancil!"

"Sorry, Pop. We'll take turns. Flip a coin to see who goes first."

Bomanz lost. He settled down with his pack as a backrest. "Going to have to spread the dig out. Going straight down like this, it'll cave in first heavy rain."

"Yeah. Be a lot of mud. Ought to think about a drainage trench. Hey, Pop, there's nobody in this thing. Looks like the rest of his armor, too." Stancil had recovered a gauntlet and uncovered part of a greave.

"Yeah? I hate to turn it in."

"Turn it in? Why? Tokar could get a fortune for it."

"Maybe so. But what if friend Men fu did spot it? He'll tell Besand out of spite. We've got to stay on his good side. We don't *need* this stuff."

"Not to mention he might have planted it."

"What?"

"It shouldn't be here, right? And no body inside the armor. And the soil is loose."

Bomanz grunted. Besand was capable of a frame. "Leave everything the way it is. I'll go get him."

* * *

"Sour-faced old fart," Stancil muttered as the Monitor departed. "I bet he did plant it."

"No sense cussing. We can't do anything." Bomanz settled against his pack.

"What're you doing?"

"Loafing. I don't feel like digging anymore." He ached all over. It had been a busy morning.

"We should get what we can while the weather is good."

"Go ahead."

"Pop . . ." Stancil thought better of it. "How come you and Mom fight all the time?"

Bomanz let his thoughts drift. The truth was elusive. Stance would not remember the good years. "I guess because people change and we don't want them to." He could find no better words. "You start out with a woman; she's magical and mysterious and marvelous, the way they sing it. Then you get to know each other. The excitement goes away. It gets comfortable. Then even that fades. She starts to sag and turn grey and get lined and you feel cheated. You remember the fey, shy one you met and talked with till her father threatened to plant a boot in your ass. You resent this stranger. So you take a poke. I guess it's the same for your mother. Inside, I'm still twenty, Stance. Only if I pass a mirror, or if my body won't do what I want, do I realize that I'm an old man. I don't see the potbelly and the varicose veins and the grey hair where I've got any left. She has to live with it.

"Every time I see a mirror I'm amazed. I end up wondering who's taken over the outside of me. A disgusting old goat, from the look of him. The kind I used to snicker at when I was twenty. He scares me, Stance. He looks like a dying man. I'm trapped inside him, and I'm not ready to go."

Stancil sat down. His father never talked about his feelings. "Does it have to be that way?"

Maybe not, but it always is. . . . "Thinking about Glory, Stance? I don't know. You can't get out of getting old. You can't get out of having a relationship change."

"Maybe none of it has to be. If we manage this . . ."

"Don't tell me about maybes, Stance. I've been living on

maybes for thirty years.'' His ulcer took a sample nibble from his gut. ''Maybe Besand is right. For the wrong reasons.''

''Pop! What are you talking about? You've given your whole life to this.''

''What I'm saying, Stance, is that I'm scared. It's one thing to chase a dream. It's another to catch it. You never get what you expect. I have a premonition of disaster. The dream might be stillborn.''

Stancil's expression ran through a series of changes. ''But you've got to . . .''

''I don't have to do anything but be Bomanz the antiquary. Your mother and I don't have much longer. This dig should yield enough to keep us.''

''If you went ahead, you'd have a lot more years and a lot more . . .''

''I'm scared, Stance. Of going either way. That happens when you get older. Change is threatening.''

''Pop . . .''

''I'm talking about the death of dreams, son. About losing the big, wild make-believes that keep you going. The impossible dreams. That kind of jolly pretend is dead. For me. All I can see is rotten teeth in a killer's smile.''

Stancil hoisted himself out of the pit. He plucked a strand of sweetgrass, sucked it while gazing into the sky. ''Pop, how did you feel right before you married Mom?''

''Numb.''

Stancil laughed. ''Okay, how about when you went to ask her father? On the way there?''

''I thought I was going to dribble down my leg. You never met your grandfather. He's the one who got them started telling troll stories.''

''Something like you feel now?''

''Something. Yes. But it's not the same. I was younger, and I had a reward to look forward to.''

''And you don't now? Aren't the stakes bigger?''

''Both ways. Win or lose.''

''Know what? You're having what they call a crisis of self-confidence. That's all. Couple of days and you'll be raring to go again.''

That evening, after Stancil had gone out, Bomanz told

Jasmine, "That's a wise boy we've got. We talked today. Really talked, for the first time. He surprised me."

"Why? He's your son, isn't he?"

The dream came stronger than ever before, more quickly than ever. It wakened Bomanz twice in one night. He gave up trying to sleep. He went and sat on the front stoop, taking in the moonlight. The night was bright. He could make out rude buildings along the dirty street.

Some town, he thought, remembering the glories of Oar. The Guard, us antiquaries, and a few people who scratch a living serving us and the pilgrims. Hardly any of those anymore, even with the Domination fashionable. The Barrowland is so disreputable nobody wants to look at it.

He heard footsteps. A shadow approached. "Bo?"

"Besand?"

"Uhm." The Monitor settled on the next step down. "What're you doing?"

"Couldn't sleep. Been thinking about how the Barrowland has gotten so blighted even self-respecting Resurrectionists don't come here anymore. You? You're not taking the night patrol yourself, are you?"

"Couldn't sleep either. That damned comet."

Bomanz searched the sky.

"Can't see it from here. Have to go around back. You're right. Nobody knows we're here anymore. Us or those things in the ground over there. I don't know what's worse. Neglect or plain stupidity."

"Uhm?" Something was gnawing at the Monitor.

"Bo, they're not replacing me because I'm old or incompetent, though I guess I'm enough of both. They're moving me out so somebody's nephew can have a post. An exile for a black sheep. That hurts, Bo. That really hurts. They've forgotten what this place is. They're telling me I wasted my whole life doing a job any idiot can sleep his way through."

"The world is full of fools."

"Fools die."

"Eh?"

"They laugh when I talk about the comet or about Resurrectionists striking this summer. They can't believe that I believe. They don't believe there's anything under those mounds. Not anything still alive."

"Bring them out here. Walk them through the Barrowland after dark."

"I tried. They told me to quit whining if I wanted a pension."

"You've done all you can, then. It's on their heads."

"I took an oath, Bo. I was serious about it then, and I'm serious now. This job is all I have. You've got Jasmine and Stance. I might as well have been a monk. Now they're discarding me for some young . . ." He began making strange noises.

Sobs? Bomanz thought. From the Monitor? From this man with a heart of flint and all the mercy of a shark? He took Besand's elbow. "Let's go look at the comet. I haven't seen it yet."

Besand got hold of himself. "You haven't? That's hard to believe."

"Why? I haven't been up late. Stancil has done the night work."

"Never mind. Slipping into my antagonistic character again. We should've been lawyers, you and I. We've got the argumentative turn of mind."

"You could be right. Spent a lot of time lately wondering what I'm doing out here."

"What *are* you doing here, Bo?"

"I was going to get rich. I was going to study the old books, open a few rich graves, go back to Oar and buy into my uncle's drayage business." Idly, Bomanz wondered how much of his faked past Besand accepted. He had lived it so long that he now remembered some fraudulent anecdotes as factual unless he thought hard.

"What happened?"

"Laziness. Plain old-fashioned laziness. I found out there's a big difference between dreaming and getting in there and doing. It was easier to dig just enough to get by and spend the rest of the time loafing." Bomanz made a sour face. He was striking near the truth. His researches were, in fact, partly an excuse for not competing. He simply did not have the drive of a Tokar.

"You haven't had too bad a life. One or two hard winters when Stancil was a pup. But we all went through those. A helping hand here or there and we all survived. There she is." Besand indicated the sky over the Barrowland.

Bomanz gasped. It was exactly what he had seen in his dreams. "Showy, isn't it?"

"Wait till it gets close. It'll fill half the sky."

"Pretty, too."

"Stunning, I'd say. But also a harbinger. An ill omen. The old writers say it'll keep returning till the Dominator is freed."

"I've lived with that stuff most of my life, Besand, and even I find it hard to believe there's anything to it. Wait! I get that spooky feeling around the Barrowland, too. But I just can't believe those creatures could rise again after four hundred years in the ground."

"Bo, maybe you are honest. If you are, take a hint. When I leave, you leave. Take the TelleKurre stuff and head for Oar."

"You're starting to sound like Stance."

"I mean it. Some idiot unbeliever kid takes over here, all Hell is going to break loose. Literally. Get out while you can."

"You could be right. I'm thinking about going back. But what would I do? I don't know Oar anymore. The way Stance tells it, I'd get lost. Hell, this is home now. I never really realized that. This dump is home."

"I know what you mean."

Bomanz looked at that great silver blade in the sky. Soon now. . . .

"What's going on out there? Who is that?" came from Bomanz's back door. "You clear off, hear? I'll have the Guard after you."

"It's me, Jasmine."

Besand laughed. "And the Monitor, mistress. The Guard is here already."

"Bo, what're you doing?"

"Talking. Looking at the stars."

"I'll be getting along," Besand said. "See you tomorrow."

From his tone Bomanz knew tomorrow would be a day of normal harassments.

"Take care." He settled on the dewy back step, let the cool night wash over him. Birds called in the Old Forest, their voices lonely. A cricket chirruped optimistically. Humid air barely stirred the remnants of his hair. Jasmine came out and sat beside him. "Couldn't sleep," he told her.

"Me either."

"Must be going around." He glanced at the comet, was startled by an instant of deja vu. "Remember the summer we came here? When we stayed up to see the comet? It was a night like this."

She took his hand, entwined her fingers with his. "You're reading my mind. Our first month anniversary. Those were fool kids, those two."

"They still are, inside."

Chapter Eleven: THE BARROWLAND

For Corbie the unravelling came quickly now. When he kept his mind on business. But more and more he became distracted by that old silk map. Those strange old names. In TelleKurre they had a ring absent in modern tongues. Soulcatcher. Stormbringer. Moonbiter. The Hanged Man. They seemed so much more potent in the old tongue.

But they were dead. The only great ones left were the Lady and the monster who started it all, out there under the earth.

Often he went to a small window and stared toward the Barrowland. The devil in the earth. Calling, perhaps. Surrounded by lesser champions, few of them recalled in the legends and few the old wizard identified. Bomanz had been interested only in the Lady.

So many fetishes. And a dragon. And fallen champions of the White Rose, their shades set to eternal guard duty. It seemed so much more dramatic than the struggle today.

Corbie laughed. The past was always more interesting than the present. For those who lived through the first great struggle it must have seemed deadly slow, too. Only in the final battle were the legends and legacies created. A few days out of decades.

He worked less now, now that he had a sound place to live and a little saved. He spent more time wandering, especially by night.

Case came calling one morning, before Corbie was fully wakened. He allowed the youth inside. "Tea?"

"All right."

"You're nervous. What is it?"

"Colonel Sweet wants you."

"Chess again? Or work?"

"Neither. He's worried about your wandering around at night. I told him I go with you and all you do is look at the stars and stuff. Guess he's getting paranoid."

Corbie smiled a smile he did not feel. "Just doing his job. Guess my life looks odd. Getting past it. Lost in my own mind. Do I act senile sometimes? Here. Sugar?"

"Please." Sugar was a treat. The Guard could not provide it.

"Any rush? I haven't eaten."

"He didn't put it that way."

"Good." More time to prepare. Fool. He should have guessed his walks would attract attention. The Guard was paranoid by design.

Corbie prepared oats and bacon, which he shared with Case. For all they were well paid, the Guard ate poorly. Because of ongoing foul weather the Oar road was all but impassable. The army quartermasters strove valiantly but often could not get through.

"Well, let's see the man," Corbie said. And: "That's the last bacon. The Colonel better think about farming here, just in case."

''They talked about it.'' Corbie had befriended Case partly because he served at headquarters. Colonel Sweet would play chess and talk old times, but he never revealed any plans.

''And?''

''Not enough land. Not enough fodder.''

''Pigs. They get fat on acorns.''

''Need herdsmen. Else the tribemen would get them.''

''I guess so.''

The Colonel ushered Corbie into his private quarters. Corbie joked, ''Don't you ever work? Sir?''

''The operation runs itself. Been rolling four centuries, that's the way it goes. I have a problem, Corbie.''

Corbie grimaced. ''Sir?''

''Appearances, Corbie. This is a world that lives by perceptions. You aren't presenting a proper appearance.''

''Sir?''

''We had a visitor last month. From Charm.''

''I didn't know that.''

''Neither did anyone else. Except me. What you might call a prolonged surprise inspection. They happen occasionally.'' Sweet settled behind his worktable, pushed aside the chess set over which they had contested so often. He drew a long sheet of southern paper from a cubby at his right knee. Corbie glimpsed printing in a crabbed hand.

''Taken? Sir?''

Corbie never sirred anyone except as an afterthought. The habit disturbed Sweet. ''Yes. With the Lady's carte blanche. He did not abuse it. But he did make recommendations. And he did mention people whose behavior he found unacceptable. Your name was first on the list. What the hell are you doing, wandering around all night?''

''Thinking. I can't sleep. The war did something. The things I saw. . . . The guerrillas. You don't want to go to sleep because *they* might attack. If you do sleep, you dream about the blood. Homes and fields burning. Animals and children screaming. That was the worst. The babies crying. I still hear the babies crying.'' He exaggerated very little. Each time he went to bed he had to get past the crying of babes.

He told most of the truth and wound it into an imaginative lie. Babies crying. The babies who haunted him were his own, innocents abandoned in a moment of fear of commitment.

"I know," Sweet replied. "I know. At Rust they killed their children rather than let us capture them. The hardest men in the regiment wept when they saw the mothers hurling their infants down from the walls, then jumping after them. I never married. I have no children. But I know what you mean. Did you have any?"

"A son," Corbie said, in a voice both soft and strained, from a body almost shaking with pain. "And a daughter. Twins, they were. Long ago and far away."

"And what became of them?"

"I don't know. I would hope they're living still. They would be about Case's age."

Sweet raised an eyebrow but let the remark slide past. "And their mother?"

Corbie's eyes became iron. Hot iron, like a brand. "Dead."

"I'm sorry."

Corbie did not respond. His expression suggested he was not sorry himself.

"You understand what I'm saying, Corbie?" Sweet asked. "You were noticed by one of the Taken. That's never healthy."

"I get the message. Which was it?"

"I can't say. Which of the Taken are where when could be of interest to the Rebel."

Corbie snorted. "What Rebel? We wiped them out at Charm."

"Perhaps. But there is that White Rose."

"I thought they were going to get her?"

"Yeah. The stories you hear. Going to have her in chains before the month is out. Been saying that since first we heard of her. She's light on her feet. Maybe light enough." Sweet's smile faded. "At least I won't be around next time the comet comes. Brandy?"

"Yes."

"Chess? Or do you have a job?"

"Not right away. I'll go you one game."

Halfway through, Sweet said, "Remember what I said.

Eh? The Taken claimed he was leaving. But there's no guarantee. Could be behind a bush someplace watching."

"I'll pay more attention to what I'm doing."

He would. The last thing he wanted was a Taken interested in *him*. He had come too far to waste himself now.

Chapter Twelve: THE PLAIN OF FEAR

I had the watch. My belly gnawed, weighted by lead. All day dots had traversed the sky, high up. A pair were there now, patroling. The continuous presence of Taken was not a good omen.

Closer, two manta pairs planed the afternoon air. They would ride the updrafts up, then circle down, taunting the Taken, trying to lure them across the boundary. They resented outsiders. The more so these, because these would crush them but for Darling—another intruder.

Walking trees were on the move beyond the creek. The dead menhirs glistened, somehow changed from their usual dullness. Things were happening on the Plain. No outsider could comprehend their import fully.

One great shadow clung to the desert. Way up there, daring the Taken, a lone windwhale hovered. An occasional, barely perceptible bass roar tumbled down. I'd never heard one talk before. They do so only when enraged.

A breeze muttered and whimpered in the coral. Old Father Tree sang counterpoint to the windwhale.

A menhir spoke behind me. "Your enemies come soon." I shivered. It recalled the flavor of a nightmare I have been having lately. I can recall no specifics afterward, only that it is filled with terror.

I refused to be unsettled by the sneaky stone. Much.

What are they? Where did they come from? Why are they different from normal stones? For that matter, why is the Plain ridiculously different? Why so bellicose? We are here on sufferance only, allied against a greater enemy. Shatter the Lady and see how our friendship prospers.

"How soon?"

"When they are ready."

"Brilliant, old stone. Positively illuminating."

My sarcasm did not go unnoticed, just unremarked. The menhirs have their own flare for sarcasm and the sharp-edged tongue.

"Five armies," said the voice. "They will not wait long."

I indicated the sky. "The Taken cruise at will. Unchallenged."

"They have not challenged." True. But a weak excuse. Allies should be allies. More, windwhales and mantas usually consider appearance on the Plain sufficient challenge. It occurred to me the Taken might have bought them off.

"Not so." The menhir had moved. Its shadow now fell across my toes. I finally looked. This one was just ten feet tall. A real runt.

It had guessed my thought. Damn.

It continued telling me what I already knew. "It is not possible to deal from a position of strength always. Take care. There has been a call to the Peoples to reassess your acceptance on the Plain."

So. This overtalkative hunk was an emissary. The natives were scared. Some thought they could save themselves trouble by booting us out.

"Yes."

"The Peoples" doesn't properly describe the parliament of species that makes decisions here, but I know no better title.

If the menhirs are to be believed—and they lie only by omission or indirection—over forty intelligent species inhabit the Plain of Fear. Those I know include menhirs, walking trees, windwhales and mantas, a handful of humans (both primitives and hermits), two kinds of lizard, a bird like a buzzard, a giant white bat, and an extremely scarce critter that looks like a camel-centaur put together backward. I mean, the humanoid half is behind. The creature runs toward what most would take as its fanny.

No doubt I have encountered others without recognizing them.

Goblin says there is a tiny rock monkey that lives in the hearts of the great coral reefs. He claims it looks like a miniature One-Eye. But Goblin is not to be trusted where One-Eye is concerned.

"I am charged with delivering a warning," the menhir said. "There are strangers on the Plain."

I asked questions. When it did not answer I turned irritably. It was gone. "Damned stone. . . ."

Tracker and his mutt stood in the mouth of the Hole, watching the Taken.

Darling interviewed Tracker thoroughly, I'm told. I missed that. She was satisfied.

I had an argument with Elmo. Elmo liked Tracker. "Reminds me of Raven," he said. "We could use a few hundred Ravens."

"Reminds *me* of Raven, too. And that's what I don't like." But what good arguing? We cannot always like everyone. Darling thinks he is all right. Elmo thinks so. The Lieutenant accepts him. Why should I be different? Hell, if he is from the same mold as Raven, the Lady is in trouble.

He will be tested soon enough. Darling has something in mind. Something preemptive, I suspect. Possibly toward Rust.

Rust. Where the Limper had raised his stella.

The Limper. Back from the dead. I did everything but burn the body. Should have done that, I guess. Bloody hell.

The scary part is wondering if he is the only one. Did others survive apparent certain death? Are they hidden away now, waiting to astound the world?

A shadow fell across my feet. I returned to the living. Tracker stood beside me. "You look distressed," he said. He did show one every courtesy, I must admit.

I looked toward those patroling reminders of the struggle. I said, "I am a soldier, grown old and tired and confused. I have been fighting since before you were born. And I have yet to see anything gained."

He smiled a thin, almost secretive smile. It made me

uncomfortable. Everything he did made me uncomfortable. Even his damned dog made me uncomfortable, and it did nothing but sleep. Much as it loafed, how had it managed the journey from Oar? Too much like work. I swear, that dog won't even get in a hurry to eat.

"Be of good faith, Croaker," Tracker said. "She *will* fall." He spoke with absolute conviction. "She hasn't the strength to tame the world."

There was that scariness again. True or not, the way he expressed the sentiment was disturbing.

"We'll bring them all down." He indicated the Taken. "They aren't real, like those of old."

Toadkiller Dog sneezed on Tracker's boot. He looked down. I thought he would kick the mutt. But instead he bent to scratch the dog's ear.

"Toadkiller Dog. What kind of name is that?"

"Oh, it's an old joke. From when we were both a lot younger. He took a shine to it. Insists on it now."

Tracker seemed only half there. His eyes were vacant, his gaze far away, though he continued to watch the Taken. Weird.

At least he admitted to having been young. There was a hint of human vulnerability in that. It is the apparent invulnerability of characters like Tracker and Raven that rattles me.

Chapter Thirteen: THE PLAIN OF FEAR

"Yo! Croaker!" The Lieutenant had come outside.

"What?"

"Let Tracker cover you." I had only minutes left in my watch. "Darling wants you."

I glanced at Tracker. He shrugged. "Go ahead." He assumed a stance facing westward. I swear, it was like he turned the vigilance on. As though on the instant he became the ultimate sentinel.

Even Toadkiller Dog opened an eye and went to watching.

I brushed the dog's scalp with my fingers as I left, what I thought a friendly gesture. He growled. "Be like that," I said, and joined the Lieutenant.

He seemed disturbed. Generally, he is a cold customer. "What is it?"

"She's got one of her wild hairs."

Oh, boy. "What?"

"Rust."

"Oh yeah! Brilliant! Get it all over with fast! I thought that was just talk. I trust you tried to argue her out of it?"

You would think a man would grow accustomed to stench after having lived with it for years. But as we descended into the Hole my nose wrinkled and tightened. You just can't keep a bunch of people stuffed in a pit without ventilation. We have precious little.

"I tried. She says, 'Load the wagon. Let me worry about the mule being blind.' "

"She's right most of the time."

"She's a damned military genius. But that don't mean she can pull off any cockamamie scheme she dreams up. Some dreams are nightmares. Hell, Croaker. The Limper is out there."

Which is where we started when we reached the conference room. Silent and I bore the brunt because we are Darling's favorites. Seldom do I see such unanimity among my brethren. Even Goblin and One-Eye spoke with a single voice, and those two will fight over whether it is night or day with the sun at high noon.

Darling prowled like a caged beast. She had doubts. They nagged her.

"Two Taken in Rust," I argued. "That's what Corder said. One of them our oldest and nastiest enemy."

"Break them and we will shatter their entire plan of campaign," she countered.

"Break them? Girl, you're talking about the Limper. I proved he is invincible before."

"No. You proved that he will survive unless you are thorough. You might have burned him."

Yeah. Or cut him into pieces and fed him to the fish, or given him a swim in a vat of acid or a dust bath in quicklime. But those things take time. We had the Lady herself coming down on us. We barely got away as it was.

"Assuming we can get there undetected—which I do not believe for a moment—and manage total surprise, how long before all the Taken get on us?" I signed vigorously, more angry than frightened. I never refuse Darling, ever. But this time I was ready.

Her eyes flashed. For the first time ever I saw her battle her temper. She signed, "If you will not accept orders you should not be here. I am not the Lady. I do not sacrifice pawns for small gain. I agree, there is great risk in this operation. But far less than you argue. With potential impact far greater than you suppose."

"Convince me."

"That I cannot do. If you are captured, you must not know."

I was primed. "You just telling me that is enough for the Taken to get on a trail." Maybe I was more scared than I could admit. Or maybe it was just an all-time case of the contraries.

"No," she signed. There was something more, but she held it back.

Silent dropped a hand on my shoulder. He had given up. The Lieutenant joined him. "You're overstepping yourself, Croaker."

Darling repeated, "If you will not accept orders, Croaker, leave."

She meant it. Really! I stood with mouth open, stunned.

"All right!" I stamped out. I went to my quarters, shuffled those obstinate old papers and, of course, found not a damned thing new.

They left me alone for a while. Then Elmo came. He did not announce himself. I just glanced up and found him leaning against the door frame. By then I was half ashamed of my performance. "Yeah?"

"Mail call," he said, and tossed me another of those oilskin packets.

I snapped it out of the air. He departed without explaining its appearance. I placed it on my worktable, wondered. Who? I knew no one in Oar.

Was it some sort of trick?

The Lady is patient and clever. I would not put past her some grand maneuver using me.

I guess I must have thought about it an hour before, reluctantly, I opened the packet.

Chapter Fourteen: THE STORY OF BOMANZ

Croaker:

Bomanz and Tokar stood in one corner of the shop. "What do you think?" Bomanz asked. "Bring a good price?"

Tokar stared at the *pièce de résistance* of Bomanz's new TelleKurre collection, a skeleton in perfectly restored armor. 'It's marvelous, Bo. How did you do it?"

"Wired the joints together. See the forehead jewel? I'm not up on Domination heraldry, but wouldn't a ruby mean somebody important?"

"A king. That would be the skull of King Broke."

"His bones, too. And armor."

"You're rich, Bo. I'll just take a commission on this one. A wedding present to the family. You took me serious when I said come up with something good."

"The Monitor confiscated the best. We had Shapeshifter's armor."

Tokar had brought helpers this trip, a pair of hulking gorilla teamsters. They were carrying antiques to wagons outside. Their back-and-forth made Bomanz nervous.

"Really? Damn! I'd give my left arm for that."

Bomanz spread his hands apologetically. "What could I do? Besand keeps me on a short leash. Anyway, you know my policy. I'm stretching it to deal with a future daughter-in-law's brother."

"How's that?"

Stuck my foot in it now, Bomanz thought. He ploughed ahead. "Besand has heard you're a Resurrectionist. Stance and I are getting a hard time."

"Now that's sick. I'm sorry, Bo. Resurrectionist! I shot my mouth off once, years ago, and said even the Dominator would be better for Oar than our clown Mayor. One stupid remark! They never let you forget. It's not enough that they hounded my father into an early grave. Now they have to torment me and my friends."

Bomanz had no idea what Tokar was talking about. He would have to ask Stance. But it reassured him; which was all he really wanted.

"Tokar, keep the profits from this lot. For Stance and Glory. As my wedding present. Have they set a date?"

"Nothing definite. After his sabbatical and thesis. Come winter, I guess. Thinking about coming down?"

"Thinking about moving back to Oar. I don't have enough fight left to break in a new Monitor."

Tokar chuckled. "Probably won't be much call for Domination artifacts after this summer anyway. I'll see if I can find you a place. You do work like the king here, you won't have trouble making a living."

"You really like it? I was thinking about doing his horse, too." Bomanz felt a surge of pride in his craftsmanship.

"Horse? Really? They buried his horse with him?"

"Armor and all. I don't know who put the TelleKurre in the ground, but they didn't loot. We've got a whole box of coins and jewelry and badges."

"Domination coinage? That's hotter than hot. Most of it was melted down. A Domination coin in good shape can bring fifty times its metal value."

"Leave King Whosis here. I'll put his horse together for him. Pick him up next trip."

"I won't be long, either. I'll unload and zip right back. Where's Stance, anyway? I wanted to say hello." Tokar waved one of those leather wallets.

"Glory?"

"Glory. She ought to write romances. Going to break me, buying paper."

"He's out to the dig. Let's go. Jasmine! I'm taking Tokar out to the dig."

During the walk Bomanz kept glancing over his shoulder. The comet was now so bright it could be seen, barely, by day. "Going to be one hell of a sight when it peaks out," he predicted.

"I expect so." Tokar's smile made Bomanz nervous. I'm imagining, he told himself.

Stancil used his back to open the shop door. He dumped a load of weapons. "We're getting mined out, Pop. Pretty much all common junk last night."

Bomanz twisted a strand of copper wire, wriggled out of the framework supporting the horse skeleton. "Then let Men fu take over. Not much more room here anyway."

The shop was almost impassable. Bomanz would not have to dig for years, were that his inclination.

"Looking good," Stance said of the horse, tarrying before going for another armful from a borrowed cart. "You'll have to show me how to get the king on top so I can put them together when I go back."

"I may do it myself."

"Thought you'd decided to stay."

"Maybe. I don't know. When are we going to start that thesis?"

"I'm working on it. Making notes. Once I get organized I can write it up like that." He snapped his fingers. "Don't worry. I've got plenty of time." He went outside again.

Jasmine brought tea. "I thought I heard Stance."

Bomanz jerked his head. "Outside."

She looked for a place to set teapot and cups. "You're going to have to get this mess organized."

"I keep telling myself that."

Stancil returned. "Enough odds and ends here to make a suit of armor. Long as nobody tries to wear it."

"Tea?" his mother asked.

"Sure. Pop, I came past headquarters. That new Monitor is here."

"Already?"

"You're going to love him. He brought a coach and three wagons filled with clothing for his mistress. And a platoon of servants."

"What? Ha! He'll die when Besand shows him his quarters." The Monitor lived in a cell more fit for a monk than for the most powerful man in the province.

"He deserves it."

"You know him?"

"By reputation. Polite people call him the Jackal. If I'd known it was him . . . What could I have done? Nothing. He's lucky his family got him sent here. Somebody would have killed him if he'd stayed around the city."

"Not popular, eh?"

"You'll find out if you stay. Come back, Pop."

"I've got a job to do, Stance."

"How much longer?"

"A couple of days. Or forever. You know. I've got to get that name."

"Pop, we could try now. While things are confused."

"No experiments, Stance. I want it cold. I won't take chances with the Ten."

Stancil wanted to argue but sipped tea instead. He went out to the cart again. When he returned, he said, "Tokar should be turned around by now. Maybe he'll bring more than two wagons."

Bomanz chuckled. "Maybe he'll bring more than wagons, you mean? Like maybe a sister?"

"I was thinking that, yes."

"How are you going to get a thesis written?"

"There's always a spare moment."

Bomanz ran a dust cloth over the jewel in the brow of his

dead king's horse. "Enough for now, Dobbin. Going out to the dig."

"Swing by and check the excitement," Stancil suggested.

"I wouldn't miss it."

Besand came to the dig that afternoon. He caught Bomanz napping. "What is this?" he demanded. "Sleeping on the job?"

Bomanz sat up. "You know me. Just getting out of the house. I hear the new man showed up.'

Besand spat. "Don't mention him."

"Bad?"

"Worse than I expected. Mark me, Bo. Today writes the end of an era. Those fools will rue it."

"You decide what you're going to do?"

"Go fishing. Bloody go fishing. As far from here as I can get. Take a day to break him in, then head south."

"I always wanted to retire to one of the Jewel Cities. I've never seen the sea. So you're headed out right away, eh?"

"You don't have to sound so damned cheerful about it. You and your Resurrectionist friends have won, but I'll go knowing you didn't beat me on my own ground."

"We haven't fought much lately. That's no reason to make up for lost time."

"Yeah. Yeah. That was uncalled for. Sorry. It's frustration. I'm helpless, and everything is going under."

"It can't be that bad."

"It can. I have my sources, Bo. I'm not some lone crazy. There are knowledgeable men in Oar who fear the same things I do. They say the Resurrectionists are going to try something. You'll see, too. Unless you get out."

"I probably will. Stancil knows this guy. But I can't go before we finish the dig."

Besand gave him a narrow-eyed look. "Bo, I ought to make you clean up before I go. Looks like Hell puked here."

Bomanz was not a fastidious worker. For a hundred feet around his pit the earth was littered with bones, useless scraps of old gear, and miscellaneous trash. A gruesome sight. Bomanz did not notice.

"Why bother? It'll be overgrown in a year. Besides, I don't want to make Men fu work any harder than he has to."

"You're all heart, Bo."

"I work at it."

"See you around."

"All right." And Bomanz tried to puzzle out what he had done wrong, what Besand had come for and not found. He shrugged, snuggled into the grass, closed his eyes.

The woman beckoned. Never had the dream been so clear. And never so successful. He went to her and took her hand, and she led him along a cool green tree-lined path. Thin shafts of sunlight stabbed through the foliage. Golden dust danced in the beams. She spoke, but he could not decipher her words. He did not mind. He was content.

Gold became silver. Silver became a great blunt blade stabbing a nighttime sky, obscuring the weaker stars. The comet came down, came down . . . and a great female face opened upon him. It was shouting. Shouting angrily. And he could not hear. . . .

The comet vanished. A full moon rode the diamond-studded sky. A great shadow crossed the stars, obscuring the Milky Way. A head, Bomanz realized. A head of darkness. A wolf's head, snapping at the moon. . . . Then it was gone. He was with the woman again, walking that forest path, tripping over sunbeams. She was promising him something. . . .

He wakened. Jasmine was shaking him. "Bo! You're dreaming again. Wake up."

"I'm all right," he mumbled. "It wasn't that bad."

"You've got to stop eating so many onions. A man your age, and with an ulcer."

Bomanz sat up, patted his paunch. The ulcer had not bothered him lately. Maybe he had too much else on his mind. He swung his feet to the floor and stared into the darkness.

"What are you doing?"

"Thinking about going out to see Stance."

"You need your rest."

"Bull. Old as I am? Old people don't need to rest. Can't

afford to. Don't have the time left to waste.'' He felt for his boots.

Jasmine muttered something typical. He ignored her. He had that down to a fine art. She added, ''Take care out there.''

''Eh?''

''Be careful. I don't feel comfortable now that Besand is gone.''

''He only left this morning.''

''Yes, but . . .''

Bomanz left the house muttering about superstitious old women who could not stand change.

He took a random roundabout route, occasionally pausing to watch the comet. It was spectacular. A great mane of glory. He wondered if his dream had been trying to tell him something. A shadow devouring the moon. Not solid enough, he decided.

Nearing the edge of town, he heard voices. He softened his step. People were not usually out at this time of night.

They were inside an abandoned shack. A candle flickered inside. Pilgrims, he supposed. He found a peephole, but he could see nothing save a man's back. Something about those slumped shoulders. . . . Besand? Of course not. Too wide. More like that one ape of Tokar's. . . .

He could not identify the voices, which were mostly whispers. One did sound a lot like Men fu's habitual whine. The words were distinct enough, though.

''Look, we did everything we could to get him out of here. You take a man's job and home, he ought to realize he's not wanted. But he won't go.''

A second voice: ''Then it's time for heroic measures.''

Whiny voice: ''That's going too far.''

Short of disgust. ''Yellow. I'll do it. Where is he?''

''Holed up in the old stable. The loft. Fixed himself a pallet, like an old dog in a corner.''

A grunt as someone rose. Feet moving. Bomanz grabbed his belly, mouse-stepped away and hid in a shadow. A hulking figure crossed the road. Comet light glittered upon a naked blade.

Bomanz scuttled to a more distant shadow and stopped to think.

What did it mean? Murder, surely. But who? Why? Who had moved into the abandoned stable? Pilgrims and transients used the empty places all the time. . . . Who were those men?

Possibilities occurred. He banished them. They were too grim. When his nerves returned, he hurried to the dig.

Stancil's lantern was there, but he was nowhere in sight. "Stance?" No answer. "Stancil? Where are you?" Still no answer. Almost in panic, he shouted, "Stancil!"

"That you, Pop?"

"Where are you?"

"Taking a crap."

Bomanz sighed, sat down. His son appeared a moment later, brushing sweat off his forehead. Why? It was a cool night.

"Stance, did Besand change his mind? I saw him leave this morning. A while ago I heard men plotting to kill somebody. Sounded like they meant him."

"Kill? Who?"

"I don't know. One of them might have been Men fu. There were three or four of them. Did he come back?"

"I don't think so. You didn't dream something, did you? What are you doing out in the middle of the night, anyway?"

"That nightmare again. I couldn't sleep. I didn't imagine it. Those men were going to kill somebody because he wouldn't leave."

"That doesn't make sense, Pop."

"I don't care. . . ." Bomanz whirled. He heard the strange noise again. A figure staggered into the light. It took three steps and fell.

"Besand! It is Besand. What did I tell you?"

The former Monitor had a bloody wound across his chest. "I'm okay," he said. "I'll be okay. Just shock. It's not as bad as it looks."

"What happened?"

"Tried to kill me. Told you all hell would break loose. Told you they'd make a play. Beat them this round, though. Got their assassin instead."

"I thought you left. I saw you leave."

"I changed my mind. Couldn't go. I took an oath, Bo. They took away my job but not my conscience. I've got to stop them."

Bomanz met his son's gaze. Stancil shook his head. "Pop, look at his wrist."

Bomanz looked. "I don't see anything."

"That's the point. His amulet is gone."

"He turned it in when he left. Didn't you?"

"No," Besand said. "Lost it in the fight. Couldn't find it in the dark." He made that funny sound.

"Pop, he's bad hurt. I better go to the barracks."

"Stance," Besand gasped. "Don't tell *him*. Get Corporal Husky."

"Right." Stancil hurried off.

The light of the comet filled the night with ghosts. The Barrowland seemed to twist and crawl. Momentary shapes drifted amongst the brush. Bomanz shuddered and tried to convince himself that his imagination was acting up now.

Dawn was approaching. Besand was over his shock, sipping broth Jasmine had sent. Corporal Husky came to report the result of his investigation. "Couldn't find anything, sir. Not no body, not no amulet. Not even no sign of no fight. It's like it never happened."

"I sure as hell didn't try to kill myself."

Bomanz became thoughtful. Had he not overheard the conspirators, he would have doubted Besand. The man was capable of staging an assault for sympathy.

"I believe you, sir. I was just saying what I found."

"They blew their best chance. We're warned now. Keep alert."

"Better not forget who's in charge now," Bomanz interjected. "Don't get anybody in trouble with our new leader."

"That rockbrain. Do what you can, Husky. Don't crawl out on a limb."

"Yes, sir." The corporal departed.

Stancil said, "Pop, you ought to get back to the house. You're looking grey."

Bomanz rose. "You all right now?" he asked.

Besand replied, "I'll be fine. Don't worry about me. The sun is up. That kind don't try anything in broad daylight."

Don't bet on it, Bomanz thought. Not if they're devotees of the Domination. They'll bring the darkness to high noon.

Out of earshot, Stancil said, "I was thinking last night, Pop. Before this got started. About our name problem. And suddenly it hit me. There's an old stone in Oar. A big one with runic carvings and pictographs. Been around forever. Nobody knows what it is or where it came from. Nobody really cares."

"So?"

"Let me show you what's carved on it." Stancil picked up a twig, brushed a dusty area clear of debris. He started drawing. "There's a crude star in a circle at the top. Then some lines of runes nobody can read. I can't remember those. Then some pictures." He sketched rapidly.

"That's pretty rough."

"So is the original. But look. This one. Stick figure with a broken leg. Here. A worm? Here, a man superimposed over an animal. Here, a man with a lightning bolt. You see? The Limper. Nightcrawler. Shifter. Stormbringer."

"Maybe. And maybe you're reaching."

Stancil kept drawing. "Okay. That's the way they are on the rock. The four I named. In the same order as on your chart. Look here. At your empty spots. They could be the Taken whose graves we haven't identified." He tapped what looked like a simple circle, a stick figure with its head cocked, and a beast head with a circle in its mouth.

"The positions match," Bomanz admitted.

"So?"

"So what?"

"You're being intentionally thick, Pop. A circle is a zero, maybe. Maybe a sign for the one called the Faceless Man or Nameless man. And here the Hanged Man. And here Moondog or Moonbiter?"

"I see it, Stance. I'm just not sure I want to." He told Stance about having dreamed of a great wolf's head snapping at the moon.

"You see? Your own mind is trying to tell you. Go check the evidence. See if it don't fit this way."

"I don't have to."

"Why not?"

"I know it by heart. It fits."

"Then what's the matter?"

"I'm not sure I want to do it anymore."

"Pop. . . . Pop, if you won't, I will. I mean it. I'm not going to let you throw away thirty-seven years. What's changed, anyway? You gave up a hell of a future to come out here. Can you just write that off?"

"I'm used to this life. I don't mind it."

"Pop. . . . I've met people who knew you back when. They all say you could have been a great wizard. They wonder what happened to you. They know that you had some great secret plan and went off to chase it. They figure you're dead now, 'cause anybody with your talent would've been heard from. Right now I'm wondering if they're not right."

Bomanz sighed. Stancil would never understand. Not without getting old under the threat of the noose.

"I mean it, Pop. I'll do it myself."

"No, you won't. You have neither the knowledge nor the skill. I'll do it. I guess it's fated."

"Let's go!"

"Not so eager. This isn't a tea party. It'll be dangerous. I need rest and time to get into the right frame of mind. I have to assemble my equipment and prepare the stage."

"Pop. . . ."

"Stancil, who is the expert? Who is going to do this?"

"I guess you are."

"Then shut your mouth and keep it shut. The quickest I could try is tomorrow night. Assuming I stay comfortable with those names."

Stancil looked pained and impatient.

"What's the hurry? What's your stake in it?"

"I just . . . I think Tokar is bringing Glory. I wanted everything out of the way when she got here."

Bomanz raised a despairing eyebrow. "Let's go to the house. I'm exhausted." He glanced back at Besand, who was staring into the Barrowland. The man was stiff with defiance. "Keep him out of my hair."

"He won't be getting around too good for a while."

Later Bomanz muttered, "I wonder what it was all about, anyway? Really Resurrectionists?"

Stancil said, "The Resurrectionists are a myth Besand's bunch use to keep themselves employed."

Bomanz recalled some university acquaintances. "Don't be too sure."

When they reached the house, Stance trudged upstairs to study the chart. Bomanz ate a small meal. Before lying down, he told Jasmine, "Keep an eye on Stance. He's acting funny."

"Funny? How?"

"I don't know. Just funny. Pushy about the Barrowland. Don't let him find my gear. He might try to open the path himself."

"He wouldn't."

"I hope not. But watch him."

Chapter Fifteen: THE BARROWLAND

Case heard Corbie was back at last. He ran to the old man's home. Corbie greeted him with a hug. "How you been, lad?"

"We thought you were gone for good." Corbie had been away eight months.

"I tried to get back. There's damned near no roads anymore."

"I know. The Colonel asked the Taken to fly supplies in."

"I heard. The military government in Oar got off their butts when that hit. Sent a whole regiment to start a new road. It's about a third of the way built. I came up on part of it."

Case donned his serious face. "Was it really your daughter?"

"No," Corbie said. On departing he had announced that he was off to meet a woman who might be his daughter. He claimed to have given over his savings to a man who would find his children and bring them to Oar.

"You sound disappointed."

He was. His researches had not worked out well. Too many records were missing.

"What sort of winter was it, Case?"

"Bad."

"It was bad down there, too. I worried for you all."

"We had trouble with the tribes. That was the worst part. You can always stay inside and throw another log on. But you can't eat if thieves steal your stores."

"I thought it might come to that."

"We watched your house. They broke in some of the empty places."

"Thank you." Corbie's eyes narrowed. His home had been violated? How thoroughly? A careful searcher might have found enough to hang him. He glanced out a window. "Looks like rain."

"It always looks like rain. When it don't look like snow. It got twelve feet deep last winter. People are worried. What's happened to the weather?"

"Old folks say it goes this way, after the Great Comet. The winters turn bad for a few years. Down in Oar it never got that cold. Plenty of snow, though."

"Wasn't that cold here. Just snowed so much you couldn't get out. I like to went crazy. The whole Barrowland looked like a frozen lake. You could hardly tell where the Great Barrow was."

"Uhm? I have to unpack yet. If you don't mind? Let everyone know I'm back. I'm near broke. I'll need work."

"Will do, Corbie."

Corbie watched from a window as Case ambled back to the Guard compound, taking an elevated walkway built since his departure. The mud below explained it. That and Colonel Sweet's penchant for keeping his men occupied. Once Case vanished he went to the second floor.

Nothing had been disturbed. Good. He peeped out a window, toward the Barrowland.

How it had changed in just a few years. A few more and you would not be able to find it.

He grunted, stared the harder. Then he retrieved the silken map from its hiding place, studied it, then the Barrowland again. After a time he fished sweat-stained papers from inside his shirt, where he had carried them since stealing them from the university in Oar. He spread them over the map.

Late that afternoon he rose, donned a cloak, gathered the cane he now carried, and went out. He limped through the water and mud and drizzle till he reached a point overlooking the Great Tragic River.

It was in flood, as always. Its bed had continued to shift. After a time he cursed, smote an old oak with his cane, and turned back.

The day had gone grey with the hour. It would be dark before he got home.

"Damned complications," he muttered. "I never counted on this. What the hell am I going to do?"

Take the high risk. The one chance he wished most to avoid, though its possible necessity was his real reason for having wintered in Oar.

For the first time in years he wondered if the game were worth the candle.

Whatever his course, it would be dark before he got home.

Chapter Sixteen: THE PLAIN OF FEAR

You get mad and walk out on Darling, you can miss a lot. Elmo, One-Eye, Goblin, Otto, those guys like to bait me. They were not about to clue me in. They got everybody else to go along. Even Tracker, who seemed to be taking a shine to me and chattered at me more than everybody else combined, would not drop a hint. So when the day came, I went topside in total ignorance.

I'd packed the usual field gear. Our traditions are heavy infantry, though mostly we ride these days. All of us are too old to lug eighty pounds of gear. I dragged mine to the cavern that serves as a stable and smells like the grandfather of them all—and found that not one animal was saddled. Well, one. Darling's.

The stable boy just grinned when I asked what was going on. "Go on up," he said. "Sir."

"Yeah? Rotten bastards. They play games with me? I'll get them. They damned well better start remembering who keeps the Annals around here." I bitched and moaned all the way into the pre-moonset shadows that lurked around the tunnel mouth. There I found the rest of the outfit, all already up, with light gear. Each man carried his weapons and a sack of dried food.

"What you doing, Croaker?" One-Eye asked with suppressed laughter. "Look like you're taking everything you own. You a turtle? Carry your house on your back?"

And Elmo: "We ain't moving, boy. Just going on a raid."

"You're a bunch of sadists, you know that?" I stepped into the wan light. The moon was half an hour from setting. Far, Taken drifted on the night. Those son-of-a-bitches were determined to keep a close watch. Nearer, a whole horde of menhirs had gathered. They looked like a graveyard out on the desert, there were so many of them. There were a lot of walking trees, too.

More, though there was no breeze, I could hear Old Father Tree tinkling. No doubt that meant something. A menhir might have explained. But the stones remain close-mouthed about themselves and their fellow species. Especially about Father Tree. Most of them won't admit he exists.

"Better lighten your load, Croaker," the Lieutenant said. He would not explain either.

"You going too?" I asked, surprised.

"Yep. Move it. We don't have long. Weapons and field medical kit should do it. Scoot."

I met Darling going down. She smiled. Grouchy as I was, I

smiled back. I can't stay mad at her. I have known her since
she was so high. Since Raven rescued her from the Limper's
thugs long ago, in the Forsberg campaigns. I cannot see the
woman that is without recalling the child that was. I get all
sentimental and soft.

They tell me I suffer from a crippling romantic streak.
Looking back, I'm almost inclined to agree. All those silly
stories I wrote about the Lady. . . .

The moon was on the rim of the world when I returned
topside. A whisper of excitement coursed among the men.
Darling was up there with them, astride her flashy white
mare, moving around, gesturing at those who understood
sign. Above, the spots of luminescence that are characteristic
of windwhale tentacles drifted lower than I'd ever heard tell
of. Except in horror stories about starved whales dropping
down to drag their tentacles on the ground, ripping up every
plant and animal in their path.

"Hey!" I said. "We'd better look out. That sucker is
coming down." A vast shadow blotted out thousands of stars.
And it was expanding. Mantas swarmed around it. Big ones,
little ones, in-between ones—more than I'd ever seen.

My expostulation drew laughter. I turned surly again. I
moved among the men, harassing them about the medical kits
I expect them to carry on a mission. I was in a better mood
when I finished. They all had them.

The windwhale kept coming down.

The moon disappeared. The instant it did the menhirs
began to move. Moments later they began to glow on the side
toward us. The side away from the Taken.

Darling rode along the pathway they marked. When she
passed a menhir its light went out. I suspect it moved to the
far end of the line.

I had no time to check. Elmo and the Lieutenant herded us
into a line of our own. Above, the night filled with the
squeaks and flutter of mantas squabbling for flying room.

The windwhale settled astride the creek.

My god, it was big. Big! I had no idea. . . . It stretched
from the coral over the creek another two hundred yards.
Four, five hundred yards long, all total. And seventy to a
hundred wide.

A menhir spoke. I could not make out its words. But the men began moving forward.

In a minute my worst suspicions were confirmed. They were climbing the creature's flank, onto its back, where mantas normally nested.

It smelled. Smelled unlike anything I've ever smelled before, and strongly. Richly, you might say. Not necessarily a bad smell, but overpowering. And it felt strange to the touch. Not hairy, scaly, horny. Not exactly slimy, but still spongy and slick, like a full, exposed intestine. There were plenty of handholds. Our fingers and boots did not bother it.

The menhir mumbled and grumbled like an old first sergeant, both issuing orders and relaying complaints from the windwhale. I got the impression the windwhale was a naturally grouchy sort. He did not like this any more than did I. Can't say I blame him.

Up top there were more menhirs, each balanced precariously. As I arrived, one menhir told me to go to another of its kind. That one told me to sit about twenty feet away. The last men climbed aboard only moments later.

The menhirs vanished.

I began to feel odd. At first blush I thought that was because the whale was lifting off. When I flew with the Lady or Whisper or Soulcatcher, my stomach was in continual rebellion. But this was a different malaise. It took a while to understand it as an absence.

Darling's null was fading. It had been with me so long it had become part of my life. . . .

What was happening?

We were going up. I felt the breeze shift. The stars turned ponderously. Then, suddenly, the whole north lighted up.

Mantas were attacking the Taken. A whole mess of them. The stroke was a complete surprise, for all the Taken must have sensed their presence. But the mantas were not doing that sort of thing. . . .

Oh, hell, I thought. They're pushing them our way. . . .

I grinned. Not our way at all. Toward Darling and her null, in a place unexpected.

As the thought occurred I saw the flash of vain sorceries,

saw a carpet stagger, flutter earthward. A score of mantas swarmed it.

Maybe Darling was not as dumb as I thought. Maybe these Taken could be taken out. A profit, for sure, if nothing else went right.

But what were we doing? The lightning illuminated my companions. Nearest me were Tracker and Toadkiller Dog. Tracker seemed bored. But Toadkiller Dog was as alert as I had seen him. He was sitting up, watching the display. The only time I ever saw him not on his belly was at mealtime.

His tongue was out. He panted. Had he been human, I would have said he was grinning.

The second Taken tried to impress the mantas with his power. He was too immensely outnumbered. And below, Darling was moving. That second Taken suddenly entered her null. Down he went. The manta swarm pursued.

Both would survive landing. But then they would be afoot at the heart of the Plain, which tonight had taken a stand. Their chances of walking out looked grim.

The windwhale was up a couple thousand feet now, moving northeast, gaining speed. How far to the edge of the Plain nearest Rust? Two hundred miles? Fine. We might make it before dawn. But what about the last thirty miles, beyond the Plain?

Tracker started singing. His voice was soft at first. His song was old. Soldiers of the north countries had sung it for generations. It was a dirge, a song-before-death sung in memory of those about to die. I heard it in Forsberg, sung on both sides. Another voice took it up. Then another and another. Perhaps fifteen men knew it, of forty or so.

The windwhale glided northward. Far, far below, the Plain of Fear slid away, utterly invisible.

I began to sweat, though the upper air was cold.

Chapter Seventeen: RUST

My first false assumption was that the Limper would be home when we called. Darling's maneuver against the Taken obviated that. I should have recalled that the Taken touch one another over long distances, mind to mind. Limper and Benefice passed nearby as we moved north.

"Down!" Goblin squealed when we were fifty miles short of the edge of the Plain. "Taken. Nobody move."

As always, old Croaker considered himself the exception to the rule. For the Annals, of course. I crept nearer the side of our monster mount, peered out into the night. Way below, two shadows raced down our backtrack. Once they were past I took a cussing from Elmo, the Lieutenant, Goblin, One-Eye, and anybody else who wanted a piece. I settled back beside Tracker. He just grinned and shrugged.

He came ever more to life as action approached.

My second false assumption was that the windwhale would drop us at the edge of the Plain. I was up again as that drew near, ignoring naughty remarks directed my way. But the windwhale did not go down. It did not descend for many minutes yet. I began to babble sillinesses when I resumed my place by Tracker.

He had his till-now mysterious case open. It contained a small arsenal. He checked his weapons. One long-bladed knife did not please him. He began applying a whetstone.

How many times had Raven done the same in the brief year he spent with the Company?

The whale's descent was sudden. Elmo and the Lieutenant passed among us, telling us to get off in a hurry. Elmo told me, "Stick close to me, Croaker. You too, Tracker. One-Eye. You feel anything down there?"

"Nothing. Goblin has his sleeping spell ready. Their sentries will be snoring when we touch down."

"Unless they aren't and raise the alarm," I muttered. Damn, but didn't I have it for the dark side?

No problems. We grounded. Men poured over the side. They spread out as if this part had been rehearsed. Parts may have been while I was sulking.

I could do nothing but what Elmo told me.

The early going reminded me of another barracks raid, long ago, south of the Sea of Torments, ere we enlisted with the Lady. We had slaughtered the Urban Cohorts of the Jewel City Beryl, our wizards keeping them snoozing while we murdered them.

Not work I enjoy, I'll tell you. Most of them were just kids who enlisted for want of something better to do. But they were the enemy, and we were making a grand gesture. A grander gesture than I had supposed Darling could order, or had in mind.

The sky began to lighten. Not one man of an entire regiment, save perhaps a few AWOL for the night, survived. Out on the main parade of the compound, which stood well outside Rust proper, Elmo and the Lieutenant began to yell. Hurry, hurry. More to do. This squad to wreck the stellae of the Taken. That squad to plunder regimental headquarters. Another to set out stuff to fire the barracks buildings. Still another to search the Limper's quarters for documents. Hurry, hurry. Got to get gone before the Taken return. Darling cannot distract them forever.

Somebody screwed up. Naturally. It always happens. Somebody fired one barracks early. Smoke rose.

Over in Rust, we soon learned, there was another regiment. In minutes a squadron of horse were galloping our way. And again, someone had screwed up. The gates were not secured. Almost without warning the horsemen were among us.

Men shouted. Weapons clanged. Arrows flew. Horses shrieked. The Lady's men got out, leaving half their number behind.

Now Elmo and the Lieutenant were in a hurry for sure. Those boys were going for help.

While we were scattering the imperials the windwhale lifted off. Maybe half a dozen men managed to scramble aboard. It rose just enough to clear the rooftops, then headed south. There was not yet enough light to betray it.

You can imagine the cussing and shouting. Even Toadkiller Dog found the energy to snarl. I slumped in defeat, dropped my butt onto a hitching rail, sat there shaking my head. A few men sped arrows after the monster. It did not notice.

Tracker leaned on the rail beside me. I grumped, "You wouldn't think something that big would be chicken." I mean, a windwhale can destroy a city.

"Do not impart motives to a creature you do not understand. You have to see its reasoning."

"What?"

"Not reasoning. I don't know the right word." He reminded me of a four-year-old struggling with a difficult concept. "It's outside the lands it knows. Beyond bounds its enemies believe it can breech. It runs for fear it will be seen and a secret betrayed. It has never worked with men. How can it remember them in a desperate moment?"

He was right, probably. But at the moment I was more interested in him than in his theory. That I would have stumbled across after I settled down. He made it seem one huge and incredibly difficult piece of thinking.

I wondered about his mind. Was he just slightly more than a half-wit? Was his Ravenlike act not a product of personality but of simpleness?

The Lieutenant stood on the parade ground, hands on hips, watching the windwhale leave us in the enemy's palm. After a minute he shouted, "Officers! Assemble!" After we gathered, he said, "We're in for it. As I see it, we have one hope. That that big bastard gets in touch with the menhirs when it gets back. And that *they* decide we're worth saving. So what we do is hold out till nightfall. And hope."

One-Eye made an obscene noise. "I think we better run for it."

"Yeah? And let the imperials track us? We're how far

from home? You think we can make it with the Limper and his pals after us?''

"They'll be after us here."

"Maybe. And maybe they'll keep them busy out there. At least, if we're here, they'll know where to find us. Elmo, survey the walls. See if we can hold them. Goblin, Silent, get those fires put out. The rest of you, clean out the Taken's documents. Elmo! Post sentries. One-Eye. Your job is to figure out how we can get help from Rust. Croaker, give him a hand. You know who we have where. Come on. Move.''

A good man, the Lieutenant. He kept his cool when, like all of us, what he wanted to do was run in circles and scream.

We didn't have a chance, really. This was the end of it. Even if we held off the troops from the city, there was Benefice and the Limper. Goblin, One-Eye, and Silent would be of no value against them. The Lieutenant knew that, too. He did not have them put their heads together to plot a surprise.

We could not get the fire controlled. The barracks had to burn itself out. While I tended two wounded men the others made the compound as defensible as thirty men could. Finished doctoring, I went poking through the Limper's documents. I found nothing immediately interesting.

"About a hundred men coming out of Rust!" someone shouted.

The Lieutenant snapped, "Make this place look abandoned!" Men scurried.

I popped up to the wall top for a quick peek at the scrub woods north of us. One-Eye was out there, creeping toward the city, hoping to get to Corder's friends.

Even after having been triply decimated in the great sieges and occupied for years, Rust remained adamant in its hatred for the Lady.

The imperials were careful. They sent scouts around the wall. They sent a few men up close to draw fire. Only after an hour of cautious maneuver did they rush the half-open gate.

The Lieutenant let fifteen get inside before tripping the portcullis. Those went down in a storm of arrows. Then we hustled to the wall and let fly at those milling around outside.

Another dozen fell. The others retreated beyond bowshot. There they milled and grumbled and tried to decide what next.

Tracker remained nearby all that time. I saw him loose only four arrows. Each ripped right through an imperial. He might not be bright, but he could use a bow.

"If they're smart," I told him, "they'll set a picket line and wait for the Limper. No point them getting hurt when he can handle us."

Tracker grunted. Toadkiller Dog opened one eye, grumbled deep in his throat. Down the way, Goblin and Silent crouched with heads together, alternately popping up to look outside. I figured they were plotting.

Tracker stood up, grunted again. I looked myself. More imperials were leaving Rust. Hundreds more.

Nothing happened for an hour, except that more and more troops appeared. They surrounded us.

Goblin and Silent unleashed their wizardry. It took the form of a cloud of moths. I could not discern their provenance. They just gathered around the two. When they were maybe a thousand strong, they fluttered away.

For a while there was a lot of screaming outside. When that died I ambled over and asked a grim-faced Goblin, "What happened?"

"Somebody with a touch of talent," he squeaked. "Almost as good as us."

"We in trouble?"

"In trouble? Us? We got it whipped, Croaker. We got them on the run. They just don't know it yet."

"I meant . . ."

"He won't hit back. He don't want to give himself away. There's two of us and only one of him."

The imperials began assembling artillery pieces. The compound had not been built to withstand bombardment.

Time passed. The sun climbed. We watched the sky. When would doom come riding in on a carpet?

Certain the imperials would not immediately attack, the Lieutenant had some of us gather our plunder on the parade ground, ready to board a windwhale. Whether he believed it or not, he insisted we would be evacuated after sunset. He would not entertain the possibility that the Taken would arrive first.

He did keep morale up.

The first missile fell an hour after noon. A ball of fire smacked down a dozen feet short of the wall. Another arced after it. It fell on the parade ground, sputtered, fizzled.

"Going to burn us out," I muttered to Tracker. A third missile came. It burned cheerfully, but also upon the parade.

Tracker and Toadkiller Dog stood and stared over the ramparts, the dog stretching on his hind legs. After a while Tracker sat down, opened his wooden case, withdrew a half dozen overly long arrows. He stood again, stared toward the artillery engines, arrow across his bow.

It was a long flight, but reachable even with my weapon. But I could have plinked all day and not come close.

Tracker fell into a state of concentration almost trancelike. He lifted and bent his bow, pulled it to the head of his arrow, let fly.

A cry rolled up the slope. The artillerymen gathered around one of their number.

Tracker loosed shafts smoothly and quickly. I'd guess he put four in the air at one time. Each found a target. Then he sat down. "That's that."

"Say what?"

"No more good arrows."

"Maybe that's enough to discourage them."

It was. For a while. About long enough for them to move back and put up some protective mantlets. Then the missiles came again. One found a building. The heat was vicious.

The Lieutenant prowled the wall restlessly. I joined his silent prayer that the imperials would not get worked up and rush us. There would be no way to stop them.

Chapter Eighteen: SIEGE

The sun was settling. We were alive still. No Taken carpet had come swooping out of the Plain. We had begun to believe there was a chance.

Something hammered on the gate, a great loud pounding, like the hammer of doom. One-Eye roared up, "Let me in, damnit!"

Somebody scooted down and opened up. He came to the ramparts. "Well?" Goblin demanded.

"I don't know. Too many imperials. Not enough Rebels. They wanted to argue it out."

"How did you get through?" I asked.

"Walked," he snapped. Then, less belligerently, "Trade secret, Croaker."

Sorcery. Of course.

The Lieutenant paused to hear One-Eye's report, resumed his ceaseless prowl. I watched the imperials. There were indications they were out of patience.

One-Eye evidently supported my suspicion with direct evidence. He, Goblin, and Silent started plotting.

I am not certain what they did. Not moths, but the results were similar. A big outcry, soon stifled. But now we had three spook doctors to work the mine. The extra man sought the imperial who negated the spell.

A man ran toward the city, aflame. Goblin and One-Eye howled victoriously. Not two minutes later an artillery engine burst into flames. Then another. I watched our wizards closely.

Silent remained all business. But Goblin and One-Eye were getting carried away, having a good time. I feared they would go too far, that the imperials would attack in hope of over-whelming them.

They came, but later than I expected. They waited till nightfall. And then they were more cautious than the situation demanded.

Meantime, smoke began to waft up over the ruined walls of Rust. One-Eye's mission had succeeded. Somebody was doing something. Some of the imperials pulled out and hurried back to deal with it.

As the stars came out I told Tracker, "Guess we'll soon know if the Lieutenant was right."

He just looked puzzled.

Imperial horns sounded signals. Companies moved toward the wall. He and I stood to our bows, seeking targets that were difficult in the darkness, though there was a bit of moon. Out of the nowhere, he asked, "What's she like, Croaker?"

"What? Who?" I let fly.

"The Lady. They say you met her."

"Yeah. A long time ago."

"Well? What's she like?" He loosed. A cry answered the twang of his bowstring. He seemed perfectly calm. Seemed unaware that he might die in minutes. That disturbed me.

"About what you'd expect," I replied. What could I say? My contacts with her were but sketchy memories now. "Hard and beautiful."

The answer did not satisfy him. It never satisfies anyone. But it is the best I can give.

"What did she look like?"

"I don't know, Tracker. I was scared shitless. And she did things to my mind. I saw a young, beautiful woman. But you can see those anywhere."

His bow twanged, was answered by another cry. He shrugged. "I sort of wondered." He began loosing more quickly. The imperials were close now.

I swear, he never missed. I loosed when I saw something, but . . . He has eyes like an owl. All I saw was shadows among shadows.

Goblin, One-Eye, and Silent did what they could. Their witcheries painted the field with short-lived little flares and screams. What they could do was not enough. Ladders slapped against the wall. Most went right back over again. But men came up a few. Then there were a dozen more. I scattered arrows into the darkness, almost randomly, as quickly as I could, then drew my sword.

The rest of the men did likewise.

The Lieutenant shouted, "It's here!"

I flicked a glance at the stars. Yes. A vast shape had appeared overhead. It was settling. The Lieutenant had guessed right.

Now all we had to do was get aboard.

Some of the young men broke for the parade ground. The Lieutenant's curses did not slow them. Neither did Elmo's snarls and threats. The Lieutenant yelled for the rest of us to follow.

Goblin and One-Eye loosed something nasty. For a moment I thought it was some cruel conjured demon. It looked vile enough. And it did stall the imperials. But like much of their magic, it was illusion, not substance. The enemy soon caught on.

But we had us a head start. The men reached the parade before the imperials recollected themselves. They roared, certain they had us.

I reached the windwhale as it touched down. Silent snagged my arm as I started to scramble aboard. He indicated the documents we had scrounged. "Oh, damn! There isn't time."

Men scrambled past me during my moment of indecision. Then I tossed sword and bow topside and began pitching bundles up to Silent, who got somebody to relay them to the top.

A gang of imperials charged toward us. I started for an abandoned sword, saw I could not reach it in time, thought: Oh, shit—not now; not here.

Tracker stepped between me and them. His blade was like something out of legend. He killed three men in the blink of an eye, wounded another two before the imperials decided they faced someone preternatural. He took the offensive, though still outnumbered. Never have I seen a sword used with such skill, style, economy, and grace. It was a part of him, an extension of his will. Nothing could stand before it. For that moment I could believe old tales about magic swords.

Silent kicked me in the back, signed at me, "Quit gawking and get moving." I tossed up the last two bundles, began scaling the monster.

The men Tracker faced received reinforcements. He retreated. From up top someone sped arrows down. But I did not think he would make it. I kicked at a man who had gotten behind him. Another took his place, leapt at me. . . .

Toadkiller Dog came out of nowhere. He locked his jaws in my assailant's throat. The man gurgled, responded as he might have if bitten by a krite. He lasted only a second.

Toadkiller Dog dropped away. I climbed a few feet, still trying to guard Tracker's back. He reached up. I caught his hand and heaved.

There were awful shouts and screams among the imperials. It was too dark to see why. I figured One-Eye, Goblin, and Silent were earning their keep.

Tracker flung up past me, took a firm hold, helped me. I climbed a few feet, looked down.

The ground was fifteen feet below. The windwhale was going up fast. The imperials stood around gawking. I fought my way to the top.

I looked down again as someone dragged me to safety. The fires in Rust were beneath us. Several hundred feet below. We were going up fast. No wonder my hands were cold.

Chills were not the reason I lay down shaking, though.

After it passed, I asked, "Anybody hurt? Where's my medical kit?"

Where, I wondered, were the Taken? How had we gotten through the day without a visit from our beloved enemy the Limper?

Going home I noticed more than I did coming north. I felt the life beneath me, the grumble and hum within the monster. I noted pre-adolescent mantas peeping from nesting places among the appendages which forested parts of the whale's back. And I saw the Plain in a different light, with the moon up to illuminate it.

It was another world, spare and crystalline at times, luminescent at others, sparkling and glowing in spots. What looked like lava pools lay to the west. Beyond, the flash and curl of a change storm illuminated the horizon. I suppose we were crossing its backtrail. Later, deeper into the Plain, the desert became more mundane.

Our steed was not the cowardly windwhale. This one was smaller and smelled less strongly. It was more spritely, too, and less tentative in its movements.

About twenty miles from home Goblin squealed, "Taken!" and everyone went flat. The whale climbed. I peeked over its side.

Taken for sure, but not interested in us. There was a lot of flash and roar way down there. Patches of desert were aflame. I saw the long, creepy shadows of walking trees on the move, the shapes of mantas rushing across the light. The Taken themselves were afoot, except one desperado aloft battling the mantas. The one aloft was not the Limper. I would have recognized his tattered brown even at that distance.

Whisper, surely. Trying to escort the others out of enemy territory. Great. They would be busy for a few days.

The windwhale began to descend. (For the sake of these Annals, I wish part of a passage had taken place by day so I could record more details.) It touched down shortly. From the ground a menhir called, "Get down. Hurry."

Getting off was more trouble than boarding. The wounded now realized they were hurt. Everyone was tired and stiff. And Tracker would not move.

He was catatonic. Nothing reached him. He just sat there, staring at infinity. "What the hell?" Elmo demanded. "What's wrong with him?"

"I don't know. Maybe he got hit." I was baffled. And the more so once we got him into some light so I could examine him. There was nothing physically wrong. He had come through without a bruise.

Darling came outside. She signed, "You were right, Croaker. I am sorry. I thought it would be a stroke so bold it would fire the whole world." Of Elmo, she asked, "How many lost?"

"Four men. I don't know if they were killed or just got left." He seemed ashamed. The Black Company does not leave its brethren behind.

"Toadkiller Dog," Tracker said. "We left Toadkiller Dog."

One-Eye disparaged the mutt. Tracker rose angrily. He had salvaged nothing but his sword. His magnificent case and arsenal remained in Rust with his mongrel.

"Here now," the Lieutenant snapped. "None of that. One-Eye, go below. Croaker, keep an eye on this man. Ask Darling if the guys who ran out yesterday made it back."

Elmo and I both did.

Her answer was not reassuring. The great cowardly windwhale dumped them a hundred miles north, according to the menhirs. At least it descended before forcing them off.

They were walking home. The menhirs promised to shield them from the natural wickedness of the Plain.

We all went down into the Hole bickering. There is nothing like failure to set the sparks flying.

Failure, of course, can be relative. The damage we did was considerable. The repercussions would echo a long time. The Taken had to be badly rattled. Our capture of so many documents would force a restructuring of their plan of campaign. But still the mission was unsatisfactory. Now the Taken knew windwhales were capable of ranging beyond traditional bounds. Now the Taken knew we had resources beyond those they had suspected.

When you gamble, you do not show all your cards till after the final bet.

I scrounged around and found the captured papers, took them to my quarters. I did not feel like participating in the conference room post-mortem. It was sure to get nasty—even with everyone agreeing.

I shed my weapons, lighted a lamp, picked one of the document bundles, turned to my worktable. And there lay another of those packets from the west.

Chapter Nineteen:
BOMANZ'S TALE

Croaker:

Bomanz walked his dreams with a woman who could not make him understand her words. The green path of promise led past moon-eating dogs, hanged men, and sentries without faces. Through breaks in the foliage he glimpsed a sky-spanning comet.

He did not sleep well. The dream invariably awaited him when he dozed off. He did not know why he could not slide down into deep sleep. As nightmares went, this was mild.

Most of the symbolism was obvious, and most of it he refused to heed.

Night had fallen when Jasmine brought tea and asked, "Are you going to lie here all week?"

"I might."

"How are you going to sleep tonight?"

"I probably won't till late. I'll work in the shop. What's Stance been up to?"

"He slept a while, went and brought a load from the site, pottered around the shop, ate, and went back out when somebody came to say Men fu was out there again."

"What about Besand?"

"It's all over town. The new Monitor is furious because he didn't leave. Says he won't do anything about it. The Guards are calling him a horse's ass. They won't take his orders. He's getting madder and madder."

"Maybe he'll learn something. Thanks for the tea. Is there anything to eat?"

"Leftover chicken. Get it yourself. I'm going to bed."

Grumbling, Bomanz ate cold, greasy chicken wings, washing them down with tepid beer. He thought about his dream. His ulcer gave him a nip. His head started aching. "Here we go," he muttered, and dragged himself upstairs.

He spent several hours reviewing the rituals he would use to leave his body and slide through the hazards of the Barrowland. . . . Would the dragon be a problem? Indications were, it was meant for physical intruders. Finally: "It'll work. As long as that sixth barrow is Moondog's." He sighed, leaned back, closed his eyes.

The dream began. And midway through he found himself staring into green ophidian eyes. Wise, cruel, mocking eyes. He started awake.

"Pop? You up there?"

"Yeah. Come on up."

Stancil pushed into the room. He looked awful.

"What happened?"

"The Barrowland. . . . The ghosts are walking."

"They do that when the comet gets close. I didn't expect them so soon. Must be going to get frisky this time. That's no call to get shook up."

"Wasn't that. I expected that. That I could handle. No. It's Besand and Men fu."

"What?"

"Men fu tried to get into the Barrowland with Besand's amulet."

"I was right! That little . . . Go on."

"He was at the dig. He had the amulet. He was scared to death. He saw me coming and headed downhill. When he got near where the moat used to be, Besand came out of nowhere, screaming and waving a sword. Men fu started running. Besand kept after him. It's pretty bright out there, but I lost track when they got up around the Howler's barrow. Besand must have caught him. I heard them yelling and rolling around in the brush. Then they started screaming."

Stancil stopped. Bomanz waited.

"I don't know how to describe it, Pop. I never heard sounds like that. All the ghosts piled onto the Howler's barrow. It went on a long time. Then the screaming started getting closer."

Stancil, Bomanz concluded, had been shaken deeply. Shaken the way a man is when his basic beliefs are uprooted. Odd. "Go on."

"It was Besand. He had the amulet, but it didn't help. He didn't make it across the moat. He dropped it. The ghosts jumped him. He's dead, Pop. The Guards were all out there. . . . They couldn't do anything but look. The Monitor wouldn't give them amulets so they could get him."

Bomanz folded his hands on the tabletop, stared at them. "So now we have two men dead. Three counting the one last night. How many will we have tomorrow night? Will I have to face a platoon of new ghosts?"

"You're going to do it tomorrow night?"

"That's right. With Besand gone there's no reason to delay it. Is there?"

"Pop. . . . Maybe you shouldn't. Maybe the knowledge out there should stay buried."

"What's this? My son parroting *my* misgivings?"

"Pop, let's don't fight. Maybe I pushed too hard. Maybe I was wrong. You know more about the Barrowland than me."

Bomanz stared at his son. More boldly than he felt, he said, "I'm going in. It's time to put doubts aside and get on with it. There's the list. See if there's an area of inquiry that I've forgotten."

"Pop. . . ."

"Don't argue with me, boy." It had taken him all evening to shed the ingrained Bomanz persona and surface the wizard so long and artfully hidden. But he was out now.

Bomanz went to a corner where a few seemingly innocuous objects were piled. He stood taller than usual. He moved more precisely, more quickly. He began piling things on the table. "When you go back to Oar, you can tell my old classmates what became of me." He smiled thinly. He could recall a few who would shudder even now, knowing he had studied at the Lady's knee. He'd never forgotten, never forgiven. And they knew him that well.

Stancil's pallor had disappeared. Now he was uncertain. This side of the father had not been seen since before the son's birth. It was outside his experience. "Do you want to go out there, Pop?"

"You brought back the essential details. Besand is dead. Men fu is dead. The Guards aren't going to get excited."

"I thought he was your friend."

"Besand? Besand had no friends. He had a mission. . . . What're you looking at?"

"A man with a mission?"

"Could be. Something kept me here. Take this stuff downstairs. We'll do it in the shop."

"Where do you want it?"

"Doesn't matter. Besand was the only one who could have separated it from the junk."

Stancil went out. Later, Bomanz finished a series of mental exercises and wondered what had become of the boy. Stance hadn't returned. He shrugged, went on.

He smiled. He was ready. It was going to be simple.

The town was in an uproar. A Guard had tried to assassinate the new Monitor. The Monitor was so bewildered and frightened he had locked himself in his quarters. Crazy rumors abounded.

Bomanz walked through it with such calm dignity that he startled people who had known him for years. He went to the edge of the Barrowland, considered his long-time antagonist. Besand lay where he had fallen. The flies were thick. Bomanz threw a handful of dirt. The insects scattered. He nodded thoughtfully. Besand's amulet had disappeared again.

Bomanz located Corporal Husky. "If you can't do anything to get Besand out, then toss dirt in on him. There's a mountain around my pit."

"Yes, sir," Husky said, and only later seemed startled by his easy acquiescence.

Bomanz walked the perimeter of the Barrowland. The sun shone a little oddly through the comet's tail. Colors were a trifle strange. But there were no ghosts aprowl now. He saw no reason not to make his communication attempt. He returned to the village.

Wagons stood before the shop. Teamsters were busy loading them. Jasmine shrilled inside, cursing someone who had taken something he shouldn't. "Damn you, Tokar," Bomanz muttered. "Why today? You could have waited till it was over." He felt a fleeting concern. He could not rely on Stance if the boy were distracted. He shoved into the shop.

"It's grand!" Tokar said of the horse. "Absolutely magnificent. You're a genius, Bo."

"You're a pain in the butt. What's going on here? Who the hell are all these people?"

"My drivers. My brother Clete. My sister Glory. Stance's Glory. And our baby sister Snoopy. We called her that because she was always spying on us."

"Pleased to meet you all. Where's Stance?"

Jasmine said, "I sent him to get something for supper. With this crowd I'll have to start cooking early."

Bomanz sighed. Just what he needed, this night of nights. A house full of guests. "You. Put that back where you got it. You. Snoopy? Keep your hands off of stuff."

Tokar asked, "What's with you, Bo?"

Bomanz raised one eyebrow, met the man's gaze, did not answer. "Where's the driver with the big shoulders?"

"Not with me anymore." Tokar frowned.

"Thought not. I'll be upstairs if something critical comes up." He stamped through the shop, went up, settled in his chair, willed himself to sleep. His dreams were subtle. It seemed he could hear at last, but could not recall what he heard. . . .

Stancil entered the upstairs room. Bomanz asked, "What are we going to do? That crowd is gumming up the works."

"How long do you need, Pop?"

"This could go all night every night for weeks if it works out." He was pleased. Stancil had recovered his courage.

"Can't hardly run them off."

"And can't go anywhere else, either." The Guards were in a hard, bitter mood.

"How noisy will you be, Pop? Could we do it here, on the quiet?"

"Guess we'll have to try. Going to be crowded. Get the stuff from the shop. I'll make room."

Bomanz's shoulders slumped when Stancil left. He was getting nervous. Not about the thing he would challenge, but about his own foresight. He kept thinking he had forgotten something. But he had reviewed four decades of notes without detecting a flaw in his chosen approach. Any reasonably educated apprentice should be able to follow his formulation. He spat into a corner. "Antiquarian's cowardice," he muttered. "Old-fashioned fear of the unknown."

Stancil returned. "Mom's got them into a game of Throws."

"I wondered what Snoopy was yelling about. Got everything?"

"Yes."

"Okay. Go down and kibbitz. I'll be there after I set up. We'll do it after they're in bed."

"Okay."

"Stance? Are you ready?"

"I'm okay, Pop. I just had the jitters last night. It's not every day I see a man killed by ghosts."

"Better get a feel for that kind of thing. It happens."

Stancil looked blank.

"You're sneaking studies on Black Campus, aren't you?" Black Campus was that hidden side of the university on which wizards learned their trade. Officially, it did not exist. Legally, it was prohibited. But it was there. Bomanz was a laureate graduate.

Stancil gave one sharp nod and left.

"I thought so," Bomanz whispered, and wondered: How black are you, son?

He pottered around till he had triple-checked everything, till he realized that caution had become an excuse for not socializing. "You're something," he mumbled to himself.

One last look. Chart laid out. Candles. Bowl of quicksilver. Silver dagger. Herbs. Censers. . . . He still had that feeling. "What the hell could I have missed?"

Throws was essentially four-player checkers. The board was four times the usual size. Players played from each side. An element of chance was added by throwing a die before each move. If a player's throw came up six, he could move any combination of pieces six moves. Checkers rules generally applied, except that a jump could be declined.

Snoopy appealed to Bomanz the moment he appeared. "They're ganging up on me!" She was playing opposite Jasmine. Glory and Tokar were on her flanks. Bomanz watched a few moves. Tokar and the older sister were in cahoots. Conventional elimination tactics.

On impulse Bomanz controlled the fall of the die when it came to Snoopy. She threw a six, squealed, sent men charging all over. Bomanz wondered if he had been that rich in adolescent enthusiasm and optimism. He eyed the girl. How old? Fourteen?

He made Tokar throw a one, let Jasmine and Glory have what fate decreed, then gave Snoopy another six and Tokar another one. After a third time around Tokar grumbled, "This is getting ridiculous." The balance of the game had shifted. Glory was about to abandon him and side with her sister against Jasmine.

Jasmine gave Bomanz the fish-eye when Snoopy threw yet another six. He winked, let Tokar throw free. A two. Tokar grumbled, "I'm on the comeback trail now."

Bomanz wandered into the kitchen, poured himself a mug of beer. He returned to find Snoopy on the edge of disaster again. Her play was so frenetic she had to throw fours or better to survive.

Tokar, on the other hand, played a tediously conservative game, advancing in echelon, trying to occupy his flankers' king rows. A man much like himself, Bomanz reflected. First he plays to make sure he doesn't lose; then he worries about the win.

He watched Tokar roll a six and send a piece on an extravagant tour in which he took three men from his nominal ally, Glory.

Treacherous, too, Bomanz thought. That's worth keeping in mind. He asked Stancil, "Where's Clete?"

Tokar said, "He decided to stay with the teamsters. Thought we were crowding you too much."

"I see."

Jasmine won that game, and Tokar the next, whereupon the antique merchant said, "That's all for me. Take my seat, Bo. See you all in the morning."

Glory said. "I'm done, too. Can we go for a walk, Stance?"

Stancil glanced at his father. Bomanz nodded. "Don't go far. The Guards are in a bad mood."

"We won't," Stance said. His father smiled at his eager

departure. It had been that way for him and Jasmine, long ago.

Jasmine observed, "A lovely girl. Stance is lucky."

"Thank you," Tokar said. "We think she's lucky, too."

Snoopy made a sour face. Bomanz allowed himself a wry smile. Somebody had a crush on Stancil. "Three-handed game?" he suggested. "Take turns playing the dummy till somebody is out?"

He let chance have its way with the players' throws but turned five and sixes for the dummy. Snoopy went out and took the dummy. Jasmine seemed amused. Snoopy squealed delightedly when she won. "Glory, I won!" she enthused when her sister and Stancil returned. "I beat them."

Stancil looked at the board, at his father. "Pop. . . ."

"I fought all the way. She got the lucky throws."

Stancil smiled a disbelieving smile.

Glory said, "That's enough, Snoopy. Bedtime. This isn't the city. People go to bed early here."

"Aw. . . ." The girl complained but went. Bomanz sighed. Being sociable was a strain.

His heartbeat quickened as he anticipated the night's work.

Stancil completed a third reading of his written instructions. "Got it?" Bomanz asked.

"I guess."

"Timing isn't important—as long as you're late, not early. If we were going to conjure some damnfool demon, you'd study your lines for a week."

"Lines?" Stancil would do nothing but tend candles and observe. He was there to help if his father got into trouble.

Bomanz had spent the past two hours neutralizing spells along the path he intended to follow. The Moondog name had been a gold strike.

"Is it open?" Stancil asked.

"Wide. It almost pulls you. I'll let you go yourself later in the week."

Bomanz took a deep breath, exhaled. He surveyed the room. He still had that nagging feeling of having forgotten something. He hadn't a hint what it might be. "Okay."

He settled into the chair, closed his eyes. "Dumni," he

murmured. ''Um muji dumni. Haikon. Dumni. Um muji dumni.''

Stancil pinched herbs into a diminutive charcoal brazier. Pungent smoke filled the room. Bomanz relaxed, let the lethargy steal over him. He achieved a quick separation, drifted up, hovered beneath the rafters, watched Stancil. The boy showed promise.

Bo checked his ties with his body. Good. Excellent! He could hear with both his spiritual and physical ears. He tested the duality further as he drifted downstairs. Each sound Stance made came through clearly.

He paused in the shop, stared at Glory and Snoopy. He envied them their youth and innocence.

Outside, the comet's glow filled the night. Bomanz felt its power showering the earth. How much more spectacular would it become by the time the world entered its mane?

Suddenly, *she* was there, beckoning urgently. He reexamined his ties to his flesh. Yes. Still in trance. Not dreaming. He felt vaguely ill at ease.

She led him to the Barrowland, following the path he had opened. He reeled under the awesome power buried there, away from the might radiating from the menhirs and fetishes. Seen from his spiritual viewpoint, they took the form of cruel, hideous monsters leashed on short chains.

Ghosts stalked the Barrowland. They howled beside Bomanz, trying to breach his spells. The power of the comet and the might of the warding spells joined in a thunder which permeated Bomanz's being. How mighty were the ancients, he thought, that all this should remain after so long.

They approached the dead soldiers represented by pawns on Bomanz's chart. He thought he heard footsteps behind him. . . . He looked back, saw nothing, realized he was hearing Stancil back at the house.

A knight's ghost challenged him. Its hatred was as timeless and relentless as the pounding surf along a cold, bleak shore. He sidled around.

Great green eyes stared into his own. Ancient, wise, merciless eyes, arrogant, mocking, and contemptuous. The dragon exposed its teeth in a sneer.

This is it, Bomanz thought. What I overlooked. . . . But

no. The dragon could not touch him. He sensed its irritation, its conviction that he would make a tasty morsel in the flesh. He hurried after the woman.

No doubt about it. She was the Lady. She had been trying to reach him, too. Best be wary. She wanted more than a grateful chela.

They entered the crypt. It was massive, spacious, filled with all the clutter that had been the Dominator's in life. Clearly, that life had not been spartan.

He pursued the woman around a furniture pile—and found her vanished. "Where? . . ."

He saw them. Side by side, on separate stone slabs. Shackled. Enveloped by crackling, humming forces. Neither breathed, yet neither betrayed the grey·of death. They seemed suspended, marking time.

Legend exaggerated only slightly. The Lady's impact, even in this state, was immense. "Bo, you have a grown son." Part of him wanted to stand on its hind legs and howl like an adolescent in rut.

He heard steps again. Damn that Stancil. Couldn't he stand still? He was making racket enough for three people.

The woman's eyes opened. Her lips formed a glorious smile. Bomanz forgot Stancil.

Welcome, said a voice within his mind. *We have waited a long time, haven't we?*

Dumbstruck, he simply nodded.

I have watched you. Yes, I see everything in this forsaken wilderness. I tried to help. The barriers were too many and too great. That cursed White Rose. She was no fool.

Bomanz glanced at the Dominator. That huge, handsome warrior-emperor slept on. Bomanz envied him his physical perfection.

He sleeps a deeper sleep.

Did he hear mockery? He could not read her face. The glamor was too much for him. He·suspected that had been true for many men, and that it was true that she had been the driving force of the Domination.

I was. And next time . . .

"Next time?"

Mirth surrounded him like the tinkle of wind chimes in a

gentle breeze. *You came to learn, O wizard. How will you repay your teacher?*

Here was the moment for which he had lived. His triumph lay before him. One part to go. . . .

You were crafty. You were so careful, took so long, even that Monitor discounted you. I applaud you, wizard.

The hard part. Binding this creature to his will.

Wind-chimes laughter. *You don't plan to bargain? You mean to compel?*

"If I have to."

You won't give me anything?

"I can't give you what you want."

Mirth again. Silver-bells mirth. *You can't compel me.*

Bomanz shrugged imaginary shoulders. She was wrong. He had a lever. He had stumbled onto it as a youth, had recognized its significance immediately, and had set his feet on the long path leading to this moment.

He had found a cipher. He had broken it and it had given him the Lady's patronym, a name common in pre-Domination histories. Circumstances implicated one of that family's several daughters as the Lady. A little historical detective work had completed the task.

So he had solved a mystery that had baffled thousands for hundreds of years.

Knowing her true name gave him the power to compel the Lady. In wizardry, the true name is identical with the thing. . . .

I could have shrieked. It seemed my correspondent ended on the brink of the very revelation for which I had been searching these many years. Damn his black heart.

This time there was a postscript, a little something more than story. The letter-writer had added what looked like chicken scratches. That they were meant to communicate I had no doubt. But I could make nothing of them.

As always, there was neither signature nor seal.

Chapter Twenty: THE BARROWLAND

The rain never ceased. Mostly it was little more than a drizzle. When the day went especially well, it slackened to a falling mist. But always there was precipitation. Corbie went out anyway, though he complained often about aches in his leg.

"If the weather bothers you so, why stay here?" Case asked. "You said you think your kids live in Opal. Why not go down there and look for them yourself? At least the weather would be decent."

It was a tough question. Corbie had yet to create a convincing answer. He had not yet found one that would do himself, let alone enemies who might ask.

There was nothing Corbie was afraid to do. In another life, as another man, he had challenged the hellmakers themselves, unafraid. Swords and sorcery and death could not intimidate him. Only people, and love, could terrify him.

"Habit, I guess," he said. Weakly. "Maybe I could live in Oar. Maybe. I don't deal well with people, Case. I don't like them that much. I couldn't stand the Jewel Cities. Did I tell you I was down there once?"

Case had heard the story several times. He suspected Corbie had been more than down there. He thought one of the Jewel Cities was Corbie's original home. "Yeah. When the big Rebel push in Forsberg started. You told me about seeing the Tower on the way up."

"That's right. I did. Memory's slipping. Cities. I don't like them, lad. Don't like them. Too many people. Sometimes there's too many of them *here*. Was when I first came.

Nowadays it's about right. About right. Maybe too much fuss
and bother because of the undead over there.'' He poked his
chin toward the Great Barrow. ''But otherwise about right.
One or two of you guys I can talk to. Nobody else to get in
my way.''

Case nodded. He thought he understood while not understanding. He had known other old veterans. Most had had
their peculiarities. ''Hey! Corbie. You ever run into the Black
Company when you was up here?''

Corbie froze, stared with such intensity the young soldier
blushed. ''Uh . . . What's the matter, Corbie? I say something wrong?''

Corbie resumed walking, his limp not slowing a furiously
increased pace. ''It was odd. Like you were reading my
mind. Yes. I ran into those guys. Bad people. *Very* bad
people.''

''My dad told us stories about them. He was with them
during the long retreat to Charm. Lords, the Windy Country,
the Stair of Tear, all those battles. When he got leave time
after the battle at Charm, he came home. Told awful stories
about those guys.''

''I missed that part. I got left behind at Roses, when Shifter
and the Limper lost the battle. Who was your dad with?
You've never talked about him much.''

''Nightcrawler. I don't talk about him because we never
got along.''

Corbie smiled. ''Sons seldom get on with their fathers.
And that's the voice of experience speaking.''

''What did your father do?''

Corbie laughed. ''He was a farmer. Of sorts. But I'd rather
not talk about him.''

''What are we doing out here, Corbie?''

Double-checking Bomanz's surveys. But Corbie could not
tell the lad that. Nor could he think of an adequate lie.
''Walking in the rain.''

''Corbie . . .''

''Can we keep it quiet for a while, Case? Please?''

''Sure.''

Corbie limped all the way around the Barrowland, maintaining a respectful distance, never being too obvious. He did not

use equipment. That would bring Colonel Sweet on the run. Instead, he consulted the wizard's chart in his mind. The thing blazed with its own life there, those arcane TelleKurre symbols glowing with a wild and dangerous life. Studying the remains of the Barrowland, he could find but a third of the map's referents. The rest had been undone by time and weather.

Corbie was no man to have trouble with his nerve. But he was afraid now. Near the end of their stroll he said, "Case, I want a favor. Perhaps a double favor."

"Sir?"

"Sir? Call me Corbie."

"You sounded so serious."

"It is serious."

"Say on, then."

"Can you be trusted to keep your mouth shut?"

"If necessary."

"I want to extract a conditional vow of silence."

"I don't understand."

"Case, I want to tell you something. In case something happens to me."

"Corbie!"

"I'm not a young man, Case. And I have a lot wrong with me. I've been through a lot. I feel it catching up. I don't *expect* to go soon. But things happen. If something should, there's something I don't want to die with me."

"Okay, Corbie."

"If I suggested something, can you keep it to yourself? Even if you think you maybe shouldn't? Can you do something for me?"

"You're making it hard, not telling me."

"I know. It's not fair. The only other man I trust is Colonel Sweet. And his position wouldn't let him make such a promise."

"It's not illegal?"

"Not strictly speaking."

"I guess."

"Don't guess, Case."

"All right. You have my word."

"Good. Thank you. It *is* appreciated, never doubt that.

Two things. First. If something happens to me, go to the room on the second floor of my home. If I have left an oilskin packet on the table there, see that it gets to a blacksmith named Sand, in Oar.''

Case looked suitably dubious and baffled.

''Second, after you do that—and only after—tell the Colonel the undead are stirring.''

Case stopped walking.

''Case.'' There was a note of command in Corbie's voice the youth had not heard before.

''Yes. All right.''

''That's it.''

''Corbie . . .''

''No questions now. In a few weeks, maybe I can explain everything. All right?''

''Okay.''

''Not a word now. And remember. Packet to Sand the blacksmith. Then word to the Colonel. Tell you what. If I can, I'll leave the Colonel a letter, too.''

Case merely nodded.

Corbie took a deep breath. It had been twenty years since he had attempted the simplest divining spell. Never had he tried anything on the order of what he now faced. Back in those ancient times, when he was another man, or boy, sorcery was a diversion for wealthy youths who would rather play wizard than pursue legitimate studies.

All was ready. The tools of the sorcerer appropriate to the task lay on the table on the second floor of the house that Bomanz built. It was fitting that he follow the old one.

He touched the oilskin packet left for Case, the opaque letter to Sweet, and prayed neither would touch the young man's hands. But if what he suspected were true, it was better the enemy knew than the world be surprised.

There was nothing left to do but do it. He gulped half a cup of cold tea, took his seat. He closed his eyes, began a chant taught him when he was younger than Case. His was not the method Bomanz had used, but it was as effective.

His body would not relax, would not cease distracting him.

But at last the full lethargy closed in. His ka loosed its ten thousand anchors to his flesh.

Part of him insisted he was a fool for attempting this without the skills of a master. But he hadn't the time for the training a Bomanz required. He had learned what he could during his absence from the Old Forest.

Free of the flesh, yet connected by invisible bonds that would draw him back. If his luck held. He moved away carefully. He conformed to the rule of bodies exactly. He used the stairway, the doorway, and the sidewalks built by the Guard. Maintain the pretense of flesh and the flesh would be harder to forget.

The world looked different. Each object had its unique aura. He found it difficult to concentrate on the grand task.

He moved to the bounds of the Barrowland. He shuddered under the impact of thrumming old spells that kept the Dominator and several lesser minions bound. The power there! Carefully, he walked the boundary till he found the way that Bomanz had opened, still not fully healed.

He stepped over the line.

He drew the instant attention of every spirit, benign and malign, chained within the Barrowland. There were far more than he expected. Far more than the wizard's map indicated. Those soldier symbols that surrounded the Great Barrow. . . . They were not statues. They were men, soldiers of the White Rose, who had been set as spirit guards perpetually standing between the world and the monster that would devour it. How driven must they have been. Now dedicated to their cause.

The path wound past the former resting places of old Taken, outer circle, inner circle, twisting. Within the inner circle he saw the true forms of several lesser monsters that had served the Domination. The path stretched like a trail of pale silver mist. Behind him that mist became more dense, his passage strengthening the way.

Ahead, stronger spells. And all those men who had gone into the earth to surround the Dominator. And beyond them, the greater fear. The dragon thing that, on Bomanz's map, lay coiled around the crypt in the heart of the Great Barrow.

Spirits shrieked at him in TelleKurre, in UchiTelle, in languages he did not know and tongues vaguely like some

still current. One and all, they cursed him. One and all, he
ignored them. There was a thing in a chamber beneath the
greatest mound. He had to see if it lay as restless as he
suspected.

The dragon. Oh, by all the gods that never were, that
dragon was real. Real, alive, of flesh, yet it sensed and saw
him. The silver trail curved past its jaws, through the gap
between teeth and tail. It beat at him with a palpable will. But
he would not be stayed.

No more guardians. Just the crypt. And the monster man
inside was constrained. He had survived the worst. . . .

The old devil should be sleeping. Hadn't the Lady defeated
him in his attempt to escape through Juniper? Hadn't she put
him back down?

It was a tomb like many around the world. Perhaps a bit
richer. The White Rose had laid her opponents down in style.
There were no sarcophagi, though. There. That empty table
was where the Lady would have lain.

The other boasted a sleeping man. A big man, and handsome,
but with the mark of the beast upon him, even in repose. A
face full of hot hatred, of the anger of defeat.

Ah, then. His suspicions were groundless. The monster
slept indeed. . . .

The Dominator sat up. And smiled. His smile was the most
wicked Corbie had ever seen. Then the undead extended a
hand in welcome. Corbie ran.

Mocking laughter pursued him.

Panic was an emotion entirely unfamiliar. Seldom had he
experienced it. He could not control it. He was only vaguely
aware of passing the dragon and the hate-filled spirits of
White Rose soldiers. He barely sensed the Dominator's creatures beyond, all howling in delight.

Even in his panic he clung to the misty trail. He made only
one misstep. . . .

But that was sufficient.

The storm broke over the Barrowland. It was the most
furious in living memory. The lightning clashed with the
ferocity of heavenly armies, hammers and spears and swords

of fire smiting earth and sky. The downpour was incessant and impenetrable.

One mighty bolt struck the Barrowland. Earth and shrubbery flew a hundred yards into the air. The earth staggered. The Eternal Guard scrambled to arms terrified, sure the old evil had broken its chains.

On the Barrowland two large shapes, one four-footed, one bipedal, formed in the afterglow of the lightning strike. In a moment both raced along a twisting path, leaving no mark upon water or mud. They passed the bounds of the Barrowland, fled toward the forest.

No one saw them. When the Guard reached the Barrowland, carrying weapons and lanterns and fear like vast loads of lead, the storm had waned. The lightning had ceased its boisterous brawl. The rain had fallen off to normal.

Colonel Sweet and his men spent hours roaming the bounds of the Barrowland. No one found a thing.

The Eternal Guard returned to its compound cursing the gods and weather.

On the second floor of Corbie's house Corbie's body continued to breathe one breath each five minutes. His heart barely turned over. He would be a long time dying without his spirit.

Chapter Twenty-One: THE PLAIN OF FEAR

I asked to see Darling and got an immediate audience. She expected me to come in raising hell about ill-advised military actions by outfits that could not afford losses. She expected lessons in the importance of maintaining cadres and forces-in-being. I surprised her by coming with neither. Here she was, primed to weather the worst, to get it over so she could get back to business, and I disappointed her.

Instead, I took her the letters from Oar, which I had shared with no one yet. She expressed curiosity. I signed: "Read them."

It took a while. The Lieutenant ducked in and out, growing more impatient each time. She finished, looked at me. "Well?" she signed.

"That comes from the core of the documents I am missing. Along with a few other things, that story is what I have been hunting. Soulcatcher gave me to believe that the weapon we want is hidden inside this story."

"It is not complete."

"No. But does it not give you pause?"

"You have no idea who the writer is?"

"No. And no way to find out, short of looking him up. Or her." Actually, I had a couple of suspicions, but each seemed more unlikely than the other.

"These have come with swift regularity," Darling observed. "After all this time." That made me suspect she shared one of my suspicions. That "all this time."

"The couriers believe they were forwarded over a more spread period."

"It is interesting, but not yet useful. We must await more."

"It will not hurt to consider what it means. The end part of the last, there. That is beyond me. I have to work on that. It may be critical. Unless it is meant to baffle someone who intercepts the fragment."

She shuffled out the last sheet, stared at it. A sudden light illuminated her face. "It is the finger speech, Croaker," she signed. "The letters. See? The speaking hand, as it forms the alphabet."

I circled behind her. I saw it now, and felt abysmally stupid for having missed it. Once you saw that, it was easy to read. If you knew your sign. It said:

This may be the last communication, Croaker. There is something I must do. The risks are grave. The chances hang against me, but I must go ahead. If you do not receive the final installment, about Bomanz's last days, you will have to come collect it. I will conceal one copy within the home of the wizard, as the story describes. You may find another in Oar. Ask for the blacksmith named Sand.

Wish me luck. By now you must have found a place of safety. I would not bring you forth unless the fate of the world hinged upon it.

There was no signature here, either.

Darling and I stared at one another. I asked, "What do you think? What should I do?"

"Wait."

"And if no further episodes are forthcoming?"

"Then you must go looking."

"Yes." Fear. The world was marshaled against us. The Rust raid would have the Taken in a vengeful frenzy.

"It may be the great hope, Croaker."

"The Barrowland, Darling. Only the Tower itself could be more dangerous."

"Perhaps I should accompany you."

"No! You will not be risked. Not under any circumstances. The movement can survive the loss of one beat-up, worn-out old physician. It cannot without the White Rose."

She hugged me hard, backed off, signed, "I am not the White Rose, Croaker. She is dead four centuries. I am Darling."

"Our enemies call you the White Rose. Our friends do. There is power in a name." I waved the letters. "That is what this is about. One name. What you have been named you must be."

"I am Darling," she insisted.

"To me, maybe. To Silent. To a few others. But to the world you are the White Rose, the hope and the salvation." It occurred to me that a name was missing. The name Darling wore before she became a ward of the Company. Always she had been Darling, because that was what Raven called her. Had he known her birthname? If so, it no longer mattered. She was safe. She was the last alive to know it, if even she remembered. The village where we found her, mauled by the Limper's troops, was not the sort that kept written records.

"Go," she signed. "Study. Think. Be of good faith. Somewhere, soon, you will find the thread."

Chapter Twenty-Two: THE PLAIN OF FEAR

The men who fled Rust with the cowardly windwhale eventually arrived. We learned that the Taken had escaped the Plain, all in a rage because but one carpet survived. Their offensive would be delayed till the carpets were replaced. And carpets are among the greatest and most costly magicks. I suspect the Limper had to do a lot of explaining to the Lady.

I drafted One-Eye, Goblin, and Silent into an expanded project. I translated. They extracted proper names, assembled them in charts. My quarters became all but impenetrable. And barely livable while they were there, for Goblin and One-Eye had had a couple of tastes of life outside Darling's null. They were at one another constantly.

And I began having nightmares.

One evening I posed a challenge, half as a result of no further courier arriving, half as busywork meant to stop Goblin and One-Eye from driving me mad. I said, "I may have to leave the Plain. Can you do something so I don't attract any special attention?"

They had their questions. I answered most honestly. They wanted to go too, as if a journey west was established fact. I said, "No way are you going. A thousand miles of this crap? I'd commit suicide before we got off the Plain. Or murder one of you. Which I'm considering anyway."

Goblin squeaked. He pretended mortal terror. One-Eye said, "Get within ten feet of me and I'll turn you into a lizard."

I made a rude noise. "You can barely turn food into shit."

Goblin cackled. "Chickens and cows do better. You can fertilize with theirs."

"You got no room to talk, runt," I snapped.

"Getting touchy in his old age," One-Eye observed. "Must be rheumatiz. Got the rheumatiz, Croaker?"

"He'll wish his problem was rheumatism if he keeps on," Goblin promised. "It's bad enough I have to put up with you. But you're at least predictable."

"Predictable?"

"Like the seasons."

They were off. I sped Silent a look of appeal. The son-of-a-bitch ignored me.

Next day Goblin ambled in wearing a smug smile. "We figured something out, Croaker. In case you do go wandering."

"Like what?"

"We'll need your amulets."

I had two that they had given me long ago. One was supposed to warn me of the proximity of the Taken. It worked quite well. The other, ostensibly, was protective, but it also let them locate me from a distance. Silent tracked it the time Catcher sent Raven and me to ambush Limper and Whisper in the Forest of Cloud, when Limper tried to go over to the Rebel.

Long ago and far away. Memories of a younger Croaker.

"We'll work up some modifications. So you can't be located magically. Let me have them. Later we'll have to go outside to test them."

I eyed him narrowly.

He said, "You'll have to come so we can test them by trying to find you."

"Yeah? Sounds like a drummed-up excuse to get outside the null."

"Maybe." He grinned.

Whatever, Darling liked the notion. Next evening we headed up the creek, skirting Old Father Tree. "He looks a little peaked," I said.

"Caught the side wash of a Taken spell during the brouhaha," One-Eye explained. "I don't think he was pleased."

The old tree tinkled. I stopped, considered it. It had to be thousands of years old. Trees grow very slow on the Plain. What stories it would tell!

"Come on, Croaker," Goblin called. "Old Father ain't talking." He grinned his frog grin.

They know me too well. Know when I see anything old I wonder what it has seen. Damn them, anyhow.

We left the watercourse five miles from the Hole, quartered westward into desert where the coral was especially dense and dangerous. I guess there were five hundred species, in reefs so close they were almost impenetrable. The colors were riotous. Fingers, fronds, branches of coral soared thirty feet into the air. I remain eternally amazed that the wind does not topple them.

In a small sandy place surrounded by coral, One-Eye called a halt. "This is far enough. We'll be safe here."

I wondered. Our progress had been followed by mantas and the creatures that resemble buzzards. Never will I trust such beasts completely.

Long, long ago, after the Battle at Charm, the Company crossed the Plain en route to assignments in the east. I saw horrible things happen. I could not shake the memories.

Goblin and One-Eye played games but also tended to business. They remind me of active children. Always into something, just to be doing. I lay back and watched the clouds. Soon I fell asleep.

Goblin wakened me. He returned my amulets. "We're going to play hide-and-seek," he said. "We'll give you a head start. If we've done everything right, we won't be able to find you."

"Now that's wonderful," I replied. "Me alone out here, wandering around lost." I was just carping. I could find the Hole. As a nasty practical joke I was tempted to head straight there.

This was business, though.

I set off to the southwest, toward the buttes. I crossed the westward trail and went into hiding among quiescent walking trees. Only after darkness fell did I give up waiting. I walked back to the Hole, wondering what had become of my companions. I startled the sentry when I arrived.

"Goblin and One-Eye come in?"

"No. I thought they were with you."

"They were." Concerned, I went below, asked the Lieutenant's advice.

"Go find them," he told me.

"How?"

He looked at me like I was a half-wit. "Leave your silly amulets, go outside the null, and wait."

"Oh. Okay."

So I went back outside, walked up the creek, grumbling. My feet ached. I was not used to so much hiking. Good for me, I told myself. Had to be in shape if there was a trip to Oar in the cards.

I reached the edge of the coral reefs. "One-Eye! Goblin! You guys around?"

No answer. I was not going on looking, though. The coral would kill me. I circled north, assuming they had moved away from the Hole. Each few minutes I dropped to my knees, hoping to spot a menhir's silhouette. The menhirs would know what had become of them.

Once I saw some flash and fury from the corner of my eye and, without thinking, ran that way, thinking it was Goblin and One-Eye squabbling. But a direct look revealed the distant rage of a change storm.

I stopped immediately, belatedly remembering that only death hurries on the Plain by night.

I was lucky. Just steps onward the sand became spongy, loose. I squatted, sniffed a handful. It held the smell of old death. I backed away carefully. Who knows what lay in waiting beneath that sand?

"Better plant somewhere and wait for the sun," I muttered. I was no longer certain of my position.

I found some rocks that would break the wind, some brush for firewood, and pitched camp. The fire was more to declare myself to beasts than to keep warm. The night was not cold.

Firemaking was a symbolic statement out there.

Once the flames rose I found that the place had been used before. Smoke had blackened the rocks. Native humans, probably. They wander in small bands. We have little intercourse with them. They have no interest in the world struggle.

Will failed me sometime after the second hour. I fell asleep.

The nightmare found me. And found me unshielded by amulets or null.

She came.

It had been years. Last time it was to report the final defeat of her husband in the affair at Juniper.

A golden cloud, like dust motes dancing in a sunbeam. An all-over feeling of being awake while sleeping. Calmness and fear together. An inability to move. All the old symptoms.

A beautiful woman formed in the cloud, a woman out of daydream. The sort you hope to meet someday, knowing there is no chance. I cannot say what she wore, if she wore anything. My universe consisted of her face and the terror its presence inspired.

Her smile was not at all cold. Long ago, for some reason, she took an interest in me. I supposed she retained some residue of the old affection, as one does for a pet long dead.

"Physician." Breeze in the reeds beside the waters of eternity. The whisper of angels. But never could she make me forget the reality whence the voice sprang.

Nor was she ever so gauche as to tempt me, either with promises or herself. That, perhaps, is one reason I think she felt a certain fondness. When she used me, she gave it to me straight going in.

I could not respond.

"You are safe. Long ago, by your standard of time, I said I would remain in touch. I have been unable. You cut me off. I have been trying for weeks."

The nightmares explained.

"What?" I squeaked like Goblin.

"Join me at Charm. Be my historian."

As always when she touched me, I was baffled. She seemed to consider me outside the struggle while yet a part of it. On the Stair of Tear, on the eve of the most savage sorcerous struggle ever I witnessed, she came to promise me I would come to no harm. She seemed intrigued with my lesser role as Company historian. Back when, she insisted I record events as they happened. Without regard to pleasing anyone. I had done so within the limits of my prejudices.

"The heat in the crucible is rising, physician. Your White Rose is crafty. Her attack behind the Limper was a grand stroke. But insignificant on the broader canvas. Don't you agree?"

How could I argue? I did agree.

"As your spies have no doubt reported, five armies stand poised to cleanse the Plain of Fear. It is a strange and unpredictable land. But it will not withstand what is being marshaled."

Again I could not argue, for I believed her. I could but do what Darling so often spoke of: Buy time. "You may be surprised."

"Perhaps. Surprises have been calculated into my plans. Come out of that cold waste, Croaker. Come to the Tower. Become my historian."

This was as near temptation as ever she had come. She spoke to a part of me I do not understand, a part almost willing to betray comrades of decades. If I went, there was so much I would *know*. So many answers illuminated. So many curiosities satisfied.

"You escaped us at Queen's Bridge."

Heat climbed my neck. During our years on the run the Lady's forces had overtaken us several times. Queen's Bridge was the worst. A hundred brothers had fallen there. And to my shame, I left the Annals behind, buried in the river bank. Four hundred years worth of Company history, abandoned.

There was just so much that could be carried away. The papers down in the Hole were critical to our future. I took them instead of the Annals. But I suffer frequent bouts of guilt. I must answer the shades of brethren who have gone before. Those Annals *are* the Black Company. While they exist, the Company lives.

"We escaped and escaped, and will continue to escape. It is fated."

She smiled, amused. "I have read your Annals, Croaker. New and old."

I began throwing wood onto the embers of my fire. I was not dreaming. "You have them?" Till that moment I had silenced guilt with promises to recover them.

"They were found after the battle. They came to me. I was pleased. You are honest, as historians go."

"Thank you. I try."

"Come to Charm. There is a place for you in the Tower. You can see the grand canvas from here."

"I can't."

"I cannot shield you there. If you stay, you must face what befalls your Rebel friends. The Limper commands that campaign. I will not interfere. He is not what he was. You hurt him. And he had to be hurt more to be saved. He has not forgiven you that, Croaker."

"I know." How many times had she used my name? In all our contacts previously, over years, she had used it but once.

"Don't let him take you."

A slight, twisted bit of humor rose from somewhere inside me. "You are a failure, Lady."

She was taken aback.

"Fool that I am, I recorded my romances in the Annals. You read them. You know I never characterized you as black. Not, I think, as I would characterize your husband. I suspect an unconsciously sensed truth lies beneath the silliness of those romances."

"Indeed?"

"I don't think you *are* black. I think you're just trying. I think that, for all the wickedness you've done, part of the child that was remains untainted. A spark remains, and you can't extinguish it."

Unchallenged, I became more daring. "I think you've selected me as a symbolic sop to that spark. I am a reclamation project meant to satisfy a hidden streak of decency, the way my friend Raven reclaimed a child who became the White Rose. You read the Annals. You know to what depths Raven sank once he concentrated all decency in one cup. Better, perhaps, that he had had none at all. Juniper might still exist. So might he."

"Juniper was a boil overdue for lancing. I am not come to be mocked, physician. I will not be made to look weak even before an audience of one."

I started to protest.

"For I know that this, too, will end up in your Annals."

She knew me. But then, she had had me before the Eye.

"Come to the Tower, Croaker. I demand no oath."

"Lady . . ."

"Even the Taken bind themselves with deadly oaths. You may remain free. Just do what you do. Heal, and record the truth. What you would do anywhere. You have value not to be wasted out there."

Now there was a sentiment with which I could agree wholeheartedly. I would take it back and rub some people's noses in it. "Say what?"

She started to speak. I raised a warning hand. I had spoken to myself, not to her. Was that a footfall? Yes. Something big coming. Something moving slowly, wearily.

She sensed it, too. An eye blink and she was gone, her departure sucking something from my mind, so that once more I was not certain I had not dreamed everything, for all that every word remained immutably inscribed on the stone of my mind.

I shuffled brush onto my fire, backed into a crack behind the dagger that was the only weapon I'd had sense enough to bring.

It came closer. Then paused. Then came on. My heartbeat increased. Something thrust into the firelight.

"Toadkiller Dog! What the hell, hey? What're you doing? Come on in out of the cold, boy." The words tumbled out, bearing fear away. "Boy, will Tracker be glad to see you. What happened to you?"

He came forward cautiously, looking twice as mangy as ever. He dropped onto his belly, rested his chin on forepaws, closed one eye.

"I don't have any food. I'm sort of lost myself. You're damned lucky, know that? Making it this far. The plain is a bad place to be on your own."

Right then that old mongrel looked like he agreed. Body language, if you will. He had survived, but it had not been easy.

I told him, "Sun comes up, we'll head back. Goblin and One-Eye got lost; it's their own tough luck."

After Toadkiller Dog's arrival I rested better. I guess the

old alliance is imprinted on people, too. I was confident he
would warn me if trouble beckoned.

Come morning we found the creek and headed for the
Hole. I stopped, as I often do, to approach Old Father Tree for
a little one-sided conversation about what he had seen during
his long sentinelship. The dog would not come anywhere
near. Weird. But so what? Weird is the order of the day on
the Plain.

I found One-Eye and Goblin snoring, sleeping in. They had
returned to the Hole only minutes after my departure in search
of them. Bastards. I would redress the balance when the
chance came.

I drove them crazy by not mentioning my night out.

"Did it work?" I demanded. Down the tunnel Tracker was
having a noisy reunion with his mutt.

"Sort of," Goblin said. He was not enthusiastic.

"Sort of? What's *sort of*? Does it work or doesn't it?"

"Well, what we got is a problem. Mainly, we can keep the
Taken from locating you. From getting a fix on you, so to
speak."

Obfuscation is a sure sign of trouble with this guy. "But?
Butt me the *but*, Goblin."

"If you go outside the null, there's no hiding the fact that
you are out."

"Great. Real great. What good are you guys, anyway?"

"It's not that bad," One-Eye said. "You wouldn't attract
any attention unless they find out you're out from some other
source. I mean, they wouldn't be watching for you, would
they? No reason to. So it's just as good as if we got it to do
everything we wanted."

"Crap! You better start praying that next letter comes
through. Because if I go out and get my ass killed, guess
who's going to haunt whom forever?"

"Darling wouldn't send you out."

"Bet? She'll go through three or four days of soul-searching.
But she'll send me. Because that last letter will give us the
key."

Sudden fear. Had the Lady probed my mind?

"What's the matter, Croaker?"

I was saved a lie by Tracker's advent. He bounced in and

pumped my hand like a mad fool. "Thank you, Croaker. Thanks for bringing him home." Out he went.

"What the hell was that?" Goblin asked.

"I brought his dog home."

"Weird."

One-Eye chortled. "The pot calling the kettle black."

"Yeah? Lizard snot. Want me to tell you about weird?"

"Stow it," I said. "If I get sent out of here I want this stuff in perfect order. I just wish we had people who could read this junk."

"Maybe I can help." Tracker was back. The big dumb lout. A devil with a sword, but probably unable to write his own name.

"How?"

"I could read some of that stuff. I know some old language. My father taught me." He grinned as if at a huge joke. He selected a piece written in TelleKurre. He read it aloud. The ancient language rolled off his tongue naturally, as I had heard it spoken among the old Taken. Then he translated. It was a memo to a castle kitchen about a meal to be prepared for visiting notables. I went over it painstakingly. His translation was faultless. Better than I could do. A third of the words evaded me.

"Well. Welcome to the team. I'll tell Darling." I slipped out, exchanging a puzzled glance with One-Eye behind Tracker's back.

Stranger and stranger. What was this man? Besides weird. At first encounter he reminded me of Raven, and fit the role. When I came to think of him as big, slow, and clumsy, he fit that role. Was he a reflection of the image in his beholder?

A good fighter, though, bless him. Worth ten of anyone else we have.

Chapter Twenty-Three: THE PLAIN OF FEAR

It was the time of the Monthly Meeting. The big confab during which nothing gets done. During which all heads yammer of pet projects on which action cannot be taken. After six or eight hours of which Darling closes debate by telling us what to do.

The usual charts were up. One showed where our agents believed the Taken to be. Another showed incursions reported by the menhirs. Both showed a lot of white, areas of Plain unknown to us. A third chart showed the month's change storms, a pet project of the Lieutenant's. He was looking for something. As always, most were along the periphery. But there was an unusually large number, and higher than normal percentage, in this chart's interior. Seasonal? A genuine shift? Who knew? We had not been watching long enough. The menhirs will not bother explaining such trivia.

Darling took charge immediately. She signed, "The operation in Rust had the effect I hoped. Our agents have reported anti-imperial outbreaks almost everywhere. They have diverted some attention from us. But the armies of the Taken keep building. Whisper has become especially aggressive in her incursions."

Imperial troops entered the Plain almost every day, probing for a response and preparing their men for the Plain's perils. Whisper's operations, as always, were very professional. Militarily, she is to be feared far more than the Limper.

Limper is a loser. That is not his fault, entirely, but the stigma has attached itself. Winner or loser, though, he is running the other side.

"Word came this morning that Whisper has established a garrison a day's march inside the boundary. She is erecting fortifications, daring our response."

Her strategy was apparent. Establish a network of mutually supporting fortresses; build it slowly until it is spread out over the Plain. She was dangerous, that woman. Especially if she sold the idea to the Limper and got all the armies into the act.

As a strategy it goes back to the dawn of time, having been used again and again where regular armies face partisans in wild country. It is a patient strategy that depends on the will of the conqueror to persevere. It works where that will exists and fails where it does not.

Here it will work. The enemy has twenty-some years to root us out. And feels no need to hold the Plain once done with us.

Us? Let us say, instead, Darling. The rest of us are nothing in the equation. If Darling falls, there is no Rebellion.

"They are taking away time," Darling signed. "We need decades. We have to do something."

Here it comes, I thought. She had on that look. She was going to announce the result of much soul-searching. So I was not struck down with astonishment when she signed, "I am sending Croaker to recover the rest of his correspondent's story." News of the letters had spread. Darling will gossip. "Goblin and One-Eye will accompany and support him."

"What? There ain't no way . . ."

"Croaker."

"I won't do it. Look at me. I'm a nothing guy. Who's going to notice me? One old guy wandering around. The world is full of them. But three guys? One of them black? One of them a runt with . . ."

Goblin and One-Eye sped me milk-curdling looks.

I snickered. My outburst put them in a tight place. Though they wanted to go no more than I wanted them along, they now dared not agree with me publicly. Worse, they had to agree with each other. Ego!

But my point remained. Goblin and One-Eye are known characters. For that matter, so am I, but as I pointed out, I'm not physically remarkable.

Darling signed, "Danger will encourage their cooperation."

I fled to my last citadel. "The Lady touched me on the desert that night I was out, Darling. *She* is watching for me."

Darling thought a moment, signed back, "That changes nothing. We must have that last piece of story before the Taken close in."

She was right about that. But . . .

She signed, "You three will go. Be careful."

Tracker followed the debate with Otto's help. He offered, "I'll go. I know the north. Especially the Great Forest. That's where I got my name." Behind him, Toadkiller Dog yawned.

"Croaker?" Darling asked.

I was not yet resigned to going. So I passed it back to her. "Up to you."

"You could use a fighter," she signed. "Tell him you accept."

I mumbled and muttered, faced Tracker. "She says you go."

He looked pleased.

As far as Darling was concerned, that was that. The thing was settled. They hastened down the agenda to a report from Corder suggesting Tanner was ripe for a raid like that on Rust.

I fussed and fumed and no one paid me any mind, except Goblin and One-Eye, who sent me looks saying I would rue my insults.

No fooling around. We left fourteen hours later. With everything arranged for us. Dragged out of bed soon after midnight, I quickly found myself topside, beside the coral, watching a small windwhale descend. A menhir yammered behind me, instructing me in the care and stroking of the windwhale ego. I ignored him. This had come on too swiftly. I was being shoved into the saddle before I'd made up my mind to go. I was living behind events.

I had my weapons, my amulets, money, food. Everything I should need. Likewise Goblin and One-Eye, who had provided themselves with a supplementary arsenal of thaumaturgic gewgaws. The plan was to purchase a wagon and team after the windwhale dropped us behind enemy lines. All the junk they were bringing, I grumbled, we might need two.

Tracker traveled light, though. Food, an array of weapons selected from what we had on hand, and his mutt.

The windwhale rose. Night enveloped us. I felt lost. I hadn't gotten so much as a good-bye hug.

The windwhale went up where the air was chill and thin. To the east, the south, and northwest I spied the glimmer of change storms. They *were* becoming more common.

I guess I was getting blasé about windwhale-riding. Shivering, huddling into myself, ignoring Tracker, who was a positive chatterbox yammering about trivia, I fell asleep. I wakened to a shaking hand and Tracker's face inches from mine.

"Wake up, Croaker," he kept saying. "Wake up. One-Eye says we got trouble."

I rose, expecting to find Taken circling us.

We were surrounded, but by four windwhales and a score of mantas. "Where did they come from?"

"Showed up while you were sleeping."

"What's the trouble?"

Tracker pointed, off what I guess you would call our starboard bow.

Change storm. Shaping.

"Just popped out of nowhere," Goblin said, joining us, too nervous to remember he was mad at me. "Looks like a bad one, too, the rate it's growing."

The change storm was no more than four hundred yards in diameter now, but the pastel-lightninged fury in its heart said it would grow swiftly and terribly. Its touch would be more than normally dramatic. Varicolored light painted faces and windwhales bizarrely. Our convoy shifted course. The windwhales are not as much affected as humans, but they prefer to dodge trouble where possible. It was clear, though, that fringes of the monster would brush us.

Even as I recognized and thought about it, the storm's size increased. Six hundred yards in diameter. Eight hundred. Roiling, boiling color within what looked like black smoke. Serpents of silent lightning snapped and snarled soundlessly around one another.

The bottom of the change storm touched ground.

All those lightnings found their voices. And the storm

expanded even more rapidly, hurling in another direction that growth which should have gone earthward. It was terrible with energy, this one.

Change storms seldom came nearer than eight miles to the Hole. They are impressive enough from that distance, when you catch only a whiff that crackles in your hair and makes your nerves go frazzled. In olden times, when we still served the Lady, I talked to veterans of Whisper's campaigns who told me of suffering through the storms. I never wholly credited their tales.

I did so as the boundary of the storm gained on us.

One of the mantas was caught. You could see through it, its bones white against sudden darkness. Then it *changed*.

Everything changed. Rocks and trees became protean. Small things that followed and pestered us shifted form. . . .

There is a hypothesis which states that the strange species of the Plain have appeared as a result of change storms. It has been proposed, too, that the change storms are responsible for the Plain itself. That each gnaws a bit more off our normal world.

The whales gave up trying to outrun the storm and plunged earthward, below the curve of expanding storm, getting down where the fall would be shorter if they changed into something unable to fly. Standard procedure for anyone caught in a change storm. Stay low and don't move.

Whisper's veterans spoke of lizards growing to elephant size, of spiders becoming monstrous, of poisonous serpents sprouting wings, of intelligent creatures going mad and trying to murder everything about them.

I was scared.

Not too scared to observe, though. After the manta showed us its bones it resumed its normal form, but grew. As did a second when the boundary overtook it. Did that mean a common tendency toward growth on a storm's outward pulse?

The storm caught our windwhale, which was the slowest getting down. Young it was, but conscientious about its burden. The crackle in my hair peaked. I thought my nerves would betray me completely. A glance at Tracker convinced me we were going to have a major case of panic.

Goblin or One-Eye, one, decided to be a hero and stay the

storm. Might as well have ordered the sea to turn. The crash
and roar of a major sorcery vanished in the rage of the storm.

There was an instant of utter stillness when the boundary
reached me. Then a roar out of hell. The winds inside were
ferocious. I thought of nothing but getting down and hanging
on. Around me gear was flying about, changing shape as it
flew. Then I spied Goblin. And nearly threw up.

Goblin indeed. His head had swelled ten times normal size.
The rest of him looked inside out. Around him swarmed a
horde of the parasites that live on a windwhale's back, some
as big as pigeons.

Tracker and Toadkiller Dog were worse. The mutt had
become something half as big as an elephant, fanged, possessed of the most evil eyes I've ever seen. He looked at me
with a starved lust that chilled my soul. And Tracker had
become something demonic, vaguely apelike yet certainly
much more. Both looked like creatures from an artist's or
sorcerer's nightmares.

One-Eye was the least changed. He swelled, but remained
One-Eye. Perhaps he is well-rooted in the world, being so
damned old. Near as I can tell, he is pushing a hundred fifty.

The thing that was Toadkiller Dog crept toward me with
teeth bared. . . . The windwhale touched down. Impact sent
everyone tumbling. The wind screamed around us. The strange
lightning hammered earth and air. The landing area itself was
in a protean mood. Rocks crawled. Trees changed shape. The
animals of that part of the Plain were out and gamboling in
revised forms, one-time prey turning upon predator. The
horror show was illuminated by a shifting, sometimes ghastly
light.

Then the vacuum at the heart of the storm enveloped us.
Everything froze in the form it had at the last instant. Nothing
moved. Tracker and Toadkiller Dog were down on the ground,
thrown there after impact. One-Eye and Goblin faced one
another, in the first phase of letting their feud go beyond its
customary gamesmanship. The other windwhales lay nearby,
not visibly affected. A manta plunged out of the color above,
crashed.

That stasis lasted maybe three minutes. In the stillness
sanity returned. Then the change storm began to collapse.

The devolution of the storm was slower than its growth. But saner, too. We suffered it for several hours. And then it was done. And our sole casualty was the one manta that had crashed. But damn, was it ever a shaking experience.

"Damn lucky," I told the others, as we inventoried our possessions. "Lucky we weren't all killed."

"No luck to it, Croaker," One-Eye replied. "The moment these monsters saw a storm coming they headed for safe ground. A place where there would be nothing that could kill us. Or them."

Goblin nodded. They were doing a lot of agreeing lately. But we all recalled how close they had come to murder.

I asked, "What did I look like? I didn't feel any change, except a sort of nervous turmoil. Like being drunk, drugged, and half-crazy all at the same time."

"Looked like Croaker to me," One-Eye said. "Only twice as ugly."

"And dull," Goblin added. "You made the most inspiring speech about the glories the Black Company won during the campaign against Chew."

I laughed. "Come on."

"Really. You were just Croaker. Maybe those amulets are good for something."

Tracker was going over his weaponry. Toadkiller Dog was napping near his feet. I pointed. One-Eye signed, "Didn't see."

Goblin signed, "He grew up and got claws."

They did not seem concerned. I decided I should not be. After all, the whale lice were the nastiest thing after the mutt.

The windwhales remained grounded, for the sun was rising. Their backs assumed the dun color of the earth, complete with sage-colored patches, and we waited for the night. The mantas nested down on the other four whales. None came near us. You get the feeling humans make them uncomfortable.

Chapter Twenty-Four: THE WIDE WORLD

They never tell me anything. But I should complain? Secrecy is our armor. Need to know. All that crap. In our outfit it is the iron rule of survival.

Our escort was not along just to help us break out of the Plain of Fear. They had their own mission. What I had not been told was that Whisper's headquarters was to be attacked.

Whisper had no warning. Our companion windwhales dropped away slowly as the edge of the Plain approached. Their mantas dropped with them. They caught favorable winds and pulled ahead. We climbed higher, into the pure shivers and gasp for breaths.

The mantas struck first. In twos and threes they crossed the town at treetop level, loosing their bolts into Whisper's quarters. Rock and timbers flew like the dust around stamping hooves. Fires broke out.

The monsters of the upper air rolled in behind as soldiers and civilians hit the streets. They unleashed bolts of their own. But the real horror was their tentacles.

The windwhales gorged upon men and animals. They ripped houses and fortifications apart. They yanked trees out by their roots. And they pounded away at Whisper with their bolts.

The mantas, meantime, rose a thousand feet and plunged again, in their pairs and threes, this time to strike at Whisper as she responded.

Her response, though it did set a broad patch of one windwhale's flank gruesomely aglow, pinpointed her for the mantas. They slapped her around good, though she did bring one down.

We passed over, the flash and fires illuminating our monster's belly. If anyone in the crucible spotted us, I doubt they guessed we were going on. Goblin and One-Eye detected no interest in anything but survival.

It continued as we lost sight of the town. Goblin said they had Whisper on the run, too busy saving her own ass to help her men.

"Glad they never pulled any of this crap on us," I said.

"It's a one-shot," Goblin countered. "Next time they'll be ready."

"I'd have thought they'd be now, because of Rust."

"Maybe Whisper has an ego problem."

No maybe about it. I had dealt with her. It was her weak spot. She would have made no preparations because she believed we feared her too much. She was, after all, the most brilliant of the Taken.

Our mighty steed ploughed the night, back brushing the stars, body gurgling, chugging, humming. I began to feel optimistic.

At dawn we dropped into a canyon in the Windy Country, another big desert. Unlike the Plain, though, it is normal. A big emptiness where the wind blows all the time. We ate and slept. When night fell we resumed our journey.

We left the desert south of Lords, turned north over the Forest of Cloud, avoiding settlements. Beyond the Forest of Cloud, though, the windwhale descended. And we were on our own.

I wish we could have gone the whole way airborne. But that was as far as Darling and the windwhales were willing to risk. Beyond lay heavily inhabited country. We could not hope to come down and pass the daylight hours unseen. So from there on we would travel the old-fashioned way.

The free city of Roses was about fifteen miles away.

Roses has been free throughout history, a republican plutocracy. Even the Lady did not see fit to buck tradition. One huge battle took place nearby, during the northern campaigns, but the site was of Rebel choosing, not ours. We lost. For several months Roses lost its independence. Then the Lady's victory at Charm ended Rebel dominion. All in all, though unaligned, Roses is a friend of the Lady.

Crafty bitch.

We hiked. Our journey was an all-day affair. Neither I nor Goblin nor One-Eye were in good shape. Too much loafing. Getting too old.

"This isn't smart," I said as we approached a gate in Roses' pale red walls, toward sunset. "We've all been here before. You two should be well-remembered, what with having robbed half the citizens."

"Robbed?" One-Eye protested. "Who robbed? . . ."

"Both of you clowns. Selling those damned guaranteed-to-work amulets when we were after Raker."

Raker was a one-time Rebel general. He had beaten the crap out of the Limper farther north; then the Company, with a little help from Soulcatcher, had sucked him into a trap in Roses. Both Goblin and One-Eye had preyed on the populace. One-Eye was an old hand at that. Back when we were in the south, beyond the Sea of Torments, he had been involved in every shady scheme he could find. Most of his ill-gotten gains he soon lost at cards. He is the world's worst cardplayer.

You'd think by one-fifty he would learn to count them.

The plan was for us to lay up at some sleazy no-questions-asked inn. Tracker and I would go out next day and buy a wagon and team. Then we would head out the way we had come, pick up what gear we had been unable to carry, and circle the city by heading north.

That was the plan. Goblin and One-Eye did not stick to it.

Rule Number One for a soldier: Stick to the mission. The mission is paramount.

For Goblin and One-Eye all rules are made to be broken. When Tracker and I returned, with Toadkiller Dog loafing along behind, it was late afternoon. We parked. Tracker stood by while I went upstairs.

No Goblin. No One-Eye.

The proprietor told me they had left soon after I had, chattering about finding some women.

My fault. I was in charge. I should have foreseen it. It had been a long, long, long time. I paid for another two nights, just in case. Then I turned animals and wagon over to the holster's boy, had supper with a silent Tracker, and retreated to our room with several quarts of beer. We shared it, Tracker, me, and Toadkiller Dog.

"You going looking for them?" Tracker asked.

"No. If they haven't come back in two days or pulled the roof in on us, we'll go ahead without them. I don't want to be seen around them. There'll be people here who remember them."

We got pleasantly buzzed. Toadkiller Dog seemed capable of drinking people under the table. Loved his beer, that dog. Actually got up and moved around when he didn't have to.

Next morning, no Goblin. No One-Eye. But plenty of rumors. We entered the common room late, after the morning crowd and before the noontime rush. The hostler had no other ears to bend.

"You guys hear about the ruckus over in the east end last night?"

I groaned before he got to the meat of it. I knew.

"Yeah. Regular wahoo war party. Fires. Sorcery. Lynch mob. Excitement like this old town hain't seen since that time they were after that General What's-it the Lady wanted."

After he went to pester another customer, I told Tracker, "We'd better get out now."

"What about Goblin and One-Eye?"

"They can take care of themselves. If they got themselves lynched, tough. I'm not going poking around and getting myself a stretched neck, too. If they got away, they know the plan. They can catch up."

"I thought the Black Company didn't leave its dead behind."

"We don't." I said it, but maintained my determination to let the wizards stew in what juice they had concocted. I did not doubt that they had survived. They had been in trouble before, a thousand times. A good hike might have a salutary effect on their feel for mission discipline.

Meal finished, I informed the proprietor that Tracker and I were departing, but that our companions would keep the room. Then I led a protesting Tracker to the wagon, put him aboard, and when the boy had the hitch ready, headed for the western gate.

It was the long way, through tortuous streets, over a dozen arched bridges spanning canals, but it led away from yesterday's silliness. As we went I told Tracker how we had tricked Raker into a noose. He appreciated it.

"That was the Company's trademark," I concluded. "Get the enemy to do something stupid. We were the best when it came to fighting, but we only fought when nothing else worked."

"But you were paid to fight." Things were black-and-white to Tracker. Sometimes I thought he had spent too much time in the woods.

"We were paid for results. If we could do the job without fighting, all the better. What you do is, you study your enemy. Find a weakness, then work on it. Darling is good at that. Though working on the Taken is easier than you would think. They're all vulnerable through their egos."

"What about the Lady?"

"I couldn't say. She doesn't seem to have a handle. A touch of vanity, but I don't see how to get hold of it. Maybe through her drive to dominate. By getting her to overextend herself. I don't know. She's cautious. And smart. Like when she sucked the Rebel in at Charm. Killed three birds with one stone. Not only did she eliminate the Rebel; she exposed the unreliable among the Taken and squashed the Dominator's attempt to use them to get free."

"What about him?"

"He isn't a problem. He's probably more vulnerable than the Lady, though. He don't seem to think. He's like a bull. So damned strong that's all he needs. Oh, a little guile, like at Juniper, but mostly just the hammer-strokes type."

Tracker nodded thoughtfully. "Could be something to what you say."

Chapter Twenty-Five: THE BARROWLAND

Corbie miscalculated. He forgot that others beside Case were interested in his fate.

When he failed to show for work various places, people came looking for him. They pounded on doors, tapped on windows, and got no response. One tried the door. It was locked. Now there was genuine concern.

Some argued for kicking a break-in up the chain of command, others for moving now. The latter view prevailed. They broke the lock and spread out inside.

They found a place obsessive in its neatness, spartan in its furnishings. The first man upstairs yelped, ''Here he is. He's had a stroke or something.''

The pack crowded into the little upstairs room. Corbie sat at a table on which lay an oilskin packet and a book. ''A book!'' someone said. ''He was weirder than we thought.''

A man touched Corbie's throat, felt a feeble pulse, noted that Corbie was taking shallow breaths spaced far more widely than those of a man sleeping. ''Guess he did have a stroke. Like he was sitting here reading and it hit him.''

''Had an uncle went like that,'' someone said. ''When I was a kid. Telling us a story and just went white and keeled over.''

''He's still alive. We better do something. Maybe he'll be all right.''

A big rush downstairs, men tumbling over men.

Case heard when the group rushed into headquarters. He was on duty. The news put him in a quandary. He had promised Corbie. . . . But he could not run off.

Sweet's personal interest got the news bucked up the ladder fast. The Colonel came out of his office. He noted Case looking stricken. "You heard. Come along. Let's have a look. You men. Find the barber. Find the vet."

Made you reflect on the value of men when the army provided a vet but not a physician.

The day had begun auspiciously, with a clear sky. That was rare. Now it was cloudy. A few raindrops fell, spotting the wooden walks. As Case followed Sweet, and a dozen men followed him, he barely noted the Colonel's remarks about necessary improvements.

A crowd surrounded Corbie's place. "Bad news travels fast," Case said. "Sir."

"Doesn't it? Make a hole here, men. Coming through." He paused inside. "He always this tidy?"

"Yes, sir. He was obsessive about order and doing things by the numbers."

"I wondered. He stretched the rules a bit with his night walks."

Case gnawed his lip and wondered if he ought to give the Colonel Corbie's message. He decided it was not yet time.

"Upstairs?" the Colonel asked one of the men who had found Corbie.

"Yes, sir."

Case was up the stairs already. He spied Corbie's oilskin packet, without thinking started to slide it inside his jacket.

"Son."

Case turned. Sweet stood in the doorway, frowning.

"What are you doing?"

The Colonel was the most intimidating figure Case could imagine. More so than his father, who had been a harsh and exacting man. He did not know how to respond. He stood there shaking.

The Colonel extended a hand. Case handed the packet over. "What were you doing, son?"

"Uh . . . Sir . . . One day . . . "

"Well?" Sweet examined Corbie without touching him. "Well? Out with it."

"He asked me to deliver a letter for him if anything happened to him. Like he thought his time was running out.

He said it would be in an oilskin packet. On account of the rain and everything. Sir.''

"I see.'' The Colonel slipped fingers under Corbie's chin, lifted. He returned the packet to the table, peeled back one of Corbie's eyelids. The pupil revealed was a pinprick. "Hmm.'' He felt Corbie's forehead. "Hmm.'' He flicked several reflex points with his finger or fist. Corbie did not respond. "Curious. Doesn't look like a stroke.''

"What else could it be, sir?''

Colonel Sweet straightened. "Maybe you'd know better than I.''

"Sir?''

"You say Corbie expected something.''

"Not exactly. He was afraid something would happen. Talked like he was getting old and his time was running out. Maybe he had something wrong he never told nobody about.''

"Maybe. Ah. Holts.'' The horse doctor had arrived. He followed the course the Colonel had, straightened, shrugged.

"Beyond me, Colonel.''

"We'd better move him where we can keep an eye on him. Your job, son,'' he told Case. "If he doesn't come out of it soon, we'll have to force-feed him.'' He poked around the room, checked the titles of the dozen or so books. "A learned man, Corbie. I thought so. A study in contrasts. I've often wondered what he really was.''

Case was nervous for Corbie now. "Sir, I think that way back he was somebody in one of the Jewel Cities, but his luck turned and he joined the army.''

"We'll talk about it after we move him. Come along.''

Case followed. The Colonel seemed very thoughtful. Maybe he *should* give him Corbie's message.

Chapter Twenty-Six: ON THE ROAD

After three days during which Tracker and I returned to our landing place, loaded the wagon, then headed north on the Salient Road, I began to wonder if I had not erred. Still no Goblin or One-Eye.

I need not have been concerned. They caught up near Meystrikt, a fortress in the Salient the Company once held on behalf of the Lady. We were off the road, in some woods, getting ready for supper. We heard a ruckus on the road.

A voice undeniably Goblin's shouted, "And I *insist* it's your fault, you maggot-lipped excuse for fish bait. I'd turn your brain into pudding for getting me into it if you had one."

"My fault. My fault. Gods! He even lies to himself. I had to talk him into his own idea? Look there, guano breath. Meystrikt is around that hill. They'll remember us even better than they did in Roses. Now I'm going to ask you once. How do we get through without getting our throats cut?"

After an initial relief I halted my rush toward the road. I told Tracker, "They're riding. Where do you suppose they got horses?" I tried finding a bright side. "Maybe they got into a game and got away with cheating. If One-Eye let Goblin do it." One-Eye is as inept at cheating as at games of chance themselves. There are times I think he has a positive death wish.

"You and your damned amulet," Goblin squeaked. "The Lady can't find him. That's great. But neither can we."

"*My* amulet? *My* amulet? Who the hell gave it to him in the first place?"

"Who designed the spell that's on it now?"

"Who cast it? Tell me that, toad face. Tell me that."

I moved to the edge of the woods. They had passed already. Tracker joined me. Even Toadkiller Dog came to watch.

"Freeze, Rebel!" I shouted. "First one moves is dead meat."

Stupid, Croaker. Real stupid. Their response was swift and gaudy. It damned near killed me.

They vanished in shining clouds. Around Tracker and me insects erupted. More kinds of bugs than I imagined existed, every one interested only in having me for supper.

Toadkiller Dog snarled and snapped.

"Knock it off, you clowns," I yelled. "It's me. Croaker."

"Who's Croaker?" One-Eye asked Goblin. "You know anybody named Croaker?"

"Yeah. But I don't think we ought to stop," Goblin replied, after sticking his head out of the shining to check. "He deserves it."

"Sure," One-Eye agreed. "But Tracker is innocent. I can't fine-tune it enough to get just Croaker."

The bugs returned to routine bug business. Eating each other, I guess. I constrained my anger and greeted One-Eye and Goblin, both of whom had donned expressions of innocence and contrition. "What you got to say for yourselves, guys? Nice horses. Think the people they belong to will come looking for them?"

"Wait up," Goblin squawked. "Don't go accusing us of . . ."

"I know you guys. Get down off those animals and come eat. We'll decide what to do with them tomorrow."

I turned my back on them. Tracker had returned to our cook fire already. He dished up supper. I went to work on it, my temper still frayed. Stupid move, stealing horses. What with the uproar they had caused already. . . . The Lady has agents everywhere. We may not be enemies of the grand sort, but we are what she has. Someone was bound to conclude that the Black Company was back in the north.

I fell asleep contemplating turning back. The least likely direction for hunters to look would be on the route to the Plain of Fear. But I could not give the order. Too much depended on us. Though now my earlier optimism stood in serious jeopardy.

Damned irresponsible clowns.

Way back down the line the Captain, who perished at Juniper, must have felt the same. We all gave him cause.

I braced for a golden dream. I slept restlessly. No dream came. Next morning I packed Goblin and One-Eye into the wagon, beneath all the clutter we deemed necessary for our expedition, abandoned the horses, and took the wagon past Meystrikt. Toadkiller Dog ran point. Tracker strolled along beside. I drove. Under the tucker, Goblin and One-Eye sputtered and grumbled. The garrison at the fort merely asked where we were bound, in such a bored manner I knew they did not care.

These lands had been tamed since last I passed through. This garrison could not conceive of trouble lifting its naughty head.

Relieved, I turned up the road that led to Elm and Oar. And to the Great Forest beyond.

Chapter Twenty-Seven: OAR

"Don't this weather ever let up?" One-Eye whined. For a week we had slogged northward, had been victimized by daily showers. The roads were bad and promised to get worse. Practicing my Forsberger on wayside farmers, I learned that this weather had been common for years. It made getting crops to town difficult and, worse, left the grains at risk from disease. There had been an outbreak of the firedance in Oar already, a malady traceable to infected rye. There were a lot of insects, too. Especially mosquitos.

The winters, though abnormal in snow and rainfall, were milder than when we had been stationed here. Mild winters do not augur well for pest control. On the other hand, game species were diminished because they could not forage in the deep snows.

Cycles. Just cycles, the old-timers assured me. The bad winters come around after the Great Comet passes. But even they thought this a cycle among cycles.

Today's weather is already the most impressive of all time.

"Deal," Goblin said, and he did not mean cards. That fortress, which the Company took from the Rebel years ago, loomed ahead. The road meanders beneath its scowling walls. I was troubled, as always I was when our path neared an imperial bastion. But there was no need this time. The Lady was so confident of Forsberg that the great fortress stood abandoned. In fact, close up, it looked ragged. Its neighbors were stealing it piece by piece, after the custom of peasants the world over. I expect that is the only return they get on taxes, though they may have to wait generations for the worm to turn.

"Oar tomorrow," I said as we left the wagon outside an inn a few miles past Deal. "And this time there will be no screwups. Hear?"

One-Eye had the grace to look abashed. But Goblin was ready to argue.

"Keep it up," I said. "I'll have Tracker thrash you and tie you up. We aren't playing games."

"Life is a game, Croaker," One-Eye said. "You take it too damned serious." But he behaved himself, both that night and the next day when we entered Oar.

I found a place well outside areas we frequented before. It catered to small-time traders and travelers. We drew no especial attention. Tracker and I kept a watch on Goblin and One-Eye. They did not seem inclined to play the fool again, though.

Next day I went looking for a smith named Sand. Tracker accompanied me. Goblin and One-Eye stayed behind, constrained by the most terrible threats I could invent.

Sand's place was easily found. He was a longtime member

of his trade, well-known among his peers. We followed directions. They led me through familiar streets. Here the Company had had some adventures.

I discussed them with Tracker as we walked. I noted, "Been a lot of rebuilding since then. We tore the place up good."

Toadkiller Dog was on point, as often he was of late. He stopped suddenly, looked around suspiciously, took a few tentative steps, sank onto his belly. "Trouble," Tracker said.

"What kind?" There was nothing obvious to the eye.

"I don't know. He can't talk. He's just doing his watch-out-for-trouble act."

"Okay. Don't cost anything to be careful." We turned into a place that sold and repaired harness and tack. Tracker yakked about needing a saddle for a hunter of large beasts. I stood in the doorway watching the street.

I saw nothing unusual. The normal run of people went about their normal business. But after a while I noted that Sand's smithy had no custom. That no smithery sounds came forth. He was supposed to supervise a platoon of apprentices and journeymen.

"Hey. Proprietor. Whatever happened to the smith over there? Last time we were here he did us some work. Place looks empty."

"Grey boys is what happened." He looked uncomfortable. Grey boys are imperials. The troops in the north wear grey. "Fool didn't learn back when. Was into the Rebellion."

"Too bad. He was a good smith. What leads regular folks to get into politics, anyway? People like us, we got trouble enough just trying to make a living."

"I heard that, brother." The tackmaker shook his head. "Tell you this. You got smithery needs doing, take your custom elsewhere. The grey boys been hanging around, taking anybody who comes around."

About then an imperial strolled around the side of the smithy and crossed to a pasty stall. "Damned clumsy," I said. "And crude."

The tackmaker looked at me askance. Tracker covered well, drawing him back to business. Not as dumb as he appeared, I noted. Maybe just not socially adept.

Later, after Tracker expressed a desire to think on the deal the tackmaker offered and we departed, Tracker asked, "What now?"

"We could bring up Goblin and One-Eye after dark, use their sleeping spell, go in and see what's to see. But it don't seem likely the imperials would leave anything interesting. We could find out what they did with Sand and try to reach him. Or we could go on to the Barrowland."

"Sounds the safest."

"On the other hand, we wouldn't know what we were headed into. Sand's being taken could mean anything. We better talk it over with the others. Catalog our resources."

Tracker grunted. "How long before that sutler gets suspicious? The more he thinks about it, the more he's going to realize we were interested in the smith."

"Maybe. I'm not going to sweat it."

Oar is a city like most of substantial size. Crowded. Filled with distractions. I understood how Goblin and One-Eye had been seduced by Roses. The last major city the Company dared visit was Chimney. Six years ago. Since then it has been all the hard times and small towns you can imagine. I battled temptations of my own. I knew places of interest in Oar.

Tracker kept me on the straight line. I've never met a man less interested in the traps which tempt men.

Goblin thought we should put the imperials to sleep, give them the question. One-Eye wanted to get out of town. Their solidarity had perished like frost in the sun.

"Logically," I said, "they would get a stronger guard after dark. But if we drag you down there now, somebody is sure to recognize you."

"Then find that old boy who brought the first letter," Goblin said.

"Good idea. But. Think about it. Assuming he had perfect luck, he'd still be a long way from here. He didn't catch a ride like we did. No go. We get out. Oar is making me nervous." Too many temptations, too many chances to be recognized. And just too many people. Isolation had grown on me out there on the Plain.

Goblin wanted to argue. He had heard the north roads were terrible.

"I know," I countered. "I also know the army is building a new route to the Barrowland. And they've pushed its north end far enough so traders are using it."

No more argument. They wanted out as much as I. Only Tracker now seemed reluctant. He who first thought it best to go.

Chapter Twenty-Eight: TO THE BARROWLAND

Oar's weather was less than exciting. Farther north it became misery curdled, though the imperial engineers had done their best to make the forest road usable. Much of it was corduroy, of logs trimmed and tarred and laid side by side. In areas where snow became obnoxious, there were frameworks to support canvas coverings.

"Amazing scope," One-Eye said.

"Uhm." There was supposed to be zero concern about the Dominator since the Lady's triumph at Juniper. This seemed a lot of effort to keep a road open.

The new road swung many miles west of the old because the Great Tragic River had shifted its bed and continued doing so. The trip from Oar to the Barrowland was fifteen miles longer. The last forty-five were not wholly finished. We endured some rough going.

We encountered the occasional trader headed south. They all shook their heads and told us we were wasting our time. The fortunes to be had had evaporated. The tribes had hunted the furbearers to extinction.

Tracker had been preoccupied since we left Oar. I could not draw out why. Maybe superstition. The Barrowland remains a great dread to Forsberg's lower classes. The Dominator is the bogeyman mothers conjure to frighten children. Though he has been gone four hundred years, his stamp remains indelible.

It took a week to cover the final forty-five miles. I was growing time-concerned. We might not get done and home before winter.

We were scarcely out of the forest, into the clearing at the Barrowland. I stopped. "It's changed."

Goblin and One-Eye crept up behind me. "Yuck," Goblin squeaked. "It sure has."

It seemed almost abandoned. A swamp now, with only the highest points of the Barrowland proper still identifiable. When last we visited, a horde of imperials was clearing, repairing, studying with a relentless clatter and bustle.

Near silence reigned. That bothered me more than the decayed state of the Barrowland. Slow, steady drizzle under deep grey skies. Cold. And no sound.

The corduroy was completed here. We rolled forward. Not till we entered the town, buildings now for the most part paintless and dilapidated, did we see a soul. A voice called, "Halt and state your business."

I stopped. "Where are you?"

Toadkiller Dog, more than normally ambitious, loped to a derelict structure and sniffed. A grumbling Guard stepped into the drizzle. "Here."

"Oh. You startled me. Name is Candle. Of Candle, Smith, Smith, Tailor, and Sons. Traders."

"Yeah? These others?"

"Smith and Tailor inside here. That's Tracker. He works for us. We're from Roses. We heard the road north was open again."

"Now you know better." He chuckled. I learned that he was in a good humor because of the weather. It was a nice day for the Barrowland.

"What's the procedure?" I asked. "Where do we put up?"

"Blue Willy is the only place. They'll be glad for the custom. Get yourself settled. Report to headquarters by tomorrow."

"Right. Where is the Blue Willy?"

He told me. I snapped the traces. The wagon rolled. "Seem pretty lax," I said.

"Where are you going to run?" One-Eye countered. "They know we're here. There's only one way out. We don't play by their book, they stick the stopper in the bottle."

The place did have that feel.

It also had a feel that went with its weather. Down. Depressing. Smiles were scarce, and those mostly commercial.

The hostler at Blue Willy didn't ask names, just payment up front. Other traders ignored us, though the fur trade, traditionally, is an Oar monopoly.

Next day a few locals came around to examine our goods. I had loaded up with what I had heard would sell well, but we got few nibbles. Only the liquor drew any offers. I asked how to get in touch with the tribes.

"You wait. They come when they come."

That done, I went to Guard headquarters. It was unchanged, though the surrounding compound seemed seedier.

The first man I encountered was one I remembered. He was the one with whom I had to do business. "Candle's the name," I said. "Of Candle, Smith, Smith, Tailor, and Sons, out of Roses. Traders. I was told to report here."

He looked at me oddly, like something way back was nagging him. He remembered something. I did not want him worrying it like a cavity in a tooth. He might come up with an answer. "Been some changes since I was here in the army."

"Going to the dogs," he grumbled. "The dogs. Worse every day. You think anybody cares? We're going to rot out here. How many in your party?"

"Four. And one dog."

Wrong move. He scowled. No sense of humor. "Names?"

"Candle. One Smith. Tailor. Tracker. He works for us. And Toadkiller Dog. Got to call him by his whole name or he gets upset."

"Funny man, eh?"

"Hey. No offense. But this place needs some sunshine."

"Yeah. Can you read?"

I nodded.

"Rules are posted over there. You got two choices. Obey them. Or be dead. Case!"

A soldier came from a back office. "Yeah, Sarge?"

"New trader. Go check him out. You at Blue Willy, Candle?"

"Yes." The list of rules had not changed. It was the same paper, almost too faded to read. Basically, it said don't mess with the Barrowland. Try it and if *it* don't kill you, we will.

"Sir?" the trooper said. "When you're ready?"

"I'm ready."

We returned to Blue Willy. The soldier looked our gear over. The only things that intrigued him were my bow and the fact that we were well armed. "Why so many weapons?"

"Been talk about trouble with the tribesmen."

"Must have gotten exaggerated. Just stealing." Goblin and One-Eye attracted no special attention. I was pleased. "You read the rules. Stick to them."

"I know them of old," I said. "I was stationed here when I was in the army."

He looked at me a bit narrowly, nodded, departed.

We all sighed. Goblin took the spell of concealment off the gear he and One-Eye had brought. The empty corner behind Tracker filled with clutter.

"He might come right back," I protested.

"We don't want to hold any spell any longer than we have to," One-Eye said. "There might be somebody around who could detect it."

"Right." I cracked the shutters to our one window. The hinges shrieked. "Grease," I suggested. I looked across the town. We were on the third floor of the tallest building outside the Guard compound. I could see the Bomanz house. "Guys. Look at this."

They looked.

"In damned fine shape, eh?" When last seen it was a candidate for demolition. Superstitious fear had kept it unused. I recalled pottering around in there several times. "Feel like a stroll, Tracker?"

"No."

"Whatever makes you comfortable"—I wondered if he had enemies here—"I'd feel better if you were along."

He strapped on his sword. Out we went, down, into the street—if that expanse of mud could be so called. The corduroy ran only to the compound, with a branch as far as Blue Willy. Beyond, there were walkways only.

We pretended to sightsee. I told Tracker stories about my last visit, most cast near the truth. I was trying to assume a foreign persona, voluble and jolly. I wondered if I was wasting my time. I saw no one interested in what I might say.

The Bomanz house had been lovingly restored. It did not appear to be occupied, though. Or guarded. Or set up as a monument. Curious. Come supper I asked our host. He had me pegged as a nostalgic fool already. He told us, "Some old boy moved in there about five years ago. Cripple. Did scut work for the Guard. Fixed the place up in his spare time."

"What happened to him?"

"While back, couple four months I guess, he had a stroke or something. They found him still alive but like a vegetable. They took him over to the compound. Far as I know, he's still there. Feeding him like a baby. That kid that was here to inspect you is the one to ask. Him and Corbie was friends."

"Corbie, eh? Thanks. Another pitcher."

"Come on, Croaker," One-Eye said in a low voice. "Lay off the beer. The guy makes it himself. It's terrible."

He was right. But I was getting adjusted for some heavy thinking.

We had to get into that house. That meant night moves and wizards' skills. It also meant our greatest risks since Goblin and One-Eye went silly in Roses.

One-Eye asked Goblin, "Think we're up against a haunt?"

Goblin sucked his lip. "Have to look."

"What's this?" I asked.

"I'd have to see the man to know for sure, Croaker, but what happened to that Corbie don't sound like a stroke."

Goblin nodded. "Sounds like somebody pulled out of body and caught."

"Maybe we can arrange to see him. What about the house?"

"First thing is to make sure there isn't a big-time haunt. Like maybe Bomanz's ghost."

That kind of talk makes me nervous. I do not believe in ghosts. Or do not want to.

"If he was caught out, or pulled out, you have to wonder how and why. The fact that that's where Bomanz lived has to be considered. Something left over from his time could have gotten this Corbie. Could be what gets us if we're not careful.''

"Complications," I grumbled. "Always the complications."

Goblin snickered.

"You watch yourself," I said. "Or I just might sell you to the highest bidder."

An hour later a savage storm arrived. It howled and hammered at the inn. The roof leaked under the downpour. When I reported that, our host blew up, though not at me. Evidently making repairs was not easy under current conditions, yet repairs had to be made lest a place deteriorate entirely.

"The damned winter firewood is the worst," he complained. "Can't leave it set out. Either gets buried under snow or so damned waterlogged you can't dry it out. In a month this place will be loaded ceiling to floor. At least filling the place up makes it less hard to heat."

Along about midnight, after the Guard had changed watches and the oncoming had had time to grow bored and sleepy, we slipped out. Goblin made sure everyone inside the inn was asleep.

Toadkiller Dog trotted ahead, seeking witnesses. He found only one. Goblin took care of him, too. On a night like that nobody was out. I wished I was not.

"Make sure nobody can see any light," I said after we slipped inside. "At a guess, I'd say we start upstairs."

"At a guess," One-Eye countered, "I'd say we find out if there are any haunts or booby traps first."

I glanced at the door. I hadn't thought about that before pushing through.

Chapter Twenty-Nine: THE BARROWLAND, BACK WHEN

The Colonel summoned Case. He shook as he stood before Sweet's desk. "There are questions to be answered, lad," Sweet said. "Start by telling me what you know about Corbie."

Case swallowed. "Yes, sir." He told. And told much more when Sweet insisted on rehashing every word that had passed between them. He told everything but the part about the message and the oilskin.

"Curious," Sweet said. "Very. Is that all?"

Case shifted nervously. "What's this about, sir?"

"Let's say what we found in the oilskin was interesting."

"Sir?"

"It appeared to be a long letter, though no one could read it. It was in a language nobody knows. It could be the language of the Jewel Cities. What I want to know is, who was supposed to get it? Was it unique or part of a series? Our friend is in trouble, lad. If he recovers, he's in hot water. Deep. Real bums don't write long letters to anybody."

"Well, sir, like I said, he was trying to track down his kids. And he may have come from Opal. . . ."

"I know. There is circumstantial evidence on his side. Maybe he can satisfy me when he comes around. On the other hand, this being the Barrowland, anything remarkable becomes suspicious. Question, son. And you must answer satisfactorily or you're in hot water, too. Why did you try to hide the packet?"

The crux. The moment from which there was no escape. He had prayed it would not arrive. Now, facing it, Case knew his loyalty to Corbie was unequal to the test.

"He asked me if, if anything happened to him, I would get a letter delivered to Oar. A letter in oilskin."

"He did expect trouble, then?"

"I don't know. I don't know what was in the letter or why he wanted it delivered. He just gave me a name. And then he said to tell you something after the letter was delivered."

"Ah?"

"I don't remember his exact words. He said to tell you the thing in the Great Barrow isn't asleep anymore."

Sweet came out of his seat as though stung. "He did? And how did he know? Never mind. The name. Now! Who was the packet to go to?"

"A smith in Oar. Named Sand. That's all I know, sir. I swear."

"Right." Sweet seemed distracted. "Back to your duties, lad. Tell Major Klief I want him."

"Yes, sir."

Next morning Case watched Major Klief and a detail ride out, under orders to arrest Sand Smith. He felt terribly guilty. And yet, just how had he betrayed anyone? He might have been betrayed himself if Corbie was a spy.

He assuaged his guilt by tending Corbie with religious devotion, keeping him clean and fed.

Chapter Thirty: A BARROWLAND NIGHT

It took Goblin and One-Eye only minutes to examine the house. "No traps," One-Eye announced. "No ghost, either. Some old resonances of sorcery overlaid by more recent ones. Upstairs."

I produced a scrap of paper. Upon it were my notes from

the Bomanz letters. We went upstairs. Confident though they were, Goblin and One-Eye let me go first. Some friends.

I checked to make certain the window was shuttered before permitting a light. Then: "Do your stuff. I'll poke around." Tracker and Toadkiller Dog remained in the doorway. It was not a big room.

I examined book titles before starting a serious search. The man had had eclectic tastes. Or had collected what was cheapest, perhaps.

I found no papers.

The place did not look ransacked. "One-Eye. Can you tell if this place was searched?"

"Probably not. Why?"

"The papers aren't here."

"You looked where he hid stuff? Like he said?"

"All but one." A spear stood in a corner. Sure enough, when I twisted it, its head came off and revealed a hollow shaft. Out came the map mentioned in the story. We spread it on the table.

Chills crept up my back.

This was real history. This chart had shaped today's world. Despite my limited grasp of TelleKurre and my even more feeble knowledge of wizardly symbols, I felt the power mapped there. For me, at least, it radiated something that left me teetering on the boundary between discomfort and true dread.

Goblin and One-Eye did not feel it. Or were too intrigued. They put their heads together and examined the route Bomanz used to reach the Lady.

"Thirty-seven years of work," I said.

"What?"

"It took him thirty-seven years to accumulate that information." I noticed something. "What's this?" It was something that should not have been there, as I recalled the story. "I see. Our correspondent added notes of his own."

One-Eye looked at me. Then he looked at the chart. Then he looked at me again. Then he bent to examine the route on the map. "That has to be it. No other answer."

"What?"

"I know what happened."

Tracker stirred uncomfortably.

"Well?"

"He tried to go in there. The only way you can. And couldn't get out."

He had written me saying there was something he had to do, that the risks were great. Was One-Eye right?

Brave man.

No papers. Unless they were hidden better than I thought. I would have Goblin and One-Eye search. I made them reroll the chart and return it to the spear shaft, then said, "I'm open to suggestions."

"About what?" Goblin squeaked.

"About how to get this guy away from the Eternal Guard. And how we get his soul back inside him so we can ask him questions. Like that."

They did not look enthused. One-Eye said, "Somebody will have to go in there to see what's wrong. Then spring him and guide him out."

"I see." Too well. We had to lay hands on the living body before doing that. "Look this place over. See what you can find that's hidden."

It took them half an hour. I became a nervous wreck. "Too much time, too much time," I kept saying. They ignored me.

The search produced one scrap of paper, very old, which contained a cipher key. It was folded into one of the books, not really hidden. I tucked it away. It might be used on the papers back at the Hole.

We got out. We got back to Blue Willy without being detected. We all heaved sighs of relief once we reached our room.

"What now?" Goblin asked.

"Sleep on it. Tomorrow is soon enough to start worrying." I was wrong, of course. I was worrying already.

With each step forward it became more complicated.

Chapter Thirty-One: NIGHT IN THE BARROWLAND

The thunder and lightning continued to strut about. The sound and flash penetrated the walls as though they were paper. I slept restlessly, my nerves frazzled more than they should be. The others were dead to the world. Why couldn't I be?

It started as a pinprick in a corner, a mote of golden light. The mote multiplied. I wanted to lunge across and hammer on Goblin or One-Eye, calling them liars. The amulet was supposed to keep me invisible. . . .

Faintest, most ghostly of whispers, like the cry of a ghost down a long, cold cavern. "Physician. Where are you?"

I did not respond. I wanted to pull my blanket over my head, but could not move.

She remained diffuse, wavering, uncertain. Maybe she did have trouble spotting me. When her face did assume substance momentarily, she did not look my way. Her eyes seemed blind.

"You have gone from the Plain of Fear," she called in that faraway voice. "You are in the north somewhere. You left a broad trail. You are foolish, my friend. I will find you. Don't you know that? You cannot hide. Even an emptiness can be seen."

She had no idea where I was. I did the right thing by not responding. She wanted me to betray myself.

"My patience is not unlimited, Croaker. But you may come to the Tower still. Make it soon, though. Your White Rose does not have long."

I finally managed to pull my blanket to my chin. What a

sight I must have made. Amusing, in retrospect. Like a little boy afraid of ghosts.

The glow slowly faded. With it went the nervousness that had plagued me since returning from the Bomanz house.

As I settled down I glanced at Toadkiller Dog. I caught lightning glinting off a single open eye.

So. For the first time there was a witness to one of the visitations. But a mutt.

I don't think anybody believed me about them, ever, except that what I reported always panned out true.

I slept.

Goblin wakened me. "Breakfast."

We ate. We made a show of looking for markets for our goods, of seeking a longer term connection for future loads. Business was not good, except our host offered to purchase distilled spirits regularly. There was a demand among the Eternal Guard. The soldiers had little to do but drink.

Lunch. And while we ate and prepared our thoughts for the head-butting session to follow, soldiers entered the inn. They asked the landlord if any of his guests had been out last night. Good old landlord denied the possibility. He claimed he was the lightest of sleepers. He knew if anyone came or went.

That was good enough for the soldiers. They left.

"What was that?" I asked when next the proprietor passed our way.

"Somebody broke into Corbie's house last night," he said. Then his eyes narrowed. He remembered other questions. My mistake.

"Curious," I said. "Why would anyone do that?"

"Yes. Why?" He went about his business, but remained thoughtful.

I, too, was thoughtful. How had they detected our visit? We were careful to leave no traces.

Goblin and One-Eye were disturbed, too. Only Tracker did not seem bothered. His lone discomfort was being there, near the Barrowland.

"What can we do?" I asked. "We're surrounded and outnumbered, and maybe now we're suspect. How do we lay hands on this Corbie?"

"That's no problem," One-Eye said. "The real trouble is

getting away after we do. If we could call in a windwhale just in time . . ."

"Tell me how it's not so hard."

"The middle of the night we go over to the Guard compound, use the sleep spell, get our man and his papers, call his spirit back, and get him out. But then what? Eh, Croaker? Then what?"

"Where do we run?" I mused. "And how?"

"There is one answer," Tracker said. "The forest. The Guard couldn't find us in the forest. If we could cross the Great Tragic, we'd be safe. They don't have the manpower for a hunt."

I nibbled the edge of a fingernail. Something to what Tracker said. I assumed he knew the woodlands and tribes well enough for us to survive with the burden of an injured man. But jumping past that only led to other problems.

There were still a thousand miles to cross to reach the Plain of Fear. With the empire alert. "Wait here," I told everybody, and left.

I hurried to the imperial compound, entered the office I had visited before, shook myself dry, examined a map on the wall. The kid who had checked us for contraband came over. "Help you somehow?"

"I don't think so. Just wanted to check the map. It pretty accurate?"

"Not anymore. The river has shifted more than a mile this way. And most of the flood plain isn't covered with woods anymore. All washed away."

"Hmm." I laid fingers on, making estimates.

"What do you want to know that for?"

"Business," I lied. "Heard we might be able to contact one of the bigger tribes around a place called Eagle Rocks."

"That's forty-five miles. You wouldn't make it. They'd kill you and take what you had. The only reason they don't bother the Guard and the road is that those have the Lady's protection. If this coming winter is as bad as the last few, that won't stop them, either."

"Uhm. Well, it was an idea. You the one called Case?"

"Yes." His eyes narrowed suspiciously.

"Heard you been taking care of some guy. . . ." I let it

drop. His reaction was not what I expected. "Well, that's what they're saying around town. Thanks for the advice." I got out. But I feared I had goofed.

I soon *knew* I had goofed.

A squad commanded by a major showed up at the inn only minutes after my return. They had the bunch of us under arrest before we knew what was happening. Goblin and One-Eye barely had time to cast spells of concealment on their gear.

We played ignorant. We cursed and grumbled and whined. It did us no good. Our captors knew less about why we were being grabbed than we did. Just following orders.

The landlord had a look which made me certain he had reported us as suspicious. I expect Case said something about my visit that tipped a balance somewhere. Whatever, we were on our way to cells.

Ten minutes after the door clanged shut, the very commander of the Eternal Guard turned up. I sighed in relief. He hadn't been here before. At least he was no one we knew. He shouldn't know us.

We had had time to rehearse using the deaf speech. All but Tracker. But Tracker seemed lost within himself. They had not allowed his mutt to accompany him. He had been angry about that. Scared the crap out of the guys who arrested us. For a minute they thought they would have to fight him.

The commander studied us, then introduced himself. "I'm Colonel Sweet. I command the Eternal Guard." Case hovered behind him, anxious. "I asked you men here because aspects of your behavior have been unusual."

"Have we unwittingly broken a rule not publicly posted?" I asked.

"Not at all. Not at all. The matter is entirely circumstantial. What you might call a question of undeclared intent."

"You've lost me, sir."

He began pacing up and down the passageway outside our cell. Up and down. "There is the old saw about actions speaking louder than words. I've had reports on you from several sources. About your excessive curiosity about matters not connected with your business."

I did my best to appear baffled. "What's unusual about

asking questions in new country? My associates haven't been here before. It's been years since I was. Things have changed. Anyway, this is one of the most interesting places in the empire.''

"Also one of the most dangerous, trader. Candle, is it? Mr. Candle, you were stationed here in service. What unit?''

That I could answer without hesitation. "Drake Crest. Colonel Lot. Second Battalion." I *was* here, after all.

"Yes. The Roses mercenary brigade. What was the Colonel's favorite drink?''

Oh, boy. "I was a pikeman, Colonel. I didn't drink with the brigadier.''

"Right.'' He paced. I could not tell if that answer worked or not. Drake Crest hadn't been a flashy, storied outfit like the Black Company. Who the hell would remember anything about them? After a time. "You must understand my position. With that thing buried out there paranoia becomes an occupational hazard.'' He pointed in the direction the Great Barrow must lie. Then he stalked off.

"What the hell was all that?'' Goblin asked.

"I don't know. And I'm not sure I want to find out. Somehow, we got ourselves into big trouble.'' That for the benefit of eavesdroppers.

Goblin accepted his cue. "Damnit, Candle, I told you we shouldn't come up here. I told you the Oar people would have an arrangement with the Guard.''

One-Eye jumped in then. They really ragged me. Meantime, we talked it over with the finger speech, decided to wait the Colonel out.

Not much choice anyway, without tipping our hands.

Chapter Thirty-Two:
IMPRISONED IN THE BARROWLAND

It was bad. Far worse than we suspected. Those Guard guys were paranoid plus. I mean, they didn't have an inkling who we were. But they did not let that slow them.

Half a platoon showed up suddenly. Rattle and clang at the door. No talk. Grim faces. We had trouble.

"I don't think they're going to turn us loose," Goblin said.

"Out," a sergeant told us.

We went out. All but Tracker. Tracker just sat there. I tried a funny. "He misses his dog."

Nobody laughed.

One of the Guards punched Tracker's arm. Tracker took a long time turning, looking at the man, his face an emotional blank.

"You shouldn't ought to have done that," I said.

"Shut up," the sergeant snapped. "Get him moving."

The man who had punched Tracker went to hit him again.

It might have been a love tap in slowed motion. Tracker reached around the moving fist, caught the advancing wrist, broke it. The Guardsman shrieked. Tracker tossed him aside. His face remained a blank. His gaze followed the man belatedly. He seemed to begin wondering what was happening.

The other Guards gaped. Then a couple jumped in with bared weapons.

"Hey! Take it easy!" I yelled. "Tracker . . ."

Still in that sort of mental nowhere, Tracker took their weapons away, tossed them into a corner, and beat the crap out of both men. The sergeant was torn between awe and outrage.

I tried to mollify him. "He's not very bright. You can't come at him like that. You have to explain things slow like, two or three times."

"I'll explain!" He started to send the rest of his men into the cell.

"You get him mad, you're going to get somebody killed." I talked fast, and wondered what the hell it was with Tracker and his damned pooch. That mutt went away, Tracker became a moron. With homicidal tendencies.

The sergeant let sense override anger. "You get him under control."

I worked on it. I knew the immediate future boded no good from the attitude of the soldiers, but was not overly worried. Goblin and One-Eye could handle whatever trouble developed. The thing to do now was keep our heads and lives.

I wanted to tend the three injured soldiers, but dared not. Just looking at One-Eye and Goblin would give clues enough for the other side to figure out, eventually, who we were. No sense giving them more. I concentrated on Tracker. Once I got him to focus on me it was no great task to get through, to calm him down, to explain that we were going somewhere with the soldiers.

He said, "They shouldn't ought to do me like that, Croaker." He sounded like a child whose feelings had been hurt. I grimaced. But the Guards did not react to the name.

They surrounded us, all with hands upon weapons, except those trying to get their injured companions to the horse doctor who served as the Guard's physician. Some of them were itching to get even. I worked hard to keep Tracker calm.

The place they took us did not encourage me. It was a sodden cellar beneath the headquarters. It looked like a caricature of a torture chamber. I suspect it was meant to intimidate. Having seen real torture and real torture implements, I recognized half the equipment as prop or unusually antiquated. But there were some serviceable implements, too. I exchanged glances with Goblin and One-Eye.

Tracker said, "I don't like it here. I want to go outside. I want to see Toadkiller Dog."

"Stand easy. We'll be out in a little while."

Goblin grinned his famous grin, though it was a little

lopsided. Yes. We would be out soon. Maybe feet first, but out.

Colonel Sweet was there. He did not seem pleased by our reaction to his stage. He said, "I want to talk to you men. You didn't seem eager to chat earlier. Are these surroundings more amenable?"

"Not exactly. They make one wonder, though. Is this the penalty for stepping on the heels of the gentlemen traders of Oar? I didn't realize they had the blessing of the Guard in their monopoly."

"Games. No games, Mr. Candle. Straight answers. Now. Or my men will make your next few hours extremely unpleasant."

"Ask. But I have a bad feeling I don't have the answers you want to hear."

"Then that will be your misfortune."

I glanced at Goblin. He had gone into a sort of trance.

The Colonel said, "I do not believe you when you say you're just traders. The pattern of your questions indicate an inordinate interest in a man named Corbie and his house. Corbie, let it be noted, is suspected of being either a Rebel agent or Resurrectionist. Tell me about him."

I did, almost completely, and truthfully: "I never heard of him before we got here."

I think he believed me. But he shook his head slowly.

"You see. You won't believe me even when you know I'm telling the truth."

"But how much are you telling? That is the question. The White Rose compartments its organization. You could have had no idea who Corbie was and still have come looking for him. Has he been out of touch for a while?"

This sucker was sharp.

My face must have been too studiedly blank. He nodded to himself, scanned the four of us, zeroed in on One-Eye. "The black man. Pretty old, isn't he?"

I was surprised he did not make more of One-Eye's skin color. Black men are extremely rare north of the Sea of Torments. Chances are the Colonel had not seen one before. That a black man, very old, is one of the cornerstones of the Black Company is not exactly a secret.

I did not answer.

"We'll start with him. He looks least likely to stand up."

Tracker asked, "You want me to kill them, Croaker?"

"I want you to keep your mouth shut and stand still, that's what I want." Damn. But Sweet missed the name. Either that or I was less famous than I thought and overdue for ego deflation.

Sweet did seem amazed that Tracker was so confident.

"Take him to the rack." He indicated One-Eye.

One-Eye chuckled and extended his hands to the men who approached him. Goblin snickered. Their amusement disturbed everyone. Me not least, for I knew their senses of humor.

Sweet looked me in the eye. "They find this amusing? Why?"

"If you don't indulge a sudden whim of civilized behavior, you're going to find out."

He was tempted to back down, but decided we were running some colossal bluff.

They took One-Eye to the rack. He grinned and climbed up himself. Goblin squeaked, "I been waiting to see you on one of those things for thirty years. Damned my luck if somebody else doesn't get to turn the crank when the chance finally comes."

"We'll see who turns that crank on who, horse apple," One-Eye replied.

They bantered back and forth. Tracker and I stood like posts. The imperials became ever more disturbed. Sweet, obviously, wondered if he shouldn't take One-Eye down and work on me.

They strapped One-Eye down. Goblin cackled, danced a little jig. "Stretch him till he's ten feet tall, guys," he said. "You'll still have a mental midget."

Somebody swung a backhand Goblin's way. He leaned only slightly. When the man pulled his hand back, having missed entirely and been only lightly brushed by a warding hand, he looked at his own paw in astonishment.

Ten thousand pinpricks of blood had appeared. They formed a pattern. Almost a tattoo. And that tattoo showed two serpents intertwined, each with its fangs buried in the other's neck. If necks are what snakes have behind their heads.

A distraction. I recognized it, of course. After the first moment, I concentrated on One-Eye. He just grinned.

The men who were to stretch him turned back after a moment, whipped by their Colonel's snarl. Sweet was damned uncomfortable now. He had a suspicion he faced something extraordinary, but he refused to be intimidated.

As the torturers stepped up to One-Eye his naked belly heaved. And a big, nasty spider crawled out of his navel. It came out in a ball, dragging itself with two legs, then unwrapped the others from around a body half the size of my thumb. It stepped aside and another crawled forth. The first ambled down One-Eye's leg, toward the man who held the crank to which One-Eye's ankles were strapped. The fellow's eyes just kept getting bigger. He turned to his commanding officer.

Absolute silence filled the cellar. I don't think the imperials even remembered to breathe.

Another spider crawled out of One-Eye's heaving belly. And another. And he seemed diminished just a bit more each time. His faced changed, slowly shifting toward what a spider's face looks like if you look real close. Most people do not have the nerve.

Goblin giggled.

"Turn the crank!" Sweet roared.

The man at One-Eye's feet tried. The first spider scuttled up the lever onto his hand. He shrieked, flung his hand around, hurled the arachnid into the shadows.

"Colonel," I said in as businesslike a voice as I could muster, "this has gone far enough. Let's not get someone hurt."

There was a whole mob of them and four of us and Sweet wanted badly to rely on that. But already several men were edging toward the exit. Most were edging away from us. Everyone stared at Sweet.

Damned Goblin. Had to let his enthusiasm get away. He squeaked, "Hold on, Croaker. This is a once-in-a-lifetime chance. Let them stretch One-Eye a little."

I saw the light dawn behind Sweet's eyes, though he tried

to conceal it. "Damn you, Goblin. Now you've done it. We're going to have a talk after this is over. Colonel. What will it be? I have the edge here. As you now know."

He elected for the better part of valor. "Release him," he told the man nearest One-Eye.

There were spiders all over One-Eye. He had them popping out of his mouth and ears now. Getting enthusiastic, he had them turning up as gaudy as you can imagine, hunters, web-spinners, jumpers. All big and revolting. Sweet's men refused to go near him.

I told Tracker, "Go stand in the doorway. Don't let any-body out." He had no trouble understanding that. I released One-Eye. I had to keep reminding myself the arachnids were illusions.

Some illusions. I *felt* the little creepies. . . . Belatedly, I realized One-Eye's legions were marching on Goblin. "Damn it, One-Eye! Grow up!" The son-of-a-bitch wasn't satisfied to bluff the imperials. He had to play games with Goblin, too. I wheeled on Goblin. "If you do one damned thing to get involved in this, I'll see you never leave the Hole again. Colonel Sweet. I can't say I've enjoyed your hospitality. If you and your men will come over here? We'll just be on our way."

Reluctantly, Sweet gestured. Half of his men refused to move toward the spiders. "One-Eye. Game time is over. It's get-out-alive time. Would you mind?"

One-Eye gestured. His eight-legged troops rushed into the shadows behind the rack, where they vanished into that mad oblivion from which such things spring. One-Eye strutted over to stand by Tracker. He was cocky now. For weeks we would hear about how he had saved us. If we lived to get away tonight.

I shooed Goblin over, then joined them myself. I told Goblin and One-Eye, "I want no sound to escape this room. And I want that door sealed like it was part of the wall. Then I want to know where we find this character Corbie."

"You got it," One-Eye said. Eye twinkling, he added, "So long, Colonel. It was fun."

Sweet forebore making threats. Sensible man.

Fixing the room took the wizards ten minutes, which I

found inordinately long. I became mildly suspicious, but forgot that notion when they said they were done and that the man we wanted was in another building nearby.

I should have harkened to my suspicions.

Five minutes later we stood in the doorway of the building where Corbie was supposed to be. We had encountered no difficulty getting there. "One second, Croaker," One-Eye said. He faced the building we had vacated, snapped his fingers.

The whole damned place fell in.

"You bastard," I whispered. "What did you do that for?"

"Now there's nobody who knows who we are."

"Whose fault was it they did know?"

"Chopped off the head of the snake, too. Be so much confusion we could walk off with the Lady's jewelry if we wanted."

"Yeah?" There would be those who knew we were brought in. They would wonder some if they saw us wandering around. "Tell me, O genius. Did you locate the documents I want before you tumbled the place down? If they're in there, you're the gent who's going to dig them out."

His face dropped.

Yes. I expected that. Because that is my kind of luck. And that is the way One-Eye is. He never thinks things through.

"We'll worry about Corbie first," I said. "Inside."

As we pushed through the door we encountered Case coming to investigate the uproar.

Chapter Thirty-Three:
MISSING MAN

"Hi, fellow," One-Eye said, punching a finger into the soldier's chest, pushing him back. "Yeah. It's your old pals."

Behind me, Tracker stared across the compound. The collapse of the headquarters building was complete. Fire snapped and crackled inside. Toadkiller Dog loped around the end of the ruin.

"Look at that." I punched Goblin's arm. "He's running." I faced Case. "Show us your friend Corbie."

He did not want to do that.

"You don't want to argue. We're not in the mood. Move it or we walk over you."

The compound had begun to fill with yammering soldiers. None noticed us. Toadkiller Dog loped up, sniffed Tracker's calves, made a sound deep in his throat. Tracker's face gleamed.

We pushed in behind Case. "To Corbie," I reminded him.

He led us to a room where a single oil lamp illuminated a man on a bed, neatly blanketed. Case turned the lamp up.

"Oh, holy shit," I murmured. I plopped my butt on the edge of the bed. "It ain't possible. One-Eye?" But One-Eye was in another universe. He just stood there with his mouth open. Like Goblin.

Finally, Goblin squeaked, "But he's dead. He died six years ago."

Corbie was the Raven who played such a grand part in the Company past. The Raven who had set Darling on her present course.

Even I had been convinced he was dead, and I was by

179

nature suspicious of Raven. He had tried the same stunt
before.

"Nine lives," One-Eye remarked.

"Should have suspected when we heard the name Corbie,"
I said.

"What?"

"It's a joke. His kind. Corbie. Crow. Rook. Raven. All
pretty much the same thing. Right? He waved it under our
noses."

Seeing him there illuminated mysteries that had plagued me
for years. Now I knew why papers I had salvaged would not
come together. He had removed the key pieces before faking
his last death.

"Even Darling didn't know this time," I mused. The
shock had begun to wear off. I found myself reflecting that on
several occasions after the letters began arriving I had skirted
the suspicion that he was alive.

A raft of questions rose. Darling not knowing. Why not?
That did not seem like Raven. But more, why abandon her to
our mercy, as he had, when for so long he had tried to keep
her away?

There was more here than met the eye. More than Raven
just running off so he could poke into doings at the Barrowland.
Unfortunately, I could question neither of my witnesses.

"How long has he been this way?" One-Eye asked Case
The soldier's eyes were wide. He knew who we were now.
Maybe my ego did not need deflating after all.

"Months."

"There was a letter," I said. "There were papers. What
became of them?"

"The Colonel."

"And what did the Colonel do? Did he inform the Taken?
Did he contact the Lady?"

The trooper was about to get stubborn. "You're in trouble
here, kid. We don't want to hurt you. You did right by our
friend. Speak up."

"He didn't. That I know of. He couldn't read any of that
stuff. He was waiting for Corbie to wake up."

"He would have waited a long time," One-Eye said.

"Give us some room, Croaker. First order of business is going to be finding Raven."

"There anyone else in this building this time of night?" I asked Case.

"Not unless the bakers come in for flour. But it's stored in the cellars down to the other end. They wouldn't come around here."

"Right." I wondered how much his information could be trusted. "Tracker. You and Toadkiller Dog go stand lookout."

"One problem," One-Eye said. "Before we do anything, we need Bomanz's map."

"Oh, boy." I slipped into the hallway, to the exit, peeped out. The headquarters building was afire, sputtering halfheartedly in the rain. Most of the Guard were fighting the fire. I shuddered. Our documents were in there. If the Lady's luck held, they would burn. I returned to the room. "One-Eye, you have a more immediate problem. My documents. You better get after them. I'll try for the chart.

"Tracker, you watch the door here. Keep the kid in and everybody else out. All right?" He nodded. He needed no special coaching while Toadkiller Dog was around.

I slipped out, into the confusion. No one paid me any heed. I wondered if this was not the time to take Raven out. I exited the compound unchallenged, dashed through the drizzle to Blue Willy. The proprietor seemed astounded to see me. I did not pause to tell him what I thought of his hospitality, just went upstairs, groped around inside the concealment spell till I found the spear with the hollow shaft. Back down. One vituperous look for the landlord, then into the rain again.

By the time I returned, the fire was under control. Soldiers had begun to pull the rubble apart. Still no one challenged me. I slipped into the building where Raven lay, handed One-Eye the spear. "You do anything about those papers?"

"Not yet."

"Damn it. . . ."

"They're in a box in the Colonel's office, Croaker. What the hell do you want?"

"Ah. Tracker. Take the kid into the hallway. You guys. I want a spell where he has to do what he's told whether he wants to or not."

"What?" One-Eye asked.

"I want to send him after those papers. Can you fix it so he's got to do it and come back?"

Case was in the doorway, listening bleakly.

"Sure. No problem."

"Do it. Son, you understand? One-Eye will put a spell on you. You go help clean up that mess till you can get the box. Bring it back and we'll take the spell off."

He looked like getting stubborn again.

"You have a choice, of course. You can die an unpleasant death instead."

"I don't think he believes you, Croaker. I'd better give him a taste."

Case's expression told me he did believe. The more he thought about who we were, the more terrified he became.

How had we developed such a fierce reputation? I guess stories grow in the retelling. "I think he'll cooperate. Right, son?"

He nodded, stubbornness dead.

He looked like a good kid. Too bad he had given his loyalty to the other side.

"Do it, One-Eye. Let's get on with this."

While One-Eye worked, Goblin asked, "What do we do after we finish here, Croaker?"

"Hell, I don't know. Play it by ear. Right now don't worry about the mules, just load the wagon. Step at a time. Step at a time."

"Ready," One-Eye said.

I beckoned the youth, opened the outside door. "Get out there and do it, kid." I patted his behind. He went, but with a look that could have curdled milk.

"He's not happy with you, Croaker."

"Screw it. Get in there with Raven. Do what you have to do. Time is wasting. Come daylight this place will see some life."

I watched Case. Tracker guarded the door to the room. No one interrupted us. Case eventually found what I wanted, slipped away from the work detail. "Good job, son," I told him, taking the box. "In the room with your friend."

We entered moments before One-Eye came out of a trance. "Well?" I asked.

He took a moment to orient himself. "Going to be harder than I thought. But I think we can bring him out." He indicated the chart Goblin had spread atop Raven's stomach. "He's about here, caught, just inside the inner circle." He shook his head. "You ever hear him tell about having any background in the trade?"

"No. But there were times I wondered. Like in Roses, when he tracked Raker through a snowstorm."

"He learned something somewhere. Weren't no parlor trick, what he did. But it was too big for his skills." For a moment he was thoughtful. "It's weird in there, Croaker. Really weird. He isn't alone by a long shot. Won't be able to give you any details till we go in ourselves but . . ."

"What? Wait. Go in yourselves? What're you talking about?"

"Figured you understood Goblin and I would have to follow him in. In order to bring him out."

"Why both of you?"

"One to cover in case the point man gets in trouble."

Goblin nodded. They were all business now. Meaning they were scared crapless.

"How long is all this going to take?"

"No telling. Quite a while. We ought to get out of here first. Out in the woods."

I wanted to argue but did not. Instead, I went and checked the compound.

They had begun bringing the bodies out of the rubble. I watched a while, got an idea. Five minutes later Case and I stepped out carrying a litter. A blanket covered what appeared to be a large broken body. Goblin's face lay exposed. He did a great corpse. One-Eye's feet stuck out the other end. Tracker carried Raven.

The documents were under the blanket with Goblin and One-Eye.

I did not expect to pull it off. But the grim business around the collapsed building preoccupied the Guard. They had reached the cellars.

I did get challenged at the compound gate. Goblin used his

Glen Cook

sleep spell. I doubted we would be remembered. Civilians were all over, helping and hindering the rescue effort.

That was the bad news. A few down in that cellar were still alive.

"Goblin, you and One-Eye get our gear. Take the kid. Tracker and I will get the wagon."

All went well. Too well, I thought, being naturally pessimistic after the way things had been going. We put Raven in the wagon and headed south.

The moment we entered the forest One-Eye said, "So we've made our getaway. Now. About Raven?"

I was without a single idea. "You call it. How close do you have to be?"

"Very." He saw I was thinking about getting out of the country first. "Darling?"

The reminder was unnecessary.

I won't say Raven was the center of her life. She will not discuss him except in the most general way. But there are nights she cries herself to sleep, remembering something. If it is for loss of Raven, we could not bring him home like this. It would break her heart all the way.

Anyway, we needed him now. He knew better than we what the hell was going on.

I appealed to Tracker for suggestions. He had none. He did not, in fact, appear pleased with what we planned. Like he expected Raven to become competition, or something.

"We've got him," One-Eye said, indicating Case, whom we had dragged along rather than leave dead. "Let's use him."

Good idea.

Twenty minutes later we had the wagon well off the road, up on rocks so it would not sink into the soggy earth. One-Eye and Goblin wound spells of concealment around it and camouflaged it with brush. We piled gear into packs, placed Raven on the litter. Case and I carried him. Tracker and Toadkiller Dog led us through the woods.

It could not have been more than three miles, yet I ached everywhere before we finished. Too old. Too out of shape. And the weather was one-hundred-ninety-proof misery. I had had enough rain to last me the rest of my life. Tracker led us to a place just east of the Barrowland. I could walk downhill a hundred yards and see its remnants. I could walk a hundred yards the other way and see the Great Tragic. Only the one narrow stretch of high ground barred it from reaching the Barrowland.

We got tents up and boughs inside so we did not have to sit on wet earth. Goblin and One-Eye took the smaller tent. The rest of us crowded into the other. Once reasonably free of the rain, I settled down to probe the rescued documents. First to catch my eye was an oilskin packet. "Case. This the letter Raven wanted you to deliver?"

He nodded sullenly. He was not talking.

Poor boy. He believed he was guilty of treason. I hoped he wouldn't get a case of the heroics.

Well, might as well keep busy while Goblin and One-Eye did their job. Start with the easy part first.

Chapter Thirty-Four: BOMANZ'S STORY

Croaker:

Bomanz faced the Lady from another angle. He saw a ghost of fear touch her matchless features. "Ardath," he said, and saw her fear become resignation.

Ardath was my sister.

"You had a twin. You murdered her and took her name. Your true name is Ardath."

You will regret this. I will find your name. . . .

"Why do you threaten me? I mean you no harm."

You harm me by thwarting me. Free me.

"Come, come. Don't be childish. Why force my hand? That will cost us both agony and energy. I only want to rediscover the knowledge interred with you. Teaching me will cost you nothing. It won't harm you. It might even prepare the world for your return.''

The world prepares already. Bomanz!

He chuckled. ''That's a mask, like the antiquarian. That's not my name. Ardath. Must we fight?''

Wise men say to accept the inevitable with grace. If I must, I must. I will try to be gracious.

When pigs fly, Bomanz thought.

The Lady's smile was mocking. She sent something. He did not catch it. Other voices filled his mind. For an instant he thought the Dominator was awakening. But the voices were in his physical ears, back at the house. ''Oh, damn!''

Wind-chimes mirth.

''Clete is in position.'' The voice was Tokar's. Its presence in the attic enraged Bomanz. He started running.

''Help me get him out of the chair.'' Stancil.

''Won't you wake him up?'' Glory.

''His spirit is out in the Barrowland. He won't know anything unless we run into each other out there.''

Wrong, Bomanz thought. Wrong, you insidious, ungrateful wart. Your old man isn't stupid. He responds to the signs even when he doesn't want to see them.

The dragon's head swung as he hurtled past. Mockery pursued him. The hatred of dead knights pounded him as he hurried on.

''Get him into the corner. Toker, the amulet is under the hearthstone in the shack. That damned Men fu! He almost blew it. I want to get my hands on the fool who sent him up here. That greedy idiot wasn't interested in anything but himself.''

''At least he took the Monitor with him.'' Glory.

''Pure accident. Pure luck.''

''The time. The time,'' Tokar said. ''Clete's men are hitting the barracks.''

''Get out of here, then. Glory, will you do something besides stare at the old man? I've got to get in there before Tokar reaches the Barrowland. The Great Ones have to be told what we're doing.''

Bomanz passed the barrow of Moondog. He felt the rest-
lessness within. He raced on.

A ghost danced beside him. A slump-shouldered, evil-faced
ghost who damned him a thousand times. "I don't have time
for it, Besand. But you were right." He crossed the old moat,
passed his dig. Strangers dotted the landscape. Resurrectionist strangers. Where had they come from? Out of hiding in
the Old Forest?

Faster. Got to go faster, he thought. That fool Stance is
going to try to follow me in.

He ran like nightmare, floating through subjectively eternal
steps. The comet glared down. It felt strong enough to cast
shadows.

"Read the instructions again to make sure," Stancil said.
"Timing isn't critical as long as you don't do anything early."

"Shouldn't we tie him up or something? Just in case?"

"We don't have time. Don't worry about him. He won't
come out till way too late."

"He makes me nervous."

"Then throw a rug over him and come on. And try to keep
your voice down. You don't want to waken Mother."

Bomanz charged the lights of the town. . . . It occurred to
him that in this state he did not have to be a stubby-legged fat
man short on breath. He changed his perception and his
velocity increased. Soon he encountered Tokar, who was
trotting toward the Barrowland with Besand's amulet. Bomanz
judged his own startling swiftness by Tokar's apparent
sluggishness. He was moving fast.

Headquarters was afire. There was heavy fighting around
the barracks. Tokar's teamsters were leading the attackers. A
few Guardsmen had broken out of the trap. Trouble was
seeping into the town.

Bomanz reached his shop. Upstairs, Stancil told Glory,
"Begin now." As Bo started up the stair, Stancil said, "Dumni.
Um muji dumni." Bomanz smashed into his own body. He
seized command of his muscles, surged off the floor.

Glory shrieked.

Bomanz hurled her toward a wall. Her career shattered
priceless antiques.

Bomanz squealed in agony as all the pains of an old body hit his consciousness. Damn! His ulcer was tearing his gut apart!

He seized his son's throat as he turned, silencing him before he finished the cantrip.

Stancil was younger, stronger. He rose. And Glory threw herself at Bomanz. Bomanz darted backward. "Don't anybody move," he snapped.

Stancil rubbed his throat and croaked something.

"You don't think I would? Try me. I don't care who you are. You're not going to free that thing out there."

"How did you know?" Stancil croaked.

"You've been acting strange. You have strange friends. I hoped I was wrong, but I don't take chances. You should have remembered that."

Stancil drew a knife. His eyes hardened. "I'm sorry, Pop. Some things are more important than people."

Bomanz's temples throbbed. "Behave yourself. I don't have time for this. I have to stop Tokar."

Glory drew a knife of her own. She sidled a step closer.

"You're trying my patience, son."

The girl jumped. Bomanz uttered a word of power. She plunged headlong into the table, slid to the floor, almost inhumanly limp. In seconds she was limper still. She mewled like an injured kitten.

Stancil dropped to one knee. "I'm sorry, Glory. I'm sorry."

Bomanz ignored his own emotional agony. He salvaged the quicksilver spilled from the bowl that had been atop the table, mouthed words which transformed its surface into a mirror of events afar.

Tokar was two thirds of the way to the Barrowland.

"You killed her," Stancil said. "You killed her."

"I warned you, this is a cruel business." And: "You made a bet and lost. Sit your butt in the corner and behave."

"You killed her."

Remorse smashed in even before his son forced him to act. He tried to soften the impact, but the melting of bones was all or nothing.

Stancil fell across his lover.

His father fell to his knees beside him. "Why did you make me do it? You fools. You bloody damned fools! You

were using me. You didn't have sense enough to make sure
of me, and you want to deal with something like the Lady? I
don't know. I don't know. What am I going to tell Jasmine?
How can I explain?'' He looked around wildly, an animal
tormented. ''Kill myself. That's all I can do. Save her the
pain of learning what her son was. . . . Can't. Got to stop
Tokar.''

There was fighting in the street outside. Bomanz ignored it.
He scrabbled after quicksilver.

Tokar was at the edge of the moat, staring into the
Barrowland. Bomanz saw the fear and uncertainty in him.

Tokar found his courage. He gripped the amulet and crossed
the line.

Bomanz began building a killing sending.

His glance crossed the doorway, spied a frightened Snoopy
watching from the dark landing. ''Oh, child. Child, get out of
here.''

''I'm scared. They're killing each other outside.''

We're killing each other in here, too, he thought. Please go
away. ''Go find Jasmine.''

A horrendous crash came from the shop. Men cursed. Steel
met steel. Bomanz heard the voice of one of Tokar's teamsters.
The man was deploying a defense of the house.

The Guard had made a comeback.

Snoopy whimpered.

''Stay out of here, child. Stay out. Go down with Jasmine.''

''I'm scared.''

''So am I. And I won't be able to help if you get in my
way. Please go downstairs.''

She ground her teeth and rattled away. Bomanz sighed.
That was close. If she had seen Stance and Glory . . .

The uproar redoubled. Men screamed. Bomanz heard Corporal Husky bellowing orders. He turned to the bowl. Tokar
had disappeared. He could not relocate the man. In passing he
surveyed the land between the town and the Barrowland. A
few Resurrectionists were rushing toward the fighting, apparently to help. Others were in headlong flight. Remnants of the
Guard were in pursuit.

Boots pounded upstairs. Again Bomanz interrupted the

preparation of his sending. Husky appeared in the doorway.
Bomanz started to order him out. He was in no mood to
argue. He swung a great bloody sword. . . .

Bomanz used the word of power. Again a man's bones
turned to jelly. Then again and again as Husky's troopers
tried to avenge him. Bomanz dropped four before the rush
ended.

He tried to get back to his sending. . . .

This time the interruption was nothing physical. It was a
reverberation along the pathway he had opened into the Lady's
crypt. Tokar was on the Great Barrow and in contact with the
creature it contained.

"Too late," he murmured. "Too damned late." But he
made the sending anyway. Maybe Tokar would die before he
could release those monsters.

Jasmine cursed. Snoopy screamed. Bomanz piled over the
fallen Guardsmen and charged downstairs. Snoopy screamed
again.

Bo entered his bedroom. One of Tokar's men held a knife
across Jasmine's throat. A pair of Guardsmen sought an
opening.

Bomanz had no patience left. He killed all three.

The house rattled. Teacups clinked in the kitchen. It was a
gentle tremor, but a harbinger strong enough to warn Bomanz.

His sending had not arrived in time.

Resigned, he said, "Get out of the house. There's going to
be a quake."

Jasmine looked at him askance. She held the hysterical
girl.

"I'll explain later. If we survive. Just get out of the
house." He whirled and dashed into the street, charged toward
the Barrowland.

Imagining himself tall and lean and fleet did no good now.
He was Bomanz in the flesh, a short, fat old man easily
winded. He fell twice as tremors shook the town. Each was
stronger than the last.

The fires still burned, but the fighting had died away. The
survivors on both sides knew it was too late for a decision of
the sword. They stared toward the Barrowland, awaiting the
unfolding of events.

Bomanz joined the watchers.

The comet burned so brightly the Barrowland was clearly illuminated.

A tremendous shock rattled the earth. Bomanz staggered. Out on the Barrowland the mound containing Soulcatcher exploded. A painful glow burned from within. A figure rose from the rubble, stood limned against the glow.

People prayed or cursed according to predilection.

The tremors continued. Barrow after barrow opened. One by one, the Ten Who Were Taken appeared against the night. "Tokar," Bomanz murmured, "I hope you rot in Hell."

There was only one chance left. One impossible chance. It rode on the time-bowed shoulders of a pudgy little man whose powers were not at their sharpest.

He marshaled his most potent spells, his greatest magicks, all the mystical tricks he had worked out during thirty-seven years worth of lonely nights. And he started walking toward the Barrowland.

Hands reached out to detain him. They found no purchase. From the crowd an old woman called, "Bo, no! Please!"

He kept walking.

The Barrowland seethed. Ghosts howled among the ruins. The Great Barrow shook its hump. Earth exploded upward, flaming. A great winged serpent rose against the night. A great scream poured from its mouth. Torrents of dragonfire inundated the Barrowland.

Wise green eyes watched Bomanz's progress.

The fat little man walked into the holocaust, unleashing his arsenal of spells. Fire enveloped him.

Chapter Thirty-Five: THE BARROWLAND, FROM BAD TO WORSE

Returning Raven's letter to the oilskin, I lay back on my bough bed, let my mind go blank. So dramatic, the way Raven told it. I wondered about his sources, though. The wife? Someone had to note the tale's ending and had to hide what was found later. What *had* become of the wife, anyway? She has no place in legend. Neither does the son, for that matter. The popular stories mention only Bomanz himself.

Something there, though. Something I missed? Ah. Yes. A congruence with personal experience. The name Bomanz had relied upon. The one that, evidently, proved insufficiently powerful.

I'd heard it before. In equally furious circumstances.

In Juniper, as the contest between the Lady and the Dominator neared its climax, with her ensconced in a castle on one side of the city and the Dominator trying to escape through another on the far side, we discovered the Taken meant to do the Company evil once the crisis subsided. Under orders from the Captain we deserted. We seized a ship. As we sailed away, with husband and wife contesting above the burning city, the struggle peaked. The Lady proved the stronger.

The voice of the Dominator shook the world as he vented a last spate of frustration. He had called her by the name Bomanz had thought puissant. Apparently, even the Dominator could be mistaken.

One sister killed another and, maybe or maybe not, took her place. Soulcatcher, our one-time mentor and plotter to usurp the Lady, it proved during the great struggle at Charm, was another sister. Three sisters, then. At least. One named Ardath, but evidently not the one who became the Lady.

Maybe the beginnings of something here. All those lists, back in the Hole. And the genealogies. Find a woman named Ardath. Then discover who her sisters were.

"It's a beginning," I murmured. "Feeble, but a beginning."

"What?"

I had forgotten Case. He had not taken advantage. I suppose he was too frightened.

"Nothing." It had grown dark outside. The drizzle persisted. Out on the Barrowland ghostly lights drifted about. I shuddered. That did not seem right. I wondered how Goblin and One-Eye were getting on. I did not dare go ask. Over in a corner Tracker snored softly. Toadkiller Dog lay against his belly, making sleeping dog noises, but I caught a glint of eye which said he was not unalert.

I invested a little more attention in Case. He was shaking, and not just with the chill. He was sure we would kill him. I reached over, rested a hand on his shoulder. "It's all right, son. You won't be harmed. We owe you for looking out for Raven."

"He's really Raven? The Raven that was the White Rose's father?"

The lad knew the legends. "Yeah. Foster-father, though."

"Then he didn't lie about everything. He *was* in the Forsberg campaigns."

That struck me as humorous. I chuckled, then said, "Knowing Raven, he didn't lie about much. Just edited the truth."

"You'll really let me go?"

"When we're safe."

"Oh." He did not sound reassured.

"Let's say when we get to the edge of the Plain of Fear. You'll find plenty of friends out there."

He wanted to get into a quasi-political discussion about why we insisted on resisting the Lady. I refused. I am no evangelist. I can't make converts. I have too much trouble understanding myself and unravelling my own motives. Maybe Raven could explain after Goblin and One-Eye brought him out.

The night seemed endless, but after three eternities which took me up to midnight I heard unsteady footsteps. "Croaker?"

"In," I said. It was Goblin. Without a light I could not read him well, but got the impression that his news was not good. "Trouble?"

"Yes. We can't get him out."

"What the hell are you talking about? What do you mean?"

"I mean we don't have the skills. We don't have the talent. This's going to take someone bigger than we are. We aren't much, Croaker. Showmen. With a few handy spells. Maybe Silent could do something. His is a different sort of magic."

"Maybe you'd better back up. Where's One-Eye?"

"Resting. It was rough on him. Really rocked him, what he saw in there."

"What was that?"

"I don't know. I was just his lifeline. And I had to pull him out before he got trapped, too. All I know is, we can't get Raven without help."

"Shit," I said. "Double damned floating sheep shit. Goblin, we can't win this one unless we have Raven to help. I don't have what it takes either. I'll never translate half those papers."

"Not even with Tracker's help?"

"He reads TelleKurre. That's it. I can do that, only I take longer. Raven must know the dialects. Some of the stuff he was translating was in them. Also, there's the question of what he was doing *here*. Why he faked his death again and took off. On Darling."

Maybe I was jumping to conclusions. I do that. Or maybe I was indulging in the human penchant for oversimplification, figuring that if we just had Raven back our troubles were solved. "What are we going to do?" I wondered aloud.

Goblin rose. "I don't know, Croaker. Let's let One-Eye get his feet under him again and find out what we're up against. We can go from there."

"Right."

He slipped out. I lay down and tried to sleep.

Whenever I dropped off I had nightmares about the thing lying in the mud and slime the Barrowland had become.

Chapter Thirty-Six: HARD TIMES

One-Eye looked gruesome. "It was grim," he said. "Get the chart out, Croaker." I did. He indicated a point. "He's here. And stuck. Looks like he went all the way to the center along Bomanz's trail, then got in trouble on his way out."

"How? I don't understand what's going on here."

"I wish you could go in there. A realm of terrible shadows. . . . Guess I should be glad you can't. You'd try it."

"What's that crack mean?"

"Mean's you're too curious for your own good. Like old Bomanz. No. Be still." He paused a moment.

"Croaker, something that was trapped there, one of the minions of the Taken, was situated near Bomanz's path. *He* was too strong for it. But Raven was an amateur. I think Goblin, Silent, and I together would have trouble with this thing, and we're more skilled than Raven could be. He underestimated the dangers and overestimated himself. As he was leaving, this thing usurped his position and left him in its place."

I frowned, not quite understanding.

One-Eye explained, "Something used him to keep the balance of the old spells. So he's stuck in a net of old-time sorcery. And it's out here."

A sinking feeling. A feeling edging despair. "Out? And you don't know? . . ."

"Nothing. The chart indicates nothing. Bomanz must have been contemptuous of the lesser evils. He hasn't marked a dozen. There should have been scores."

The literature supported that. "What did he tell you? Were you able to communicate?"

"No. He was aware of a presence. But he's in a sinkhole of spells. I couldn't contact him without getting caught myself. There's a small imbalance there, like what went out might have been a hair more than what stayed in. I did try to get close to him. That was why Goblin had to yank me out. I did sense a great fear, not due to his situation. Only anger there. I think he got caught only because he was in so big a hurry he didn't pay attention to his surroundings."

I got the message. Been to the center, and in flight. What lay at the center? "You think whatever got away might try to open the Great Barrow?"

"It might try engineering it."

I had a brainstorm. "Why not sneak Darling out here? She could . . ."

One-Eye gave me a don't-be-stupid look. Right. Raven was the least of the things a null would loose.

"The big guy would love that," Goblin chided. "Purely love it."

"There's nothing we can do for Raven here," One-Eye said. "Someday we might find a wizard who can. Till then?" He shrugged. "Better make a pact of silence. Darling might forget her mission if she finds out."

"Agreed," I said. Then: "But . . ."

"But what?"

"I've been thinking about that. Darling and Raven. There's something there we don't see, I think. I mean, considering the way he always was, why did he cut out and come here? On the face of it, to sneak around the Lady and her gang. But why would he leave Darling in the dark? You see what I'm saying? Maybe she wouldn't be as upset as we think. Or maybe for different reasons."

One-Eye looked dubious. Goblin nodded. Tracker looked baffled, as usual.

"What about his body?" I asked.

"A definite encumbrance," One-Eye replied. "And I can't say but what taking him to the Plain might not snap the connection between flesh and spirit."

"Stop." I looked at Case. He looked at me. Here we had another double bind.

I knew one sure way of solving Raven's body problem. And of getting him brought out. Betray him to the Lady. That might solve several other problems, too. Like the escaped whatever, and the threat of another escape attempt by her husband. It might buy Darling time, too, for the Lady's attention would shift dramatically.

But what would become of Raven then?

He could be the key to our success or failure. Give him up to save him? Play the very long odds that we could somehow get him in hand again before his knowledge could hurt us? Ever a quandary. Ever a quandary.

Goblin suggested, "Let's give it another look. This time I'll take the point. One-Eye will cover."

One-Eye's sour look said they had had a knock-down-drag-out about this before. I kept my mouth shut. It was their area of expertise.

"Well?" Goblin demanded.

"If you think it's worthwhile."

"I do. Anyway, there's nothing to lose. Different viewpoint might help, too. I might catch something he missed."

"Having only one eye don't blind me," One-Eye snarled. Goblin glowered. This had arisen before, too.

"Don't waste time," I said. "We can't stay put forever."

Sometimes decisions get made for you.

Deep in the night. Wind in the trees. Chill fingering into the shelter, waking me to shiver till I fell asleep again. Rain pattering steadily, but not restfully. Gods, was I sick of rain. How could the Eternal Guard maintain any semblance of sanity?

A hand shook me. Tracker whispered, "Company coming. Trouble." Toadkiller Dog was at the tent flap, hackles up.

I listened. Nothing. But no point not taking his word. Better safe than dead. "What about Goblin and One-Eye?"

"Not finished yet."

"Oh-oh." I scrambled for clothing, for weapons. Tracker said, "I'll go scout them and try to scare or lead them off. You warn the others. Get ready to run." He slipped out of the tent behind Toadkiller Dog. Damned beast showed some life now!

Our whispering wakened Case. Neither of us spoke. I wondered what he would risk. I covered my head with my blanket and left. Sufficient unto the day the evil thereof.

Into the other tent, where I found both men in trances. "Shit. Now what?" Did I dare try waking One-Eye? Softly: "One-Eye. This is Croaker. We've got trouble."

Ah. His good eye opened. For a moment he seemed disoriented. Then: "What're you doing here?"

"Trouble. Tracker says there's somebody in the woods."

A cry came through the rain. One-Eye bolted upright. "The power!" he spat. "What the hell?"

"What is it?"

"Somebody just ripped off a spell almost like one of the Taken."

"Can you get Goblin out? Fast?"

"I can . . ." Another cry ripped through the woods. This one stretched out and out, and seemed as much of despair as of agony. "I'll get him."

He sounded like all hope had gone.

Taken. Had to be. Sniffed out our tracks. Closing in. But the cries. . . . First one somebody Tracker ambushed? Second one Tracker gotten? Didn't sound like him.

One-Eye lay down and closed his eye. In moments he was back in trance, though his face betrayed the fear on his surface mind. He was good, to go under such tension.

There was a third cry from the woods. Baffled, I moved to where I could look into the rain. I saw nothing. Moments later Goblin stirred.

He looked awful. But his determination showed he had gotten the word. He forced himself upright though it was obvious he was not ready. His mouth kept opening and closing. I had a feeling he wanted to tell me something.

One-Eye came out after him but recovered more quickly. "What's happened?" he asked.

"Another yell."

"Drop everything? Run for it?"

"We can't. We have to get some of this stuff back to the Plain. Otherwise we might as well surrender right here."

"Right. Get it together. I'll take care here."

Getting things together was not much of a job. I had unpacked very little. . . . Something roared out in the woods. I froze. "What the hell?" Sounded like something bigger than four lions. A moment later there were screams.

No sense. No sense at all. I could see Tracker raising nine kinds of hell with the Guard, but not if they had one of the Taken with them.

Goblin and One-Eye showed up as I began knocking the tent down. Goblin still looked like hell. One-Eye carried half his stuff. "Where's the kid?" he asked.

I had paid no attention to his absence. It hadn't surprised me. "Gone. How are we going to carry Raven?"

My answer stepped out of the woods. Tracker. Looking a little the worse for wear, but still healthy. Toadkiller Dog was covered with blood. He seemed more animated than I had seen before. "Let's get him out of here," Tracker said, and moved to take one end of the litter.

"Your stuff."

"No time."

"What about the wagon?" I lifted the other end.

"Forget it. I'm sure they found it. March."

We marched, letting him lead the way. I asked, "What was all that uproar?"

"Caught them by surprise."

"But . . ."

"Even the Taken can be surprised. Save your breath. He isn't dead."

For a few hours it was put one foot in front of the other and don't look back. Tracker set a tough pace. In a corner of my mind where the observer still dwelt, I noted that Toadkiller Dog kept the pace with ease.

Goblin collapsed first. Once or twice he had tried to catch me and pass something along, but he just did not have the energy. When he went down, Tracker stopped, looked back irritably. Toadkiller Dog lay down in the wet leaves, rumbling. Tracker shrugged, set his end of the litter down.

That was *my* cue to drop. Like a stone. And damn the rain and mud. I couldn't get any wetter.

Gods, my arms and shoulders ached. Needles of fire drove

into me where the muscles start swooping up to the neck.
"This isn't going to work," I said after I caught some breath.
"We're too old and weak."

Tracker considered the forest. Toadkiller Dog rose, sniffed
the wet wind. I struggled up long enough to look back the
way we had come, trying to guess which direction we had
run.

South, of course. North made no sense and east or west
would have put us in the Barrowland or river. But if we kept
heading south we would encounter the old Oar road where it
curved in beside the Great Tragic. That stretch was sure to be
patrolled.

With my breath partially restored and my breathing no
longer roaring in my ears, I could hear the river. It was no
more than a hundred yards away, churning and grumbling as
always.

Tracker came out of a reflective mood. "Guile, then.
Guile."

"I'm hungry," One-Eye said, and I realized I was too.
"Reckon we'll get a lot hungrier, though." He smiled feebly.
He now had enough strength to look Goblin over. "Croaker.
Want to come check him out?"

Funny that they aren't enemies when the pinch comes.

Chapter Thirty-Seven: THE FOREST AND BEYOND

Two days passed before we ate, courtesy of Tracker's skill as
a hunter. Two days we spent dodging patrols. Tracker knew
those woods well. We disappeared into their deeps and drifted
southward at a more relaxed pace. After the two days Tracker
felt confident enough to let us have a fire. It was not much,

though, because finding burnable wood was a pain. Its value was more psychological than physical.

Misery balanced by rising hope. That was the story of our two weeks in the Old Forest. Hell, trekking overland, off the road, was as fast or faster than using the road itself. We felt halfway optimistic when we neared the southern verge.

I am tempted to dwell on the misery and the arguments about Raven. One-Eye and Goblin were convinced we were doing him no good. Yet they could come up with no alternative to dragging him along.

I carried another weight in my belly, like a big stone.

Goblin got to me that second night while Tracker and Toadkiller Dog were hunting. He whispered, "I got farther in than One-Eye did. Almost to the center. I know why Raven didn't get out."

"Yeah?"

"He saw too much. What he went to see, probably. The Dominator is not asleep. I . . ." He shuddered. It took him a moment to get hold of himself. "I saw him, Croaker. Looking back at me. And laughing. If it hadn't been for One-Eye . . . I'd have been caught just like Raven."

"Oh, my," I said softly, mind abuzz with the implications. "Awake? And working?"

"Yes. Don't talk about it. Not to anybody till you can tell Darling."

There was a hint of fatalism in him then. He doubted he would be around long. Scary. "One-Eye know?"

"I'll tell him. Got to make sure word gets back."

"Why not just tell us all?"

"Not Tracker. There's something wrong with Tracker. . . . Croaker. Another thing. The old-time wizard. He's in there, too."

"Bomanz?"

"Yes. Alive. Like he's frozen or something. Not dead, but not able to do anything. . . . The dragon . . ." He shut up.

Tracker arrived, carrying a brace of squirrels. We barely let them warm before we attacked them.

We rested a day before tackling the tamed lands. Henceforth it would be scurry from one smidgen of cover to the next, mouselike, by night. I wondered what the hell the point might be. The Plain of Fear might as well be in another world.

That night I had a golden dream.

I do not recall anything except that *she* touched me, and somehow tried to warn me. I think exhaustion more than my amulet blocked the message. Nothing stuck. I wakened retaining only a vague sense of having missed something critical.

End of the line. End of the game. Two hours out of the Great Forest I knew our time was approaching. Darkness was inadequate insulation. Nor were my amulets sufficient.

The Taken were in the air. I felt them on the prowl once it was too late to turn back. And they knew their quarry was afoot. We could hear the distant clamor of battalions moving to bar retreat into the forest.

My amulet warned me of the near passage of Taken repeatedly. When it did not, as it seemed not always to do—perhaps because the new Taken did not affect it— Toadkiller Dog gave warning. He could smell the bastards coming a league away.

The other amulet did help. That and Tracker's genius for laying a crooked trail.

But the circle closed. And closed. And we knew that it would not be long before there were no gaps through which we could slide.

"What do we do, Croaker?" One-Eye asked. His voice was shaky. He knew. But he wanted to be told. And I could neither give the order nor do it myself.

These men were my friends. We had been together all my adult life. I could not tell them to kill themselves. I could not cut them down.

But I could not allow them to be captured, either.

A vague notion formed. A foolish one, really. At first I thought it simple desperation silliness. What good?

Then something touched me. I gasped. The others felt it, too. Even Tracker and his mutt. They jumped as if stung. I gasped again. "It's her. She's here. Oh, damn." But that made up my mind. *I* might be able to buy time.

Before I could reflect and thus chicken out, I shucked my

amulets, shoved them into Goblin's hands, pushed our precious documents at One-Eye. "Thanks, guys. Take care. Maybe I'll see you."

"What the hell you doing?"

Bow in hand—the bow she had given me so long ago—I leaped into darkness. Soft protests pursued me. I caught the edge of Tracker asking what the hell was going on. Then I was away.

There was a road not far off, and a little sliver of moon up top. I got onto the one and trotted by the light of the other, pushing my tired old body to its limit, trying to build as big a margin as possible before the inevitable befell me.

She would protect me for a time. I hoped. And once caught, I might stall on behalf of the others.

I felt sorry for them, though. Neither Goblin nor One-Eye was strong enough to help carry Raven. Tracker could not manage alone. If they made it to the Plain of Fear, they would not be able to evade the unenviable duty of explaining everything to Darling.

I wondered if any of them would have what it took to finish Raven. . . . Bile rose. My legs were going watery. I tried to fill my mind with nothingness, stared at the road three steps ahead of my feet, puffed hard, kept on. Count steps. By hundreds, over and over.

A horse. I could steal a horse. I kept telling myself that, concentrated on that, damning the stitch in my side, till shadows loomed before me and imperials began to shout, and I hared off into a wheat field with the Lady's hounds abay behind me.

I nearly gave them the slip. Nearly. But then the shadow descended from the heavens. Air whistled past a carpet. And a moment later darkness devoured me.

I welcomed it as the end of my miseries, hoping it was permanent.

It was light when I regained consciousness. I was in a cold place, but all places are cold in the north countries. I was dry. For the first time in weeks, I was dry. I harkened back to my run and recalled the sliver of moon. A sky clear enough for a moon. Amazing.

I cracked one eye. I was in a room with walls of stone. It
had the look of a cell. Beneath me, a surface neither hard nor
wet. How long since I had lain on a dry bed? Blue Willy.

I became aware of an odor. Food! Hot food, on a platter
just inches from my head, atop a small stand. Some mess that
looked like overcooked stew. Gods, did it smell good!

I rose so swiftly my head spun. I almost passed out. Food!
The hell with anything else. I ate like the starved animal I
was.

I had not quite finished when the door slammed inward.
Exploded inward, ringing off the wall. A huge dark form
stamped through. For a moment I sat with spoon halfway
between bowl and mouth. This thing was human? It stepped
to one side, weapon ready.

Four imperials followed, but I hardly noticed, so taken was
I with the giant. Man, all right, but bigger than any I'd ever
seen. And looking lithe and spritely as an elf for all his size.

The imperials paired to either side of the doorway, presented arms.

"What?" I demanded, determined to go down with a
defiant grin. "No drumrolls? No trumpets?" I presumed I
was about to meet my captor.

I can call them when I call them. Whisper came through
the doorway.

I was more startled by seeing her than by the dramatic
advent of her giant thug. She was supposed to be holding the
western boundary of the Plain. . . . Unless . . . I could not
think it. But the worm of doubt gnawed anyway. I had been
out of touch a long time.

"Where are the documents?" she demanded, without
preamble.

A grin smeared my face. I had succeeded. They had not
caught the others. . . . But elation faded swiftly. There were
more imperials behind Whisper, and they bore a litter. Raven.
They dumped him roughly onto a cot opposite mine.

Their hospitality was not niggardly. It was a grand cell.
Plenty of room for the prisoner to stretch his legs.

I found my grin. "Now, you shouldn't ask questions like
that. Mama wouldn't like it. Remember how angry she became last time?"

Whisper was always a cool one. Even when she led the Rebel, she never let emotion get in the way. She did remind me, "Your death can be an unpleasant one, physician."

"Dead is dead."

A slow smile spread upon her colorless lips. She was not a lovely woman. That nasty smile did not improve her looks.

I got the message. Down in the dark inside me something howled and gibbered like a monkey getting roasted. I resisted its call to terror. Now, if ever there was one, was a time to act as a brother of the Black Company. I had to buy time. Had to give the others the longest head start possible.

She might have read my mind as she stood there staring, smiling. "They won't get far. They can hide from witchery, but they cannot hide from the hounds."

My heart sank.

As if cued, a messenger arrived. He whispered to Whisper. She nodded. Then she turned to me. "I go to collect them now. Think on the Limper in my absence. For once I have drained you of knowledge, I may deliver you to him." Smile again.

"You never were a nice lady," I said, but it came feebly and got said to her departing back. Her menagerie went with her.

I checked Raven. He seemed unchanged.

I lay on my cot, closed my eyes, tried to push everything out of my mind. It had worked once before when I needed contact with the Lady.

Where was she? I knew she was near enough to sense last night. But now? Was she playing some game?

But she had said no special consideration. . . . Still. There is consideration and consideration.

Chapter Thirty-Eight: THE FORTRESS AT DEAL

Bam! The old door trick. This time I had heard the man-mountain stomping down the hall, so I did not react except to ask, "Don't you ever knock, Bruno?"

No response. Till Whisper stepped inside. "Get up, physician."

I would have made a crude remark, but something in her voice chilled me beyond the chill due my straits. I rose.

She looked terrible. Not that she was much different physically. But something inside had gone dead and cold and frightened. "What was that thing?" she demanded.

I was baffled. "What thing?"

"The thing you were traveling with. Speak."

I could not, for I hadn't the slightest notion what she was blathering about.

"We caught up. Or my men did. I arrived only in time to count the bodies. What shreds twenty hounds and a hundred men in armor, in minutes, then disappears from mortal ken?"

Gods, One-Eye and Goblin must have outdone themselves. Still I did not speak.

"You came from the Barrowland. Where you were tampering. Did you call something forth?" She sounded as though she were musing. "It's time we found out. It's time we found out how tough you really are, soldier."

She faced the giant. "Bring him."

I gave it my best shot by playing my dirtiest. I pretended meek for just long enough to let him relax. Then I stomped his foot, running the side of my boot down his shin. Then I spun away and kicked at his crotch.

Guess I'm getting old and slow. Course, he was a lot faster than a man his size should be. He leaned back, caught my foot, and threw me across the room. Two imperials got me up and started dragging me. I went with the satisfaction of seeing the big man limp.

I tried a few more tricks, just to slow things up. They did little more than get me knocked around. The imperials strapped me down in a high-backed wooden chair in a room where Whisper had set up to practice her magicks. I saw nothing especially villainous. That only made the anticipation worse.

They got two or three good screams out of me and were working themselves up to get unpleasant when the tableau suddenly broke up. The imperials ripped me out of the chair, hustled me toward my cell. I was too foggy to wonder.

Till, in the hallway a few yards short of that cell, we encountered the Lady.

Yes. So. My message had gotten through. I'd thought the brief touch I'd made a response in wishful thinking at the time. But here she was.

The imperials ran. Is she that terrible to her own people?

Whisper stood her ground.

Whatever passed between them did so unspoken. Whisper helped me to my feet, pushed me into the cell. Her face was stone but her eyes were asmoulder.

"Curses. Foiled again," I croaked, and fell onto my cot.

It was plain daylight when the door closed. It was night when I wakened and she was standing over me, wearing her guise of beauty. She said, "I warned you."

"Yes." I tried to sit up. I had aches everywhere, both from maltreatment and from pushing an old body beyond its limits before my capture.

"Stay. I would not have come had my own interests not demanded it."

"I would not have called otherwise."

"Again you do me a favor."

"Only in the interest of self-preservation."

"You may, as they say, have jumped from the frying pan into the fire. Whisper lost many men today. To what?"

"I don't know. Goblin and One-Eye . . ." I shut up.

Damn groggy head. Damn sympathetic voice. Said too much already.

"It wasn't them. They haven't the skill to raise anything like that. I saw the bodies."

"I don't know, then."

"I believe you. Even so . . . I've seen wounds like those before. I'll show you before we leave for the Tower." Was there ever any doubt about that? "When you make your examination, reflect on the fact that the last time men died in such fashion my husband ruled the world."

None of this added up. But I was not worried about it. I was worried about my own future.

"*He* has begun to move already. Long before I expected. Will he never lie quietly and let me get on with my work?"

Some sums started toting. One-Eye saying something had gotten out. Raven having been caught because of it. . . . "Dumb shit Raven, you did it again." On his own, trying to care for Darling, he had damned near let the Dominator break through at Juniper. "What did you do this time?"

Why would it follow and protect One-Eye and them?

"This is Raven, then?"

Screwup Number Two for Croaker. Why can't I keep my big damned mouth shut?

She bent over him, rested a hand on his forehead. I watched from beneath my brows, unfocused. I could not look at her direct. She did have the power to sway stone.

"I will return soon," she said, heading for the door. "Fear not. You will be safe in my absence."

The door closed.

"Sure," I murmured. "Safe from Whisper, maybe. But how safe from you?" I looked around the room, wondering if I might end my life.

Whisper took me out to look at the carnage where hounds and imperials had overhauled One-Eye and Goblin. Not pleasant, I'll tell you. The last I saw the like was when we went up against the forvalaka in Beryl, ere we joined the Lady. I wondered if that monster was back and tracking One-Eye again. But he had slain it during the Battle at Charm. Hadn't he?

But the Limper survived. . . .

Hell, yes, he did. And two days after the Lady took off—I was imprisoned in the old fortress at Deal, I'd learned—he made an appearance. A little friendly visit, just for old time's sake.

I sensed his presence before I actually saw him. And terror nearly unmanned me.

How had he known? . . . Whisper. Almost certainly Whisper.

He came to my cell, buoyed on a miniature carpet. His name no longer really described him. He could not get around without that carpet. He was but the shadow of a being, human wreckage animated by sorcery and a mad, burning will.

He floated into my cell, hovered there considering me. I did my best to appear unintimidated, failed.

A ghost of a voice stirred the air. "Your time has come. It will be a prolonged and painful ending to your tale. And I will enjoy every moment."

"I doubt it." Had to keep up the show. "Mama won't like you messing with her prisoner."

"She is not here, physician." He began to drift backward. "We will begin soon. After time for reflection." A snatch of insane chuckle drifted in behind him. I am not sure if he or Whisper was the source. She was in the hallway, watching.

A voice said, "But she *is* here."

They froze. Whisper went pallid. Limper sort of folded in upon himself.

The Lady materialized out of nowhere, appearing first as golden sparkles. She said nothing more. The Taken did not speak either, for there was nothing they could say.

I wanted to interject one of my remarks, but the better part of valor prevailed. Instead, I tried to make myself small. A roach. Beneath notice.

But roaches get squished beneath the uncaring foot. . . .

The Lady finally spoke. "Limper, you were given an assignment. Nowhere in your brief is there an allowance for you to leave your command. Yet you have done so. Again. And the results are the same as when you slipped off to Roses to sabotage Soulcatcher."

Limper wilted even more.

That was one damned long time ago. One of our sneaky tricks on the Rebel of the day. What happened was, the Rebel attacked Limper's headquarters while he was away from his demense trying to undermine Soulcatcher.

So Darling was whooping it up on the Plain.

My spirits rose. It was the confirmation I'd had that the movement had not collapsed.

"Go," the Lady said. "And know this. There will be no more understanding. Henceforth we live by the iron rules as my husband made them. Next time will be the last time. For you or anyone else who serves me. Do you understand? Whisper? Limper?"

They understood. They were careful to say so in so many words.

There was communication there beneath the level of mere words, not accessible to me, for they went away absolutely convinced their continued existence depended upon unquestioning and unswerving obedience not only to the letter but the spirit of their orders. They went with a crushed air.

The Lady faded the moment my cell door closed.

She appeared in the flesh shortly before nightfall. Her anger still simmered. I gathered, from hearing guards gossip, that Whisper had been ordered back to the Plain, too. Things had turned bad out there. The Taken on the scene could not cope.

"Give them hell, Darling," I murmured. "Give them hell." I was working hard on resigning myself to whatever fate's horror shop stocked for me.

Guards brought me out of the cell soon after nightfall. They brought Raven, too. I asked no questions. They would not have answered.

The Lady's carpet rested in the fortress' main court. The soldiers placed Raven upon it, tied him down. A glum sergeant gestured for me to board. I did so, surprising him by knowing what to do. My heart was in my heels. I knew my destination.

The Tower.

I waited half an hour. Finally she came. She looked thoughtful. Even a little disturbed and uncertain. She took her place at the leading edge of the carpet. We rose.

Riding a windwhale is more comfortable and much less trying to the nerves. A windwhale has substance, has scale.

We rose perhaps a thousand feet and began running south. I doubt we were making more than thirty miles per hour. It would be a long flight, then, unless she chose to break it.

After an hour she faced me. I could barely discern her features. She said, "I visited the Barrowland, Croaker."

I did not respond, not knowing what was expected.

"What have you done? What have you people set free?"

"Nothing."

She looked at Raven. "Perhaps there is a way." After a time: "I know the thing that is loose. . . . Sleep, physician. We'll talk another time." And I went to sleep. And when I wakened I was in another cell. And knew, by the uniforms, that my new prison was the Tower at Charm.

Chapter Thirty-Nine: A GUEST AT CHARM

A colonel of the Lady's household force came for me. He was almost polite. Even back when, her troops never were sure of my status. Poor babies. I had no niche in their ordered and hierarchical universe.

The Colonel said, "She wants you now." He had a dozen men with him. They did not look like an honor guard. Neither did they act like executioners.

Not that it mattered. I would go if they had to carry me.

I left with a backward glance. Raven was holding his own.

The Colonel left me at a doorway into the inner Tower, the Tower inside the Tower, into which few men pass, and from which fewer return. "March," he said. "I hear you've done this before. You know the drill."

I stepped through the doorway. When I looked back I saw only stone wall. For a moment I became disoriented. That passed and I was in another place. And she was there, framed by what appeared to be a window, though her parts of the Tower are completely ensheathed within the rest.

"Come here."

I went. She pointed. I looked out that non-window on a burning city. Taken soared above it, hurling magicks that died. Their target was a phalanx of windwhales that were devastating the city.

Darling was riding one of the whales. They were staying within her null, where they were invulnerable.

"They are not, though," the Lady said, reading my thoughts. "Mortal weapons will reach them. And your bandit girl. But it does not matter. I've decided to suspend operations."

I laughed. "Then we've won."

I do believe that was the first time I ever saw her piqued with me. A mistake, mocking her. It could make her reassess emotionally a decision made strategically.

"You have won nothing. If that is the perception a shift of focus will generate, then I will not break off. I will adjust the campaign's focus instead."

Damn you, Croaker. Learn to keep your big goddamn mouth shut around people like this. You will jack-jaw your way right into a meat grinder.

After regaining her self-control, she faced me. The Lady, from just two feet away. "Be sarcastic in your writing if you like. But when you speak, be prepared to pay a price."

"I understand."

"I thought you would." She faced the scene again. In that far city—it looked like Frost—a flaming windwhale fell after being caught in a storm of shafts hurled by ballistae bigger than any I'd ever seen. Two could play the suck-in game. "How well did your translations go?"

"What?"

"The documents you found in the Forest of Cloud, gave to my late sister Soulcatcher, took from her again, gave to your friend Raven, and took from him in turn. The papers you thought would give you the tool of victory."

"*Those* documents. Ha. Not well at all."

"You couldn't have. What you sought isn't there."

"But . . ."

"You were misled. Yes. I know. Bomanz put them together, so they must hold my true name. Yes? But that has been eradicated—except, perhaps, in the mind of my husband." She became remote suddenly. "The victory at Juniper cost."

"He learned the lesson Bomanz did too late."

"So. You noticed. *He* has information enough to pry an answer from what happened. . . . No. My name isn't there. *His* is. *That* was why they so excited my sister. She saw an opportunity to supplant us both. She knew me. We were children together, after all. And protected from one another only by the most tangled web that could be woven. When she enlisted you in Beryl she had no greater ambition than to undermine me. But when you delivered those documents . . ."

She was thinking aloud as much as explaining.

I was stricken by a sudden insight. "*You* don't know his name!"

"It was never a love match, physician. It was the shakiest of alliances. Tell me. How do I get those papers?"

"You don't."

"Then we all lose. This is true, Croaker. While we argue and while our respective allies strive to slash one another's throats, the enemy of us all is shedding his chains. All this dying will be for naught if the Dominator wins free."

"Destroy him."

"That's impossible."

"In the town where I was born there is a folk tale about a man so mighty he dared mock the gods. In the end his might proved sheer hubris, for there is one against whom even the gods are powerless."

"What's the point?"

"To twist an old saw, death conquers all. Not even the Dominator can wrestle death and win every time."

"There are ways," she admitted. "But not without those papers. You will return to your quarters now, and reflect. I will speak to you again."

I was dismissed that suddenly. She faced the dying city. Suddenly, I knew my way out. A powerful impulse drove me toward the door. A moment of dizziness and I was outside.

The Colonel came puffing along the corridor. He returned me to my cell.

I planted myself on my bunk and reflected, as ordered.

There was evidence enough that the Dominator was stirring, but . . . The business about the documents not holding the lever we had counted on—that was the shocker. That I had to swallow or reject, and my choice might have critical repercussions.

She was leading me for her own ends. Of course. I conceived numerous possibilities, none pleasant, but all making a sort of sense. . . .

She'd said it. If the Dominator broke out, we were all in the soup, good guys and bad.

I fell asleep. There were dreams, but I do not recall them. I awakened to find a hot meal freshly delivered, sitting atop a desk that had not been there before. On that desk was a generous supply of writing materials.

She expected me to resume my Annals.

I devoured half the food before noting Raven's absence. The old nerves began to rattle. Why was he gone? Where to? What use did she have for him? Leverage?

Time is funny inside the Tower.

The usual Colonel arrived as I finished eating. The usual soldiers accompanied him. He announced, "She wants you again."

"Already? I just came back from there."

"Four days ago."

I touched my cheek. I have been affecting only a partial beard of late. My face was brushy. So. One long sleep. "Any chance I could get a razor?"

The Colonel smiled thinly. "What do you think? A barber can come in. Will you come along?"

I got a vote? Of course not. I followed rather than be dragged.

The drill was the same. I found her at a window again. The scene showed some corner of the Plain where one of Whisper's fortifications was besieged. It had no heavy ballistae. A windwhale hovered overhead, keeping the garrison in hiding. Walking trees were dismantling the outer wall by the simple mechanism of growing it to death. The way a jungle destroys an abandoned city, though ten thousand times faster than the unthinking forest.

"The entire desert has risen against me," she said. "Whisper's outposts have suffered an annoying variety of attacks."

"I suspect your intrusions are resented. I thought you were going to disengage."

"I tried. Your deaf peasant isn't cooperating. Have you been thinking?"

"I've been sleeping is what I've been doing. As you know."

"Yes. So. There were matters which demanded attention. Now I can devote myself to the problem at hand." The look in her eye made me want to run. . . . She gestured. I froze. She told me to back up, to sit in a nearby chair. I sat, unable to shake the spell, though I knew what was coming.

She stood before me, one eye closed. The open eye grew bigger and bigger, reached out, devoured me. . . .

I think I screamed.

The moment had been inevitable since my capture, though I had held a foolish hope otherwise. Now she would drain my mind like a spider drains a fly. . . .

I recovered in my cell, feeling as though I had been to hell and back. My head throbbed. It was a major undertaking to rise and stagger to my medical kit, which had been returned after my captors removed the lethals. I prepared an infusion of willow inner bark, which took forever because I had no fire over which to heat the water.

Someone came in as I nursed and cursed the first weak, bitter cup. I did not recognize him. He seemed surprised to see me up. "Hello," he said. "Quick recovery."

"Who the hell are you?"

"Physician. Supposed to check you once an hour. You weren't expected to recover for a long time. Headache?"

"Goddamn well right."

"Cranky. Good." He placed his bag next to my kit, which he glanced through as he opened his. "What did you take?"

I told him, asked, "What do you mean, good?"

"Sometimes they come out listless. Never recover."

"Yeah?" I thought about whipping him just for the hell of it. Just to vent my spleen. But what was the point? Some guard would come bouncing in and make my pains the worse. Too much like work, anyway.

"Are you something special?"

"*I* think so."

A flicker of a smile. "Drink this. Better than the bark tea." I downed the drink he offered. "*She* is most concerned. Never before have I seen her care what became of one subjected to the deep probe."

"How about that?" I was having trouble keeping my foul mood. The drink he'd given me was good stuff, and fast. "What was that concoction? I could use it by the barrel."

"It's addictive. Rendered from the juice of the top four leaves of the parsifal plant."

"Never heard of it."

"Rather scarce." He was examining me at the time. "Grows in some place called the Hollow Hills. The natives use it as a narcotic."

The Company had been through those terrible hills once upon a time. "Didn't know there *were* natives."

"They're as scarce as the plant. There's been talk in council of growing it commercially after the fighting ends. As a medicinal." He clucked his tongue, which reminded me of the toothless ancient who had taught me medicine. Funny. I hadn't thought of him in ages.

Funnier still, all sorts of old odd memories were streaking to the surface, like bottom fish scared toward the light. The Lady had stirred my mind good.

I did not pursue his remark about raising the weed commercially, though that was at odds with my notion of the Lady. The black hearts don't worry about relieving pain.

"How do you feel about her?"

"The Lady? Right now? Not very charitable. How about you?"

He ignored that. "She expects to see you as soon as you recover."

"Does a bear shit in the woods?" I countered. "I get the idea I'm not exactly a prisoner. How about I get some air on the roof? Can't hardly run away from there."

"I'll see if it's permitted. Meantime, take some exercise here."

Hah. The only exercise I get is jumping to conclusions. I just wanted to get somewhere outside four walls. "Am I still among the living?" I asked when he finished examining me.

"For the time being. Though with your attitude I am amazed you survived in an outfit like yours."

"They love me. Worship me. Wouldn't harm a hair on my head." His mention of the outfit put my mood on the downswing. I asked, "You know how long it's been since I was captured?"

"No. I think you've been here more than a week. Could be longer."

So. Guess at least ten days since my capture. Give the boys the benefit of the doubt, have them moving light and hard, and they had maybe covered four hundred miles. Just one giant step out of many. Crap.

Stalling was pointless now. The Lady knew everything I did. I wondered if any of it had been of any use. Or much of a surprise.

"How is my friend?" I asked, suffering a sudden guilt.

"I don't know. He was moved north because his connection with his spirit was becoming attenuated. I'm sure the subject will arise when next you visit the Lady. I'm finished. Have a nice stay."

"Sarky bastard."

He grinned as he left.

Must run in the profession.

The Colonel stepped in a few minutes later. "I hear you want to go to the roof."

"Yeah."

"Inform the sentry when you would like to go." He had something else on his mind. After a pause he asked, "Isn't there any military discipline in your outfit?"

He was irked because I had not been sirring him. Various smart remarks occurred. I stifled them. My status might not remain enigmatic. "Yes. Though not so much as in earlier days. Not enough of us left since Juniper to make that stuff worth the trouble."

Sly shot, Croaker. Put them on the defensive. Tell them the

Company fell to its current pitiful state laboring for the Lady. Remind them that it was the empire's satraps who turned first. That must be common knowledge by now, among the officer corps. Something they should think about occasionally.

"Pity, that," the Colonel said.

"You my personal watchdog?"

"Yes. She sets great store by you for some reason."

"I wrote her a poem once," I lied. "I also got the goods on her."

He frowned, decided I was bullshitting.

"Thanks," I said, by way of extending an olive branch. "I'll write for a while before I go." I was way behind. Except for a bit at Blue Willy I had done nothing but jot an occasional note since leaving the Plain.

I wrote till cramps compelled me to stop. Then I ate, for a guard brought a meal as I sanded my last sheet. Done gobbling, I went to the door, told the lad there I was ready to go topside. When he opened up I discovered I was not locked in.

But where the hell could I go if I got out? Silly even thinking of escape.

I had a feeling I was about to take on the official historian job. Like it or no, it would be the least of many evils.

Some tough decisions stared me in the eye. I wanted time to think them over. The Lady understood. Certainly she had the power and talent to be more foresighted than a physician who had spent six years out of touch.

Sunset. Fire in the west, clouds in raging flame. The sky a wealth of unusual colors. A chill breeze from the north, just enough to shiver and refresh. My guardian stayed well away, permitting the illusion of freedom. I walked to the northern parapet.

There was little evidence of the great battle fought below. Where once trenches, palisades, earthworks, and siege engines had stood, and burned, and tens of thousands had died, there was parkland. A single black stone stella marked the site, five hundred yards from the Tower.

The crash and roar returned. I remembered the Rebel horde, relentless, like the sea, wave after wave; smashing upon unyielding cliffs of defenders. I recalled the feuding Taken, their fey and fell deaths, the wild and terrible sorceries. . .

"It was a battle of battles, was it not?"

I did not turn as she joined me. "It was. I never did it justice."

"They will sing of it." She glanced up. Stars had begun to appear. In the twilight her face seemed pale and strained. Never before had I seen her in any but the most self-possessed mood.

"What is it?" Now I did turn, and saw a group of soldiers some distance away, watching, either awed or aghast.

"I have performed a divination. Several, in fact, for I did not get satisfactory results."

"And?"

"Perhaps I got no results at all."

I waited. You do not press the most powerful being in the world. That she was on the verge of confiding in a mortal was stunning enough.

"All is flux. I divined three possible futures. We are headed for a crisis, a history-shaping hour."

I turned slightly toward her. Violet light shaded her face. Dark hair tumbled down over one cheek. It was not artifice, for once, and the impulse to touch, to hold, perhaps to comfort, was powerful. "Three futures?"

"Three. I could not find my place in any."

What do you say at a moment like that? That maybe there was an error? *You* accuse the Lady of making a mistake.

"In one, your deaf child triumphs. But it is the least likely chance, and she and all hers perish gaining the victory. In another, my husband breaks the grasp of the grave and reestablishes his Domination. That darkness lasts ten thousand years. In the third vision, he is destroyed forever and all. It is the strongest vision, the demanding vision. But the price is great. . . . Are there gods, Croaker? I never believed in gods."

"I don't know, Lady. No religion I ever encountered made any sense. None are consistent. Most gods are megalomaniacs and paranoid psychotics by their worshipers' description. I don't see how they could survive their own insanity. But it's not impossible that human beings are incapable of interpreting a power so much greater than themselves. Maybe religions are twisted and perverted shadows of truth. Maybe there *are* forces which shape the world. I myself have never understood why, in a universe so vast, a god would *care* about something so trivial as worship or human destiny."

"When I was a child . . . my sisters and I had a teacher."

Did I pay attention? You bet your sweet ass I did. I was ears from my toenails to the top of my pointy head. "A teacher?"

"Yes. He argued that *we* are the gods, that we create our own destiny. That what we are determines what will become of us. In a peasantlike vernacular, we all paint ourselves into corners from which there is no escape simply by being ourselves and interacting with other selves."

"Interesting."

"Well. Yes. There is a god of sorts, Croaker. Do you know? Not a mover and shaker, though. Simply a negator. An ender of tales. He has a hunger than cannot be sated. The universe itself will slide down his maw."

"Death?"

"I do not want to die, Croaker. All that I am shrieks against the unrighteousness of death. All that I am, was, and probably will be, is shaped by my passion to evade the end of me." She laughed quietly, but there was a thread of hysteria there. She gestured, indicating the shadowed killing ground below. "I would have built a world in which I was safe. And the cornerstone of my citadel would have been death."

The end of the dream was drawing close. I could not imagine a world without me in it, either. And the inner me was outraged. Is outraged. I have no trouble imagining someone becoming obsessed with escaping death. "I understand."

"Maybe. We're all equals at the dark gate, no? The sands run for us all. Life is but a flicker shouting into the jaws of eternity. But it seems so damned unfair!"

Old Father Tree entered my thoughts. *He* would perish in time. Yes. Death is insatiable and cruel.

"Have you reflected?" she asked.

"I think so. I'm no necromancer. But I've seen roads I don't want to walk."

"Yes. You're free to go, Croaker."

Shock. Even my heels tingled with disbelief. "Say what?"

"You're free. The Tower gate is open. You need but walk out it. But you're also free to remain, to reenter the lists in the struggle that envelopes us all."

There was almost no light left except for some sun hitting very high clouds. Against the deep indigo in the east a squadron of bright pinpricks moved westward. They seemed headed toward the Tower.

I gabbled something that made no sense.

"Will she, nihil she, the Lady of Charm is at war with her husband once more," she said. "And till that struggle is lost or won, there is no other. You see the Taken returning. The armies of the east are marching toward the Barrowland. Those beyond the Plain have been ordered to withdraw to garrisons farther east. Your deaf child is in no danger unless she comes looking for it. There is an armistice. Perhaps eternally." Weak smile. "If there is no Lady, there is no one for the White Rose to battle."

She left me then, in total confusion, and went to greet her champions. The carpets came down out of the darkness, settling like autumn leaves. I moved a little nearer till my personal guardian indicated that my relationship with the Lady was insufficiently close to permit eavesdropping.

The wind grew more chill, blowing out of the north. And I wondered if it might not be autumn for us all.

Chapter Forty: MAKING UP MY MIND

She never once demanded anything. Even her hints were so oblique they left everything to me to work out. Two days after our evening on the ramparts I asked the Colonel if I might see her. He said he would ask. I suspect he was under instructions. Otherwise there would have been arguments.

Another day passed before he came to say the Lady had time for me.

I closed my inkwell, cleaned my quill, and rose. "Thank you." He looked at me oddly. "Is something wrong?"

"No. Just . . ."

I understood. "I don't know either. I'm sure she has some special use for me."

That brightened the Colonel's day. That he could comprehend.

The usual routine. This time I entered her demesne as she stood at a window opening on a world of wet gloom. Grey rain, choppy brown water, and hulking to the left, shapes barely discernible, trees clinging precariously to a high river bank. Cold and misery leaked out of that portraiture. It had a too familiar smell.

"The Great Tragic River," she said. "In full flood. But it's always in flood, isn't it?" She beckoned. I followed. Since my last visit a large table had been added. Atop it was a miniature of the Barrowland, a representation so good it was spooky. You almost expected to see little Guards scurrying around the compound.

"You see?" she asked.

"No. Though I've been there twice, I'm not familiar with

THE WHITE ROSE 223

much but the town and the compound. What am I supposed to see?''

"The river. Your friend Raven evidently recognized its import." With one delicate finger she sketched a loop well to the east of the river's course, which curved into the ridge where we had camped.

"At the time of my triumph in Juniper the river's bed lay here. A year later the weather turned. The river flooded continuously. And crept this way. Today it's devouring this ridge. I examined it myself. The ridge is entirely earthen, without bones of stone. It won't last. Once it goes, the river will cut into the Barrowland. All the spells of the White Rose won't keep it from opening the Great Barrow. Each fetish swept away will make it that much easier for my husband to rise.''

I grunted. "Against Nature there is no defense."

"There is. If one foresees. The White Rose did not. I did not when I attempted to bind him more securely. Now it's too late. So. You wanted to speak to me?''

"Yes. I have to leave the Tower.''

"So. You didn't have to come to me about that. You're free to stay or go.''

"I'm going because there're things I have to do. As you well know. If I walk, I'll probably get them done too late. It's a long hike to the Plain. Not to mention risky. I want to beg transportation.''

She smiled, and this smile was genuine, radiant, subtly different from previous smiles. "Good. I thought you would see where the future lies. How soon can you be ready?''

"Five minutes. There is one question. Raven.''

"Raven has been hospitalized at the compound at the Barrowland. Nothing can be done for him right now. Every effort will be made when an opportunity arises. Sufficient?''

I could not argue, of course.

"Good. Transport will be available. You will have a unique chauffeur. The Lady herself.''

"I . . .''

"I, too, have been thinking. My best next step is to meet your White Rose. I'm going with you.''

After gulping quarts of air, I managed, "They'd jump all over you."

"Not if they don't know me. They wouldn't, unless they were told."

Well, no one was likely to recognize her. I am unique in having met her and lived to brag on it. But . . . Gods, the heaps and bales of *buts*. "If you entered the null, all your spells would fall apart."

"No. New spells wouldn't work. Spells in place would be safe."

I did not understand and said so.

"A simple glamor will fade on entering the null. It is being actively maintained. A spell which changes and leaves changed, but which isn't active on entering the null, won't be affected."

Something off in the badlands of my mind tickled me. I could not run it down. "If you turned into a frog and hopped in there, you'd stay a frog?"

"If the transformation was actual and not just an illusion."

"I see." I hung a red flag on that, told me to worry it later.

"I will become a companion acquired along the way. Say, someone who can help with your documents."

There had to be levels of deceit. Or something. I could not imagine her putting her life into my hands. I do believe I gawked.

She nodded. "You begin to understand."

"You trust me too much."

"I know you better than you know yourself. You're an honorable man, by your own lights, with enough cynicism to believe there can be a lesser of two evils. You *have* been under the Eye."

I shuddered.

She did not apologize. We both knew an apology would be false.

"Well?" she asked.

"I'm not sure why you want to do this. It makes no sense."

"There is a new situation in the world. Once there were only two poles, your peasant girl and I, with a line of conflict drawn between. But that which stirs in the north adds another point. It can be seen as a lengthening of the line, with my point near the middle, or as a triangle. The point that is my husband intends destroying both your White Rose and myself. I submit that she and I ought to eliminate the greater danger before . . ."

"Enough. I see. But I don't see Darling being that pragmatic. There's a lot of hatred in her."

"Perhaps. But it's worth a try. Will you help?"

Having been within a stone's throw of the old darkness and seen the ghosts astalk on the Barrowland, yes, I would do most anything to keep that dread spook from shedding his grave. But how, how, how trust *her*?

She did that trick they all have, of seeming to read my mind. "You will have me within the null."

"Right. I'll need to think some more."

"Take your time. I can't leave for some time." I suspect she wanted to establish safeguards against a palace revolution.

Chapter Forty-One: A TOWN CALLED HORSE

Fourteen days passed before we took air for Horse, a modest town lying between the Windy Country and the Plain of Fear, about a hundred miles west of the latter. Horse is a caravan stage for those traders mad enough to traipse through those two wildernesses. Of late, the city has been the logistical headquarters for Whisper's operations. What skeleton forces were not on the road to the Barrowland were in garrison there.

Damned northbound fools were going to get wet.

We drifted in after an eventless passage, me with eyes agog. Despite the removal of vast armies, Whisper's base was an anthive swirling around newly created carpets.

They came in a dozen varieties. In one field I saw a W formation of five monsters, each a hundred yards long and forty wide. A wood and metal jungle topped each. Elsewhere, other carpets in unusual shapes sat upon ground that looked to have been graded. Most were far longer than they were wide and bigger than the traditional. All had a variety of appurtenances, and all were enveloped in a light copper cage.

"What is all that?" I asked.

"Adaptation to enemy tactics. Your peasant girl isn't the only one who can change methods." She stepped down, stretched. I did the same. Those hours in the air leave you stiff. "We may get the chance to test them, despite my having backed off the Plain."

"What?"

"A large Rebel force is headed for Horse. Several thousand men and everything the desert has to offer."

Several thousand men? Where did they come from? Had things changed that much?

"They have." That damned mind-reading trick again. "The cities I abandoned poured men into her forces."

"What did you mean, test?"

"I'm willing to stop fighting. But I won't run away from a fight. If she persists in heading west, I'll show her that, null or no null, she can be crushed."

We were near one of the new carpets. I ambled over. In shape it was like a boat, about fifty feet long. It had real seats. Two faced forward, one aft. In front there was a small ballista. Aft there was a much heavier engine. Clamped to the carpet's sides and underbelly were eight spears thirty feet long. Each had a bulge the size of a nail keg five feet behind its head. Everything was painted blacker than the Dominator's heart. This boat-carpet had fins like a fish. Some humorist had painted eyes and teeth up front.

Others nearby followed similar designs, though different artisans had followed different muses in crafting the flying boats. One, instead of fish fins, had what looked like round, translucent, whisper thin dried seed pods fifteen feet across.

The Lady had no time to let me inspect her equipment and no inclination to let me wander around unchaperoned. Not as a matter of trust, but of protection. I might suffer a fatal accident if I did not stay in her shadow.

All the Taken were in Horse. Even my oldest friends.

Bold, bold Darling. Audacity. Becoming her signature, that. She had the entire strength of the Plain just twenty miles from Horse, and she was closing in. Her advance was ponderous, though, limited to the speed of the walking trees.

We went out onto the field where the carpets waited, arranged in formal array around the monsters I had spotted first. The Lady said, "I planned a small demonstration raid on your headquarters. But this will be more convincing, I think."

Men were busy around the carpets. The big ones they were loading with huge pieces of pottery which looked like those big urn-planters with the little cup-holes in the upper half for small plants. They were fifteen feet tall; the planter sites were sealed with paraffin, and the bottom boasted a twenty foot pole with a crossbar on its end. Scores were being mounted in racks.

I did a fast count. More carpets than Taken. "All these are going up? How?"

"Benefice will handle the big ones. Like the Howler before him, he has an outstanding capacity for managing a large carpet. The other four bigs will be slaved to his. Come. This one is ours."

I said something intelligent like, "Urk?!"

"I want you to see it."

"We might be recognized."

Taken circled the long, skinny boat-carpets. Soldiers were aboard them, in the second and third seats. The men facing aft checked their ballistae, munitions, cranked a spring-powered device apparently meant to help restretch bowstrings after missiles were discharged. I could see no apparent task assigned the men in the middle seats. "What's the cagework for?"

"You'll learn soon enough."

"But . . ."

"Come to it fresh, Croaker. Without preconceptions."

I followed her around our carpet. I do not know what she

checked, but she seemed satisfied. The men who had prepared it were pleased by her nod.

"Up, Croaker. Into the second seat. Fasten yourself securely.
It'll get exciting before it's over."

Oh yeah.

"We're the pathfinders," she said as she buckled into the
front seat. A grizzled old sergeant took the rear position. He
looked at me doubtfully, but said nothing. The Taken assumed the front seat aboard every carpet. The bigs, as the
Lady called them, had crews of four. Benefice rode the carpet
at the center point of the W.

"Ready?" the Lady shouted.

"Right."

"Aye," the sergeant said.

Our carpet began to move.

Lumbering is the only word to describe the first few seconds.
The carpet was heavy and, till it managed some forward
motion, did not want to lift.

The Lady looked back and grinned as the earth dropped
away. She was enjoying herself. She began shouting instructions which explained the bewildering bunch of pedals and
levers surrounding me.

Push and pull on these two in combination and the carpet
began to roll around its long axis. Twist those and it turned
right or left. The idea was to use combinations somehow to
guide the craft.

"What for?" I shouted into the wind. The words ripped
away. We had donned goggles which protected our eyes but
did nothing for the rest of our faces. I expected a case of
windburn before the game was played out.

We were two thousand feet up, five miles from Horse, well
ahead of the Taken. I could see traces of dust raised by
Darling's army. Again I shouted, "What for?"

The bottom fell out.

The Lady had extinguished the spells which made the
carpet go. "That's why. You'll fly the boat when we hit the
null."

What the hell?

She gave me a half dozen shots at getting the hang of it,

and I did see the theory, before she whipped toward the Rebel army.

We circled once, at screaming speed, well outside the null. I was astounded at what Darling had put together. About fifty windwhales, including some monsters over a thousand feet long. Mantas by the hundred. A vast wedge of walking trees. Battalions of human soldiers. Menhirs by the hundred, flickering around the walking trees, shielding them. Thousands of things that leaped and hopped and glided and flopped and flew. So gruesome and wondrous a sight.

On the westward leg of our circle I spied the imperial force, two thousand men in a phalanx on the foreslope of a ridge a mile ahead of the Rebel. A joke, them standing against Darling.

A few bold mantas cruised the edge of the null, sniping with bolts that fell short or just missed. I judged Darling herself to be aboard a windwhale about a thousand feet up. She had grown stronger, for her null's diameter had expanded since my departure from the Plain. All that bewildering Rebel array marched within its protection.

The Lady had called us pathfinders. Our carpet was not equipped like the others, but I did not know what she meant. Till she did it.

We climbed straight up. Little black balls trailing streamers of red or blue smoke scattered behind us, shoveled overboard hastily by the old sergeant. Must have been three hundred. The smoke balls scattered, hovered just feet short of the null. So. Markers by which the Taken could navigate.

And here they came. Way up, the smaller surrounding the W formation of bigs.

The men on the bigs began releasing the giant pots. Down, down, down went a score. We followed, sliding along outside the smudge pots. As they plummeted, the flowerpots turned pole-downward. Mantas and whales slid out of their way.

When the pole hit ground it drove a plunger. The paraffin seals burst. Liquid squirted. The plunger hit a striker. The fluid ignited. Gouts of fire. And when that fire reached something inside the pots, they exploded. Shards cut down men and monsters.

I watched the blooming of those flowers of fire, aghast.

Above, the Taken wheeled for a second pass. There was no magic in this. The null was useless.

The second fall drew lightning from whales and mantas. Their first few successes cured them, though, for the pots they hit exploded in the air. Mantas went down. One whale was in grave trouble till others maneuvered overhead and sprayed it with ballast water.

The Taken made a third pass, again dropping pots. They would hammer Darling's troops into slime unless she did something.

She went up after the Taken.

The smoke pots slid around the flanks of the null, outlining it completely.

The Lady climbed at shrieking speed.

The W of bigs went away. The smaller carpets took on more altitude. The Lady brought us into position behind Whisper and the Limper. Clearly, she had anticipated Darling's response.

My emotions were mixed, to say the least.

Whisper's carpet tipped its nose downward. Limper followed. Then the Lady. Others of the Taken followed us.

Whisper dove toward one especially monstrous windwhale. Faster and faster she flew. Three hundred yards from the null two thirty-foot spears ripped away from her carpet, impelled by sorcery. When they hit the null they continued on in a normal ballistic trajectory.

Whisper made no effort to avoid the null. Into it she plunged, the man in her second seat guiding the carpet's fall with those fish fins.

Whisper's spears struck near the windwhale's head. Both burst into flames.

Fire is anathema to those monsters, for the gas that lifts them is violently explosive.

The Limper trailed Whisper with élan. He loosed two spears outside the null and another two inside, just dropped as his second-seat man took the carpet within inches of the windwhale.

Only one lance failed to strike home.

The whale had five fires burning upon its back.

Storms of lightning crackled round Whisper and Limper.

Then *we* hit the null. Our buoying spells failed. Panic snatched at me. Up to me? . . .

We were headed for the burning whale. I jerked and banged and kicked levers.

"Not so violently!" the Lady yelled. "Smoothly. Gently."

I got it in hand as the whale roared upward past us.

Lightning crackled. We passed between two smaller whales. They missed us. The Lady discharged her little ballista. Its bolt struck one of those monsters. What the hell was the point? I wondered. That was not a bee sting to one of them.

But that quarrel had a wire attached, running off a reel. . . .

Wham!

I was blinded momentarily. My hair crackled. Direct hit from a manta bolt. . . . We're dead, I thought.

The metal cage surrounding us absorbed the lightning's energy and passed it along the unwinding wire.

A manta was on our tail, only yards behind. The sergeant ripped off a shaft. It took our pursuer under the wing. The beast began to slide and flutter like a one-winged butterfly.

"Watch where we're going!" the Lady yelled. I turned around. A windwhale back rushed toward us. Fledgling mantas scurried in panic. Rebel bowmen threw up a barrage of arrows.

I hit and yanked every damned lever and pedal, and pissed my pants. Maybe that did it. We scraped the thing's flank, but did not crash.

Now the damned carpet began spinning and tumbling. Earth, sky, windwhales swirled around us. In one glimpse, way up, I saw a windwhale's side explode, saw the monster fold in the middle, raining gobbets of fire. Two more whales trailed smoke. . . . But it was a picture there and gone in a moment. I could find none of it when the carpet again rolled to where I could see the sky.

We began our plunge from high enough that I had time to calm down. I fiddled with levers and pedals, got some of the wild spin off. . . .

Then it did not matter. We were out of the null and it was the Lady's craft again.

I looked back to see how the sergeant was. He gave me a dirty look, shook his head pityingly.

The look the Lady gave me was not encouraging either.

We climbed and moved westward. The Taken assembled, observed the results of their attack.

Only the one windwhale was destroyed. The other two managed to get under friends who doused them with ballast water. Even so, the survivors were demoralized. They had done the Taken no injury at all.

Still, they came on.

This time the Taken dropped to the surface and attacked from below, building speed from several miles away, then curving up through the null. I maneuvered between whales with a more delicate hand but still fell dangerously near the ground.

"What are we doing this for?" I yelled. We were not attacking; we were just following Whisper and Limper.

"For the hell of it. For the sheer hell of it. And so you can write about it."

"I'll fake it."

She laughed.

We went high and circled.

Darling took the whales back down. That second pass slew two more. Down low the Taken could not throw themselves all the way through the null. None but Limper, that is. He played the daredevil. He backed off five miles and built a tremendous velocity before hitting the null.

He made that pass while the bigs were dropping the last of their pots.

I've never heard Darling called stupid. She did not do the stupid thing this time.

Despite all the flash and excitement, it was clear that she could, if she wanted, press on to Horse. The Taken had expended most of their munitions. Limper and the bigs were headed back to rearm. The others circled. . . . Horse was Darling's if she was willing to pay the price.

She decided it was too dear.

Wise choice. My guess is, it would have cost her half her force. And windwhales are too rare to give up for a prize so insignificant.

She turned back.

The Lady broke away and let her go, though she could have maintained the attacks almost indefinitely.

We touched down. I scrambled over the side even before the Lady and in a calculated, melodramatic gesture, kissed the ground. She laughed.

She had had a great time.

"You let them go."

"I made my point."

"She'll shift tactics."

"Of course she will. But for the moment the hammer is in my hand. By not using it I've told her something. She'll have thought it over by the time we get there."

"I suppose."

"You didn't do badly for a novice. Go get drunk or something. And stay out of Limper's way."

"Yeah."

What I did was go to the quarters assigned me and try to stop shaking.

Chapter Forty-Two:
HOMECOMING

The Lady and I entered the Plain of Fear twelve days after the aerial skirmish near Horse. We traveled on horseback, on second-grade nags, along the old trade trail the denizens of the Plain respect with free passage most of the time. Clad in castoffs, for the trail, the Lady was no longer a beauty. No kick-out-of-bed dog, but no eye-catcher.

We entered the Plain aware that by a pessimistic estimate, we had about three months before the Great Tragic River opened the Great Barrow.

The menhirs noted our presence immediately. I sensed them out there, observing. I had to point it out. For this venture the Lady had schooled herself to eschew anything but the most direct and raw sensory input. She would train herself to mortal ways during our ride so she would make no mistake once we reached the Hole.

The woman has guts.

I guess anyone willing to play heads-up power games with the Dominator has to have them.

I ignored the lurking menhirs and concentrated on explaining the ways of the Plain, revealing the thousand little traps that, at the least, might betray the Lady. It was what a man would do on bringing a newcomer to the land. It would not seem unusual.

Three days into the Plain we narrowly missed being caught in a change storm. She was awed. "What was that?" she asked.

I explained the best I could. Along with all the speculations. She, of course, had heard it all before. But seeing is believing, as they say.

Not long after that we came on the first of the coral reefs, which meant we were in the deep Plain, among the great strangenesses. "What name will you use?" I asked. "I better get used to it."

"I think Ardath." She grinned.

"You have a cruel sense of humor."

"Perhaps."

I do believe she was having fun at pretending to be ordinary. Like some great lord's lady slumming. She even took her turns at the cook fire. To my stomach's despair.

I wondered what the menhirs made of our relationship. No matter the pretense, there was a brittleness, a formality, that was hard to overcome. And the best we could fake was a partnership, which I am certain they found strange. When did man and woman travel together thus, without sharing bedroll and such?

The question of pursuing verisimilitude that far never arose. And just as well. My panic, my terror, at the suggestion would have been such that nothing else would have arisen.

Ten miles from the Hole we breasted a hill and encountered

a menhir. It stood beside the way, twenty feet of weird stone, doing nothing. The Lady asked in touristy fashion, "Is that one of the talking stones?"

"Yep. Hi, rock. I'm home."

Old rock didn't have anything to say. We passed on. When I looked back it was gone.

Little had changed. As we crested the last ridge, though, we saw a forest of walking trees crowding the creek. A stand of menhirs both living and dead guarded the crossing. The backwards camel-centaurs gamboled among them. Old Father Tree stood by himself, tinkling, though there was not a breath of wind. Up high, a single buzzardlike avian soared against shattered clouds, watching. One or another of its kind had followed us for days. Of a human presence there was no sign. What did Darling do with her army? She could not pack those men into the Hole.

For a moment I was frightened that I had returned to an untenanted keep. Then, as we splashed across the creek, Elmo and Silent stepped out of the coral.

I dove off my animal and gathered them into a monster hug. They returned it, and in best Black Company tradition did not ask a single question.

"Goddamn," I said. "Goddamn, it's good to see you. I heard you guys was wiped out out west somewhere."

Elmo looked at the Lady with just the slightest hint of curiosity.

"Oh. Elmo. Silent. This is Ardath."

She smiled. "So pleased to meet you. Croaker has said so much about you."

I had not said a word. But she had read the Annals. She dismounted and offered her hand. Each took it, baffled, for only Darling, in their experience, expected treatment as an equal.

"Well, let's go down," I said. "Let's go down. I've got a thousand things to report."

"Yeah?" Elmo said. And that said a lot, for he looked up our backtrail as he said it.

Some people who had gone away with me had not come back.

"I don't know. We had half the Taken after us. We got

separated. I couldn't find them again. But I never heard anything about them being captured. Let's go down. See Darling. I've got incredible news. And get me something to eat. We've been eating each other's cooking forever, and she's a worse cook than I am.''

"Guck," Elmo said, and slapped me across the back. "And you lived?"

"I'm one tough old buzzard, Elmo. You ought to know. Shit, man, I . . .'' I realized I was chattering like a whacko. I grinned.

Silent signed, "Welcome home, Croaker. Welcome home.''

"Come," I told the Lady as we reached the entrance to the Hole, and took her hand. "It'll seem like the pit till your eyes get used to it. And brace yourself for the smell."

Gods, the stench! Gag a maggot.

All kinds of excitement down below. It faded into studied indifference as we passed, then resumed behind us. Silent led straight to the conference room. Elmo split off to order us up something to eat.

As we entered I realized that I still held the Lady's hand. She gave me half a smile, in which there was a hell of a lot of nervousness. Talk about strutting into the dragon's lair. Bold old Croaker gave her hand a squeeze.

Darling looked ragged. So did the Lieutenant. A dozen others were there, few of whom I knew. They must have come aboard after the imperials evacuated the perimeter of the Plain.

Darling hugged me for a long time. So long I became flustered. We are not touchy people, she and I. She finally backed off and gave the Lady a look in which there was a hint of jealousy.

I signed, "This is Ardath. She will help me translate. She knows the old languages well."

Darling nodded. She asked no questions. So much was I trusted.

The food arrived. Elmo dragged in a table and chairs and shooed out everyone but myself, the Lieutenant, himself, Silent, and the Lady. He might have sent her away, too, but remained unsure of her standing with me.

We ate, and as we did I related my tale in snatches, when

my hands and mouth were not full. There were some rough moments, especially when I told Darling that Raven was alive.

In retrospect I think it was harder on me than on her. I was afraid she would get all excited and hysterical. She did nothing of the sort.

First, she flat refused to believe me. And I could understand that, for till he disappeared Raven had been the corner stone of her universe emotionally. She could not see him not including her in his biggest lie ever just so he could slip away to go poke around the Barrowland. That made no sense to her. Raven never lied to her before.

Made no sense to me, either. But then, as I have noted before, I suspected there was more in the shadows than anyone was admitting. I sniffed the faintest whiff that maybe Raven was running *from* instead of *to*.

Darling's denials did not last long. She is not one to disdain truth indefinitely only because it is unpleasant. She handled the pain far better than I anticipated, and that suggested maybe she had had a chance to bleed off some of the worst in the past.

Still, Raven's present circumstances did nothing for Darling's emotional health, already doing poorly after her defeat at Horse. That harbinger of grander defeats to come. Already she suspected she might have to face the imperials without benefit of the information I had been sent to acquire.

I conjured universal despair when I announced my failure and added, "I have it on high authority that what we sought isn't in those papers anyway. Though I can't be sure till Ardath and I finish what we have here." I did sketch what I learned from Raven's documents before losing them.

I did not lie outright. That would not be forgiven later, when the truth came out. As inevitably it must. I just overlooked a few details. I even admitted having been captured, questioned, and imprisoned.

"What the hell are you doing here, then?" Elmo demanded. "How come you're even alive?"

"They turned us loose, Ardath and me. After that business you had near Horse. That was a message. I'm supposed to deliver another."

"Such as?"

"Unless you're blind and stupid, you'll have noticed that you're not under attack. The Lady has ordered all operations against the Rebellion ceased."

"Why?"

"You haven't been paying attention. Because the Dominator is stirring."

"Come on, Croaker. We finished that business in Juniper."

"I went to the Barrowland. I saw for myself, Lieutenant. That thing is going to break loose. One of its creatures is out already, maybe dogging One-Eye and them. I'm convinced. The Dominator is a step from breaking out, and not half-assed like in Juniper." I turned to the Lady. "Ardath. What was that I figured? I lost track of how long we've been in the Plain. It was about ninety days when we came in."

"It took you eight days to get here," Elmo said.

I lifted an eyebrow.

"The menhirs."

"Of course. Eight days, then. Away from ninety for a worst-case scenario. Eighty-two days till the Great Barrow opens." I went into more detail about the Great Tragic River floods.

The Lieutenant was not convinced. Neither was Elmo. And you cannot blame them. The Lady weaves crafty, intricate plots. And they were sneaky guys who judged others by themselves. I did not proselytize. I was not wholeheartedly born-again myself.

It was of little consequence whether or not those two believed, anyway. Darling makes the decisions.

She signed for everyone to leave but me. I asked Elmo to show Ardath around and find her a place to bunk. He looked at me oddly. Like everyone else, he figured I'd brought me home a girlfriend.

I had trouble keeping a straight face. All those years they have ridden me because of a few romances written when first we entered the Lady's service. And now I'd brought her home.

I figured Darling wanted to talk about Raven. I was not wrong, but she surprised me by signing, "She has sent you to propose an alliance, has she not?"

Quick little devil. "Not exactly. Though in practice it would amount to that." I went into the details, known and reasoned, of the situation. Signing is not quick work. But Darling remained attentive and patient, not at all distracted by whatever was going on inside her. She took me over the value, or lack thereof, of my document cache. Not once did she ask about Raven. Nor about Ardath, though my friend was on her mind, too.

She signed, "She is correct in saying that our feud becomes inconsequential if the Dominator rises. My question must be, is the threat genuine or a ploy? We know just how convoluted a scheme she can manage."

"I am sure," I signed in reply. "Because Raven was sure. He had made up his mind before the Lady's people began to suspect. In fact, as far as I can tell, he developed the evidence that convinced them."

"Goblin and One-Eye. Are they safe?"

"As far as I know. I never heard of them being captured."

"They should be getting close. Those documents. They are the crux still."

"Even if they do not contain the secret of her name, but only that of her husband?"

"She wants access?"

"I would assume so. I was released for some reason, though I cannot say what the reason behind the reason was."

Darling nodded. "So I thought."

"Yet I am convinced that she is honest in this. That we must consider the Dominator the more dangerous and immediate peril. It should not be too difficult to anticipate most of the ways she could become treacherous."

"And there is Raven."

Here it comes, I thought. "Yes."

"I will reflect, Croaker."

"There is not much time."

"There is all the time in the world, in a way. I will reflect. You and your lady friend translate."

I felt I had been dismissed before we got to why she wanted to see me privately. The woman has a face like stone. You can't tell much about what is going on inside. I moved toward the door slowly.

"Croaker," she signed. "Wait."

I stopped. This was it.

"What is she, Croaker?"

Damn! Ducked around it again. Chills on my part. Guilt. I did not want to lie outright. "Just a woman."

"Not a special woman? A special friend?"

"I guess she is special. In her way."

"I see. Ask Silent to come in."

Again I went slowly, nodding. But it was not till I actually started to open the door that she beckoned me back.

In accordance with instructions, I sat. She did not. She paced. She signed, "You think I am cold toward great news. You think ill of me because I am not excited that Raven is alive."

"No. I thought it would shock you. That it would cause you great distress."

"Shock, no. I am not entirely surprised. Distressed, yes. It opens old wounds and makes them more painful."

Puzzled, I watched as she continued to prowl.

"Our Raven. He never grew up. Fearless as a stone. Utterly without the handicap of a conscience. Tough. Smart. Hard. Fierce. All those things. Yes? Yes. And a coward."

"What? How can you? . . ."

"He runs away. There were machinations around the Limper which pulled his wife in, years ago. Did he try to discover the truth and work it out? He killed people and ran away with the Black Company to kill more people. He abandoned two babies without a word of good-bye."

She was hot now. She was opening the doors on secrets and spilling stuff of which I had seen only the vaguest glimmering reflections. "Do not defend him. I have had the power to investigate, and I did," she signed.

"He fled the Black Company. For my sake? As much excuse to avoid entanglement as reason. Why did he salvage me in that village? Because of guilt over children he had abandoned. I was a safe child. And while a child I remained a safe emotional investment. But I did not remain a child, Croaker. And I knew no other man in all those years in hiding.

"I should have known better. I saw how he pushed people

away if they tried to get close in any way that was not completely one-sided and under his control. But after the horrible things he did in Juniper I thought I could be the one to redeem him. On the road south, when we were running from the dark danger of the Lady and light danger of the Company, I betrayed my true feelings. I opened the lid on a chest of dreams nurtured from a time before I was old enough to think about men.

"He became a changed man. A frightened animal caught in a cage. He was relieved when news came that the Lieutenant had appeared with some of the Company. It was not but a matter of hours before he was 'dead.'

"I suspected then. I think a part of me always knew. And that is why I am not so devastated now as you want. Yes. I know you know I cry myself to sleep sometimes. I cry for a little girl's dreams. I cry because the dreams will not die, though I am powerless to make them come true. I cry because the one thing I truly want I cannot have. Do you understand?"

I thought about Lady, and Lady's situation, and nodded. I signed nothing back.

"I am going to cry again. Go out. Please. Tell Silent to come."

I did not have to look for him. He was waiting in the conference room. I watched him go inside, wondering if I was seeing things or seeing things.

She'd certainly given me something to think about.

Chapter Forty-Three:
PICNIC

Put on any deadline and time accelerates. The clockwork of the universe runs off an overwound mainspring. Four days went down the jakes, *zip*! And I did not waste much time sleeping.

Ardath and I translated. And translated. And translated. She read, translating aloud. I wrote till my hands cramped. Occasionally Silent took over for me.

I spot-checked by slipping in documents already done, especially those both Tracker and I had worked. Not once did I catch a misinterpretation.

That fourth morning I did catch something. We were doing one of those lists. This soiree must have been so big that if held today, we'd call it a war. Or at least a riot. On and on. So-and-so of such-and-such, with Lady Who's-is, sixteen titles, four of which made sense. By the time the heralds finished proclaiming everyone, the party must have died of encroaching senility.

Anyway, along about the middle of the list I heard a little catch in her breath. Aha! I said to myself. A bolt strikes close. My ears pricked up.

She went on smoothly. Moments later I was not sure I had not imagined it. Reason told me the name that startled her would not be the one she was speaking. She was toddling along at my writing pace. Her eyes would be well ahead of my hand.

Not one of the names that followed clanged any bell.

I would go over the list later, just in case, hoping she had deleted something.

No such luck.

Come afternoon she said, "Break, Croaker. I'm going for tea. You want some?"

"Sure. Maybe a hunk of bread, too." I scribbled another half minute before realizing what had happened.

What? The Lady herself offering to fetch? Me putting in an order without thinking? I got a case of the nerves. How much was she role-playing? How much pretending for fun? It must be centuries since she got her own tea. If ever.

I rose, started to follow, halted outside my cell door.

Fifteen steps down the tunnel, in the grungy, feeble lamplight, Otto had cornered her against the wall. He was talking some shit. Why I had not foreseen the problem I do not know. I doubted that she had. Surely it was not one she faced normally.

Otto got pushy. I started to go break it up then vacillated. She might be angered by my interference.

A light step from the other direction. Elmo. He paused. Otto was too single-minded to notice us.

"Better do something," Elmo said. "We don't need that kind of trouble."

She did not appear frightened or upset. "I think maybe she can handle it."

Otto got a "no" that could not be misinterpreted. But he did not accept it. He tried to lay hands on.

He got a ladylike slap for his trouble. Which angered him. He decided to take what he wanted. As Elmo and I moved forward, he disappeared in a flurry of kicks and punches that set him down in the muck on the floor, holding his belly with one arm and that arm with the other. Ardath went on as though nothing had happened.

I said, "I told you she could handle it."

"Remind me not to overstep myself," Elmo said. Then he grinned and tapped my arm. "Bet she's mean on the horizontal. Eh?"

Damned if I did not blush. I gave him a foolish grin. It only confirmed his suspicions. What the hell. Anything would have. That is the way those things go.

We lugged Otto to my room. I thought he would puke up his guts. But he controlled himself. I checked for broken bones. He was just bruised. "All yours, Elmo," I said, for ı knew the old sergeant was rehearsing a few choice words.

He took Otto by the elbow and said, "Step down to my office, soldier." He started dirt tumbling from the tunnel overheads when he explained the facts of life.

When Ardath returned she behaved as if nothing had happened. Perhaps she missed us watching. But after half an hour she asked, "Can we take a break? Go outside? Walk?"

"You want me to come?"

She nodded. "We need to talk. Privately."

"All right."

To tell the truth, whenever I lifted my nose from my work I got a little claustrophobic myself. My venture westward reminded me how good it is to stretch one's legs. "Hungry?" I asked. "Too serious to make a picnic?"

She looked startled, then charmed, by the idea. "Good. Let's do that."

So we went to the cook and baker and filled a bucket and went topside. Though she did not notice everyone smirking, I did.

There is but one door in the Hole. To the conference room, behind which Darling's personal quarters lie. Neither my quarters nor Ardath's had so much as a curtain closure. Folks figured we were off for the privacy of the wide open spaces.

Dream on. Up there there would be more spectators than down below. They just would not be human.

The sun was maybe three hours short of setting when we stepped outside, and it smacked us right in the eyes. Rough. But I expected it. Should have warned her.

We strolled up the creek, breathing slightly sagey air and saying nothing. The desert was silent. Not even Father Tree stirred. The breeze was insufficient to sigh in the coral. After a while I said, "Well?"

"I needed to get out. The walls were closing in. The null made it worse. I feel helpless down there. It preys on the mind."

"Oh."

We rounded a coral head and encountered a menhir. One of my old buddies, I guess, for he reported, "There are strangers on the Plain, Croaker."

"No lie?" Then: "Which strangers, rock?" But it had nothing more to say.

"They're always like that?"

"Or worse. Well. The null begins to fade. Feel better?"

"I felt better the moment I stepped outside. That's the gate to Hell. How can you people live like that?"

"It isn't much, but it's home."

We came to bare earth. She halted. "What's this?"

"Old Father Tree. You know what they think we're up to, down there?"

"I know. Let them think it. Call it protective coloration. *That* is your Father Tree?" She indicated Himself.

"That's him." I walked on. "How you doing today, old-timer?"

Must be fifty times I have asked that. I mean, the old guy is remarkable, but just a tree. Right? I did not expect a response. But Father Tree's leaves started tinkling the moment I spoke.

"Come back here, Croaker." The Lady's voice was commanding, hard, a little shaken. I turned and marched. "Back to your old self?" From the corner of my eye I caught a shadow in motion, off toward the Hole. I concentrated on a bit of coral and nearby brush. "Keep your voice down. We have an eavesdropper."

"That's no surprise." She spread the ragged blanket she had brought, sat down with her toes right at the edge of the barren. She removed the rag covering the bucket. I settled beside her, positioned so I could watch that shadow. "Do you know what that is?" she asked, nodding at the tree.

"Nobody does. It's just Old Father Tree. The desert clans call him a god. We've seen no evidence of that. One-Eye and Goblin were impressed with the fact that he stands almost exactly on the geographical center of the Plain, though."

"Yes. I suppose . . . So much was lost in the fall. I should have suspected . . . My husband was not the first of his kind, Croaker. Nor the White Rose the first of hers. It is a grand cycle, I believe."

"You've lost me."

"A very long time ago, even as I measure time, there was another war like that between the Dominator and the White

Rose. The light overcame the shadow. But as always, the shadow left its taint on the victors. In order to end the struggle, they summoned a thing from another world, plane, dimension, what-have-you, the way Goblin might conjure a demon, only this thing was an adolescent god. Of sorts. In a sapling avatar. These events were legendary only in my youth, when much more of the past survived, so details are open to question. But it was a summoning of such scope, and such price, that thousands perished and counties were devastated. But they planted their captive god over the grave of their great enemy, where it would keep him enchained. This tree-god would live a million years.''

"You mean? . . . Old Father is sitting on something like the Great Barrow?"

"I did not connect the legends and the Plain till I saw that tree. Yes. This earth constrains something as virulent as my husband. So much suddenly makes sense. It all fits. The beasts. The impossible talking rocks. Coral reefs a thousand miles from the sea. It all leaked through from that other world. The change storms are the tree's dreams.''

She rattled on, not so much explaining as putting things together for herself. I gaped and remembered the change storm that caught me on the way west. Was I accursed, to be caught in a god's nightmare?

"This is crazy," I said, and at the same instant decrypted the shape I had been trying to pry from the shadows, bushes, and coral.

Silent. Squatting on his hams, motionless as a snake await-ing prey. Silent, who had been everywhere I went the last three days, like an extra shadow, seldom noticed because he *was* Silent. Well. So much for my confidence that my return with a companion had tickled no suspicions.

"This is a bad place to be, Croaker. Very bad. Tell that deaf peasant wench to move.''

"If I did that, I would have to explain why and reveal who gave *me* the advice. I doubt she would be impressed.''

"I suppose you're right. Well, it won't matter much longer. Let's eat.''

She opened a packet and set out what looked like fried rabbit. But there are no rabbits on the Plain. "For all they got kicked around, their adventure toward Horse improved the larder.'' I dug in.

Silent remained motionless in the corner of my eye. You bastard, I thought. I hope you're drooling.

Three pieces of rabbit later I slowed enough to ask, ''That about the old-timer is interesting, but does it have any relevance?''

Father Tree was raising a ruckus. I wondered why. ''Are you afraid of him?''

She did not answer. I chucked bones down the creek bank, rose. ''Back in a minute.'' I stomped over to Father Tree. ''Old-Timer, you got any seeds? Any sprouts? A little something we could take to the Barrowland to plant on top of our own villain?''

Talking to that tree, all those times heading past, was a game. I was possessed of an almost religious awe of its age, but of no conscious belief in it as anything like either the nomads or the Lady claimed. Just a gnarly old tree with weird leaves and a bad temper.

Temper?

When I touched it, to lean against it while looking up among its bizarre leaves for nuts or seeds, it bit me. Well, not with teeth. But sparks flew. The tips of my fingers stung. When I took them out of my mouth they looked burned. ''Damn,'' I muttered, and backed off a few steps. ''Nothing personal, tree. Thought you might want to help out.''

Vaguely, I was aware that a menhir now stood near Silent's lurking place. More appeared around the barren area.

Something hit me with the force of windwhale ballast dumped from a hundred feet up. I went down. Waves of power, of thought, beat upon me. I whimpered, tried to crawl toward the Lady. She extended a hand, but would not cross that boundary. . . .

Some of that power began to hint at comprehensibility. But it was like being inside fifty minds at once, with them scattered across the world. No. The Plain. And more than fifty minds. As it became more melded, more meshed . . . I was touching the menhir minds.

That all faded. The sledge of power ceased hammering the anvil that was me. I scrambled for the edge of the barren,

though I knew that line demarked no true safety. I reached the
blanket, caught my breath, finally turned to face the tree. Its
leaves tinkled in exasperation.

"What happened?"

"Basically, he told me he's doing what he can, not for our
sake but for that of his creatures. That I should go to Hell,
leave him alone, quit aggravating him or find my ass in deep
shit. Oh, my."

I had looked back to see how Silent had taken my encounter.

"I warned . . ." She glanced back, too.

"I think we maybe got trouble. Maybe they recognized
you."

Almost everyone from the Hole had appeared. They were
lining up across the trail. The menhirs were more numerous.
Walking trees were forming a circle with us at its center.

And we were unarmed, for Darling was there. We were
inside the null again.

She had on her white linen. She stepped past Elmo and the
Lieutenant and came toward me. Silent joined her. Behind
her came One-Eye, Goblin, Tracker, and Toadkiller Dog.
Those four still had the dust of the trail upon them.

They had been on the Plain for days. And I had been given
no word. . . .

You talk about your trapdoor on your gallows dropping
unexpectedly. For fifteen seconds I stood there with my
mouth open. Then I asked, "What do we do?" in a soft
squeak.

She startled me by taking my hand. "I bet and lost. I don't
know. They're your people. Bluff. Oh!" Her eyes narrowed.
Her stare fixed, became intense. Then a thin smile stretched
her lips. "I see."

"What?"

"Some answers. The shadow of what my husband is about.
You have been manipulated more than you know. He antici-
pated being found out with his weather. Once he had your
Raven, he decided to bring your peasant girl to him. . . .
Yes. I think . . . Come."

My old comrades did not appear hostile, only puzzled.

The circle continued to close.

The Lady caught my hand again, led me to the base of Old

Father Tree. She whispered, "Let there be peace between us while you observe, Ancient One. One comes whom you will remember of old." And to me: "There are many old shadows in the world. Some reach back to the dawn. Not big enough, they seldom draw attention like my husband or the Taken. Soulcatcher had minions who antedated the tree. They were interred with her. I told you I recognized the way those bodies were torn."

I stood there in the bloody light of the fading sun, baffled all to hell. She might as well have been speaking UchiTelle.

Darling, Silent, One-Eye, and Goblin came right to us. Elmo and the Lieutenant halted within a rock's throw. But Tracker and Toadkiller Dog sort of melted into the crowd.

"What is going on?" I signed at Darling, obviously frightened.

"That is what we want to find out. We have been getting disjointed, nonsensical reports from the menhirs since Goblin, One-Eye, and Tracker reached the Plain. On one hand, Goblin and One-Eye confirm everything you told me—till you parted ways."

I glanced at my two friends—and saw no friendship there. Their eyes were cold and glassy. Like somebody else had moved in behind them.

"Company," Elmo called, without shouting.

A pair of Taken, aboard boat-carpets, cruised some distance away. They came no closer. The Lady's hand twitched. She controlled herself otherwise. They remained far enough out not to be recognizable.

"More than one pair of hands is stirring this stew," I said. "Silent, get to the point. Right now you're scaring the crap out of me."

He signed, "The rumor is strong in the empire that you have sold out. That you have brought someone high-up here, to assassinate Darling. Maybe even one of the new Taken."

I could not help grinning. The planters of rumors had not dared tell the whole tale.

The grin convinced Silent. He knew me well. Which, I guess, was why *he* was watching me.

Darling, too, relaxed. But neither One-Eye nor Goblin softened.

"What's wrong with these guys, Silent? They look like zombies."

"They say you sold them out. That Tracker saw you. That if . . ."

"Bullshit! Where the hell is Tracker? Get that big stupid son-of-a-bitch out here and let him say that to my face!"

The light was weakening. The fat tomato of a sun had slipped behind the hills. Soon it would be dark. I felt a creepy tingle against my back. Was the damned tree going to act up?

Once I thought of him, I sensed an intense interest upon Old Father Tree's part. Also a sort of dreamy rage coalescing. . . .

Suddenly, menhirs flickered around all over the place, even across the creek where the brush was dense. A dog yelped. Silent signed something to Elmo. I did not catch it because his back was turned. Elmo trotted toward the turmoil.

The menhirs worked our way, forming a wall, herding something. . . . Well! Tracker and Toadkiller Dog. Tracker looked vacuously puzzled. The mutt kept trying to scoot between the menhirs. They would not let him. Our people had to stay light on their feet to keep from getting their toes squashed.

The menhirs pushed Toadkiller Dog and Tracker into the barren circle. The mongrel let out one long, despairing howl, tucked his tail between his legs, and slunk into Tracker's shadow. They stood about ten feet from Darling.

"Oh, Gods," the Lady murmured, and squeezed my hand so hard I almost yelled.

The kernel of a change storm exploded in Old Father Tree's tinkly hair.

It was huge; it was horrible; it was violent. It devoured us all, with such ferocity we could do nothing but endure it. Shapes shifted, ran, changed; yet those nearest Darling stayed exactly the same.

Tracker screamed. Toadkiller Dog unleashed a howl that spread terror like a cancer. And they changed the most, into the identical vile and violent monsters I saw while westward bound.

The Lady shouted something lost in the rage of the storm. But I caught its triumphal note. She *did* know those shapes.

I stared at her.

She had not changed.

That seemed impossible. This creature about whom I had been silly for fifteen years could not be the real woman.

Toadkiller Dog flung himself into the jaws of the storm, hideous fangs bared, trying to reach the Lady. He knew her, too. He meant to finish her while she was helpless inside the null. Tracker shambled after, just as puzzled as the Tracker that looked human had been.

One of Father Tree's great branches whipped down. It batted Toadkiller Dog the way a man might bat an attack bunny. Three times Toadkiller Dog gave it the valiant try. Three times he failed. The fourth time, what might have been the grandfather of all lightning bolts met him squarely and hurled him all the way to the creek, where he smouldered and twitched for a minute before rising and howling away into the enemy desert.

At the same time Tracker-beast went for Darling. He gathered her up and headed west. When Toadkiller Dog-beast went out of the game, Tracker got all the attention.

Old Father Tree may not be a god, but when he talks he has the voice. Coral reefs crumbled when he spoke. Everyone outside the barren grabbed their ears and screamed. For us who were closer it was less tormenting.

I do not know what he said. The language was none I knew, and it sounded like none I had ever heard. But it got through to Tracker. He put Darling down and came back, into the teeth of the storm, to stand before the god while that great voice hammered him and violent violet echoed round his misshapen bones. He bowed and did homage to the tree, and then he *did* change.

The storm died as swiftly as it had began. Everyone collapsed. Even the Lady. But unconsciousness did not come with collapse. By the wan light remaining I saw the circling Taken decide their hour had come. They fell back, gathered velocity, cut a ballistic chord through the null, each loosing four of those thirty-foot spears meant for shattering windwhales. And I sat on the hard ground drooling, hand in hand with their target.

Through sheer will, I guess, the Lady managed to murmur,

"They can read the future as well as I." Which made no sense at the time. "I overlooked that."

Eight shafts arced down.

Father Tree responded.

Two carpets disintegrated beneath their riders.

The shafts exploded so high that none of their fiery charge reached the ground.

The Taken did, though. They plunged in neat arcs into a dense coral reef east of us. Then the sleepiness came. The last thing I recall was that the glaze had left the three eyes of Goblin and One-Eye.

Chapter Forty-Four: THE QUICKENING

There were dreams. Endless, horrible dreams. Someday, if I live so long, if I survive what is yet to come, I may record them, for they were the story of a god that is a tree, and of the thing his roots bind. . . .

No. I think not. One life of struggle and horror is enough to report. And this one goes on.

The Lady stirred first. She reached over, pinched me. The pain wakened my nerves. She gasped, in a voice so soft I barely heard it, "Get up. Help me. We have to move your White Rose."

Made no sense.

"The null."

I was shivering. I thought it was reaction to whatever struck me down.

"The thing below is of this world. The tree is not."

Wasn't me shivering. It was the ground. Ever so gently and

rapidly. And now I became aware of a sound. Something far away, deep down.

I began to get the idea.

Fear is one hell of a motivator. I got my feet under me. Above, the Tinkle of Old Father Tree beat maddeningly. There was panic in his wind-chimes song.

The Lady rose too. We staggered toward Darling, supporting one another. Each groggy step spiced more life into my sluggish blood. I looked into Darling's eyes. She was aware, yet paralyzed. Her face was frozen halfway between fear and disbelief. We hoisted her up, each slipping an arm around her. The Lady began counting steps. I remember no other labor so damnably great. I do not recall another time when I ran so much on will alone.

The shaking of the earth waxed rapidly into the shudder of passing horsemen, then to a landslide's uproar, then to an earthquake. The ground around Father Tree began to writhe and buckle. A gout of flame and dust blasted upward. The tree tinkled a shriek. Blue lightning rioted in his hair. We pressed even harder in our flight down and across the creek.

Something behind us began to scream.

Images in mind. That which was rising was in agony. Father Tree subjected it to the torments of Hell. But it came on, determined to be free.

I no longer looked back. My terror was too great. I did not want to see what an ancient Dominator looked like.

We made it. Gods. Somehow the Lady and I got Darling sufficiently far away for Father Tree to regain his full otherworldly power.

The shriek rose rapidly in pitch and fury; I fell down grasping my ears. And then it went away.

After a time the Lady said, "Croaker, go see if you can help the others. It's safe. The tree won."

That quickly? Out of that much fury?

Getting my feet under me seemed an all-night job.

A blue nimbus still shimmered among Father Tree's branches. You could feel his aggravation from two hundred yards. Its weight grew as I moved nearer.

The ground around the tree's feet hardly seemed disturbed, considering the violence of moments ago. It looked freshly plowed and harrowed, was all. Some of my friends were partially buried, but no one appeared injured. Everyone was moving at least a little. Faces looked wholly stunned. Except Trucker's. That ugly character had not resumed his fake human form.

He was up early, placidly helping the others, dusting their clothing with hearty, friendly slaps. You would not have known that a short time before he had been a deadly enemy. Weird.

Nobody needed any help. Except the walking trees and menhirs. The trees had been overturned. The menhirs . . . Many of them were down, too. And unable to right themselves.

That gave me a chill.

I got me another shudder when I neared the old tree.

Reaching out of the ground, fumbling at the bark of a root, was a human hand and forearm, long, leathery, greenish, with nails grown to claws then broken and bleeding upon Father Tree. It did not belong to anyone from the Hole.

It twitched feebly, now.

Blue sparks continued to crackle above.

Something about that hand stirred the old beast within me. I wanted to run away shrieking. Or seize an axe and mutilate it. I took neither course, for I got the distinct feeling that Father Tree was watching me and glowering more than a little, and maybe blaming me personal-like for wakening the thing to which the hand belonged.

"I'm going," I said. "Know how you feel. Got my own old monster to keep down." And I backed away, bowing some each three or four steps.

"What the hell was that?"

I whirled. One-Eye was staring at me. He had a Croaker-is-up-to-another-of-his-crazies look.

"Just chatting with the tree." I looked around. People seemed to be finding their sea legs. Some of the less flustered were starting to right the walking trees. For the fallen menhirs, though, there seemed no hope. Those had gone to whatever reward a sentient stone may expect. Later they would be discovered righted, standing among the other dead menhirs near the creek ford.

I returned to Darling and the Lady. Darling was slow to

come around, too groggy to communicate yet. The Lady asked, "Everyone all right?"

"Except the guy in the ground. And he came close to making himself well." I described the hand.

She nodded. "That's a mistake not likely to be made again soon."

Silent and several others had gathered around, so we could say little that would not sound suspect. I did murmur, "What now?" In the background I heard the Lieutenant and Elmo hollering about getting some torches out to shed a little light.

She shrugged.

"What about the Taken?"

"You want to go after them?"

"Hell, no! But we can't have them running around loose in our backyard, either. No telling . . ."

"The menhirs will watch them. Won't they?"

"That depends on how pissed the old tree is. Maybe he's ready to let us go to hell in a bucket after this."

"You might find out."

"I'll go," Goblin queaked. He wanted an excuse to put a lot of yards between him and the tree.

"Don't take all night," I said. "Why don't the rest of you help Elmo and the Lieutenant?"

That got rid of some folks, but not Silent.

There was no way I was going to get Silent out of sight of Darling. He had some reservations still.

I chaffed Darling's wrists and did other silly things when time was the only cure. After some minutes I mumbled, "Seventy-eight days."

And the Lady, "Before long it will be too late."

I lifted an eyebrow.

"He can't be beaten without her. It won't be long before the hardest ride won't get her there in time."

I do not know what Silent made of that exchange. I do know that the Lady looked up at him and smiled thinly, with that look she gets when she knows your thoughts. "We need the tree." And: "We didn't get to finish our picnic."

"Huh?"

She went away for a few minutes. When she returned she

had the blanket, dirtier than ever, and the bucket. She snagged my hand and headed for the dark. "You watch for the traps," she told me.

What the hell was this game?

Chapter Forty-Five:
BARGAIN STRUCK

Later a broken boat of a moon arose. We did not go far before it did, for there was not enough starlight to risk much movement. Once the moon did rise, the Lady guided me in a slow circle toward where the Taken had come down. We halted in a clear area, sandy but not dangerous. She spread the blanket. We were outside the null. "Sit."

I sat. She sat. I asked, "What? . . ."

"Be quiet." She closed her eyes and went inside herself.

I wondered if Silent had torn himself away from Darling to stalk us. Wondered if my comrades were making crude jokes about us as they labored over the walking trees. Wondered what the hell kind of game had me caught in its toils.

You learned something out of it, anyway, Croaker.

After a while I realized she was back from wherever she had gone. "I *am* amazed," she whispered. "Who would have thought they had the guts?"

"Eh?"

"Our sky-borne friends. I expected Limper and Whisper, up to their old crimes. But I got Scorn and Blister. Though I might have suspected her, had I thought. Necromancy is her great talent."

Another round of her thinking aloud. I wondered if she did that often. I am sure she was unaccustomed to having witnesses around if she did. "What do you mean?"

She ignored me. "I wonder if they told the others?"

I harkened back, put a few things together. The Lady's divinations about three possible futures and no place in any of them. Maybe that meant there was no place in them for Taken, either. And maybe they figured they could take their futures into their own hands by ridding themselves of their mistress.

A light step startled me. But I did not get excited. I just figured Silent had chosen to follow. So I was very surprised when Darling sat down with us, unchaperoned.

How had I overlooked the return of the null? Distracted, of course.

The Lady said, as though Darling had not appeared, "They haven't yet gotten out of the coral. It's very slow going, and they're both injured. And though the coral can't kill them, it can cause a lot of pain. Right now they're lying up, waiting for first light."

"So?"

"So maybe they won't get out at all."

"Darling can read lips."

"She knows already."

Well, I have said a thousand times that the girl is not stupid.

I think Darling's knowledge was implicit in the position she took. She placed me squarely in the gap between them.

Oh yeah.

I found myself playing interpreter.

Trouble is, I cannot record what went back and forth. Because someone tampered with my memories later. I got only one chance to make notes, and those now make no sense.

Some sort of negotiation took place. I can still conjure a sense of profound astonishment at Darling's willingness to deal. Also an amazement at the Lady for the same reason.

They reached an accommodation. An uneasy one, to be sure, for the Lady henceforth stuck very close and kept me between her and anyone else while she was within the null. Great feeling, knowing you're a human shield. . . . And Darling kept near the Lady to prevent her calling on her power.

But she did turn her loose once.

That is getting ahead, slightly. First we all sneaked back, not letting anyone know there had been summit. The Lady and I returned after Darling, trying to look like we had had an energetic and thorough encounter. I could not help chuckling at some envious looks.

The Lady and I went outside the null again next morning, after Darling distracted Silent, One-Eye, and Goblin by sending them to dicker with the menhirs. Father Tree could not make up his mind. We went the other direction. And tracked Taken.

Actually, there was little tracking to do. They were not yet free of the coral. The Lady called upon that power she held over them and they ceased to be Taken.

Her patience was exhausted. Maybe she wanted them to serve as an object lesson. . . . In any event, buzzards—real buzzards—were circling before we returned to the Hole.

That easy, I thought. For her. And for me, when I tried to kill the Limper, with every damned thing going my way, impossible.

She and I went back to translating. So busy did we stay that I did not remain abreast of the news from outside. I was a little vacant, anyway, because she had expunged my memories of the meeting with Darling.

Anyhow, somehow, the White Rose got right with Father Tree. The shaky alliance survived.

One thing I did notice. The menhirs stopped ragging me about strangers on the Plain.

They meant Tracker and Toadkiller Dog all the time. And the Lady. Two of three were no longer strangers. No one knew what had become of Toadkiller Dog. Even the menhirs could not trace him.

I tried to get Tracker to explain the name. He could not remember. Not even Toadkiller Dog himself. Weird.

He was the tree's creature now.

Chapter Forty-Six: SON OF THE TREE

I was nervous. I had trouble sleeping. Days were slipping away. Out west, the Great Tragic was gnawing its banks. A four-legged monster was running to its overlord with news that it had been found out. Darling and the Lady were doing nothing.

Raven remained trapped. Bomanz remained trapped in the long fires he had called down on his own head. The end of the world tramped ever closer. And nobody was doing anything.

I completed my translations. And was no wiser than before. It seemed. Though Silent, Goblin, and One-Eye kept fooling with charts of names, cross-indexing, seeking patterns. The Lady watched over their shoulders more than did I. I fiddled with these Annals. I bothered myself with how to phrase a request for the return of those I had lost at Queen's Bridge. I fussed. I grew ever more antsy. People became irritated with me. I began taking moonlight walks to work off my nervous energy.

One night the moon was full, a fat orange bladder just scaling the hills to the east. A grand sight, especially with patrolling mantas crossing its face. For some reason the desert had a lilac luminescence upon all its edges. The air was chill. There was a dust of powder swirling on the breeze, fallen that afternoon. A change storm flickered far away to the north. . . .

A menhir appeared beside me. I jumped three feet. "Strangers on the Plain, rock?" I asked.

"None stranger than you, Croaker."

"I get a comedian. You want something?"

"No. The Father of Trees wants *you*."

"Yeah? See you." Heart pounding, I headed toward the Hole.

Another menhir blocked the path.

"Well. Since you put it that way." Faking bravery, I headed upstream.

They would have herded me. Best accept the inevitable. Less humiliation.

The wind was bitter around the barren, but when I crossed the boundary it was like stepping into summer. No wind at all, though the old tree was tinkling. And heat like a furnace.

The moon had risen enough to flood the barren with light now argent. I approached the tree. My gaze fixed on that hand and forearm, still protruding, still gripping a root, still, it seemed, betraying the occasional feeble twitch. The root had grown, though, and seemed to be enveloping the hand, as a tree used for a line post will envelope a wire tacked to it. I stopped five feet from the tree.

"Come closer," it said. In plain voice. In conversational tone and volume.

I said, "Yipe!" and looked for the exits.

About two skillion menhirs surrounded the barren. So much for running away.

"Stand still, ephemeral."

My feet froze to the ground. Ephemeral, eh?

"You asked help. You demanded help. You whined and pleaded and begged for help. Stand still and accept it. Come closer."

"Make up your mind." I took two steps. Another would have me climbing him.

"I have considered. This thing you ephemera fear, in the ground so far from here, would be a peril to my creatures if it rose. I sense no significant strength in those who resist it. Therefore . . ."

I hated to interrupt, but I just had to scream. You see, something had me by the ankle. It was squeezing so hard I felt the bones grinding. Crushing. Sorry about that, old-timer.

The universe turned blue. I rolled in a hurricane of anger. Lightning roared in Father Tree's branches. Thunder rolled across the desert. I yelled some more.

Bolts of blue hammered around me, crisping me almost as

much as my tormentor. But, at last, the hand turned me loose.

I tried to run away.

One step and down I went. I kept on, crawling, while Father Tree apologized and tried to call me back.

Like Hell. I would crawl through the menhirs if I had to. . . .

My mind filled with a waking dream, Father Tree delivering a message direct. Then the earth got quiet, except for the *wish* as menhirs vanished.

Big hoopla from the direction of the Hole. A whole gang charged out to find the cause of the uproar. Silent reached me first. "One-Eye," I said. "I need One-Eye." He is the only one beside me with medical training. And contrary though he is, I could count on him to take medical instructions.

One-Eye showed up in a moment, along with twenty others. The watch had reacted quickly. "Ankle," I told him. "Maybe crushed. Somebody get some light up here. And a damned shovel."

"A shovel? Are you off your gourd?" One-Eye demanded.

"Just get it. And do something for the pain."

Elmo materialized, still buckling buckles. "What happened, Croaker?"

"Old Tree wanted to talk. Had the rocks bring me over. Says he wants to help us. Only while I was listening, that hand got ahold of me. Like to ripped my foot off. The racket was the tree saying, 'Now stop that. That's not polite.' "

"Cut his tongue out after you fix his leg," Elmo told One-Eye. "What did it want, Croaker?"

"Your ears gone? To help with the Dominator. Said he thought it over. Decided it was in his own best interest to keep the Dominator down. Give me a hand up." One-Eye's efforts were paying dividends. He had sponged one of his wild jungle glops onto my ankle—it had swollen three times normal size already—and the pain was fading.

Elmo shook his head.

I said, "I'll break *your* damned leg if you don't get me up." So he and Silent hoisted me, but supported me.

"Bring them shovels," I said. A half dozen had appeared.

They were entrenching tools, not real ditchdiggers. "You guys insist on helping, get me back over to the tree."

Elmo growled. For a moment I thought Silent might say something. I eyed him expectantly, smiling. I had been waiting twenty-some years.

No luck.

Whatever vow he had taken, whatever it was that had driven him to abstain from speech, it had put a steel lock on Silent's jaw. I have seen him so pissed he could chew nails, so excited he lost sphincter control, but nothing has shaken his resolution against talking.

Blue still sparkled in the tree's branches. Leaves tinkled. Moonlight and torchlight mixed into weird shadows the sparks sent dancing. . . . "Around him," I told my body slaves. I had not seen it myself, so it must be beyond that trunk.

Yep. There it was, out twenty feet from the base of the tree. A sapling. It stood about eight feet tall.

One-Eye, Silent, Goblin, those guys gobbled and gaped like startled apes. But not old Elmo. "Get a few buckets of water and soak the ground good," he said. "And find an old blanket we can wrap around the roots and the dirt that comes up with them."

He caught right on. Damned farmer. "Get me back downstairs," I said. "I want to see this ankle myself, in better light."

Going back, with Elmo and Silent carrying me, we encountered the Lady. She put on a suitably solicitous act, fussing all over me. I had to endure a lot of knowing grins.

Only Darling knew the truth even then. With maybe a little suspicion on Silent's part.

Chapter Forty-Seven:
SHADOWS IN
SHADOWLAND

There was no time inside the Barrowland, only shadow and fire, light without source, and endless fear and frustration. From where he stood, snared in the web of his own device, Raven could discern a score of Domination monsters. He could see men and beasts put down in the time of the White Rose to prevent those evils from escaping. He could see the silhouette of the sorcerer Bomanz limned against frozen dragon fire. The old wizard still struggled to take one more step toward the heart of the Great Barrow. Didn't he know that he had failed generations ago?

Raven wondered how long he had been caught. Had his messages gotten through? Would help come? Was he just marking time till the darkness exploded?

If there was a clock to count the time, it was the growing distress of those set to guard against the darkness. The river gnawed ever closer. There was nothing they could do. No way for them to summon the wrath of the world.

Raven thought he would have done things differently had he been in charge back when.

Vaguely, Raven recalled some things passing nearby, shades like himself. But he knew not how long ago, or even what they were. Things moved at times, and one could tell nothing certain. The world had a whole different look from this perspective.

Never had he been so helpless, so frightened. He did not like the feeling. Always he had been master of his destiny, dependent upon no one. . . .

There was, in that world, nothing to do but think. Too

much, too often, his thoughts came back to what it meant to be Raven, to things Raven had done and not done and should have done differently. There was time to identify and at least confront all the fears and pains and weaknesses of the inside man, all of which had created the ice and iron and fearless mask he had presented to the world. All those things which had cost him everything he had valued and which had driven him into the fangs of death again and again, in self-punishment. . . .

Too late. Far too late.

When his thoughts cleared and coagulated and he reached this point, he sent shrieks of anger echoing through the spirit world. And those who surrounded him and hated him for what he might have triggered, laughed and reveled in his torment.

Chapter Forty-Eight: FLIGHT WEST

Despite my exoneration by the tree, I never quite regained my former status with my comrades. Always there was a certain reserve, perhaps as much from envy of my apparent sudden female wealth as from trust slow to heal. I cannot deny the pain it caused me. I had been with those guys since I was a boy. They were my family.

I did take some ribbing about getting onto crutches in order to get out of work. But my work would have gone on had I had no legs at all.

Those damned papers. I had them committed to memory, set to music. And still I did not have the key we sought, nor what the Lady hoped to find. The cross-referencing was taking forever. The spelling of names, in pre-Domination and

Domination times, had been free-form. KurreTelle is one of those languages where various letter combinations can represent identical sounds.

Pain in the damned fundament.

I do not know how much Darling told the others. I was not at the Big Meeting. Neither was the Lady. But word came out: The Company was moving out.

One day to get ready.

Topside, near nightfall, on my crutches, I watched the windwhales arrive. There were eighteen of them, all summoned by Father Tree. They came with their mantas and a whole panoply of Plain sentient forms. Three dropped to the ground. The Hole puked up its contents.

We began boarding. I got a ration because I had to be lifted, along with my papers, gear, and crutches. The whale was a small one. I would share it with just a few people. The Lady. Of course. We could not be separated now. And Goblin. And One-Eye. And Silent, after a bloody sign battle, for he did not want to be separated from Darling. And Tracker. And the child of the tree, for whom Tracker was guardian and I was *in loco parentis*. I think the wizards were supposed to keep an eye on the rest of us, though little they could have done had a situation presented itself.

Darling, the Lieutenant, Elmo, and the other old hands boarded a second windwhale. The third carried a handful of troops and a lot of gear.

We lifted off, joined the formation above.

A sunset from five thousand feet is unlike anything you will see from the ground. Unless you are atop a very lonely mountain. Magnificent.

With darkness came sleep. One-Eye spelled me under. I still had a good deal of swelling and pain.

Yes. We were outside the null. Our whale flew the far flank from Darling. Specifically for the Lady's benefit.

Even then she did not give herself away.

The winds were favorable and we had the blessing of Father Tree. Dawn found us passing over Horse. It was there the truth finally surfaced.

Taken came up, all in their fish-carpets, armed to the gills.

Panic noises wakened me. I got Tracker to help me stand.
After one glance at the fire of the rising sun, I spied the
Taken drifting into guardian positions around our whale.
Goblin and them expected an attack. They howled their hearts
out. Somehow One-Eye found a way for it all to be Goblin's
fault. They went at it.

But nothing happened. Almost to *my* surprise, too. The
Taken merely maintained station. I glanced at the Lady. She
startled me with a wink. Then: "We *all* have to cooperate,
whatever our differences."

Goblin heard that. He ignored One-Eye's ranting for a
moment, stared at the Taken. After a bit he looked at the
Lady. Really looked.

I saw the light dawn. In a more than normally squeaky
voice, and with a truly goofy look, he said, "I remember
you." He remembered the one time he had had a sort of
direct contact with her. Many years ago, when he tried to
contact Soulcatcher, he had caught her in the Tower, in the
Lady's presence. . . .

She smiled her most charming smile. The one that melts
statues.

Goblin threw a hand in front of his eyes, turned away from
her. He looked at me with the most awful expression. I could
not help laughing. "You always accused me. . . ."

"You didn't have to go and *do* it, Croaker!" His voice
climbed the scale till it became inaudible. He sat down abruptly.

No lightning bolt splattered him across the sky. After a
time he looked up and said, "Elmo is going to crap!" He
giggled.

Elmo was the most unremitting of them all when it came to
reminding me of my romances about the Lady.

After the humor went out of it, after One-Eye had been
through it, too, and Silent had had his worst fears confirmed,
I began to wonder about my friends.

One and all, they were westward bound on Darling's say-so.
They had not been informed, in so many words, that we were
allied with our former enemies.

Fools. Or was Darling? What happened once the Dominator was down and we were ready to go after each other
again? . . .

Whoa, Croaker. Darling learned to play cards from Raven. Raven was a cutthroat player.

It was the Forest of Cloud by nightfall. I wonder what they made of us in Lords. We passed right over. The streets filled with gawkers.

Roses passed in the night. Then the other old cities of our early years in the north. There was little talk. The Lady and I kept our heads together, growing more tense as our strange fleet neared its destination and we drew no nearer unearthing the nuggets we sought.

"How long?" I asked. I had lost track of time.

"Forty-two days," she said.

"We were in the desert that long?"

"Time flies when you're having fun."

I gave her a startled look. A joke? Even an old cliché? From her?

I hate it when they go human on you. Enemies are not supposed to do that.

She had been crawling all over me with it for a couple months.

How can you hate?

The weather stayed halfway decent till we got to Forsberg. Then it became clabbered misery.

It was solid winter up there. Good, briskly refreshing winds loaded up with pellets of powder snow. A nice abrasive for a tender face like mine. A bombardment to clear out the lice on the backs of the whales, too. Everybody cussed and fussed and grumbled and huddled for warmth that dared not be provided by man's traditional ally, fire. Only Tracker seemed untouched. "Don't anything bother that thing?" I asked.

In the oddest voice I ever heard her use, the Lady replied, "Loneliness. If you want to kill Tracker the easy way, lock him up alone and go away."

I felt a chill that had nothing to do with the weather. Whom did I know who had been alone a long time? Who, maybe, just maybe, had begun to wonder if absolute power were worth the absolute price?

I knew beyond the glimmer of doubt that she had enjoyed every second of pretend on the Plain. Even the moments of danger. I knew that had I had the hair on my ass, there in the last days, I could have become more than a pretend boyfriend. There was a growing and quiet desperation to her in that time as going back to being the Lady approached.

Some of that I might have appropriated out of ego, for a very critical time faced her. She was under a lot of stress. She knew the enemy we faced. But not all was ego. I think she actually did like me as a person.

"I got a request," I said softly, in the middle of the huddle, banishing thoughts caused by a woman pressed against me.

"What?"

"The Annals. They're all that's left of the Black Company." Depression had set in fast. "There was an obligation undertaken ages ago, when the Free Companies of Khatovar were formed. If any of us get through this alive, someone should take them back."

I do not know if she understood. But: "They're yours," she said.

I wanted to explain, but could not. *Why* take them back? I am not sure where they are supposed to go. Four hundred years the Company drifted slowly north, waxing, waning, turning over its constituents. I have no idea if Khatovar still exists or if it is a city, country, a person, or a god. The Annals from the earliest years either did not survive or went home already. I have seen nothing but digests and excerpts from the earliest century. . . . No matter. Part of the Annalist's undertaking has always been to return the Annals to Khatovar should the Company disband.

The weather worsened. By Oar it seemed actively inimical, and may have been. That thing in the earth would know we were coming.

Just north of Oar all the Taken suddenly dropped away like rocks. "What the hell?"

"Toadkiller Dog," the Lady said. "We've caught up with him. He hasn't reached his master yet."

"Can they stop him?"

"Yes."

I crutched over to the side of the whale. I do not know what I expected to see. We were up in the snow clouds.

There were a few flashes below. Then the Taken came back. The Lady looked displeased. "What happened?" I asked.

"The monster got crafty. Ran into the null where it brushes the ground. The visibility is too poor to go after him."

"Will it make much difference?"

"No." But she did not sound entirely confident.

The weather worsened. But the whales remained undaunted. We reached the Barrowland. My group went to the Guards compound. Darling's put up at Blue Willy. The boundary of the null fell just outside the compound wall.

Colonel Sweet himself greeted us. Good old Sweet who I thought was dead for sure. He had a gimp leg now. I cannot say he was convivial. But then, it was a time when nobody was.

The orderly assigned us was our old friend Case.

Chapter Forty-Nine: THE INVISIBLE MAZE

The first time Case appeared he rode the edge of panic. Me doing a kindly uncle act did not soothe him. The Lady doing her bit almost kicked him over the edge into hysteria. Having Tracker lurking around in natural form was no help either.

One-Eye, of all people, calmed him down. Got him onto the subject of Raven and how Raven was doing, and that did the job.

I had my own near case of hysteria. Hours after we put down, before I even got set up for it, the Lady brought Whisper and Limper to double-check our translations.

Whisper was supposed to see if any papers were missing. Limper was supposed to plumb his memory of olden times for connections we may have missed. He, it seems, was much into the social whirl of the early Domination.

Amazing. I could not imagine that hunk of hatred and human wreckage ever having been anything but nastiness personified.

I got Goblin to keep an eyeball on those two while I broke away to look in on Raven. Everyone else had given him a look-see already.

She was there, leaning against a wall, gnawing a fingernail, not looking anything like the great bitch who had tormented the world for lo! so many years. Like I said before, I hate it when they go human. And she was human and then some. Flat-assed scared.

"How is he?" I asked, and when I saw her mood: "What's the matter?"

"He's unchanged. They've taken good care of him. Nothing is the matter that a few miracles won't cure."

I dared raise a questioning eyebrow.

"All the exits are closed, Croaker. I'm headed down a tunnel. My choices grow ever more narrow, and each is worse than the other."

I settled on the chair Case used while watching over Raven, began playing doctor. Needlessly, but I liked to see for myself. Half-distracted, I said, "I expect it's lonely, being queen of the world."

Slight gasp. "You grow too bold."

Didn't I? "I'm sorry. Thinking out loud. An unhealthy habit known to be the cause of bruises and major hemorrhaging. He does look sound. You think Limper or Whisper will help?"

"No. But every angle has to be tried."

"What about Bomanz?"

"Bomanz?"

I looked at her. She seemed honestly puzzled. "The wizard who sprung you."

"Oh. What about him? What could a dead man contribute? I disposed of my necromancer. . . . You know something I don't?"

Not bloody likely. She had me under the Eye. Nevertheless . . .

I debated for half a minute, not wanting to give up what might be a whisker of advantage. Then: "I had it from Goblin and One-Eye that he's perfectly healthy. That he's caught in the Barrowland. Like Raven, only body and all."

"How could that be?"

Was it possible she had overlooked this while interrogating me? I guess if you do not ask the right questions, you will not get the right answers.

I reflected on all we had done together. I had sketched Raven's reports for her, but she had not read those letters. In fact . . . The originals, from which Raven drew his story, were in my quarters. Goblin and One-Eye lugged them all the way to the Plain only to see them hauled right back. Nobody had plumbed them because they repeated a story already told. . . .

"Sit," I said, rising. "Back in two shakes."

Goblin fish-eyed me when I breezed in. "Be a few minutes more. Something came up." I scrounged up the case in which Raven's documents had traveled. Only the original Bomanz manuscript resided there now. I fluttered back out, ignored by the Taken.

Nice feeling, I'll tell you, being beneath their notice. Too bad it was just because they were fighting for their existence. Like the rest of us.

"Here. This is the original manuscript. I went over it once, lightly, to check Raven's translation. It looked good to me, though he did dramatize and invent dialog. But the facts and characterizations are pure Bomanz."

She read with incredible swiftness. "Get Raven's version."

Out and back, under Goblin's scowl and growl at my departing back: "How long is a few minutes these days, Croaker?"

She went through those swiftly, too. And looked thoughtful when she finished.

"Well?" I asked.

"There may be something here. Actually, something that's not here. Two questions. Who wrote this in the first place? And where is the stone in Oar that the son mentioned?"

"I assume Bomanz did most of the original and his wife finished it."

"Wouldn't he have used first person?"

"Not necessarily. It's possible the literary conventions of the time forbade it. Raven often chided me for interjecting too much of myself into the Annals. He came of a different tradition."

"We'll accept that as a hypothesis. Next question. What became of the wife?"

"She came of a family from Oar. I would expect her to go back."

"When she was known as the wife of the man responsible for loosing me?"

"Was she? Bomanz was an assumed name."

She brushed my objection aside. "Whisper acquired those documents in Lords. As a lot. Nothing connects Bomanz with them except his story. My feeling is that they were accumulated at a later date. But his papers. What were they doing between the time they left here and the time Whisper found them? Have some ancillary items been lost? It's time we consulted Whisper."

We, however, included me out.

Whatever, a fire was ignited. Before long, Taken were roaring off to faraway places. Within two days Benefice delivered the stone mentioned by Bomanz's son. It proved useless. Some Guards appropriated it and used it for a door-step to their barracks.

I caught occasional hints of a search progressing from Oar south along the route Jasmine had taken after fleeing from the Barrowland, widowed and shamed. Hard to find tracks that old, but the Taken have remarkable skills.

Another search progressed from Lords.

I had the dubious pleasure of hanging around with the Limper while he pointed out all the mistakes we made translit-erating UchiTelle and KurreTelle names. Seems not only were spellings not uniform in those days, but neither were alphabets. And some of the folks mentioned were not of UchiTelle or KurreTelle stock, but outsiders who had adapted their names to local usage. Limper busied himself doing things backwards.

One afternoon Silent gave me the high sign. He had been spying over the Limper's shoulder, off and on, with more devotion than I.

He had found a pattern.

Chapter Fifty: GNOMEN?

Darling has a self-discipline that amazes me. All that time she was over there at Blue Willy and not once did she surrender to her desire to see Raven. You could see the ache in her whenever his name came up, but she held off for a month.

But she came, as inevitably we knew she must, with the Lady's permission. I tried to ignore her visit entirely. And I made Silent, Goblin, and One-Eye stay away too, though with Silent it was a tight thing. Eventually he did agree; it was a private thing, for her alone, and his interests would not be served by sticking his nose in.

If I would not go to her, she would come to me. For a while, while everyone else was busy elsewhere. For a hug, to remind her there were those of us who cared. To have some moral support there while she worked out something in her mind.

She signed, "I cannot deny it now, can I?" And a few minutes later: "I still have the soft place for him. But he will have to earn his way back in." Which was her equivalent of our thinking aloud.

I felt more for Silent at that moment than for Raven. Raven I'd always respected for his toughness and fearlessness, but I'd never really grown to like him. Silent I did like, and did wish well.

I signed, "Do not be brokenhearted if you find he is too old to change."

Wan smile. "My heart was broken a long time ago. No. I have no expectations. This is not a fairy-tale world."

That was all she had to say. I did not take it to heart till it began to illuminate later events.

She came and she went, in sorrow for the death of dreams, and she came no more.

In moments when his needs called him away, we copied everything the Limper left behind and compared it with our own charts. "Oh, hey," I breathed once. "Oh, hey."

Here was a lord from a far western kingdom. A Baron Senjak who had four daughters said to vie with one another in their loveliness. One wore the name Ardath.

"She lied," Goblin whispered.

"Maybe," I admitted. "More likely, she didn't know. In fact, she couldn't have known. Nor could anyone else have, really. I still don't see how Soulcatcher could have been convinced that the Dominator's true name was in here."

"Wishful thinking, maybe," One-Eye guessed.

"No," I said. "You could tell she *knew* what she had. She just didn't know how to dig it out."

"Just like us."

"Ardath is dead," I said. "That leaves three possibilities. But if push comes to shove, we only get one shot."

"Catalog what else we know."

"Soulcatcher was one sister. Name not yet known. Ardath may have been the Lady's twin. I think she was older than Catcher, though they were children together and not separated by many years. Of the fourth sister we know nothing."

Silent signed, "You have four names, given and family. Consult the genealogies. Find who married whom."

I groaned. The genealogies were over at Blue Willy. Darling had had them loaded onto the cargo whale with everything else.

Time was short. The work daunted me. You do not go into those genealogies with a woman's name and find anything easily. You have to look for a man who married the woman you are seeking and hope the recorder thought enough of her to mention her name.

"How are we going to manage all this?" I wondered. "With me the only one who can decipher these chicken tracks?" Then a brilliant idea. If I say so myself. "Tracker. We'll put Tracker on it. He don't have nothing to do but watch that sapling. He can do that over at Blue Willy and read old books at the same time."

Easier said than done. Tracker was far from his new master. Getting the message into his pea brain was a major undertaking. But once that had been accomplished there was no stopping him.

One night, as I snuggled down under the covers, *she* appeared in my quarters. "Up, Croaker."

"Huh?"

"We're going flying."

"Uh? No disrespect, but it's the middle of the night. I had a hard day."

"Up."

So you don't argue when the Lady commands.

Chapter Fifty-One: THE SIGN

A freezing rain was falling. Everything was glazed with crystal ice. "Looks like a warm snap," I said.

She was without a sense of humor that night. It took an effort to overlook my remark. She led me to a carpet. It had a crystal dome covering the forward seats. That was a feature recently added to Limper's craft.

The Lady used some small magic to melt the ice off. "Make sure it's sealed tightly," she told me.

"Looks good to me."

We lifted off.

Suddenly I was on my back. The nose of the fish pointed at unseen stars. We climbed at a dreadful rate. I expected momentarily to be so high I could not breathe.

We got that high. And higher. We broke through the clouds. And I understood the significance of the dome.

It kept in breathable air. Meaning the windwhales could no longer climb higher than the Taken. Always chipping away, the Lady and her gang.

But what the hell was *this* all about?

"There." A sigh of disappointment. A confirmation that a shadow darkened hope. She pointed.

I saw it. I knew it, for I had seen it before, in the days of the long retreat that ended in the battle before the Tower. The Great Comet. Small, but no denying its unique silver scimitar shape. "It can't be. It isn't due for twenty years. Celestial bodies don't change their cycles."

"They don't. That's axiomatic. So maybe the axiom makers are wrong."

She tilted the carpet down. "Note it in your writings, but don't mention it otherwise. Our peoples are troubled enough."

"Right." That comet has a hold on men's minds.

Back down into the yuck of a Barrowland night. We came in over the Great Barrow itself, only forty feet up. The damned river was close. The ghosts were dancing in the rain.

I sloshed into the barracks in a numb state, checked the calendar.

Twelve days to go.

The old bastard was probably out there laughing it up with his favorite hound, Toadkiller Dog.

Chapter Fifty-Two: NO SURPRISE

Something that lies down in that mind below the mind would not let me be. I tossed and turned, wakened, fell asleep, and finally, in the wee hours, it surfaced. I got up and shuffled through papers.

I found that piece that made the Lady gasp once, ploughed through that interminable guest list till I found a Lord Senjak and his daughters Ardath, Credence, and Sylith. The youngest, one Dorotea, the scribbler noted, could not attend.

"Ha!" I crowed. "The search narrows."

There was no more information, but that was a triumph. Assuming the Lady was indeed a twin and Dorotea was the youngest and Ardath dead, the odds were now fifty-fifty. A woman named Sylith or a woman named Credence. Credence? That is how it translated.

I was so excited I got no more sleep. Even that damned off-schedule comet fled my thoughts.

But excitement perished between the grinding stones of time. Nothing came from those Taken tracing Bomanz's wife and papers. I suggested the Lady go to the source himself. She was not prepared for the risk. Not yet.

Our old and stupid friend Tracker produced another gem four days after I eliminated sister Dorotea. The big goof had been reading genealogies day and night.

Silent came back from Blue Willy wearing such a look I knew something good had happened. He dragged me outside, toward town, into the null. He gave me a slip of damp paper. In Tracker's simple style, it said:

Three sisters were married. Ardath married twice, first a Baron Kaden of Dartstone, who died in battle. Six years later she married Erin NoFather, an unlanded priest of the god Vancer, from a town called Slinger, in the kingdom of Vye. Credence married Barthelme of Jaunt, a renowned sorcerer. It is in my memory that Barthelme of Jaunt became one of the Taken, but my memory is not trustworthy.

No lie.

Dorotea married Raft, Prince-in-Waiting, of Start. Sylith never married.

Tracker then proved that, slow though he might be, an occasional idea did perk through his murk of a mind.

The death rolls reveal that Ardath and her husband, Erin NoFather, an unlanded priest of the god Vancer, from a town called Slinger, in the kingdom of Vye, were slain by bandits while traveling between Lathe and Ova. My untrustworthy

*memory recalls that this took place just months before the
Dominator proclaimed himself.*

*Sylith drowned in a flood of the River Dream some years
earlier, swept away before countless witnesses. But no body
was found.*

We had an eyewitness. It never occurred to me to think of
Tracker that way, though the knowledge had been there for
the recognition. Maybe we could figure some way to get at his
memories.

*Credence perished in the fighting when the Dominator and
Lady took Jaunt in the early days of their conquests. There is
no record of Dorotea's death.*

"Damn," I said. "Old Tracker is worth something after
all."

Silent signed, "It sounds confused, but reason should provide something."

More than something. Without drawing charts, connecting
all those women, I felt confident enough to say, "We knew
Dorotea as Soulcatcher. We know Ardath wasn't the Lady.
Odds are, the sister who engineered the ambush that killed
her . . ." There was something missing still. If I just knew
which were twins. . . .

In response to my question, Silent signed, "Tracker is
looking for birth records." But he was unlikely to score
again. Lord Senjak was not KurreTelle.

"One of the purported dead didn't die. I'd put my money
on Sylith. Assuming Credence was killed because she recognized a sister who was supposed to be dead when the Dominator and Lady took Jaunt."

"Bomanz mentions a legend about the Lady killing her
twin. Is that this ambush? Or something more public?"

"Who knows?" I said. It really did get confusing. For a
moment I wondered if it mattered.

The Lady called an assembly. Our original estimate of time
available now appeared overly optimistic. She told us, "We
appear to have been misled. There is nothing in Catcher's
documents to betray my husband's name. How she reached
that assumption is beyond us now. If documents are missing,
we cannot be sure. Unless news comes from Lords or Oar

soon, we can forget that avenue. It's time to consider alternatives."

I scribbled a note, asked Whisper to pass it to the Lady. The Lady read it, then looked at me with narrowed, thoughtful eyes. "Erin NoFather," she read aloud. "An unlanded priest of the god Vancer, from Slinger, in the kingdom of Vye. This, from our amateur historian. What you found is less interesting than the fact that you found it, Croaker. That news is five hundred years old. It was worthless then. Whoever Erin NoFather was before he left Vye, he did an absolute job of eliminating traces. By the time he became interesting enough to have his antecedents investigated, he had obliterated not only Slinger but every person to have lived in that village during his lifetime. In later years he went even farther, wasting all Vye. Which is why the notion that those papers might contain his true name constituted such a surprise."

I felt about half-size, and stupid. I should have known they would have tried to unmask the Dominator before. I had surrendered some small advantage for nothing. So much for the spirit of cooperation.

One of the new Taken—I cannot keep them straight, for they all dress the same—arrived soon afterward. He or she gave the Lady a small carved chest. The Lady smiled when she opened it. "There were no papers that survived. But there were these." She dumped some odd bracelets. "Tomorrow we go after Bomanz."

Everyone else knew. I had to ask. "What are they?"

"The amulets made for the Eternal Guard in the time of the White Rose. So they could enter the Barrowland without hazard."

The resulting excitement surpassed my understanding.

"The wife must have carried them away. Though how she laid hands on them is a mystery. Break this up now. I need time to think." She shooed us like a farm wife shooes chickens.

I returned to my room. The Limper floated in behind me. He said nary a word, but ducked into the documents again. Puzzled, I looked over his shoulder. He had lists of all the names we had unearthed, written in the alphabets of the languages whence they sprang. He seemed to be playing with both substitution codes and numerology. Baffled, I went to my bed, turned my back on him, faked sleep.

As long as he was there, I knew, sleep would evade me.

Chapter Fifty-Three: THE RECOVERY

It resumed snowing that night. Real snow, half a foot an hour and no letup. The racket raised by the Guards as they strove to clear it from doorways and the carpets wakened me.

I had slept despite the Limper.

An instant of terror. I sat bolt upright. He remained at his task.

The barracks was overly warm, holding the heat because it was all but buried.

There was a bustle despite the weather. Taken had arrived while I slept. Guards not only dug but hurried about other tasks.

One-Eye joined me for a rude breakfast. I said, "So she's going ahead. Despite the weather."

"It won't get any better, Croaker. That guy out there knows what's going on." He looked grim.

"What's the matter?"

"I can count, Croaker. What do you expect from a guy with a week to live?"

My stomach tightened. Yes. I had been able to avoid thoughts of the sort so far, but . . . "We've been in tight places before. Stair of Tear. Juniper. Beryl. We made it."

"I keep telling myself."

"How's Darling?"

"Worried. What do you think? She's a bug between hammer and anvil."

"The Lady has forgotten her."

He snorted. "Don't let your special dispensation erode your common sense, Croaker."

"Sound advice," I admitted. "But unnecessary. A hawk couldn't watch her more closely."

"You going out?"

"I wouldn't miss it. Know where I can get some snowshoes?"

He grinned. For an instant the devil of years past peeped forth. "Some guys I know—mentioning no names, you know how it is—swiped a half dozen pairs from the Guard Armory last night. Duty man fell asleep on post."

I grinned and winked. So. I was not seeing enough of them to keep up, but they were not just sitting around and waiting.

"Couple pairs went off to Darling, just in case. Got four pair left. And just a smidgen of a plan."

"Yeah?"

"Yeah. You'll see. Brilliant, if I do say so myself."

"Where are the shoes? When are you going?"

"Meet us in the smokehouse after the Taken get off the ground."

Several guards came in to eat, looking exhausted, grumbling. One-Eye departed, leaving me in deep thought. What were they plotting?

The most carefully laid plans. . . . Like that.

The Lady marched into the mess hall. "Get your gloves and coats, Croaker. It's time."

I gaped.

"Are you coming?"

"But . . ." I flailed around for an excuse. "If we go, somebody will have to do without a carpet."

She gave me an odd look. "Limper is staying here. Come. Get your clothing."

I did so, in a daze, passing Goblin as we went outside. I gave him a baffled little headshake.

A moment before we lifted off the Lady reached back, offering me something. "What's this?"

"Better wear it. Unless you want to go in without an amulet."

"Oh."

It did not look like much. Some cheap jaspar and jadé on brittle leather. Yet when I secured the buckle around my wrist, I felt the power in it.

We passed over the rooftops very low. They were the only visual guides available. Out on the cleared land there was nothing. But being the Lady, she had other resources.

We took a turn around the bounds of the Barrowland. On the river side we descended till the water lay but a yard beneath us. "Lot of ice," I said.

She did not reply. She was studying the shoreline, now within the Barrowland itself. A sodden section of bank collapsed, revealing a dozen skeletons. I grimaced. In moments they were covered with snow or swept away.

"Just about on schedule, I'd guess," I said.

"Uhm." She moved on around the perimeter. A couple times I glimpsed other carpets circling. Something below caught my eye. "Down there!"

"What?"

"Thought I saw tracks."

"Maybe. Toadkiller Dog is nearby."

Oh, my.

"Time," she said, and turned toward the Great Barrow.

We put down at the mound's base. She piled out. I joined her. Other carpets descended. Soon there were four Taken, the Lady, and one scared old physician standing just yards from the despair of the world.

One of the Taken brought shovels. Snow began to fly. We took turns, nobody exempt. It was a bitch of a job, and became more so when we reached the buried scrub growth. It got worse when we reached frozen earth. We had to go slow. The Lady said Bomanz was barely covered.

It went on, it seemed, forever. Dig and dig and dig. We uncovered a withered humanoid thing the Lady assured us was Bomanz.

My shovel clicked against something my last turn. I bent to examine it, thinking it a rock. I brushed frosty earth away. . . .

And dived out of that hole, whirled, pointed. The Lady

went down. Laughter drifted upward. "Croaker found the dragon. His jaw, anyway."

I kept on retreating, toward our carpet. . . .

Something huge vaulted it, trailing a basso snarl. I flung myself to one side, into snow that swallowed me. There were cries, growls. . . . When I emerged it was over. I glimpsed Toadkiller Dog clearing the carpet in retreat, more than a little scarred.

The Lady and Taken had been ready for him.

"Why didn't somebody warn me?" I whined.

"He could have read you. I'm just sorry we didn't cripple him."

Two Taken, probably of the male vice, lifted Bomanz. He was stiff as a statue, yet there was that about him which even I could sense. A spark, or something. No one could have mistaken him for dead.

Into a carpet he went.

The anger in the mound had been a trickle, barely sensed, like the buzzing of a fly across a room. It smacked us now, one hard hammer stroke reeking madness. Not an iota of fear informed it. That thing had an absolute confidence in its ultimate victory. We were but delays and irritants.

The carpet carrying Bomanz departed. Then another. I settled into my place and willed the Lady to hurry me away.

A spate of snarling and yelling broke out toward town. Brilliant light slashed through the snowfall. "I knew it," I growled, one fear realized. Toadkiller Dog had found One-Eye and Goblin.

Another carpet lifted. The Lady boarded ours, closed the dome. "Fools," she said. "What were they doing?"

I said nothing.

She did not see. Her attention was on the carpet, which was not behaving as it should. Something seemed to pull it toward the Great Barrow. But I saw. Tracker's ugly face passed at eye level. He carried the son of the tree.

Then Toadkiller Dog reappeared, stalking Tracker. Half the monster's face was gone. He ran on three legs. But he was plenty enough to take Tracker apart.

The Lady saw Toadkiller Dog. She spun the carpet. Systematically she loosed its eight thirty foot shafts. She did not miss. And yet . . .

Dragging the missiles, engulfed in flame, Toadkiller Dog crawled into the Great Tragic River. He went under and did not come up.

"That'll keep *him* out of the way for a while."

Not ten yards away, oblivious, Tracker was clearing the peak of the Great Barrow so he could plant his sapling. "Idiots," the Lady murmured. "I'm surrounded by idiots. Even the Tree is a dolt."

She would not explain. Neither did she interfere.

I sought traces of One-Eye and Goblin as we flew homeward. I saw nothing. They were not in the compound. Of course. There had not yet been time for them to snowshoe back. But when they had not appeared an hour later, I began having trouble concentrating on the reanimation of Bomanz.

That started with repeated hot baths, both to warm his flesh and to cleanse him. I did not get to see the preliminaries. The Lady kept me with her. She did not look in till the Taken were ready for the final quickening. And that was unimpressive. The Lady made a few gestures around Bomanz—who looked pretty moth-eaten—and said a few words in a language I did not understand.

Why do sorcerers always use languages nobody understands? Even Goblin and One-Eye do it. Each has confided that he cannot follow the tongue the other uses. Maybe they make it up?

Her words worked. That old wreck came to life grittily determined to push forward against a savage wind. He marched three steps before registering his altered circumstances.

He froze. He turned slowly, face collapsing into despair. His gaze locked on the Lady. Maybe two minutes passed. Then he looked the rest of us over and considered his surroundings.

"You explain, Croaker."

"Does he speak . . ."

"Forsberger hasn't changed."

I faced Bomanz, a legend come to life. "I am Croaker. A military physician by profession. You are Bomanz. . . ."

"His name is Seth Chalk, Croaker. Let us establish that immediately."

"You are Bomanz, whose true name may be Seth Chalk, a sorcerer of Oar. Nearly a century has passed since you attempted to contact the Lady."

"Give him the whole story." The Lady used a Jewel Cities dialect likely to be outside Bomanz's capacity.

I talked till I was hoarse. The rise of the Lady's empire. The threat defeated at the battle at Charm. The threat defeated at Juniper. The present threat. He said not a word in all that time. Not once did I see in him the fat, almost obsequious shopkeeper of the story.

His first words were: "So. I did not entirely fail." He faced the Lady. "And you remain tainted by the light, Not-Ardath." He faced me again. "You will take me to the White Rose. As soon as I have eaten."

Nary a protest from the Lady.

He *ate* like a fat little shopkeeper.

The Lady herself helped me back into my wet winter coat. "Don't dawdle," she cautioned.

Hardly had we departed when Bomanz seemed to diminish. He said, "I'm too old. Don't let that back there fool you. An act. Going to play with the big boys, you have to act. What'll I do? A hundred years. Less than a week to redeem myself. How will I get a handle on things that quickly? The only principal I know is the Lady."

"Why did you think she was Ardath? Why not one of the other sisters?"

"There was more than one?"

"Four." I named them. "From your papers I've established that Soulcatcher was the one named Dorotea. . . ."

"*My* papers?"

"So called. Because the story of you wakening the Lady was prominent among them. It's always been assumed, till a few days ago, that you assembled them and your wife carried them away when she thought you had died."

"Bears investigation. I collected nothing. I risked nothing but a map of the Barrowland."

"I know the map well."

"I must see those papers. But first, your White Rose. Meanwhile, tell me about the Lady."

I had trouble staying with him. He zigged and zagged, spraying ideas. "What about her?"

"There is a detectable tension between you. Of enemies who are friends, perhaps. Lovers who are enemies? Opponents who know one another well and respect one another. If you respect her, it's with reason. It's impossible to respect total evil. It cannot respect itself."

Wow. He was right. I did respect her. So I talked a bit. And my theme was, when I noticed it, that she did remain tainted by the light. "She tried hard to be a villain. But when faced by real darkness—the thing under the mound—her weakness started to show."

"It is only slightly less difficult for us to extinguish the light within us than it is for us to conquer the darkness. A Dominator occurs once in a hundred generations. The others, like the Taken, are but imitations."

"Can you stand against the Lady?"

"Hardly. I suspect my fate is to become one of the Taken when she finds time." He'd landed on his feet, this old boy. He halted. "Lords! She's strong!"

"Who?"

"Your Darling. An incredible absorption. I feel helpless as a child."

We stamped into Blue Willy, entering through a second-floor window. The snow was banked that high.

One-Eye, Goblin, and Silent were down in the common room with Darling. The first two looked a bit shopworn. "So," I said. "You guys made it. I thought Toadkiller Dog had you for lunch."

"No problem at all," One-Eye said. "We . . ."

"What do you mean, we?" Goblin demanded. "You were worthless as tits on a boar hog. Silent . . ."

"Shut up. This is Bomanz. He wants to meet Darling."

"*The* Bomanz?" Goblin squeaked.

"The very one."

Their meeting was about a three-question interview. Darling took charge immediately. When he realized Darling was leading him, Bomanz broke it off. He told me, "Next step. I read my alleged autobiography."

"It's not yours?"

"Unlikely. Unless my memory serves me worse than I suppose."

We returned to the compound in silence. He seemed reflective. Darling has that impact on those who meet her for the first time. She is just Darling to those of us who have known her all along.

Bomanz worked his way through the original manuscript, occasionally asking about specific passages. He was unfamiliar with the UchiTelle dialect.

"You had nothing to do with that, then?"

"No. But my wife was the primary source. Question. Was the girl Snoopy traced?"

"No."

"She is the one to follow up. She is the only survivor of significance."

"I'll tell the Lady. But there isn't time for it. In a few days Hell is going to break loose out there." I wondered if Tracker had gotten the sapling planted. Much good it would do when the Great Tragic reached the mound. Brave move but dumb, Tracker.

The effects of his effort were apparent soon, though. When I got around to relaying Bomanz's suggestion about Snoopy, the Lady asked, "Have you noted the weather?"

"No."

"It's getting better. The sapling stilled my husband's ability to shape it. Too late, of course. It will be months before the river falls."

She was depressed. She merely nodded when I told her what Bomanz had to say.

"Is it that bad? Are we defeated before we enter the lists?"

"No. But the price of victory escalates. I do not want to pay that price. I don't know if I can."

I stood there perplexed, awaiting an expansion upon the subject. None was forthcoming.

After a time she said, "Sit, Croaker." I sat in the chair she indicated, next to a roaring fire diligently tended by the soldier Case. After a time she sent Case away. But still nothing was forthcoming.

"Time tightens the noose," she murmured at one point, and at another, "I'm afraid to unravel the knot."

Chapter Fifty-Four: AN EVENING AT HOME

Days passed. No one of any especial allegiance gained any apparent ground. The Lady canceled all investigations. She and the Taken conferred often. I was excluded. So was Bomanz. The Limper participated only when ordered out of my quarters.

I gave up trying to sleep there. I moved in with Goblin and One-Eye. Which shows how much the Taken distressed me. Sharing a room with those two is like living amidst an ongoing riot.

Raven, as ever, changed not the least and remained mostly forgotten by all but his loyal Case. Silent did look in occasionally, on Darling's behalf, but without enthusiasm.

Only then did I realize that Silent felt more toward Darling than loyalty and protectiveness, and he was without means of expressing those feelings. Silence was enforced upon him by more than a vow.

I could not learn which sisters were twins. As I anticipated, Tracker found nothing in the genealogies. A miracle he found what he did, the way sorcerers cover their backtrails.

Goblin and One-Eye tried hypnotizing him, hoping to plumb his ancient memories. It was like stalking ghosts in a heavy fog.

The Taken moved to stall the Great Tragic. Ice collected along the western bank, turning the force of the current. But they overtinkered and a gorge developed. It threatened to raise the river level. A two-day effort won us maybe ten hours.

Occasionally large tracks appeared around the Barrowland, soon vanished beneath drifting snow. Though the skies cleared, the air grew colder. The snow neither melted nor crusted. The Taken engineered that. A wind from the east stirred the snow continuously.

Case stopped by to tell me, "The Lady wants you, sir. Right away."

I broke off playing three-handed Tonk with Goblin and One-Eye. So far had things slowed—except the flow of time. There was nothing more we could do.

"Sir," said Case as we stepped out of hearing of the others, "be careful."

"Uhm?"

"She's in a dark mood."

"Thanks." I dallied. My own mood was dark enough. It did not need to feed on hers.

Her quarters had been refurnished. Carpets had been brought in. Hangings covered the walls. A settee of sorts stood before the fireplace, where a fire burned with a comforting crackle. The atmosphere seemed calculated. Home as we dream it to be rather than as it is.

She was seated on the couch. "Come sit with me," she said, without glancing back to see who had come in. I started to take one of the chairs. "No. Here, by me." So I settled on the couch.

"What is it?"

Her eyes were fixed on something far away. Her face said she was in pain. "I have decided."

"Yes?" I waited nervously, not sure what she meant, less sure I belonged there.

"The choices have narrowed down. I can surrender and become another of the Taken."

That was a less dire penalty than I had expected. "Or?"

"Or I can fight. A battle that can't be won. Or won only in its losing."

"If you can't win, why fight?" I would not have asked that

of one of the Company. With my own I would have known the answer.

Hers was not ours. "Because the outcome can be shaped. I can't win. But I can decide who does."

"Or at least make sure it isn't him?"

A slow nod.

Her bleak mood began to make sense. I have seen it on the battlefield, with men about to undertake a task likely to be fatal but which must be hazarded so others will not perish.

To cover my reaction, I slipped off the couch and added three small logs to the fire. But for our moods it would have been nice there in the crispy heat, watching the dancing flames.

We did that for a while. I sensed that I was not expected to talk.

"It begins at sunup," she said at last.

"What?"

"The final conflict. Laugh at me, Croaker. I'm going to try to kill a shadow. With no hope of surviving myself."

Laugh? Never. Admire. Respect. My enemy still, in the end unable to extinguish that last spark of light and so die in yet another way.

All this while she sat there primly, hands folded in her lap. She stared into the fire as if certain that eventually it would reveal the answer to some mystery. She began to shiver.

This woman for whom death held such devouring terror had chosen death over surrender.

What did that do for my confidence? Nothing good. Nothing good at all. I might have felt better had I seen the picture she did. But she did not talk about it.

In a very, very soft, tentative voice, she asked, "Croaker? Will you hold me?"

What? I didn't say it, but I sure as hell thought it.

I didn't say anything. Clumsily, uncertainly, I did as she asked.

She began crying on my shoulder, softly, quietly, shaking like a captive baby rabbit.

It was a long time before she said anything. I did not presume.

"No one has done this since I was a baby. My nurse . . ."

Another long silence.

"I've never had a friend."

Another long gap.

"I'm scared, Croaker. And alone."

"No. We'll all be with you."

"Not for the same reasons." She fell silent for good then. I held her a long time. The fire burned down and its light faded from the room. Outside, the wind began to howl.

When I finally thought she had fallen asleep, and started to disengage myself, she clung more tightly, so I stilled and continued to hold her, though half the muscles in my body ached.

Eventually she peeled herself away, rose, built up the fire. I sat. She stood behind me a while, staring at the flames. Then she rested a hand on my shoulder a moment. In a faraway voice she said, "Good night."

She went into another room. I sat for ten or fifteen minutes before putting on a last log and shuffling back into the real world.

I must have worn an odd look. Neither Goblin nor One-Eye aggravated me. I rolled into my bedroll, back to them, but did not fall asleep for a long time.

Chapter Fifty-Five: OPENING ROUNDS

I wakened startled. The null! I had been out of it so much it disturbed me by its presence. I rolled out hurriedly, discovered I was alone in the room. Not only there, but in the barracks, practically. There were a few Guards in the mess hall.

The sun was not yet up.

The wind still howled around the building. There was a marked chill in the air, though the fires were burning high. I shoveled boiled oats in and wondered what I was missing.

The Lady entered as I finished. "There you are. I thought I'd have to leave without you."

Whatever her problems the night before, she was brisk and confident and ready for business now.

The null faded while I got my coat. I dropped by my own room momentarily. The Limper was there still. I left frowning thoughtfully.

Into the carpet. Full crew today. Every carpet was fully crewed and armed. But I was more interested in the absence of snow between town and the Barrowland.,

That howling wind had blown it away.

We went up as it became light enough to see. The Lady took the carpet up till the Barrowland resembled a map taking shape as shadows vaporized. She set us to cruising in a tight circle. The wind, I noted, had faded.

The Great Barrow looked ready to collapse into the river.

"One hundred hours," she said, as though divining my thoughts. So we were reduced to counting hours.

I looked around the horizon. There. "The comet."

"They can't see it from the ground. But tonight . . . it'll have to cloud up."

Below, tiny figures scurried around one quarter of the cleared area. The Lady unrolled a map similar to Bomanz's.

"Raven," I said.

"Today. If we're lucky."

"What're they doing down there?"

"Surveying."

More than that was happening. The Guards were out in full battle regalia, forming an arc around the Barrowland. Light siege machines were being assembled. But some men were, indeed, surveying and setting up rows of lances flying colored pennons. I did not ask why. She would not explain.

A dozen windwhales hovered to the east, beyond the river. I had thought them long departed.

The sky there burned with dawn's conflagration.

"First test," the Lady said. "A feeble monster." She frowned in concentration. Our carpet began to glow.

A white horse and white rider came from the town. Darling. Accompanied by Silent and the Lieutenant. Darling rode into an aisle marked by pennons. She halted beside the last.

The earth erupted. Something that might have been first cousin to Toadkiller Dog, and even more closely related to an octopus, burst into the light. It raced over the Barrowland, toward the river, away from the null.

Darling galloped toward town.

Wizards' fury rained from the carpets. The monster was a cinder in seconds. "One," the Lady said. Below, men began another aisle of pennons.

And so it went, slowly and deliberately, all the day long. Most of the Dominator's creatures broke for the river. The few that charged the other way encountered a barricade of missile fire before succumbing to the Taken.

"Is there time to eliminate them all?" I asked as the sun was setting. I had been itchy for hours, sitting in one place.

"More than enough. But it won't stay this easy."

I probed, but she would not expand upon what she had said.

It looked slick to me. Just pick them off and keep picking them off, and go for the big guy when they were all gone. Tough he might be, but what could he do enveloped in the null?

When I staggered into the barracks, to my room, I found the Limper still at work. The Taken need less rest than we mortals, but he had to be on the edge of collapse. What the hell was he doing?

Then there was Bomanz. He had not appeared today. What was he trying to slip up his sleeve?

I was eating a supper very much like breakfast when Silent materialized. He settled opposite me, clutching a bowl of mush as if it were an alms bowl. He looked pale.

"How was it for Darling?" I asked.

He signed, "She almost enjoyed it. She took chances she should not have. One of those things almost got to her. Otto was hurt fending it off."

"He need me?"

"One-Eye managed."

"What're you doing here?"

"It is the night to bring Raven out."

"Oh." Again I had forgotten Raven. How could I number myself among his friends when I seemed so indifferent to his fate?

Silent followed me to where I was staying with One-Eye and Goblin. Those two joined us shortly. They were subdued. They had been assigned major roles in the recovery of our old friend.

I worried more about Silent. The shadow had passed over him. He was fighting it. Would he be strong enough to win?

Part of him did not want Raven rescued.

Part of me did not, either.

A very tired Lady came to ask, "Will you participate in this?"

I shook my head. "I'd just get in the way. Let me know when it's done."

She gave me a hard look, then shrugged and went away.

Very late a feeble One-Eye wakened me. I bolted up. "Well?"

"We managed. I don't know how well. But he's back."

"How was it?"

"Rough." He crawled into his bedroll. Goblin was in his already, snoring. Silent had come with them. He was against the wall, wrapped in a borrowed blanket, cutting logs. By the time I wakened fully One-Eye was sawing with the rest.

In Raven's room there was nothing to see but Raven snoring and Case looking worried. The crowd had cleared out, leaving a ripe stench behind.

"He seem all right?" I asked.

Case shrugged. "I'm no doctor."

"I am. Let me look him over."

Pulse strong enough. Breathing a little fast for a sleeper, but not disturbingly so. Pupils dilated. Muscles tense. Sweaty. "Don't look like much to worry about. Keep feeding him broth. And get hold of me as soon as he's talking. Don't let him get up. His muscles will be clay. He might hurt himself."

Case nodded and nodded.

I returned to my bedroll, lay there a long time alternately wondering about Raven and about the Limper. A lamp still burned in my former quarters. The last of the old Taken still pursued his monomaniacal quest.

Raven became the greater worry. He was going to demand an accounting of our care for Darling. And I was in a mood to challenge his right.

Chapter Fifty-Six: TIME FADING

Dawn comes early when you wish it would not. The hours flash when you want them to drag. The following day was another of executions. The only thing unusual was that the Limper came out to watch. He seemed satisfied we were doing things right. He returned to my quarters—where he sacked out in my bed.

My evening check on Raven showed little change. Case reported that he had come near wakening several times and was mumbling in his sleep.

"Keep pouring soup down him. And don't be afraid to yell if you need me."

I could not sleep. I tried roaming the barracks, but near silence reigned. A few sleepless Guards haunted the mess hall. They fell silent at my arrival. I thought about going over to Blue Willy. But I would find no better reception there. I was on everybody's list.

It could do nothing but get worse.

I knew what the Lady meant about lonely.

I wished I had the nerve to visit her now that *I* needed a hug.

I returned to my bedroll.

I did fall asleep this time; they had to threaten mayhem to get me up.

We polished off the last of the Dominator's pets before noon. The Lady ordered a holiday for the remainder of the day. Come next morning we were to rehearse for the big show. She guessed we had about forty-eight hours before the river opened the tomb. Time to rest, time to practice, and ample time to get in the first whack.

That afternoon Limper went out and flew around a while. He was in high spirits. I seized the opportunity to visit my quarters and poke around, but all I could find were a few black wood shavings and a hint of silver dust, and barely enough of either to leave traces. He had cleaned up hastily. I did not touch. No telling what curiosities might occur if I did. Otherwise, I learned nothing.

The practice for the Event was tense. Everyone turned out, including Limper and Bomanz, who had kept so low most everyone had forgotten him. The windwhales ranged above the river. Their mantas soared and swooped. Darling charged the Great Barrow down a prepared aisle, stopping just short of far enough. The Taken and Guards stood to their respective weapons.

It looked good. Looked like it would work. So why was I convinced we were in for big trouble?

The moment our carpet touched down Case was beside it. "I need your help," he told me, ignoring the Lady. "He won't listen to me. He keeps trying to get up. He fell on his face already twice."

I glanced at the Lady. She gave me a go-ahead nod.

Raven was seated on the edge of his bed when I arrived. "I hear you're being a pain in the ass. What's the point of pulling your butt out of the Barrowland if you're going to commit suicide?"

His gaze rose slowly. He did not appear to recognize me. Oh, damn, I thought. His mind is gone.

"He talked any, Case?"

"Some. He don't always make sense. He don't realize how long it's been, I think."

"Maybe we should restrain him."

"No."

Startled, we looked at Raven. He knew me now. "No

restraints, Croaker. I'll behave.'' He flopped onto his back, smiling. "How long, Case?"

"Tell him the story," I said. "I'm going to go whip up some medicine."

I just wanted away from Raven. He looked worse with his soul restored. Cadaverous. Too much a reminder of my mortality. And that was one thing I did not need on my mind more than it was.

I whipped up a couple potions. One would settle Raven's shakes. The other would knock him out if he gave Case too much trouble.

Raven gave me a dark look when I returned. I do not know how far Case had gotten. "Stay off your high horse," I told him. "You got no idea what's happened since Juniper. In fact, not a whole lot since the Battle at Charm. You being the brave and rugged loner hasn't helped. Drink this. It's for the shakes.'' I gave Case the other mixture with whispered instructions.

In a voice little above a whisper, Raven asked, "Is it true? Darling and the Lady are going after the Dominator tomorrow? Together?"

"Yes. Do-or-die time. For everybody."

"I want to . . ."

"You'll stay put. You, too, Case. We don't want Darling distracted."

I had managed to abolish worries about the tangled ramifications inherent in tomorrow's confrontations. Now they rushed in on me again. The Dominator would not be the end of it. Unless we lost. If he fell, the war with the Lady would resume instantly.

I wanted to see Darling badly, wanted in on her plans. I dared not go. The Lady was keeping me on the leash. She might interrogate me any time.

Lonely work. Lonely work.

Case went on tale-telling. Then Goblin and One-Eye dropped in to tell stories from their perspectives. The Lady even looked in. She beckoned me.

"Yes?" I asked.

"Come."

I followed her to her quarters.

Outside, night had fallen. In about eighteen hours the Great Barrow would open of its own accord. Sooner if we followed plan.

"Sit."

I sat. I said, "I'm getting fixated on it. Butterflies the size of horses. Can't think about anything else."

"I know. I considered you as a distraction, but I cared too much."

Well, that distracted *me*.

"Perhaps one of your potions?"

I shook my head. "There is no specific for fear in my arsenal. I've heard of wizards . . ."

"Those antidotes cost too dearly. We'll need our wits about us. It won't go like it did in rehearsal."

I raised an eyebrow. She did not expand. I suppose she expected a lot of improvisational behavior from her allies.

The mess sergeant appeared. His crew rolled in a grand meal they set out on a table brought in special. A last feast for the condemned? After the crowd dispersed, the Lady said, "I ordered the best for everyone. Your friends in town included. Breakfast likewise." She seemed calm enough. But she was more accustomed to high-risk confrontations. . . .

I snorted at myself. I recalled being asked for a hug. She was as scared as anybody.

She saw but did not ask—tip enough that she was focused inward.

The meal was a miracle considering what the cooks had to work with. But it was nothing grand. We exchanged no words during its course. I finished first, rested my elbows on the table, retreated into thought. She followed suit. She had eaten very little. After a few minutes she went to her bedroom. She returned with three black arrows. Each had silver inlays in Kurre Telle script. I had seen their like before. Soulcatcher gave Raven one the time we ambushed Limper and Whisper.

She said, "Use the bow I gave you. And stay close."

The arrows appeared identical. "Who?"

"My husband. They can't kill him. They lack his true name. But they'll slow him down."

"You don't think the rest of the plan will work?"

"Anything is possible. But all eventualities should be

considered.'' Her eyes met mine. There was something there. . . . We looked away. She said, ''You'd better go. Sleep well. I want you alert tomorrow.''

I laughed. ''How?''

''It's been arranged. For all but the duty section.''

''Oh.'' Sorcery. One of the Taken would put everyone to sleep. I rose. I dithered for a few seconds, putting logs on the fire. I thanked her for the meal. Finally I managed to say what was on my mind. ''I want to wish you luck. But I can't put my whole heart into it.''

Her smile was wan. ''I know.'' She followed me to the door.

Before I went out I yielded to the final impulse, turned— found her right there, hoping. I hugged her for half a minute.

Damn her for being human. But I needed that, too.

Chapter Fifty-Seven: THE LAST DAY

We were permitted to sleep in, then given an hour to breakfast, make peace with our gods, or whatever we had to do before entering battle. The Great Barrow was supposed to hold till noon. There was no rush.

I wondered what the thing in the earth was doing.

Battle muster came about eight. There were no absences. The Limper drifted around on his little carpet, his path seeming to intersect that of Whisper more often than was necessary. They had their heads together about something. Bomanz skulked around the edges of things, trying to remain invisible. I did not blame him. In his shoes I might have made a run for Oar. . . . In his shoes? Were mine more comfortable?

The man was a victim of his sense of honor. He believed he had a debt to repay.

A drumbeat announced time to take positions. I followed the Lady, noting that the remaining civilians were headed down the road to Oar with what possessions they could carry. It was going to be a crazy road. The troops the Lady had summoned were reported our side of Oar, coming in their thousands. They would arrive too late. Nobody thought to tell them to hold up.

Attentions had narrowed. The outside world no longer existed. I watched the civilians and for a moment wondered what difficulties faced us if we had to flee. But my concern did not persist. I could not worry past the Dominator.

Windwhales took station over the river. Mantas searched for updrafts. Taken carpets rose. But today my feet remained on the ground. The Lady intended meeting her husband toe to toe.

Thanks a bunch, friend. There was Croaker in her shadow with his puny bow and arrows.

Guards all in position, entrenched, behind low palisades, ditches, and artillery. Pennons all in place, to guide Darling's carefully surveyed ride. Tension mounting.

What more was there to do?

"Stay behind me," the Lady reminded. "Keep your arrows ready."

"Yeah. Good luck. If we win, I'll buy you dinner at the Gardens in Opal." I don't know what possessed me to say that. Frenzied attempt at self-distraction? It was a chilly morning, but I was sweating.

She seemed startled. Then she smiled. "If we win, I'll hold you to that." The smile was feeble. She had no cause to believe she would survive another hour.

She started walking toward the Great Barrow. Faithful pup, I dogged her.

The last spark of light would not die. She would not save herself through surrender.

Bomanz gave us a head start, then followed. Likewise, the Limper.

Neither's action was in the master plan.

The Lady did not react. Perforce, I let it go, too.

Taken carpets began to spiral down. The windwhales seemed a little bouncy, the mantas a little frenetic in their search for favorable air.

Edge of the Barrowland. My amulet did not tingle. All the old fetishes outside the Barrowland's heart had been removed. The dead now lay in peace.

Moist earth sucked at my boots. I had trouble maintaining my balance, keeping an arrow across my bow. I had one black shaft set to string, the other two gripped in the hand that held the bow.

The Lady halted a few feet from the pit whence we had dragged Bomanz. She became oblivious to the world, almost as if she were communing with the thing underground. I glanced back. Bomanz had halted a little to the north, about fifty feet from me. He had his hands in his pockets and wore a look that dared me to protest his presence. The Limper had set down about where the moat was when a moat surrounded the Barrowland. He did not want to fall when the null swept over him.

I glanced at the sun. About nine. Three hours margin if we wanted to use it.

My heart was setting records for carrying on. My hands shook so much it seemed the bones ought to rattle. I doubted I could put an arrow into an elephant from five feet.

How come I got lucky and got picked to be her buttboy?

I reviewed my life. What had I done to deserve this? So many choices I might have made differently. . . . "What?"

"Ready?" she asked.

"Never." I pasted on a sickly grin.

She tried to smile back, but she was more scared·than I was. She knew what she faced. She believed she had only moments to live.

She had guts, that woman, going on when there was nothing she could win but, perhaps, some small redemption in the eyes of the world.

Names flashed through my mind. Sylith. Credence. Which? In a moment a choice might be critical.

I am not a religious man. But I sped a silent prayer to the gods of my youth asking that it not be me required to complete the ritual of her naming.

She faced the town and raised an arm. Trumpets winded. As though anyone were not paying attention.

Her arm dropped.

Hoofbeats. Darling in-her white, with Elmo, Silent, and the Lieutenant all three dogging her, galloped the lane defined by the pennons. The null was to come sudden, then freeze. The Dominator was to be allowed to break out, but not with his power intact.

I felt the null. It hit me hard, so unaccustomed to it was I. The Lady staggered too. A mewl of fear fled her lips. She did not want to be disarmed. Not now. But it was the only way.

The ground shuddered once, gently, then geysered upward. I retreated a step. Shivering, I watched the fountain of muck disperse . . . and was amazed to see not a man but the dragon. . . .

The damned dragon! I hadn't thought about that.

It reared fifty feet high, flames boiling around its head. It roared. What now? In the null the Lady could not shield us.

The Dominator fled my mind entirely.

I drew a shaft to its head, aimed for the beast's open mouth.

A shout restrained me. I turned. Bomanz pranced and shrieked, calling insults in KurreTelle. The dragon eyeballed him. And recalled that they had unfinished business.

It struck like a snake. Flames surged ahead of it.

Fire masked Bomanz but did not harm him. He had taken his stand beyond the null.

The Lady moved a few steps to her right, to look past the dragon, whose forelegs were now free and scrabbling to drag the rest of its immense body loose. I could see nothing of our quarry. But the flying Taken were into their attack runs. Heavy fire-carrying spears were in flight already. They roared down, burst.

A thunderous voice announced, "Headed for the river."

The Lady hurried forward. Darling resumed moving, carrying the null toward the water. Ghosts cursed and pranced around me. I was too distracted to respond.

Mantas dropped in swift, dark pairs, dancing between bolts of lightning loosed by windwhales. The air went crackly, smelled dry and strange.

Suddenly Tracker was with us, muttering about having to save the tree.

I heard a rising bray of horns. I dodged a flailing dragon leg, ducked a hammering wing, looked back.

Scores of ill-clad human skeletons poured from the forest in the wake of a limping Toadkiller Dog. "I knew we hadn't seen the last of that bastard." I tried to get the Lady's attention. "The forest tribes. They're attacking the Guard." The Dominator had had at least one ace in the hole.

The Lady paid me no heed.

What the tribesmen and Guard did were of no consequence to us at the moment. We had prey on the run and dared concern ourselves with nothing else.

"In the water!" that voice thundered from above. Darling moved some more. The Lady and I scrambled over earth still rippling with the dragon's efforts to break free. It ignored us. Bomanz had its entire attention.

A windwhale dropped. Its tentacles probed the river. It caught something, dropped ballast water.

A human figure writhed in the whale's grasp, screaming. My spirits rose. We had done it. . . .

The whale lifted too high. For a moment it raised the Dominator out of the null.

Deadly mistake.

Thunder. Lightning. Terror on hot hooves. Half the town and a swath to the edge of the null shattered, scattered, burned, and blackened.

The whale exploded.

The Dominator fell. As he plunged toward both water and null, he bellowed, "Sylith! I name your name!"

I loosed an arrow.

Deadeye. One of the best wing shots I have ever made. It got him in the side. He shrieked and clawed at the shaft. Then he hit water. Manta lightning made the river boil. Another whale dropped and shoved tentacles beneath the surface. For a long moment I was terrified the Dominator would stay under and escape.

But up he came, again in a monster's grasp. This whale, too, went too high. And paid the price, though the Dominator's magic was much enfeebled, probably by my arrow. He got

off one wild spell which went astray and started fires in the
Guards compound. The Guards and tribesmen were closely
engaged nearby. The spell slew scores from both forces.

I did not get another arrow off. I was frozen. I had been
assured that the naming of a name, once suitable rituals had
been observed, could not be stilled by the null. But the Lady
had not faltered. She stood a step short of the edge of land,
staring at the thing that had been her husband. The naming of
the name Sylith had not disturbed her at all.

Not Sylith! Twice the Dominator had named her wrong. . . .
Only one left to try. But my grin was hollow. *I* would have
named her Sylith.

A third windwhale caught the Dominator. This one made
no mistake. It carried him to shore, toward Darling and her
escort. He struggled furiously. Gods! The vitality of that
man!

Behind us, men screamed. Arms clashed. The Guards had
not been as surprised as I. They were holding their ground.
The airborne Taken hastened to support them, flinging a
storm of deadly sorceries. Toadkiller Dog was the center of
their attention.

Elmo, the Lieutenant, and Silent jumped the Dominator the
moment the windwhale dropped him. That was like jumping a
tiger. He threw Elmo thirty feet. I heard the crack as he broke
the Lieutenant's spine. Silent danced away. I put another
arrow into him. He staggered, but did not go down. Dazed,
he started toward the Lady and me.

Tracker met him halfway. He set the son of the tree aside,
grabbed hold of his man, started a wrestling match of epic
scale. He and the Dominator shrieked like souls in torment.

I wanted to rush down and tend to Elmo and the Lieutenant,
but the Lady gestured for me to stay. Her gaze roved
everywhere. She expected something more.

A great shriek shook the earth. A ball of oily fire rolled
skyward. The dragon flopped like an injured worm, screaming.
Bomanz had disappeared.

To be seen was the Limper. Somehow he had dragged
himself to within a dozen feet of me without my noticing. My
fear was so great I nearly voided my bowels. His mask was
gone. The devasted wasteland of his bare face glowered with

malice. In a moment, he was thinking, he would even all scores with me. My legs turned to jelly.

He pointed a small crossbow, grinned. Then his aim drifted aside. I saw that his quarrel was close cousin to the arrow across my bow.

That electrified me, finally. I drew to the head.

He squealed, "Credence, the rite is complete. I name your name!" And then he let fly.

I loosed at the same instant. I could get the shaft off no faster, damn me. My arrow slammed into his black heart, knocked him over. But too late. Too late.

The Lady cried out.

Terror turned into unreasoning rage. I flung myself at the Limper, abandoning my bow for my sword. He did not turn to face my assault. He just held himself up on one elbow and gaped at the Lady.

I really went crazy. I guess we all can, in the right circumstances. But I had been a soldier for ages. I'd long ago learned you don't do that sort of thing and stay alive long.

The Limper was inside the null. Which meant he was barely clinging to life, barely able to sustain himself, wholly unable to defend himself. I made him pay for all the years of fear.

My first stroke half severed his neck. I kept hacking till I finished the job. Then I scattered a few limbs about, blunting my steel and madness on ancient bone. Sanity began to return. I whirled to see what had become of the Lady.

She was down on one knee, the weight of her body resting upon the other. She was trying to draw Limper's bolt. I charged over, pulled her hand away. "No. Let me. Later." This time I was less startled that the naming had not worked. This time convinced me that nothing could disarm her.

She should have been gone, damn it!

I gave myself up to a long fit of the shakes.

The Taken pounding on the forest people were having an effect. Some of the savages had begun fleeing. Toadkiller Dog was enveloped by painful sorceries. "Hang on," I told the Lady. "We're over the hump. We're going to do it." I don't know that I believed that, but it was what she needed to hear.

Tracker and the Dominator continued to roll around, grunting and cursing. Silent pranced around them with a broad-bladed spear. When chance presented itself, he cut our great enemy. Nothing could survive that forever. Darling watched, stayed close, stayed out of the Dominator's way.

I scooted back to the wreck of the Limper and dug out the shaft I'd put into his chest. He glared at me. There was life in his brain still. I booted his head into the trench left by the dragon's rising.

That beast had ceased thrashing. Still no sign of Bomanz. Never any sign of Bomanz. He found the fate he feared, second try. He slew the monster from within.

Do not think Bomanz peripheral because he kept his head down. I believe the Dominator expected the dragon to preoccupy Darling and the Lady those few moments he needed to get shut of the null. Bomanz took that away. With the same determination and distinction as the Lady facing *her* inescapable fate.

I returned to the Lady. My hands had attained their battlefield steadiness. I wished for my kit. My knife would have to do. I laid her back, started digging. That quarrel would chew on her till I got it out. For all the pain, she managed a grateful smile.

A dozen men surrounded Tracker and the Dominator now, every one stabbing. Some did not seem particular as to whom they hit.

The sands were about gone for the old evil.

I packed and bound the Lady's wound with material from her own clothing. "We'll change this as soon as we can."

The tribesmen were whipped. Toadkiller Dog was dragging himself toward the high country. That old mutt had as much staying power as his boss. Guards freed of the fighting hurried our way. They carried wood for the old doom's funeral pyre.

Chapter Fifty-Eight: END OF THE GAME

Then I spotted Raven.

"The damned fool."

He was leaning on Case, hobbling. He carried a bare sword. His face was set.

Trouble for sure. His step was not quite as feeble as he pretended.

It took no genius to guess what he had in mind. In his simple way of seeing things, he was going to make everything right with Darling by finishing off her big enemy.

The shakes came back, but this time not from fear. If somebody did not do something, I was going to be right in the middle. Right where I would have to make a choice, to act, and nothing I did would make anyone happy.

I tried distracting myself by testing the Lady's dressing.

Shadows fell upon us. I looked up into Silent's cold eyes, into Darling's more compassionate face. Silent cast a subtle glance Raven's way. He was in the middle, too.

The Lady clawed at my arm. "Lift me," she said.

I did. She was as weak as water. I had to support her.

"Not yet," she told Darling, as though Darling could hear. "He is not yet finished."

They had gotten a leg and an arm off the Dominator. Those they threw into the woodpile. Tracker hung on so they could carve on the Dominator's neck. Goblin and One-Eye stood by, waiting for the head, ready to run like hell. Some Guards planted the son of the tree. Windwhales and mantas hovered overhead. Others, with the Taken, were harassing Toadkiller Dog and the savages through the forest.

Raven was getting closer. And I was no closer to knowing where I stood.

That son-of-a-bitching Dominator was tough. He killed a dozen men before they finished carving him up. Even then he was not dead. Like Limper's, his head lived on.

Time for Goblin and One-Eye. Goblin grabbed the still-living head, sat down, held it tightly between his knees. One-Eye hammered a six-inch silver spike through its forehead, into its brain. The Dominator's lips kept forming curses.

The nail would capture his blighted soul. The head would go into the fire. When that burned out, the spike would be recovered and driven into the trunk of the son of the tree. Meaning one dark spirit would be bound for a million years.

Guards brought Limper parts to the fire, too. They did not find his head, though. The sodden walls of the trench whence the dragon had risen had collapsed upon it.

Goblin and One-Eye torched the woodpile.

The fire leapt up as if eager to fulfill its mission.

The Limper's bolt had struck the Lady four inches from the heart, midway between her left breast and collarbone. I confess to a certain pride in having drawn it under such terrible circumstances without killing her. I should have incapacitated her left arm, though.

She now lifted that arm, reached out to Darling. Silent and I were puzzled. But only for a moment.

The Lady pulled Darling to her. She had no strength, so it must be that, in a way, Darling allowed herself to be pulled. Then she whispered, "The rite is complete. I name your true name, Tonie Fisk."

Darling screamed soundlessly.

The null began to fray.

Silent's face blackened. For what seemed an eternity he stood there in obvious torment, torn between a vow, a love, a hatred, perhaps the concept of an obligation to a higher duty. Tears began coursing down his cheeks. I got an old wish, and was ready to cry myself when I did.

He spoke. "The ritual is closed." He had trouble shaping his words. "I name your true name, Dorotea Senjak. I name your true name, Dorotea Senjak."

I thought he would collapse in a faint then. But he did not.

The women did.

Raven was getting closer. So I had a pain atop all the other pains.

Silent and I stared at one another. I suspect my face was as tormented as his. Then he nodded through his tears. There was peace between us. We knelt, untangled the women. He looked worried while I felt Darling's neck. "She'll be all right," I told him. The Lady, too, but he did not care about that.

I wonder still how much each of the women expected in that moment. How much each yielded to destiny. It marked their end as powers of the world. Darling had no null. The Lady had no magic. They had canceled one another out.

I heard screaming. Carpets were raining. All those Taken had been Taken by the Lady herself, and after what had happened on the Plain, she had made certain her fate would be their fate. So now they were undone, and soon dead.

Not much magic left on that field. Tracker, too, was a goner, mauled to death by the Dominator. I believe he died happy.

But there was no end yet. No. There was Raven.

Fifty feet away, he let go of Case and bore down like nemesis itself. His gaze was fixed on the Lady, though you could tell by his very step that he was on stage, that he was going to do a deed to win back Darling.

Well, Croaker? Can you let it happen?

The Lady's hand shivered in mine. Her pulse was feeble, but it was there. Maybe . . .

Maybe he would bluff.

I picked up my bow and the arrow recovered from Limper. "Stop, Raven."

He did not. I do not think he heard me. Oh, damn. If he didn't . . . It was going to get out of hand.

"Raven!" I bent the bow.

He stopped. He stared at me as if trying to recall who I was.

That whole battleground fell into silence. Every eye fixed upon us. Silent stopped moving Darling away, took up a sword, made certain he was between her and potential danger. It was almost amusing, the two of us there, like twins, standing guard over women whose hearts we could never have.

One-Eye and Goblin began drifting our way. I had no idea where they stood. Wherever, I did not want them involved. This had to be made into Raven against Croaker.

Damn. Damn. Damn. Why couldn't he just go away?

"It's over, Raven. There ain't going to be no more killing." I think my voice began to rise in pitch. "You hear? It's lost and won."

He looked at Silent and Darling, not at me. And took a step.

"You *want* to be the next guy dead?" Damn it, nobody could ever bluff him. Could I do it? I might have to.

One-Eye stopped a careful ten feet to one side. "What are you doing, Croaker?"

I was shaking. Everything but my hands and arms, though my shoulders had begun to ache with the strain of keeping my arrow drawn. "What about Elmo?" I asked, my throat tight with emotion. "What about the Lieutenant?"

"No good," he replied, telling me what I already knew in my heart. "Gone. Why don't you put the bow down?"

"When he drops the sword." Elmo had been my best friend for more years than I cared to count. Tears began to blur my vision. "They're gone. That leaves me in charge, right? Senior officer surviving? Right? My first order is, peace breaks out. Right now. *She* made this possible. *She* gave herself up for this. Nobody touches her now. Not while I'm alive."

"Then we'll change that," Raven said. He started moving.

"Damned stubborn fool!" One-Eye shrieked. He flung himself toward Raven. I heard Goblin pattering up behind me. Too late. Both too late. Raven had a lot more fire in him than anyone suspected. And he was more than a little crazy.

I yelled, "No!" and let fly.

The arrow took Raven in the hip. In the very side he had been pretending was crippled. He wore a look of amazement as he stumbled. Lying there on the ground, his sword eight feet away, he looked up at me, still unable to believe that, in the end, I was not bluffing.

I had trouble believing it myself.

Case yelled and tried to jump me. Hardly looking at him, I whacked him up side the head with my bow. He went away and fussed over Raven.

Silence, and stillness, again. Everyone looking at me. I slung my bow. "Fix him up, One-Eye." I limped over to the Lady, knelt, lifted her. She seemed awfully light and fragile for one who had been so terrible. I followed Silent toward what was left of the town. The barracks were still burning. We made an odd parade, the two of us lugging women. "Company meeting tonight," I threw out at the Company survivors. "You all be there."

I would not have believed myself capable before I did it. I carried her all the way to Blue Willy. And my ankle never hurt till I put her down.

Chapter Fifty-Nine: LAST VOTE

I limped into the common room at what was left of Blue Willy, the Lady supported under one arm, bow used as a crutch. The ankle was killing me. I had thought it almost healed.

I deposited the Lady in a chair. She was weak and pale and only about half conscious despite the best One-Eye and I could do. I was determined not to let her out of my sight. Our situation was still fraught with peril. Her people no longer had any reason to be nice. And she was at risk herself— probably more from herself than from Raven or my comrades. She had fallen into a state of complete despair.

"Is this all?" I asked. Silent, Goblin, and One-Eye were there. And Otto the immortal, wounded as always after a Company action, with his eternal sidekick, Hagop. A youngster named Murgen, our standard-bearer. Three others from the Company. And Darling, of course, seated beside Silent. She ignored the Lady completely.

Raven and Case were back by the bar, present without having been invited. Raven wore a dark look but seemed to have himself under control. His gaze was fixed on Darling.

She looked grim. She had rebounded better than the Lady. But she had won. She ignored Raven more assiduously than she did the Lady.

There had been a showdown between them, and I had overheard his half. Darling had made very clear her displeasure with his inability to handle emotional commitment. She had not cut him off. She had not banished him from her heart. But he was not redeemed in her eyes.

He then had said some very unkind things about Silent, whom, it was obvious, she held in affection but nothing deeper.

And that had gotten her really angry. I had peeped then. And she had gone on in great length and fury about not being a prize in some men's game, like a princess in some dopey fairy tale where a gang of suitors ride around doing stupid and dangerous things vying for her hand.

Like the Lady, she had been in charge too long to accept a standard female role now. She was still the White Rose inside.

So Raven was not so happy. He had not been shut out, but he *had* been told he had a long way to go if he wanted to lay any claims.

The first task she had given him was righting himself with his children.

I halfway felt sorry for the guy. He knew only one role. Hard guy. And it had been stripped away.

One-Eye interrupted my thoughts. "This is it, Croaker. This is all. Going to be a big funeral."

It would. "Shall I preside as senior officer surviving? Or do you want to exercise your prerogative as oldest brother?"

"You do it." He was in no mood to do anything but brood.

Neither was I. But there were ten of us still alive, surrounded by potential enemies. We had decisions to make.

"All right. This is an official convocation of the Black Company, last of the Free Companies of Khatovar. We've lost our captain. First business is to elect a new commander. Then we have to decide how we're going to get out of here. Any nominations?"

"You," Otto said.

"I'm a physician."

"You're the only real officer left."

Raven started to rise.

I told him, "You sit down and keep quiet. You don't even belong here. You walked out on us fifteen years ago, remember? Come on, you guys. Who else?"

Nobody. spoke. Nobody volunteered. Nobody met my eye, either. They all knew I did not want it.

Goblin squeaked, "Is anybody against Croaker?"

Nobody blackballed me. It's wonderful to be loved. Grand to be the least of evils.

I wanted to turn it down. The option was not there. "All right. Next order of business. Getting the hell out of here. We're surrounded, guys. And the Guard will get its balance pretty soon. We've got to get gone before they start looking around for somebody to whip on. But once we get clear, then what?"

Nobody offered an opinion. These men were as much in shock as the Guards.

"All right. I know what *I* want to do. Since time immemorial one of the jobs of the Annalist has been to return the Annals to Khatovar should the Company disband or be demolished. We've been demolished. I propose a vote to disband. Some of us have assumed obligations that are going to put us at odds as soon as we don't have anybody more dangerous to fuss at." I looked at Silent. He met my gaze. He'd just moved his seat so he was more into the gap between Darling and Raven, a gesture understood by everyone but Raven himself.

I had nominated myself guardian for the Lady, for the time being. There was no way we could keep those two women in one another's company for long. I hoped we could hold the group together as far as Oar. I would be satisfied with getting to the edge of the forest. We needed every hand. Our tactical situation could not have been worse.

"Shall we disband?" I asked.

That caused a stir. Everyone but Silent argued the negative.

I interjected, "This is a formal proposition. I want those with special interests to go their own ways without the stigma of desertion. That don't mean we *have* to split. What I'm saying is, we formally shed the name the Black Company. I'll head south with the Annals, looking for Khatovar. Anyone who wants can come. Under the usual rules."

Nobody wanted to give up the name. That would be like renouncing a patronym thirty generations old.

"So we don't give it up. Who would rather not go look for Khatovar?"

Three hands rose. All belonged to troopers who had enlisted north of the Sea of Torments. Silent abstained, though he wanted to go his own way, in pursuit of his own impossible dream.

Then another hand shot up. Belatedly, Goblin had noted that One-Eye was not opposed. They started one of their arguments. I cut it short.

"I won't insist on the majority dragging everybody along. As commander, I can discharge anyone who wants to follow another path. Silent?"

He had been a brother of the Black Company longer than I. We were his friends, his family. His heart was torn.

Finally, he nodded. He would go his own road, even without promises from Darling. The three who had opposed heading for Khatovar nodded too. I entered their discharges in the Annals. "You're out," I told them. "I'll deal out your shares of money and equipment when we clear the south edge of the forest. Till then we stick together." I did not pursue it further, or in a moment I would have been hanging all over Silent, bawling my eyes out. We had been through a lot, he and I.

I wheeled on Goblin, pen poised. "Well? Do I strike your name?"

"Go on," One-Eye said. "Hurry. Do it. Get rid of him. We don't need his kind. He's never been anything but trouble."

Goblin scowled at him. "Just for that I'm not leaving. I'm

going to stay and outlive you and make your remaining days examples of misery. And I hope you live another hundred years."

I had not thought they would split. "Fine," I said, stifling a grin. "Hagop, take a couple men and round up some animals. The rest of you collect whatever might be useful. Like money, if you see any laying around."

They looked at me with eyes still dull with the impact of what had happened.

"We're getting out, guys. As soon as we can ride. Before any more trouble finds us. Hagop. Don't stint on pack animals. I want to carry off everything that isn't nailed down."

There was talk, argument, whatnot, but I closed the official debate at that point.

Cunning devil that I am, I got the Guards to do our burying. I stood over the Company graves with Silent and shed more than a few tears. "I never thought Elmo . . . He was my best friend." It had hit me. At last. Hard. Now I had done all the duties, there was nothing to hold it at bay. "He was my sponsor when I came in."

Silent lifted a hand, gently squeezed my arm. It was as much of a gesture as I could expect.

The Guards were paying their last respects to their own. Their daze was fading. Soon they would begin thinking about getting on with business. About asking the Lady what they should do. In a sense, they had been rendered unemployed.

They did not know their mistress had been disarmed. I prayed they did not learn, for I meant to use her as our ticket out.

I dreaded what might happen should her loss become general knowledge. On the broad canvas, civil wars to torment the world. On the fine, attempts at revenge upon her person.

Someday someone would begin to suspect. I just wanted the secret kept till we had a good run at getting out of the empire.

Silent took my arm again. He wanted to go. "One second," I said. I drew my sword, saluted our graves, repeated the ancient formula of parting. Then I followed him to where the others waited.

Silent's party would ride with us a while, as I'd wished. Our ways would part when we felt safe from the Guards. I did not look forward to that moment, inevitable though it was. How keep two such as Darling and the Lady in company when there was no survival imperative?

I swung into the saddle cursing my wretched aching ankle. The Lady gave me a dirty look. "Well," I said. "You're showing some spirit."

"Are you kidnapping me?"

"You want to be alone with all your folks? With maybe nothing better than a knife to keep order?" Then I forced a grin. "We've got a date. Remember? Dinner at the Gardens in Opal?"

For just a moment there was a spark of mischief behind her despair. And a look from a moment by a fire when we had come close. Then the shadow returned.

I leaned closer, trembling with the thought. I whispered, "And I need your help to get the Annals out of the Tower." I had not told anyone that I did not have them in my possession yet.

The shadow went. "Dinner? That's a promise?"

The witch could promise a lot, just with a look and her tone. I croaked, "In the Gardens. Yes."

I gave the time-honored signal. Hagop started off on point. Goblin and One-Eye followed, bickering as usual. Then Murgen, with the standard, then the Lady and I. Then most of the others, with the pack animals. Silent and Darling brought up the rear, well separated from the Lady and I.

As I urged my mount forward, I glanced back. Raven stood leaning on his cane, looking more forlorn and abandoned than he should. Case was still trying to explain it to him. The kid had no trouble understanding. I figured Raven would, once he got over the shock of not having everyone jump to do things his way, the shock of discovering that old Croaker could fill his bluff if he had to. "I'm sorry," I murmured his way, not quite sure why. Then I faced the forest and did not look back again.

I had a feeling he would be on the road himself soon enough. If Darling really meant as much to him as he wanted us to think.

*   *   *

That night, for the first time in who knows how long, the northern skies were completely clear. The Great Comet illuminated our way. Now the north knew what the rest of the empire had known for weeks.

It was on the wane already. The hour of decision had passed. The empire awaited in fear the news that it portended.

Away north. Three days later. In the dark of a moonless night. A beast with three legs limped from the Great Forest. It settled on its haunches on the remains of the Barrowland, scratched the earth with its one forepaw. The son of the tree flung a tiny change storm.

The monster fled.

But it would return another night, and another, and another after that. . . .